THE KIDS OF GOD

Dave Appleby

ISBN-13: 9781234567890
ISBN-10: 1477123456

Cover design by: Art Painter
Library of Congress Control Number: 2018675309
Printed in the United States of America

To Steph, Sam Simon, Lucy and Alexa. And Monty.

CONTENTS

Title Page   1

Copyright   2

Dedication   3

Chapter One: Worse than a Peacemaker?   7

Chapter Two: A Nose for Drudjers   17

Chapter Three: The Night of Violence   33

Chapter Four: A Right Paella of a Night   46

Chapter Five: Sodz and the Memsahib   54

Chapter Six: Breakfast with the Boss   65

Chapter Seven: Xan   84

Chapter Eight: Perspective   93

Chapter Nine: The Errand Boy   104

Chapter Ten: At the Enchanted Isle   114

Chapter Eleven: Madame and Faith   132

Chapter Twelve: You're offal   141

Chapter Thirteen: The Key to the Escape   155

Chapter Fourteen: A Proposition from Xan   168

Chapter Fifteen: Somebody Always Has To Be In Charge   187

Chapter Sixteen: The Man with the Gun   200

Chapter Seventeen: Of Pearls and Poppers   210

Chapter Eighteen: The Patron Saint of Hopeless Causes   225

Chapter Nineteen: What Nikov wants   239

Chapter Twenty: What will we do when we get out of   252
here?

Chapter Twenty One: The rescue   264

Chapter Twenty Two: Xan's secret   273

Chapter Twenty Three: Blossoming   288

Chapter Twenty Four: The Chase   296

Chapter Twenty Five: Betrayal   308

Chapter Twenty Six: Blessed are the Peacemakers   317

Chapter Twenty Seven: Exhumed   330

Chapter Twenty Eight: We're All Fucked Now   339

Chapter Twenty Nine: Brother and Sister   351

Chapter Thirty: The Trial   362

Chapter Thirty One: The Fall Guy   379

Epilogue   392

Acknowledgement   397

About The Author   399

Books By This Author   401

CHAPTER ONE: WORSE THAN A PEACEMAKER?

They said it couldn't happen here. It had.

For me it started with a knock upon the door. I didn't want to answer. It was dark outside and darkness meant that it was dangerous. But when the Peacemakers came calling, since you had to open, it was better if you opened fast. They got impatient. Didn't like delay.

I shuffled down the hallway to the door. I opened it. I stared.

He was no Peacemaker. It was much worse than that.

How did he dare?

'Out of the way,' he said. He stepped towards me. I gave way. I didn't want to. I was taken by surprise. You don't expect that sort of thing.

He put his hand out flat, the palm against my chest. He pushed. I staggered. 'Let me in,' he snarled. I felt his fingers jabbing into me. He thrust and I fell back.

'You can't come in,' I said. Too late. He was already standing upright in my narrow hallway.

'Go away. You can't come in. It's not allowed.' I was afraid.

He showed no sign that he had heard. He'd never listened.

He did what he wanted and the rest of us were scattered, gathered, dragged down in his wake.

I noticed he was soaking wet. Completely drenched. His face was streaked with mud. His sodden shirt had shrunk; I saw that it was sticking to his skin. His feet were bare, a toenail torn. The carpet where he stood was damp.

He dripped.

He smelt of rotting wood. Wet dog. Of Drudjer.

I was petrified. I couldn't move. I stood and watched him turn around and close the door. He had been just in time. The searchlight passed across, its horrid yellow thinly bleeding through the gap around the doorframe like a draught.

He faced me, and he grabbed my hand to shake it. As he pumped it up and down he screwed his arm around so that his palm was turned to face the ground: his hand on top of mine. It was his usual handshake. I remembered it. It was the way he told you who was boss.

'It's been a long time, Ed,' he said.

I shuddered. Freezing fingers. He was colder than a corpse. I gasped.

As if he read my mind he said: 'I am so fucking frigid that they cannot even see me on their infra-red'. He barked a laugh. 'So cold I'm camouflaged.'

He placed a little backpack on the floor. It was a tiny thing, the sort a starting schoolboy has strapped to his spine, to hold his sandwiches. It was the only thing about him that was dry. He said: 'I need a towel.'

'You're wet,' I said, as if he might not know.

'I swam the river.'

'Swam?' Although tonight the clouds had fled, it had been raining heavily for days. The land was saturated and the swollen river surged between its banks. I'd watched it from my window, fearing floods. 'There's quite a current underneath the bridge,' I said. I had seen whirlpools form. The stream was turbulent. 'You must be mad to swim the river when it is as high as this.'

'I need a towel,' he said again.

'You're not supposed to be here. It's forbidden.'

'Well,' he said. 'I'm here. I'm wet. I'm cold. For goodness sake.' He took another step towards me; I retreated once again. He looked towards the stairs. 'I'll just go up,' he said.

I panicked. 'No. You can't.' My terror seemed to snap me out of my paralysis. I moved in front of him to block his way. My mind was working now. At last. Too late, perhaps. 'You can't go up the stairs.'

'Of course I can.'

'The window. You'll be seen.'

Mine was an end-of-terrace townhouse, five years old, on an estate in a suburban part of town. Relentlessly anonymous. Brick built, three floors. There was a tall arched window stretching up the end wall of the house from half way up the ground floor almost to the roof. It was a feature. Standing on the staircase there was quite a view: the river and beyond. On this bank was an open space; there had been plans to plant a formal garden there but for the moment it was grassed. The architects for the estate had promised they would also build a leisure complex on the further bank. But that was then, before the country had collapsed. Now, from the stairs, I looked beyond the river to a wasteland. In the distance I could see the Kennels where the Drudjers lived.

A footbridge spanned the river. In the middle were the guards. They had binoculars and lights and guns. Their job was to prevent the Drudjers crossing. Any swimmers would be shot.

He always was a lucky man.

If I had let him go upstairs he could have looked out of my window at the guardpost on the bridge. He could have seen the guards. But what looks out, looks in. I knew the guards could see me when I stood upon the stairs. They watched me going up and down. Sometimes they waved.

As if on cue the searchlight perched upon the bridge swung in its arc and lit my window, casting broken shadows of the window-frame onto the banisters.

'The window. I'd forgotten that,' he muttered. 'I suppose we'll have to stay downstairs.' He glanced at me. 'I need a towel. For pity's sake, go fetch me one.'

I stared at him. Who did he think he was? 'You're not my boss, not any more.'

I had a spare towel in the kitchen, as it happened. Since the wife and kids had gone away there didn't seem much point in keeping tidy house. I did such laundry as I needed in the kitchen and I hung it there to dry until I needed it. Nobody cared. Not any more.

'Stay there,' I told him as I fetched the towel. I threw it to him and he caught it. 'But you can't stay here,' I said.

'Why not?'

'You know why not. It is against the law.'

He nodded thoughtfully. 'What's to be done?' he asked.

That's when I should have shouted. Had I screamed and told him to get out, somebody might have come, a Peacemaker perhaps. They would have taken him away.

They'd shoot him.

'Let me be quite clear,' he said, 'if I am caught I'll tell them that you harboured me. I'll say you gave me refuge.'

'But that isn't true.'

'You will be shot.'

'They won't believe a Drudj.'

'Perhaps they will'.

Perhaps they would. The Peacemakers weren't known for taking time to ponder all the ifs and buts. They saw the world in black and white. If he was found here in this house they'd say that I had helped him; they would shoot us both.

The world had changed. Back then we ate, we drank, we shopped, we played. Then came the Water Wars and floods of Migrants fleeing drought, all thirsting for prosperity. They dreamed of having what we had but what they dreamed of was itself a dream. They thought our world was stable; it was nothing but a house of cards. They thought we were secure, that we had banished hazard. What had we to fear? they asked. But we were more afraid than ever; we were scared of them. We felt besieged. We closed our borders. Trade collapsed. Shelves emptied. Prices rocketed. We started bickering. Fights broke out on the streets and people rioted. The government resigned and politicians argued but the truth was they were impotent. You can't administer a world gone mad.

Some units of the army mutinied. The country crumbled into a mosaic of conflicting fiefdoms. Here, in my town, there was still a mayor and council, there were still police, but they were puppets. We were governed by a set of self-appointed vigilantes. They had named themselves the Peacemakers. They made the peace all right; now they kept us in order. They patrolled the streets. Imposed decrees.

They blamed our troubles on the Drudj although the Migrants and the Drudjers were two groups that scarcely overlapped and many Drudjer families had been around for generations, rooted deeply in our land. But they had stayed, to some extent, distinct. The Drudjers had their customs and their clothes, the things they would and wouldn't eat and drink; they had their words. They could be pointed at. They could be named.

Our world was sick, the Peacemakers explained. It was infected and the only cure required the purging of the pathogens. They must be quarantined. And so it was decreed: all Drudjers had to live within the Kennels. This had always been the poorer part of town, where many of the Drudj already lived. Now any house a Drudjer owned in any other part of town was confiscated. Drudjers weren't allowed to leave the Kennels: those who worked outside were sacked or had their businesses transferred away from them. A Drudjer found outside the Kennels would be shot. Or hanged. Or crucified. Sometimes it just depended on the fancy of the man in charge.

The rules applied to us as well. By order of the Peacemakers a Citizen who helped the Drudjers could be put to death. At best they'd disappear into the cells.

I watched him dry himself. He wiped his face and he massaged his hair. He draped the towel round his neck and started to remove his shirt. He didn't even look at me.

'How's Mrs Angelo?' he asked.

I couldn't speak. I couldn't breathe. How did he dare?

'I'm told she isn't here.' How could he be so blatant and so calm?

'She hasn't left me.'

Now he looked at me. He had a sort of semi-smile upon his lips.

'It's just a holiday,' I said.

When I had lost my job my wife was furious. I was the one she blamed. Two boys: no money coming in.

It hadn't been my fault. This most unwelcome guest who now stood in my hall had been my boss. He founded Kapko Industries; I'd joined it fresh from university. We built surveillance systems culling data from the internet, from mobile phones, from social media, from hidden cameras; collecting information, analysing it, detecting patterns and extrapolating trends. Bright promises, big profits, rosy dawns.

We failed to prophesy the coming of the Peacemakers. They seized the firm and they evicted Mr Kapko from his penthouse flat. I had been glad of that: I'd never trusted him; I'd liked him even less since finding out about the things that he got up to in that flat. But then the Peacemakers expelled the Drudjers from the company. It didn't matter to them that these workers were among the keys to our success; that they had skills and knowledge which were irreplaceable. The makeshift management began to cobble teams together. The company began to miss important deadlines. Customers were offered incomplete sub-optimal solutions. Clients started to desert us. With the chaos in the general economy, that was enough to make the company collapse.

I had to find another job. It wasn't easy. Failure clung to me and also I was tainted with the fact of working for a Drudjer. Finally I crawled into a public service post. I worked at the Town Hall. They used our system. Now I operated what I'd once designed. It meant less pay of course. My wife said that it wasn't good enough. She'd sacrificed herself, she said, so I could keep my job at Kapko Industries and now I'd lost it after all she wasn't going to accept what would be second best.

But I had no intention of explaining this to him. Had he not done enough? I told him that she'd gone off to her mother's house, that it was in the countryside where it was safer, that she had the boys with her. That I had wanted her to go. 'How could we raise our boys in such a world as this?' I asked.

'It sounds as if she's left you.'

'No.' I clenched my fists. I should have hit him there and then. Why didn't I? It was my chance. He was a Drudjer, at my mercy. 'No,' I said. 'It's just a holiday. She hasn't gone for long. She's coming back when things calm down.'

There were persistent rumours that the army was approaching from the north.

I don't know why I felt I had to justify myself to him. He pushed my buttons. Always had. And now ...

He said if he was captured he would tell the Peacemakers I'd helped him. I believed he would. It was the sort of thing he'd do.

He started taking off his river-saturated clothes. I watched him fumble with the buttons of his shirt. He had a convex, hairy belly like a monkey. Strong, broad shoulders. Powerful. He must be strong, I thought, to do what he had said he'd done. To swim the river. How, I wondered, had the guards not seen him cross?

He rubbed the towel against his chest and held it up before his face. 'I'm making it all dirty. See?'

The searchlight stationed on the bridge lit up the staircase window once again in a brief dawn before it travelled on. There was a single shot, a splash. A Drudjer? Or a duck?

He started to undo his belt.

A dog barked raggedly and then another answered. I could hear a window shattering. The normal night-time soundscape nowadays: a yawning silence, peace imposed, made deeper by haphazard splinters of brutality.

'You can't stay here,' I said. 'It isn't safe.'

He paused. One foot was free, the other leg bare-thighed, its foot still tangled in his trousers. 'What you mean is that it isn't safe for you. There's nowhere safe for me. The only place a Drudjer is allowed to be is in the Kennels. That isn't safe. They've crammed us all in there. Six to a room. On average. You can't imagine. Dysentery, some say cholera. We are surrounded.'

'By the Peacemakers?'

'We have another name for them'. He paused to extricate his foot. 'They're starving us. We're dying. So, I ask, what are the odds? I stay, I die; I flee, I might get shot but there's a slender chance I will escape.' He gave a strangely sideways grin: 'You know me. I like risk'

'You don't look hungry'.

'Looks can lie'.

Not only looks, I thought.

'I'm here,' he said. 'Inside your house. You can't turn back the clock. It is like mixing ink with water; you can't separate them afterwards. You know this: it's the second law of being fucked.'

He stood there wearing nothing but his soggy undershorts and lectured me and then he bent and dried his thighs with the already filthy towel. I stared down at his back. He was tattooed of course. The ink had faded through the years. It seemed to be a battle scene; they had been popular back then. The image was distorted; as the years had passed he had grown fatter, hairier. You couldn't call him handsome.

'Just one night. I only need to stay tonight. Tomorrow morning I'll be gone. You won't see me again.'

He wiped his feet, between his toes; he skirted round the hanging nail.

'And then, when all of this is over, when the Peacemakers have been defeated, when normality returns, then you can tell the world what you have done. You will have saved my life. You'll be a hero, Ed.'

A man's voice, outside, shouting. Running feet.

I didn't want to be a hero. All I wanted was to stay alive.

He straightened up. In one swift movement he took off his boxer shorts and used the towel to rub himself. Some people have no shame, I thought. I looked away.

Another knock came on the door.

CHAPTER TWO: A NOSE FOR DRUDJERS

I froze.

'It hasn't started yet,' the Drudjer whispered.

'What?' I shot an angry look at him and put my finger to my lips. Somebody was outside and, given that there was a curfew, it was probably a Peacemaker. A Peacemaker was standing just outside my door and in the hall there was a Drudjer.

He was cowering behind the towel as if that would protect him. 'Clothes,' he mouthed. 'Give me my clothes.'

I mimed to ask if he had locked the door.

He shook his head.

Shit, shit and shit, I thought. As usual he had nothing more to lose. I had. It felt as if I was the naked one.

The clock behind me ticked. The Peacemakers don't like it if you make them wait. They don't like much.

He had to hide but where? He couldn't go upstairs; he might be seen. The door behind me led into the kitchen but that too had windows; it was overlooked by flats. There was a cupboard underneath the stairs but that was full. The downstairs loo? Too obvious. It had to be the garage.

When my wife and I had moved into the house with two boys underneath the age of five we made a door between the hallway and the garage so that we could use it as a storeroom. Kids have lots of stuff. We kept the garage door so that the frontage of the house looked just as it had always done but we constructed a false wall behind it. This kept out the draught. We sealed the concrete floor against the damp. We shelved the walls.

There were no windows in the room. It might not be the perfect place to hide but it was all I had.

I grabbed his arm and pulled. He stumbled, and he dropped the towel. There was no time to pick it up. Another knock. I called 'I'm coming!' and I bundled him into the darkness of the garage.

I picked his clothes up from the floor and held them to my chest. Where could I hide them? I spun around and fled into the kitchen, flung the clothes into the washing machine, hurled a laundry tablet after them, slammed shut the door and wrenched the dial. It started straight away. I breathed. I turned again and raced out of the kitchen down the hall. I hurtled to a stop.

There on the carpet was a damp patch. Little hint of mud. Where he'd been standing. Dripping.

I grabbed the towel that he had dropped. I fell upon my knees. If I could use the towel, I thought, although it was already soaked, to blot the stain...

Another knock.

'Come in,' I called, my voice as squeaky as boy's mid-puberty. 'It isn't locked.'

I took a breath. Play calm, I told myself.

The door swung open. I looked up.

He was a Peacemaker. He wore their ad hoc uniform. His dark-blue jeans were crisply ironed, held up by a black leather belt with a substantial buckle. At his left hip was his holstered mobile phone; the gun upon his right hip balanced it. Symmetrical. His tucked-in tee-shirt, with the logo of the Peacemakers upon the front, showed off his upper body. He had swollen biceps, sculpted pectorals; beneath the cloth there was a hint of finely chiselled abs. His chin was closely shaved; his hair cut neat and short. His face was fat, quite babyish; his mouth was wide, his lips were full and slightly parted and his nostrils flared. It was the sort of face that used to be described as sensuous.

I felt a little faint.

'Whatever are you doing?' he enquired. He added: 'Sir.'

I heard the laundry slosh in the machine.

'I'm mopping up,' I said. 'I spilt some water on the floor.'

He took a long breath through his nose. He twitched his lips. He nodded. 'I can smell the fungal perfume of decay and drains.' He frowned, looked puzzled. 'And. There's something else.'

I kept on scrubbing at the carpet but it was no use. The towel was much too wet and slimed with mud which I was spreading in a smear across the floor.

I didn't dare look up. The Peacemakers prefer it if you know your place. I kept my eyes fixed on his shoes. Designer trainers kept immaculate.

'We've had reports,' he said, 'of Drudjers in this area?' He sniffed again. 'Wet water. Mud. A hint of pepper. I can't quite pinpoint the aroma. Sir. Have you seen anyone tonight?'

I didn't trust myself to speak. I rubbed and rubbed. The dirty mark began to grow.

'Sir? Sir!' he said. 'Stand up and look at me.'

I slowly struggled to my feet. My gaze tracked slowly up his body from his knees, his thighs, his groin, his waist, his belly, up the valley in between the moulding of his chest and through the vulnerable hollow just above his sternum, up across the bulge that was his larynx, softly past his dimpled chin, his lips, his philtrum, in between his nostrils, climbing up the ridge that was his nose. I focussed on the space between his eyebrows.

Never look them in the eyes.

'How would I see somebody? I've been in all night.'

'May I come in?' He was still standing at the door. It was polite of him to ask, though it was meaningless, we both knew that. Had I said no he would have entered anyway. And then I would have angered him. When you don't have a choice it's best to yield. So I surrendered. Let him enter. But my compliance didn't mean consent.

He thanked me. 'Sir,' he said.

I clutched the useless towel. It dangled, limp and ripping. I tried not to think about what Mr Kapko had been swimming in but it was foul, repellently malodorous. The towel was soiled beyond the point of any soap. I'd never get it clean, not now. I'd have to throw it in the trash.

He hadn't closed the door, not yet, and as I looked at him the light that they had stationed on the roof of what had once been Kapko Industries shone straight towards me so that I was blinded, so that all at once I could see nothing but his silhouette. My eyes were dazzled. Then the light moved on but I could still see nothing. When I blinked my eyes were flooded with green demons, purple dancing shapes, and orange snakes.

In my imagination, I could see the Drudjer in my garage,

crouching, naked, in the dark. My nemesis.

'Can't you smell something? Sir?' the Peacemaker enquired. 'A sort of unripe, rancid pungency. Like Drudjers.'

'Drudjers?' I was startled. I forgot. I looked at him.

His eyes were staring hard at me. 'I have a nose for sniffing Drudjers out,' he said.

He was staring straight at me. I squeaked: 'What do they smell of?'

'Of disgust,' he said.

'I think it's just the towel,' I said. I held it out for him to smell and halfway through the movement stopped. If he discovered Drudjers by their scent he would detect my Drudjer from his odour on the towel.

He didn't comment on my hesitation and I hoped he hadn't noticed it. But his attention had been caught by something else. He picked up Mr Kapko's tiny backpack. 'Is this yours?'

I felt a little giddy. Something lurched. I glanced up at the bookshelves on the wall. If looks could trigger landslides I'd have buried him beneath an avalanche of books.

'My son's,' I said. 'My younger son's. He's always leaving it around. What can you do? Boys are untidy.'

'Some, perhaps,' he said. 'I never was.'

He used a disinfecting soap; its stinging scent went scorching up my nose. It made me sneeze.

'Well that's all right,' he said. 'They say you cannot sneeze and tell a lie.'

He handed me the backpack. 'It is very heavy. What is in it?'

'Bits and bobs. The sorts of things that boys collect. Like you did, I expect.'

'I never had much time for stamps or things like that. I didn't have the money.' Now, I thought, he'd started staring at my stomach. 'Sir. I wonder. Can you please explain? Your shirt is damp. Why is that?'

He moved a little closer. He was now so near to me that I could feel his warmth, his breath upon my face.

From far off, outside, in the dark, a voice cried out.

'The clothes were wet. I held them up against my chest. Before I put them into the machine.'

'Before?' he said. 'The clothes were wet before you put them into the machine?'

I nodded.

'Why?' he asked.

I thought, because he swam the river. That was what I couldn't say. Instead: 'I soaked them. Boys, you know. I don't know what they do to get so dirty. Mucky pups. It's hard to keep things clean with all the nastiness today.'

I froze, appalled at what I'd said. Sometimes my chatter runs away with me. I had complained; in this new Peacemaker utopia complaints of anything - the weather, influenza, growing old - were out of place. They didn't like it if they thought that they were being criticised.

'I didn't mean ...' I said.

He gave a tight-lipped smile. He didn't look amused. 'Your son. Is he upstairs?'

'My son?'

'The messy one. The owner of the backpack. Is he here?' He smiled again. This time he showed his teeth. They were extremely white.

It seemed to me that if I made a single false move he would leap on it. It seemed to me that all my moves were false.

'My wife's away. She's gone on holiday. Her and the boys.'

'That must cut down the washing. Sir'

'I have to do it all myself.'

'I think you should have added that before you started the machine.' He nodded at my mucky towel.

I heard the washing churning in its drum. If they arrested him, I would be asked: why is he naked? Then: why are you laundering his clothes?

They shoot you if they think that you have helped a Drudjer to escape.

'I'm sure,' I said, 'I recognise your face. I've seen you somewhere.'

'Maybe that's because I live across the road. I moved in yesterday.'

'The lawyer's house?'

'The middle of the terrace. Sir.'

Of course, I thought. The lawyer was a Drudj. He had been forced out of his home some time ago. They kept them empty for their officers.

'My house is just like yours,' he said, 'except reversed. The staircase, Sir, is on the left. It feels as if I'm looking at a mirror image. But my hallway doesn't have that door.'

He pointed to the door that led into the garage.

'No', I said. Please no, I thought.

'Is it another room?' he asked. Then he remembered: 'Sir'.

'The garage.'

'Yes. Of course. The garage. You have made a door so you have access from inside the house. That was a good idea.'

'Yes', I said.

'I doubt I will be staying long enough to make it worth my while.'

'We just keep junk in there'.

'It's useful though', he said. 'It's somewhere you could hide all sorts of contraband. Black market goods, that sort of thing.'

In hindsight, I suppose that was my chance. Perhaps I should have said right there and then: there is a Drudjer hiding in my garage. He's not wearing any clothes because ... because ... because I took them from him so he'd be less likely to escape when ... when what ... as soon as I could get a message to the relevant authorities.

'There is something that I ought to mention,' I began.

I heard a girl's voice singing a lament. It seemed a long way off. I wondered who she was.

I was too late.

He prompted me: 'To mention what?'

'What?'

'You said that you should mention something. Sir.'

What?

I had to stop him looking in the garage so I forced a laugh. 'The other difference between your house and mine is you don't have a window up the stairs,' I said, 'because your house is in the middle of the terrace. Would you like to take a look?'

He looked at me a little doubtfully and then he stepped, as delicate as you could wish, across the muddy patch of carpet to the bottom of the stairs.

I moved a little further back and to the side. The old song says there is a time to stand and there's a time to cede. It didn't mean I welcomed him.

I gestured: he should go up first.

He climbed the first flight.

'Can you see the river and the guard post on the bridge?' I asked.

'If I were you I wouldn't look,' he warned.

'It makes the whole house lighter,' I explained.

'But don't you feel,' he asked, 'that anyone can see you when you're going up and down your stairs?'

'At first it used to bother me,' I said. 'The bathroom's on the middle floor and sometimes when I've had a bath I'm naked when I run upstairs to bed.' I stopped. Remembered who he was. A Peacemaker. They can be funny when it comes to things like that.

'I'd rather that you didn't do that, Sir,' he said. 'If I were you, I'd cover up. I know the lads who man that bridge. We don't want them to see things that they shouldn't, do we? Sir.'

He shook his head. I copied him.

He started down the stairs and I retreated so that I was always in between the garage door and him. 'I have seen you before,' he said. 'You work at the Town Hall.'

'Of course, that's where we must have met.'

'You are the one who works on System K,' he said.

My mouth was dry. I licked my lips. I wondered how he knew.

'Big test tonight,' he said. 'You must be nervous.'

I'd hoped he hadn't noticed. I told him that I thought I might be coming down with something.

He backed away. 'That sneeze', he said.

I coughed.

'I won't detain you anymore. I hope that you feel better in the morning, sir. We need you at your post. Tomorrow, then.'

I nodded.

'Duty calls,' he said. He stepped up to the front door, opened it, and let the cold night. 'Remember. If you happen to see anything.' He looked out at the darkness.

Then he turned.

I moved up close to him. Go now, I urged him silently, no second thoughts.

'If I see anyone?' I offered.

'Anything,' he said. 'You would be wise to let me know.' He added: 'Sir.'

I nodded; gulped: 'I will.'

'I find it's best to keep things simple. Sir,' he said. 'To keep good separate from bad. Lines knot when they get tangled'. As he spoke he put his fingers to his throat, his thumb and index finger pressing either side into his Adam's Apple. Then he winked. Released himself. 'Knots can be dangerous.'

It made me gasp.

He walked away across the street towards his house.

I shut the door and locked it.

I started shaking. I was numb. My legs felt weak. I staggered to the stairs. I sat down awkwardly upon the bottom step, askew, my knees scrunched up, my right hip jammed into the step above. I gripped one of the balusters for steadiness.

A voice out of the darkness in the garage: 'Has he gone?'

'For now.'

The little Drudjer peered around the door. He blinked. It takes a little time for eyes that have been swamped with darkness to adjust to light. He crept into my hallway, bare-skinned, crouching, hairy as a monkey, one hand reaching out in front of him as if to feel his way, the other cupped to shield his genitals.

What had she seen in him?

'Your bloody backpack almost finished us,' I said. 'What's in it anyway?'

He carefully unzipped it, slipped his hand inside and, with the air of a magician, extracted not a rabbit but a heavy metal object, oval-shaped and of the same size as a book. It was a silver frame around the watercolour portrait of a woman.

'We almost lost our lives for that? Who is it anyway? Another of your women, I suppose.'

'She was my wife,' he said with dignity.

'I didn't know you had one.'

'She's been dead some years. And after that, I am afraid, I rather lost my way.'

He hadn't seemed directionless, I thought, when he was heading for the mother of my boys.

'I need some clothes,' he said.

'They're being washed.'

He looked at me. I'm tall and thin and he was short and stout. 'A dressing gown, perhaps?'

I hesitated.

'Oh, for goodness sake. I'm not a thief. What could I even thieve, supposing that I wanted to?' He looked around. 'Your books? Go in your downstairs loo and steal the bleach? And then what? Run away? Out there where I am being hunted? Naked? Use your common sense!'

I trudged upstairs. It seemed a long way to the top. I stared out of the window as I climbed. The guard post on the footbridge. There was something going on. Most nights they had their searchlights pointing at the river so that they could shoot at any Drudjers who were swimming to escape. Tonight the lights were aimed towards the Kennels. Maybe that was how he'd got away with it. He'd seen that they weren't watching and he took his chance. It was in character.

I hated him.

He tied me up in knots. I couldn't think straight when I was with him. He stood there, bare and ugly, and he told me what to do and even now he had me running up the stairs. I won't, I told myself. I will be buggered if I act the slave to him. He's just a bloody Drudjer after all.

Besides, I really didn't want his bollocks in my underpants.

I couldn't leave him naked though. It was disgusting, horrible.

I found the perfect thing for him to wear. I opened up the wardrobe and I saw it straight away. A dressing gown my wife had worn. She'd picked it up on holiday. Blue artificial silk, a silver dragon on the back with baggy sleeves. Cut short, mid-thigh. It might preserve his modesty but it would make him look ridiculous.

When I got back downstairs I found that he was in the garage. He had found the switch and turned the lights on. On an empty shelf he'd placed the photographic portrait of his wife. It looked as if he'd made himself at home.

'It isn't very warm,' he said.

I shrugged.

'But I suppose,' he said, 'that it will do. We need to clean it out, of course.' He coughed. 'It's rather dusty. Do you have some rugs? A solid floor can be so hard. I'll need some bedding. Do you think that you could bring a mattress down the stairs? It wouldn't be that heavy; you could slide it down.'

'You can't stay here. You have to go. As soon as I have washed your clothes.'

'Oh dear,' he said. 'I thought you understood. You don't have any other choice. I heard you talking to the Peacemaker. I heard it all. You had the chance to turn me in. You didn't take it. Too late now, you'll have to make the best of it. Because you lied.'

'I didn't lie,' I said. 'Not properly.'

'You told a whole damn pack of lies, court cards and all. If there is one thing that the Peacemakers can't stand it's being lied to. Can you hear that sound?'

He put his hand into the air as if for silence. I heard nothing. 'No. What sound?'

'Boats being burned,' he said. 'Dice being cast and rivers crossed. No going back, not now; you've passed the point of no return.'

I felt immensely sorry for myself. 'When all of this is over ...' I exclaimed.

'Yes,' he said. 'You'll be a hero. Yes. You'll tell your children how you saved a Drudjer's life.'

I didn't want to be a hero.

'After all,' he said, 'this is the only chance you'll have. It's not as if you had top billing in the movie of your life. You were a bit part player, nothing more. But now ... I know that you don't have a hero's rugged looks but heroes have been shaped from clay before. When you look back you will be glad I chose your door.'

The problem with the hero's role is the improbability of their survival. Watching movies we suspend our disbelief. But when we leave the darkened rooms, the unromantic and unblinking light of day reminds us that heroic glory has a price: short lives and brutal deaths.

'I'm giving you your only chance,' he said. 'You do the right thing now and you'll redeem yourself.'

'Redeem myself?' He was a hypocrite, like all his kind. 'I have done nothing wrong. I'm not the one who needs redemption.'

'You're a puppet of the Peacemakers,' he said.

It was ridiculous. I turned my back on him.

'I heard you telling him,' he said. 'You work on System K.'

'Named after you,' I said. 'Although it shouldn't be.'

If anybody understood the implications of my work on System K it would be Mr Kapko, boss of Kapko Industries, the firm that built the system I'd designed. Its purpose was efficiency. It tracked the energy and water usage of the buildings in a district of a town so that supply could match demand. It had an element of forecasting, allowing council officers to plan towards the future. My job was nothing more exciting than analysis. Each Friday I submitted a report which summarised the week and made predictions. It was labelled: Confidential. It was circulated to the Mayor and his top team of councillors.

But I suspected that a copy was diverted to the Peacemakers.

In recent weeks I'd taken on a little more. The system analysed the usage of utilities. Of water. Energy. And now we added data. We recorded information flowing in and out. Not the content, just the use. We didn't listen to your phone calls but we knew when you had phoned and for how long. We didn't read your emails but we knew you'd sent them. We didn't bug your private conversations but we knew what you participated in. It was enough to build a profile of your household.

It had been enough for me to know that soon the Kennels would explode. There were too many people living far too close together. Now there were too many messages. I knew the Drudjers were becoming restless. So I wrote it up in my report,

'I don't work for the Peacemakers,' I said.

'That's not the way posterity will understand it,' he replied.

I knew that he was right.

'I know you didn't want to shelter me but it's too late to turn back now. If I am caught, you're caught as well. You don't want that. They'll hurt you and they'll make you wish that you were dead and in the end you will be.'

Yes. I knew. My hand went to my throat. I nodded. I was dumb.

'But if you stick this out and we come through I promise I'll tell nobody that you were too afraid to be a hero. It's a promise.'

But he'd broken promises before.

The lights went out. There was a roar like thunder and the air inside the house shook once, as if it shrugged. The front door rattled, once.

'What's happening?' I whispered to the dark.

'It has begun,' he said.

CHAPTER THREE: THE NIGHT OF VIOLENCE

'What's happening?' I asked him as the echoes of that first explosion faded.

'They've attacked the Kennels.' He was grinning with excitement. I'd have sworn he sounded glad.

Which puzzled me.

The Kennels was a slum, a ghetto, a favela, where the poor were penned. It was a lobster pot: you might get in but you could never leave. Its boundaries to east and north were roads, upon the west there was the railway, to the south the river. Each was fenced, patrolled and spotlighted both day and night; the bridges and the paths were checkpointed. It was cut off.

Since it was built, back in the days of steam, it was the poorest district. Many Drudjers lived there in the past. That's why they picked it. Once the Peacemakers had grabbed control of law enforcement in this town, they rounded up those Drudjers who had moved away and herded them into the Kennels so what was a shanty town became an overcrowded cage. And even those who were as rich as Mr Kapko with a penthouse flat were forced to move.

The Peacemakers had turned this place into a Drudjer pen and now they were attacking it? That made no sense. And why did Mr Kapko sound triumphant?

There'd only been a single bang. It had been loud but in its aftermath came silence.

'Have they killed them all?' I whispered.

'Don't be stupid,' he replied.

Then we began to hear the screams.

Though all screams are alike, each scream has individuality. Each scream has its own provenance. There are the deep-voiced screams of hatred and of anger; there are breathless screams of fear; there are the ragged shrieks of pain, often, for the dying, punctuated by a stream of gasps; there are the sobbing screams of grief. And then, as well, beyond the beastly sounds that humans make, I heard the screams that shells make as they shred the air.

I shuddered as I heard a helicopter overhead. Its spinning wings went whoomp and whoomp. I clutched at Mr Kapko, grabbing for his hand. 'That's here,' I said. 'It's right above this house. They are attacking us!'

He disengaged himself from me and stepped away. 'Of course they're not. You will be safe enough. You're special. You are not a Drudj.'

I heard a whistle and a thud, the ground shook and there was a rattle as if somebody had hurled a grab of gravel onto corrugated iron. I ducked.

'That's mortar fire,' he said.

There was a burst of gunfire. 'That was close!' he said.

I knelt down on the floor. I told myself I ought to pray. I hadn't been inside a church in years. I had forgotten how.

He poked me with his foot. He laughed at me. 'It's too late now. You should have thought of that before. Now, there is nothing you can do.'

Another howl, as if a wolf was being crucified.

'You had your chance,' he said, 'and look what happened. This is all your fault.'

I squeaked. I didn't understand.

'You're safe at home while there are Drudjers dying in the streets,' he said.

Another blast. The garage shook. The air was sucked out of my lungs, my chest was squashed.

And then somebody hammered at the door. 'Please, please!' they roared.

I froze.

'Your chance to be a hero,' Mr Kapko said.

'But I don't want to be a hero!' I yelled back.

He reached down and he grabbed my arm and hauled me to my feet. He spoke into my face, his mouth so close that I could feel the heat of anger on his breath. 'If you survive all this you'll want your sons to have respect for you.'

'If I survive? What if I don't?'

'It doesn't matter very much if you die as a hero or a coward,' he replied. 'The dead are dead.' He grasped my arm and shook me. I was limp and flopped about. 'You'll be alright,' he told me. 'All the danger is the far side of the river.' Then, his strong hands gripping me, he hauled me, dragged me, marched me down the hallway to the door. I had no strength to stop. I was too scared. I didn't know which frightened me the most: what might be waiting for me outside in the dark or what was here right now, the monster holding me. He pushed me up against the wall and promised me that I'd be safe. And then the door was open and I found myself outside.

I gulped the cold air of the night.

I was alone. There wasn't anybody here. He had been right. The trouble was across the river. I could see the flashes. There were bangs. But that was there. In my street there was peace. It was, perhaps, as calm as anything could be this side of death. My fear subsided. It had done its job: I was alert to danger. But I wasn't overwhelmed.

I looked around. The street on which I lived was made up of two rows of terraced houses running north to south. There was a grassy island in the middle in the shape of an ellipse; a roadway circumnavigated its perimeter. The southern side was closed off by an arch. It therefore seemed a little like a London square, except it was rectangular and it was modern, and there were no buildings on the northern side, which was the grassy space that swept down to the river and the bridge which I could see out of my staircase window.

The arch had been the ornamental entrance for a foundry that, back in the days of Empire, smelted iron and worked it into products sold around the world. It's decorated brickwork advertised prosperity and permanence. But now, a tramp lived there. He'd built a tiny home inside the narrow covered walkway at the arch's top behind its castellated battlements. No one could reach him there. He sat up there like Quasimodo, though without the bells, and sprinkled rhyming curses on the heads of any passer-by. We nicknamed him 'The Officer', because he dressed in military clothes, one day combat fatigues, the next a sailor suit.

The manufactory had lost its way when people turned to cars and, later, planes. It stuck to agricultural machines. It closed when people wanted weapons. After that the land was derelict for many years. They had to decontaminate the land before they were allowed to build on it.

Now I was standing on the path before my home and peering at the far side of the street. Nine houses: every window dark. It wasn't that surprising. From the data held by System K I knew that many properties in town were now unoccupied. Some owners had been relocated to the Kennels; others had escaped into the countryside. We were becoming ghostly. No one moved. Dark mushroomed. Silence reigned.

There was another cough of gun fire and I shied. I hadn't been prepared; I hadn't seen the flash. It sounded close. Where was it coming from? I couldn't tell. The street had three brick sides and echoes bounced around.

If there was any danger it would come across the river, rushing up the grassy bank. The other way was safe; it must be. Through the archway was a major road and on its other side the Town Hall stood. That would be guarded by the Peacemakers. The Drudjers would be crazy to attack it.

What was that?

Another shriek. Too close.

The silhouette of someone running?

Then there was a bursting blaze of sparkles in the sky. Time hesitated for a semibreve. I quivered as the earth beneath me bumped.

Then I heard him tell me to: 'Go in! There is a curfew. It is dangerous out here.'

My eyes were dazzled so I couldn't see him but, despite the background noise from the reverberations, I could recognise his voice.

'What are you doing? Go inside,' I heard him urge.

I wish I could, I thought.

It was the same young man that I had seen before. He stood quite still, beside the wasteland on the road that forms the north side of the square. He held a sub-machine gun at his waist. He moved it in a lazy curve, the barrel pointing at the ground as if was a scythe and he was harvesting.

'It isn't safe,' he said. He added: 'Sir.'

I told him that I thought that I had heard somebody scream.

'I can't hear anything but screams,' he said. He sounded tired. A sudden flash lit up his dirty face, accentuating chin and cheek-bones and the shadows in the hollows of his eyes.

'What's happening?' I asked. 'What's going on?'

'It's best to stay indoors. Sir.' And another cannonade of bangs and whistles backed his words.

'Who's shooting? Who is being shot?'

'Sir,' he insisted.

'I just came out to see what the commotion was about ...'

'It's not a good idea'.

I was distracted for a moment. Something moved perhaps. I wasn't sure. Sometimes you notice what's not there.

But then I saw it move again.

'I caught a glimpse,' I said.

'A Drudjer? Here? On this side of the river?' He had changed. He added: 'Sir.' It was, all of a sudden, quite a different word.

I shook my head. 'Perhaps it was a shadow, nothing more.'

He sniffed the air. 'Yes, I can smell him. I was sure I could. I always trust my senses. He was here. Where did he go?'

'It may have been a woman. I could not be sure.'

He sniffed again. 'Perhaps he's wearing scent. But there's undoubtedly the musk of Drudjer masculinity.'

I pointed west, along the path that paralleled the river bank, towards the railway tracks. 'He went down there,' I said.

He nodded. 'It is where the trains slow down,' he said. 'That's when the Drudjers try to jump aboard.'

'Good luck,' I said.

'Good luck?' he echoed as he hurried off.

I watched until he disappeared around the corner of the road.

'He's gone,' I said. 'You're safe.'

I wasn't sure until he moved that he was there.

In hindsight I might say I should have been more careful. There were explosions just across the river, there were bullets being fired. I'd sent away the Peacemaker who called me 'Sir', the man pledged to protect me. I had seen a stranger hiding in the bush that marks the edge of my front garden. Why did I not think that he might be dangerous? In normal times he could have been a robber or a psychopath but in those days of chaos there were desperadoes, terrorists and martyrs; there were men who killed because they had to; there were men who killed because they liked it; there were tales of Drudjers who had sworn to take ten lives for every Drudjer put to death.

I should have been less reckless. All I can suppose is that I had been swamped with terror, overloaded, so it was impossible for me to think. It wasn't sensible or wise, it wasn't even typical, but this is what I did. I sent away the man who might protect me and I told the shadow hiding in my hedge that he was safe.

He stood. He wore a charcoal three piece business suit, well-polished shoes, gold cufflinks and a purple tie. His clothes were creased; his hands were shaking as he smoothed his hair.

He panted: 'too damn close.' He smelt of smoke. 'I thought I'd bowed,' he puffed, 'my final curtain call.'

'We'd better get inside,' I said. The door, I saw, had opened. He went first. I followed him.

As soon as we had reached the temporary safety of my hall I studied him. He made a piteous sight, like a dishevelled pea-cock. He was dressed in order to impress, in smart and stylish finery but when you scrutinised him he was shabby, tattered and unkempt. His suit, which fitted him so perfectly he might have grown inside it, had a missing button on the left hand cuff; it had been ripped a little at the corner of the right hand trouser pocket. On the knees there was a stain as if he'd knelt in something. There were muddy splashes on the shoes.

He looked from side to side. He didn't have a lot to see. My hallway is a narrow passage. He was standing in between the bookcase on his left side and the door into the downstairs toilet on his right. He looked at me. He looked at Mr Kapko. I supposed he smiled although it was a weak, insipid smile, its happiness diluted to the point of tastelessness.

He knelt down suddenly in front of me and took my hand and placed it on his muddled hair which, though it shone, was soft and dry. 'You must be Mr Angel.'

'Angelo.' He'd startled me. 'My name's Ed Angelo.'

'To me you are my guardian angel,' he replied. 'How can I ever thank you? ' He began to sob. 'You saved me. Just in time. I thought ... I don't like thinking what I thought.'

'Don't cry,' said Mr Kapko. 'Don't make so much fuss. You are too loud. They're only just outside the door. They'll hear your whining. Then we'll all be finished.'

'Come into the garage,' I suggested, but he wobbled when he tried to rise. He wasn't very steady on his feet. We had to stand on either side supporting him. We put him in a corner of the garage where he leaned against the back wall, clinging to an empty shelf.

'I've had a shock,' he told us, which was obvious. He asked for coffee and he told me that he liked it black with sugar 'for my nerves.'

I went to put the kettle on. He called out after me: 'perhaps a little brandy, or a scotch would do, or even gin, a smidgeon, just a soupcon, just the dibbiest of little dablets, por favor.'

'Don't talk so loudly,' Mr Kapko said.

Two Drudjers in my garage. I was serving them. It seemed that nowadays the world was upside down.

Watched kettles make a lot of noise. I tipped the coffee powder and the sugar in the mugs and tiptoed to the kitchen door. I listened. Mr Kapko muttered something but what it was I couldn't quite make out.

'Let me alone,' the other Drudjer said. 'It was too awful. I won't think about it now. Leave me alone.'

That worried me. I had so many questions. Was the whole thing not a little too convenient? How had this latest Drudjer known my name? Why had he picked my hedge to hide in? Did they know each other?

He had asked for brandy. I'd been told that Drudjers didn't drink. Perhaps if I could make him drunk I might discover what was going on. I had no brandy but there was some vodka. As the kettle boiled, at last, I splashed the water in the mug and glugged a generous amount of liquor in. I almost spilled it as I rushed it through.

He sipped his drink as if each mouthful was a fresh delight. 'Oh. That's so good. Mmm. Wow.'

I couldn't keep up with this mood-chameleon who seemed to swoop from scaredy cat to connoisseur in moments.

'Hush,' said Mr Kapko. 'Keep your voices down.'

'Sodz,' the other said. He offered me his hand. We shook. 'My name is Sodz. The pleasure's mine. It always is.'

The next explosion made us jump, all three of us. It took us by surprise, again. One interlude of peace and you believe the nightmare's ended.

Sodz was startled. 'Not again.'

'Shut up,' said Mr Kapko and we stood in silence, hiding in an empty box and listening to save our lives.

But there was nothing. Noiselessness, like darkness, is more fearsome than a scary sound. Imagination fills the emptiness with monsters.

'What I want to know,' I whispered, 'is ...' I couldn't finish. I did not know where to start. There were so many things I didn't understand.

'Do you two know each other?' I enquired.

'Where there are Kennels there are dogs,' said Mr Kapko. He had twisted lips. His nose was wrinkled as if there was something nasty in the air.

Sodz, who had been weeping, stopped.

'He calls himself a businessman, said Mr Kapko. 'Ask him what he buys and sells. This man would dig up cadavers if there was profit to be made from selling bones.'

'Free enterprise,' sniffed sullen Sodz.

'Black market goods. Exploiting need, exploiting hunger and exploiting those who suffer illnesses.'

'Providing food, providing medicines that otherwise they'd have to do without.' Sodz was forgetting his distress, forgetting fear, replacing these with anger.

'Shut your mouth,' said Mr Kapko. 'Don't speak so loud. Or do you want us to be captured?'

I felt sympathy for Sodz right then. I think it must have been the way he looked that made me pity him. The optimism of his tailored suit had been subverted by the stained reality of mud and dirt and damage.

Then I looked a little closer.

'You're not wet,' I said. 'Why not?'

'He didn't have to swim the river,' Mr Kapko said. 'He has a pass to cross the bridge.'

'I thought he was a Drudjer.'

'Barely Drudjer.' Mr Kapko said it with a sneer.

'So how is he allowed to travel to and from the Kennels?'

'He has a lot of friends.' He gestured air-quotes with his fingers.

'Friends are friends,' said Sodz. 'It is important to be friendly.'

'Profitable,' Mr Kapko said.

'I like to be the friend of ... well, of nearly everyone,' said Sodz.

'He mostly likes to be a friend of Peacemakers especially the ones who guard the bridge. They get a lot of presents. That's how he smuggles stuff into the Kennels. That is how he comes and goes.'

'But if he is a buddy of the guards,' I asked, 'why did he have to hide just now?' A bubble of suspicion started in my stomach. 'Was that an act? Just now, were you pretending to be scared? Are you some sort of spy?'

'For sake's sake shut your mouth,' said Mr Kapko. 'Muzzle it. We can't afford to make a noise.'

'I'm not a spy,' said Sodz, 'I'm not.'

'They know you're here,' I said, appalled. 'They followed you.' I looked at my surroundings. I was standing in a hollow space, a little larger than a normal tomb. It had a single door. Just one way in and when they came in through the door I would be trapped. There would be no way out. The only way that I was leaving here was as a corpse.

Plus it was fucking cold.

'He's not a spy,' said Mr Kapko. 'If he was they would be here by now.'

'Then how do you explain that one day he goes in and out, the next he's being chased?'

'He must have angered them somehow. Perhaps they wanted bigger bribes. Perhaps he has outgrown his usefulness. That's how the market works.' He sounded bitter and I thought of how the company that he had founded had been taken from him. You spend a lifetime building but it only takes a moment for it all to go.

'I had a rendezvous,' said Sodz. He stared at Mr Kapko. 'You know who.'

'Oh yes,' said Mr Kapko. 'How could I forget? He isn't just a smuggler of illicit goods. He is a gigolo.'

'Why don't you call a spade a shovel, mon cher puritan,' said Sodz. 'Why don't you say I am a ravager, a profligate, a jigger jigger, a bordello boy, a lecher, whorehound, goat, a chartered libertine,a prostitute? Fuck you, my friend. You're not so high and mighty. It's not like you've never picked a penny from the street.'

CHAPTER FOUR:
A RIGHT PAELLA
OF A NIGHT

There was an interlude of silence. In this space hostility was strong enough to smell.

'I think it's stopped,' I said.

'What time is it?' asked Mr Kapko, fidgeting. 'Too late?'

A thought occurred to me. 'You're not expecting someone else?' I asked.

'It's been a right paella of a night,' said Sodz. 'It's been as dodgy as a wobble board. What's going on?'

There was another knock upon the door.

Sodz made a movement with his hands: palm down, he moved them horizontally so that they crossed and uncrossed, as if he were brushing any blame away. 'It wasn't me!' he mouthed. His eyes were wide; he was afraid.

I couldn't think. There was a tangled throng of half-connected feelings whirling round the inside of my brain. Half way along, I found that I was moving down the hall towards the door like someone walking in their sleep, as if I was a zombie newly resurrected from the grave by Papa Kapko. I had no choice. I was reluctant but unable to resist. I told myself: if Sodz, intentionally or unwittingly, had brought the Peacemakers then there was nothing to be done. They'd catch us. We'd be shot. And if I didn't answer straight away then they would smash the door down. I was trapped.

If they were out there then I was a convict plodding to the gallows. My last few seconds. I was proud, as only those bereft of hope can be, that I could still command my legs to walk, that I could still unlock the door although my fingers fumbled. I was proud that I could open it.

There were two Drudjers standing there. One was a girl, perhaps eighteen, wrapped head to toe in black. The other was a thin boy of about the same age wearing nothing but a pair of sky blue running shorts. The boy cascaded river water but the girl seemed almost dry.

I was bewildered, too benumbed to speak.

'Please,' said the boy. I stood aside. They tumbled through the door. The river water from the boy baptised the floor. My carpet would be soiled beyond repair.

'I'm very sorry for the mess,' apologised the girl. She smiled at me. I liked her smile. It brought her eyes alive. 'Thank you for having us.'

Before I closed the door I peeked outside. Had they been seen? It seemed unlikely. Many of the houses on the street had emptied since the Siege. There was a curfew; at this time of night no one walked by unless it was a Peacemaker patrol. I hoped that he was still off chasing shadows. It was lucky that the doorstep of my house was screened off from the footbridge by the hedge that Sodz had hidden in. There was, of course, that searchlight on the Town Hall roof but that swung slowly round the sky: it wasn't difficult to dodge.

I thought I might have got away with it.

I shut the door. I locked it. Four. Now there were four. 'How many more?' I asked.

'Are we the f-f-f-f-f-f-first?' the boy said.

'Look what flotsam has been swept up by the flood,' said Sodz, appearing in the doorway of the garage. 'I heard your voices and I knew that it was you. Your voice is always such sweet music, Madame Blossom. And you've brought your little brother, I perceive.'

'B-Big b-brother,' said the boy although he did indeed seem young compared to her. He had the tattoo of two lovers kissing on his chest.

'Get him a towel,' commanded Mr Kapko. I was stunned. 'Can you not see he needs a towel?' I stared.

'If you would be so kind,' said Blossom, putting out her hand and touching me upon the wrist. I shivered. 'He's been in the water.'

'He's just wet behind the ears,' sneered Sodz.

'You're dry,' I told her. Blossom. How was that a Drudjer name?

'We had a mattress. I lay on it while he pushed. He's very cold. Please help us. We are very grateful you have let us come to you.'

'Just get the towel for Ochre,' Mr Kapko said.

'John Zombie's d-d-dead,' the boy was saying as I brought the towels downstairs. 'John Z-Z-Zombie's dead. The fool g-got h-high before he went to f-f-fight. I s-s-said to h-him: You need to th-th-th-th-think. He laughed. He said: It makes the b-b-bullets slower. But it didn't. He was always wrong. He was a s-s-stupid fool. I had to see him d-d-die. I could d-do n-nothing. He just lay there and I couldn't get to him. '

'And so you ran away,' said Sodz.

'It was the only thing I could d-do. M-m-m-m-my thanks.' He took a towel and started rubbing. 'I am s-s-so cold.'

'I brought a duvet,' I explained. 'I don't have any clothes your size. My boys are younger and I am too big for you.'

'You have a wife. Think out the coffin. Go fetch him a dress,' suggested Sodz. 'It wouldn't be the first time.'

'Th-Thank you,' said Ochre. 'The duvet will b-be f-fine.' He told his sister she should turn away, then slipped his shorts off, rubbed the towel against his bare backside, and wrapped the quilt around himself. He had a skinny rump. He wouldn't suit a dress, I thought. My wife is made of sterner stuff.

More coffee. Lots of sugar. I was running out. Back in the garage Sodz was sticking to the vodka. 'This is not for boys,' he said. 'Boys shouldn't drink. They are too young; they have no head for it.'

'I'm not a boy,' snarled Ochre through his teeth. He had stopped stuttering now he was dry.

'You're bleeding,' Blossom told him, pointing to a smear of blood upon the duvet.

'That was clean,' I grumbled. First the carpet, second this. 'When she comes home my wife will not be happy.'

Blossom asked, round-eyed with frightened eyebrows: 'When are you expecting her?'

'She's on her ... holidays,' said Mr Kapko and he laughed. 'Some people still have holidays.'

'It's just a gash,' said Ochre who had been investigating where his body leaked. 'I must have caught it on a branch. It doesn't really need a bandage but I ought to get it clean. The river's rather dirty. Do you have some antiseptic?'

Suddenly all hell broke loose: guns, cannon-fire, continuing for several seconds. Then it stopped as swiftly as it had begun. 'It means they've won,' said Mr Kapko.

'Why?' I asked.

'They always do that at the end,' he said. 'One final burst to celebrate.'

'It's been a right moqueca of a night, a classic bouillabaisse,' said Sodz.

'What happens now?' I asked.

'Where's Xan?' asked Ochre suddenly.

'Be patient. There's still time,' said Mr Kapko.

'Who is Xan?' I asked.

'We have to wait for Xan,' said Ochre.

'Well of course we do,' said Mr Kapko. 'We can't go out there yet. They will be mopping up survivors for a while. When you attack a place such as the Kennels you expect some of the people there to run away; some will escape. There will be more patrols tomorrow. This is not a time to be outside. We'll have to stay in hiding.'

'Here? You can't stay here. This is my home.'

'Stop shrieking,' Mr Kapko told me though I hadn't shrieked. 'They will be going round the streets and listening at doors.'

'Why me?' I asked. 'Why here? It cannot be coincidence. You didn't all four turn up at a single house by accident. You know each other. This was planned. Why did you pick on me?'

'I gave them your address,' said Mr Kapko.

As he spoke, a throbbing told us that the helicopter had returned. We all sat silently, each one of us locked in, unmoving, as we listened to the blades go: 'threat, threat, threat'.

He had been here of course. He must have been. I didn't want to think about it. He was arrogant. It would have been his style. Not incognito rooms in chain hotels; he would have sought more personal experiences. More intrusive. He'd have found it more exciting. He'd already told me he liked risk.

The helicopter wasn't passing. It was lingering. I hoped the infra-red detectors couldn't sense five bodies crouching at the bottom of a house.

He would have marked me out. It wasn't simply that my house was nearest to the river, to the Kennels. He'd have chosen me. He liked to pick on me. My wife. My work. I'd let him get away with it.

The helicopter stayed too long before it moved away. It was as if it knew. It was as if it was a cat and we were mice. This is the thing with hunters: they have better fun if they can tease their prey.

When it had gone at last I asked how many more I might expect. How many had been given my address?

'John Zombie's dead. Perhaps one more, that's all.'

'Xan,' Ochre breathed and Blossom looked at him.

'How long do you intend to stay?' I asked and then I knew the thought that had been itching at my mind. 'If you all fled the Peacemaker's attack why is it you,' I jabbed my finger straight at Mr K, 'came to this house before,' I stabbed my finger at his chest in emphasis, 'we heard the first explosions?'

'Luck.'

I echoed him incredulously: 'Luck?'

He looked at me, his finger to his lips.

Four onto one, I thought. If I scream loud enough, I thought, the Peacemakers will hear.

'It seems that we will have to stay a little longer than we first intended,' Mr Kapko said.

'You said you'd leave tomorrow.'

'We will leave as soon as it is safe,' he answered. 'Safe for us and safe for you.'

'When you have had a jambalaya of a night such as tonight,' said Sodz, 'whizz-bangs and everything, it takes a little while for things to settle down. We'll have to wait until the barbeque goes cold. A lot of bling was spilled tonight.'

A lot of vodka drunk, I thought.

'We have decided,' Mr Kapko said.

'Did I have any part to play in this decision?' I enquired.

He only shrugged.

'Do you have any antiseptic?' Ochre asked.

Blossom begged: 'Please help us.' She had juicy lips.

Sodz held his hand out. 'Do you want a pearl?' he asked.

It wasn't perfect, that is how I knew that it was real. It wasn't spherical, more like an egg. It wasn't milky white, as you associate with pearls, but tinged with pink, like blushing, like the dawn. It lay there, nestled in the crinkles of his palm. It was as big as any pearl I'd ever seen, a little larger than a grape.

'It must be worth a fortune,' I exclaimed.

He shrugged. 'It's only shellfish shit. But it is worth at least a few days rent. What do you say, amigo?'

Me, I didn't say a word. I reached for it. I didn't take it. I just touched it. That is not a contract. We did not shake hands or anything. I touched it with a fingertip. It was quite cool. It felt a little rough. How did that constitute agreement? I didn't even nod.

CHAPTER FIVE: SODZ AND THE MEMSAHIB

'Where did you get that?' Mr Kapko asked. He sounded shocked and angry. I was glad that he was rattled. It was petty vengeance but it tasted good.

'Well, well, well, would anybody credit it? Who would have thought that little Sodz the guttersnipe, the good-for-nothing scallywag, the scoundrel, the delinquent, Sodz who never will be good enough to mix with ritzy swankers, that Sodz, should possess more lucre in this ball of nacre than a Kapko at the very pinnacle of Drudj society.'

He was so gloriously jubilant he fidgeted.

'I told you not to see her,' Mr Kapko said. 'That's where you were. You disobeyed me.'

It was like bursting a balloon. Sodz sounded sulky. 'No. You didn't tell me not to go. You just said it was dangerous.'

'And I was right. Because of you, we're all in danger.' Mr Kapko rolled his eyes. 'I should know better. If you work with Lowlife Drudjers you will get what you deserve: catastrophe.'

I looked around. The garage had four walls, one door. It was a trap. And now, now I was caught, he used words such as 'danger' and 'catastrophe'. What had Sodz done?

If I was frightened Sodz was angry. 'She is dead. But I suppose you knew that when you warned me off. I found her dead.' He shook his head. 'I can't believe she's dead. How can she be? She is so gorgeous and so full of life. She likes to gossip,' - here he chuckled - 'and she can be sweetly vicious. She is shrewd and she loves laughing at herself. She likes cartoons and gorgonzola cheese and doggy style and opera. She loves the aria 'I'll kiss your mouth'. And she likes me. She can't be dead.'

'Who's dead?' asked Ochre. 'Xan?'

'Not Xan.' I watched as Blossom reassured her brother, reaching out to stroke his hair. 'Xan's tough. She's clever. She'll escape. You'll see. She will be fine.'

'Not Xan?' asked Ochre.

'No, not Xan,' said Blossom. 'Someone else. Sodz had a girlfriend.'

Mr Kapko scoffed: 'a client.'

'She was not just any woman.' Sodz was sniffing once again. 'She had a name: Salome. She was someone.'

Blossom handed him a tissue so that he could wipe his eyes.

He blew his nose. 'And now she's dead. And it was Papa Kapko's fault.' He pointed. He accused. 'You set me up. You knew that this would happen.'

'I knew nothing.' Mr Kapko held his hands up to display his palms. 'I don't see why you're so upset. She was a Memsahib. You're a gigolo. She was a customer. Someone you fucked. What's wrong with you? She wasn't Drudj. It wasn't like you could have made a go of it. She was the enemy.'

I was appalled. 'A Memsahib? Do you mean ...?' A Memsahib. That is what they called their wives. 'You mean that she was married to a Peacemaker?'

'She was a woman,' Sodz said, 'and a chatterbox. Her favourite meal was fish and chips and Chardonnay and she liked yellow roses and blue cheese and fat romantic novels, Brahms and Beethoven and dance and ambient, and singing karaoke and she liked old-fashioned songs and she liked me. And I liked her. And she is dead. You set me up.'

'Not Xan,' said Ochre.

'No,' his sister snapped. 'I have already told you. What is wrong with you.' She looked at him. Her eyes were sharp. 'Are you not feeling well?'

'I feel a little strange,' he said. 'May I sit down?' With Blossom's help he sat down on the floor. 'Do you think Xan will be alright?'

His sister had removed the duvet from his leg. He had a nasty gash, high on his inner thigh. There seemed to be a lot of blood. It looked as if he had been gored. I wondered what had done it. Could he have been stabbed? But it was less a puncture, more a tear. Barbed wire perhaps.

'It's just a flesh wound,' Ochre said.

'It needs a bandage,' Blossom said.

'Needs antiseptic. River water,' Ochre said.

I offered him the vodka. 'Drudjers not. Forbidden alcohol,' he said.

His sister took the bottle. 'This is medicine.' Carefully, she dribbled it across the bleeding wound.

He flinched and made a face.

'The more it hurts, the better,' Blossom said.

Sodz laughed. 'Save some for me.'

'He needs a bandage.' Blossom looked at me.

I had just washed my sheets. I didn't really need a freshly laundered pillowcase. I fetched it from the kitchen, wincing as she ripped it.

'Mrs Angelo will not be pleased,' said Mr Kapko.

'You can go to hell,' I said.

We all watched Blossom as she wrapped the cloth around her brother's thigh, her fingers deft and delicate.

'I wouldn't mind her doing that to me,' said Sodz. He licked his lips.

'You keep,' said Ochre, panting, 'Lowlife hands away.'

'He's getting stiff,' said Sodz. 'His sister. What a pervert.'

Blossom fumbled. Ochre gasped. He told her not to tie the knot too tight. When she was done he pulled the duvet back across his leg. His face was damp with sweat; his features fixed into a rictus.

Sodz bent and plucked the bottle from the floor. He toasted: 'Blossom and her little brother. What a pretty pair.'

I shook my head to rattle loose the image that was budding there of Ochre's skinny bottom pumping in and out at Blossom's opened thighs. I didn't want to have such thoughts. I wished my wife was still around.

'And Xan,' said Ochre in a whisper.

'And Salome,' Blossom said.

'Salome!' Mr Kapko scoffed. 'He has forgotten her already. You see? It wasn't serious. How could it be? She wasn't Drudj? I don't blame Sodz; it's just the way he is. He loves, with his whole heart, one woman. At a time. She's out of mind as soon as she is out of sight. Then he moves on.'

'That's right,' said Sodz. 'That is exactly who I am: a bed-post-notcher, casual casanova, one-night-wonder-man, philanderer, punani-juggling lothario. Well fuck the lot of you. Salome was the sweetest and the sauciest and she liked watching soccer and she knew an awful lot of dirty words.' He had another long swig at his bottle. 'And she liked to bake and she liked me.' He wiped his hand across his mouth. 'And she is dead. And I'm entitled to forget her for a moment. I'm allowed. I don't know any other way to do this. Fuck.' He turned the vodka bottle upside-down. He shook a few last drips from it. 'That's it,' he said. 'It's over. She is ...' But he didn't finish, he just shook his head.

'What happened, Sodz?' asked Blossom.

'I don't know.'

'You went to see her though I told you not to,' Mr Kapko said. 'I told you it was dangerous.'

'You said I ought to leave the Kennels, if I could, tonight. You told me that it wasn't safe. I thought you meant the Kennels. Because we all know, don't we, it is never safe when you are sleeping with another fellow's wife. I wanted ... She was wonderful. She liked the scent of new cut grass and she liked shopping and she liked old-fashioned sweets and she liked me. I wanted to be with her. So I went to see her in her flat.'

'In my flat,' Mr Kapko said. 'The flat she stole from me.'

Before the Siege, before the Peacemakers, he'd bought an office block above a pub to house his company. That's where I worked, though I was on the lowly second floor while he was at the top. But as we grew, as Kapko Industries expanded, he had built another floor on top of what was there already and converted it into a penthouse suite for him and Mrs K. It was luxurious, by all accounts. They said that it had views along the river almost to the sea.

That's where the big Boss of the Peacemakers was living now. It must have been his wife that Sodz was sleeping with. Salome. It was her that Sodz discovered dead.

'Had you arranged it in advance?' asked Blossom. 'Did she know when you were coming?'

'Eight o'clock.' Sodz nodded. 'I was bang on time.' He sniggered. 'And I always knew when she was coming. And I always bang on time.' He pushed the vodka bottle at me. 'More.'

'Don't be disgusting,' Ochre muttered.

'Wine,' I said. 'It's all I have.'

He nodded. 'Hope it isn't Chardonnay. I will drink anything but Chardonnay, my old amigo.'

'Let me get this straight,' said Blossom. 'When you got there, was she still alive?'

Sodz shook his head. He put his hand up to his cheek and brushed it angrily.

I went into the kitchen for the wine. As I returned there was the vaguest whimper of a boom, the sort of anticlimax that a paper bag produces when it bursts. No more.

'That's to the north,' said Mr Kapko. 'They are bombing refugees.'

'How did you get into the flat?' I asked, 'if, as you say, Salome was already dead?'

Sodz took the bottle, drank from it. 'I had the key.'

'She'd given you a key?'

'Not her.' He looked at Mr Kapko. 'Him.'

'My spare,' he muttered.

'He's the one who started it,' said Sodz. 'He fixed me up with her.'

I looked from one towards the other. Back again. Someone was hiding something.

'You unlocked the door,' said Blossom, 'and you found her dead. Was she just lying in the hallway?'

Mr Kapko shook his head. 'There is no hall. Not in the flat. The key unlocks the private door that leads onto the street. From there you walk across a vestibule to catch the lift. It only serves the top floor and it takes you straight into the living room.'

'The room is trashed,' said Sodz. He stared. I thought at first that he was looking straight at me and then I noticed that his eyes were focused far away. 'There is a man's discarded jacket, lined with purple satin. It is draped across an armchair. On the floor there is a wineglass, with its stem already snapped. The wine has stained the carpet. She will hate that. Red wine on a sheepskin rug. It makes a strange shape, like a bloody question mark.' He seemed to be immersed in reverie. He shook his head as if to wake himself. 'Pearls from a necklace have been scattered on the floor. I pick them up. No sense in wasting them. They form a trail like breadcrumbs leading to the bedroom door.'

'You followed it, of course,' I said.

'There is a strange aroma in the air. It isn't any smell I'd ever smelt before. She uses body butter: rich, thick and voluptuous. She used. That was the way she was. She smelled of decadence, of secrets, sweating flesh, of hot and humid sunsets and exhausted dawns. Not scented soap.'

'What happened next?' asked Blossom.

'She was in the bedroom. She was naked, tangled in the sheets. Her arm had tumbled to the floor. They'd strangled her. She had big bruises on her neck. Her face was ... horrible. I wondered whether she had fought. She would have fought. She was as fierce as flames. She would have scratched them. She had wicked nails. She used to dig them in my buttocks when ...' He stopped. He looked down at the floor.

I prised the bottle from his fingers. He'd already drunk more than he should have done. I found his mug and filled it and I passed it back to him.

He nodded. 'Pain relief.' He took a sip. 'That's when I heard the lift doors close. I realised that it was going down. I knew that someone must have called it. Somebody who had a key.'

'But who had killed Salome?' Blossom asked.

'I sneaked onto the balcony and squinted down and saw a Peacemaker outside the private entrance. I had walked into a trap. Whoever strangled my Salome set me up to take the blame.'

'She wasn't your Salome,' Mr Kapko pointed out.

'She wasn't yours.'

'She was a cheating wife,' I said.

'It doesn't matter what she'd done,' Sodz snapped. 'They slaughtered her. That shouldn't be the punishment for infidelity.'

'She wasn't one of us,' said Mr Kapko.

'She was kind, she liked to cuddle and she had an earthy laugh. I am a mongrel from the streets, a mutt, a ne'er do well, a brat, a rascal and a rogue and I'll eat any scrap that's tossed to me but she was choosy and she had the chance to choose and she chose me.' Sodz shed silent tears. 'And if you ever say another word about her, I will break you and I won't care who you are.'

'Don't talk. Too loud,' said Ochre, wrapping up still tighter in his duvet.

'She could talk the hind leg off a donkey and they didn't even kill her for herself. To them, she was just bait. They used her as a slaughtered lamb to tempt the wolf. I was their target.'

'Though they didn't need to kill her just to lure you in,' I pointed out.

'That was their little perquisite,' he said. 'An added bonus. I suspect that they enjoyed themselves. These are sick fucks that we are talking here. They're Peacemakers.'

'It's cold,' said Ochre. 'Please don't speak so loud.'

His sister knelt beside him, hugging him, to warm him with her breasts.

'But why?' I asked. 'Why go to all that trouble? You're a Drudjer. They could shoot you anyway.'

'How did you get away?' asked Blossom.

'What?' said Sodz.

'You're on the top floor of a tower block, surrounded,' she reminded him. 'The lift is heading back downstairs to pick up Peacemakers. What did you do? Fly from the roof?'

He looked at her. He took his time to reach across and take the bottle and to pour another glug glug glug of wine into his mug. He sniffed it, sipped it, savoured it. This was the secret agent Sodz, the gentleman, the gourmet, who was brave and dashing, bold and debonair. 'It wasn't easy. I suppose it was the rummest go, the closest shave a boyo ever had.'

'I'll tell you how he got away,' said Mr Kapko with a growl. 'He made a bargain. He betrayed us.'

'No.'

'You trade with them,' said Mr Kapko. 'You will even sleep with them providing that the price is right. Why not play

Judas? Treachery is just another deal.'

'That isn't true.'

'So how did you escape?' asked Blossom.

'It was wrong what they had done to her. I gathered up her perfumes, her cosmetics, her libretti, and I gave my gorgeous girl a send off that would suit the widow of a warrior. I piled it all around her bed. And then I set it burning. It was quick to catch alight. I opened up the windows and I fanned the flames. It started roaring. That was when I left.'

'That's why you smell of smoke,' I said.

'There is another set of stairs,' he said. 'They go down to the floor below.'

'The private stairs to Mr Kapko's office.' I'd been there. I'd seen them. I knew where they went. I'd never had the chance to use them.

'From the office there's another lift. It goes down to the ground floor, where they had reception when the company was still in business. I suspected they'd be coming up that lift as well as so I hid beneath the big desk in the corner of the room. I watched them bursting from the lift and charging up the stairs.'

He paused. He drank more wine. 'The building was in flames, you see. It was a tinderbox: a penthouse perched above an empty office block. They panicked.' He began to laugh. 'You should have seen them.'

'Not so loud,' warned Mr Kapko.

Sodz looked straight at him. 'It wasn't just because it was the penthouse. There is something special on that roof. I don't know what. Do you?'

We all watched Mr Kapko shake his head. But I was sure that he was telling lies.

Sodz simply shrugged. 'If you had seen them scampering up-stairs. I was forgotten for the moment, less important than the flames. So ... When the lift had emptied I got in and rode it to the bottom. Then I walked away. And here I am. And she is there. It's over. We will never lie in one another's arms again. We'll never kiss, and touch each other's skin, and stroke and lick and cuddle, flesh to flesh and flesh in flesh and pain and joy and ecstasy, again. No more. C'est fini, esta terminado, è finito, consummatum est.'

CHAPTER SIX:
BREAKFAST WITH
THE BOSS

I was exhausted. I had spent all night, the servant of my four guests in the garage, running up and down the stairs collecting bedding, carrying my microwave and my electric kettle from the kitchen, finding towels and flannels so that they could wash themselves at the small basin in the downstairs loo. They would be warm and clean, they were well-hidden, they could eat and drink.

With all that done, there wasn't time for me to go to bed. I drank a strong black coffee, took a shower, changed my clothes.

They would be staying in my garage. I was off to work.

You have to do what you have always done. To alter your routine makes people notice you.

I walked to work. It wasn't far. I didn't have a car. My wife had taken it. She'd seen the way the wind was blowing. Private vehicles had all but disappeared: sent to the front to fight against the Army who, so rumour said, were fast approaching from the north. The roads were empty, more or less, except for Peacemakers patrolling in the poshest cars that they could commandeer. We humble workers walked or used converted vans which acted as unscheduled buses with negotiated fares.

lack of traffic meant that you could hear the birds, ~~~adays they never seemed to bill or coo but only ~~ ~~~~k or squawk.

There's something in the freshness of a bright new dawn that heralds optimism. It's like being young. Gloom comes with age. Today, although the sun was rising and the air was cool, the morning seemed to promise melancholy. It didn't help that I was half asleep.

I left my front door, turning right and walking south, my back towards the river and the footbridge and the newly corpse-filled Kennels. I passed the house where my new neighbour lived. I wondered whether he was he sleeping in. Or was he standing at the window, watching me?

I walked beneath the arch.

My wife and I, when we had bought our house, both felt the arch was more than just a relic monumentalising a forgotten past of empire, industry and engineers. It seemed to us back then that we experienced a happier environment when walking through the arch into our street. We felt that where we lived possessed a kinder temperature, a gentler breeze, a friendlier, benigner atmosphere. We lived within a bubble of benevolence. The outside world, with all its threats and dangers, all its weirdness, started on the far side of the arch.

Not any more. Last night the world turned inside out. Now bad and good live cheek by jowl.

All was confused. Things had been well and truly broken.

Perhaps things would be mended when the Army reached us. It was coming, so they said. But it was slouching far too slowly and I wasn't sure that we could last that long.

The Officer was perched upon his keystone on the arch and as I passed beneath him he called out:

'When their years were fulfilled the Lord's host
(As in throng) fled from Egypt. And most
Of them died. But a few
Became parasites, who
Sucked the blood and the life from their host.'

He cackled and I wondered what he meant. It sounded like a warning. Had he seen the Drudjers coming to my house? It had been very dark. Unless the spotlight from the top of the Town Hall had caught them in its beam. But if it had, the Officer was in the perfect spot to see them.

It was Sodz, I thought. The other Drudjers came up from the river. Sodz had come along the road. His path went through the arch. He might have timed things so he never was illuminated by the searchlight but the Officer might easily have heard Sodz scuttle underneath.

He must have been aware there was a Drudjer on the street. He would have heard me talk to Nikov, sending him astray, Put two and two together and it's easy to come up with four. Four Drudjers in my garage.

Would he tell? Would he betray me? That's the trouble with a madman: you can never know which side he's on.

There wasn't any way to stop him so the only thing to do was hope he'd keep the secret. Cross my fingers, carry on and go to work.

I lingered for a moment on the footpath underneath the arch. In front of me there was a major road; if I turned left along it I would reach the south side of the road bridge where the High Street crossed the river. I was going straight across the road to the Town Hall. I had my office on the second floor.

There was a crowd of Peacemakers across the road. They filled the courtyard of the brutalist Town Hall. It was a pandemonium. It seemed to be some sort of celebration. I would have to cross that mob to reach reception so that I could go to work.

They were ecstatic. They had spent all night eliminating Drudjers. Now they hoisted beer cans, toasting triumph. There was mayhem, there was havoc. It was a delirium. They stamped their feet, they grinned, they yelled at one another. Young men who had fought and chased and butchered, and they hadn't had a chance to sleep, or wash, or shave, or change their clothes but they weren't tired. They stank of blood and mouthwash, sweat and medicated soap; they were as raw as daybreak. And they shouted. And they howled with laughter. And they danced. A demon thrust a can of lager at me, crying out: 'We won! We beat them. We're the best.'

'There are four Drudjers in his garage', I could hear my guilty conscience scream inside my head. In my imagination fingers pointed, eyes accused. How could they be so blind that they could not see from my face what I had done? Was this the mockery before the storm?

He rescued me. One moment I was lost among the swaggering, the triumph, then I felt his hand upon my shoulder. 'No. Not that way. This way. Sir.'

He had authority. The sea of bodies parted. He escorted me towards the side door of the building.

'But I work upstairs,' I said.

'Not anymore.'

I thought he was arresting me.

My right knee weakened and I wobbled and I felt him gripping me still tighter as his fingers dug into the hollow underneath my collarbone. He steadied me.

That door led to the basement.

We were council workers and we never went down there.

Down there was where the Peacemakers were housed. The rooms were windowless. The corridors were dark. It was a labyrinth, I had been told, in which the only way was down. They said that there were prisoners locked up down there. Interrogations. If you went down there, you stayed down there. You were forgotten.

He was there, so close behind me, as I stumbled down the stairs, that I could feel his body heat.

I wondered whether he had killed last night.

I wondered whether I was his dessert.

I asked where we were going as we reached the bottom and he pointed: 'Down that passage and the third door on the left.'

I hesitated.

'I will be beside you all the way. You won't get lost.'

I wasn't reassured.

The third door on the left was made of steel. 'It used to be an archive room,' he said, 'so it's secure.' He knocked. I didn't hear an answer but we didn't wait. He pushed the door. It opened. I supposed they were expecting us.

There was a draught of ice-cold air. I shivered.

'That's because the vault is thermostatically controlled,' he told me. 'You'll get used to it.'

There was a bellow from inside the room. It was distorted by the echoes off the floor, the ceiling and the bare brick walls. It didn't even sound like words until it ended with 'right now.'

'Sir. After you.'

He pointed out the way I was to go. Between two stacks of metal shelves. The shelves were full of metal boxes. Each box locked. The secrets of the council, I supposed. It couldn't be the Peacekeepers. They hadn't been around for long enough to have a history like this.

He marched me down towards the far end of the room. The shelves stopped just before they reached the wall. Here we turned left, passed three more rows of shelving, and arrived upon an open door.

A burst of oven-hot air slammed into my face. It made me stagger back. It made me hesitate.

They make you shiver, then they make you sweat. They do this so you won't know what comes next.

'In there,' he said.

The hot air seemed as solid as an eggshell and it felt as if I had to launch myself towards it so that I could shatter it.

And once inside the heat wrapped round me like a sticky second skin. It sheathed me and it squeezed me and I gasped for breath.

There was a table in the room and on the table there were mats and knives and forks and spoons laid out for four and at the table, staring at me, was a man.

He wasn't fat but bulky. You would never call him overweight although his belly stretched his belt; you wouldn't dare. You'd call him brawny. He was built of muscle. Beefed-up like a bull.

His head was almost spherical and bald and basted with his sweat. His skin was smooth, shaved to the silky polish of a prepubescent boy. He had no worry-lines. A pair of spectacles were balanced on his bulging cheeks. Thick lenses magnified his goggle-eyes. He didn't blink.

He snorted when he saw us.

He was half-way through his meal.

'Bring two more plates,' he spluttered as he chewed.

'Sit here,' he said, and tapped the seat beside him. 'Nikov, you sit over there, beside the door.'

I squeezed myself around the table. I was trapped.

'He looks a little nervous, Nikov.'

'That's because he's scared.'

'I'm not.'

'You would be wise to be afraid. Have you not heard about this place? Interrogation suites and whatnot. Torture cells and gallows rooms.' He scoffed. 'To hear the Drudjers talk you'd think I dined on children. Plate!'

An empty plate appeared in front of me. I jumped.

'There's nothing better than a piece of sirloin,' said the man beside me, sawing at his steak. 'I hope you like it rare.' He cut a chunk and used his fork to skewer it and dropped it from a height onto my plate so that it splattered blood. 'You're not a vegetarian, I hope. I don't like vegetarians. Too skinny to be trusted. Men are meant to be omnivorous. Look at our teeth.' He turned to me and opened up his mouth. He jabbed a meaty finger at a lower canine, ran it, right to left, along the four incisors. 'See? The front teeth here are like a dog's. They cut and tear. For eating flesh. Like dogs do. Back teeth crush and grind.' He grinned. He took his finger from his mouth and picked a roast potato from his plate and popped it onto mine. 'I don't mind eating veggies though.' He laughed. 'A man's a man when he'll accept his plate as he is given it, and chew it up, and swallow all of it. I hope you're not like prissy Nikov here.'

I glanced across at Nikov's plate. He had a salad.

'Man must eat,' my neighbour said. 'Eat or be eaten, that's the law of life. Of nature. Nothing we can do.' He grinned. 'You think a Drudjer wouldn't eat you if he had the chance? He'd gobble, gobble, gobble you all up.' He speared his knife into his meat and held it up before his mouth and used his teeth to rip a portion from it.

I had not seen steak for months. My mouth was watering so hard my eyes were weeping too. I picked my knife and fork up. I might as well. There was a massive man beside me and a waiter standing just behind my back and Nikov in between the door and me. I wasn't getting out of here.

I had just crammed a juicy chunk into my mouth, too greedy to be delicate, when Nikov asked: 'Are you the Edward Angelo who wrote last week of your concern about the overcrowding in the Kennels?'

Questioning.

He watched me, dagger-eyed. I chewed and chewed and chewed. The meat was tough. It wouldn't yield. Still Nikov waited, slicing a tomato into two. I wished I hadn't taken quite so much to eat. I wished I'd looked and seen the gristle in my meat. It was like chewing rubber. Nikov picked a gherkin from his plate and raised it to his lips and neatly bit the tip off with his pearl-white teeth. I tried to swallow my half-masticated meat. It wouldn't go.

The massive body of the man beside me radiated heat. 'He's very silent, Nikov. Rather rude.'

'Perhaps he'd like a drink, Boss.'

Instantly, the heavily perspiring Boss poured half the drink from his glass into mine. It frothed. 'I hope you like it bitter. Beer's the drink for men, don't you agree?'

I didn't really want it but I thought I was about to choke and so I drank some hoping it would shift the plug of fat and ropy sinew in my throat. I swallowed. Hard. I felt it wobble so I added more. Success. It slithered down, the ale cascading after it. An unblocked pipe, I thought. My stomach heaved. I'm going to be sick, I thought. I mustn't be, not here, not now and not in front of them. I desperately tried to keep it down. A little vomit forced its way into my mouth. I kept my lips closed tight.

The Boss was focussed on a sausage. 'He's still silent,' he observed to Nikov. 'Shall we loosen up his tongue?'

I shook my head. I choked, I gasped, I nodded.

'How about black pudding?' asked the Boss. Again he chopped his own in two and, with his fingers, placed one of the pieces on my plate. 'They use the recipe I gave them, passed down through the Brises. Take four cups of nice fresh pig's blood, salted, strained in case of clots. Stir in two cups of pork fat, finely diced, and add an onion chopped up small, some freshly ground black pepper and a teaspoon of ground allspice. Stir it well then stir it into oatmeal porridge. Plop the whole thing in the oven, bake it for an hour, then slice it up and fry in butter. Wonderful. They say it isn't healthy. Look at me! There's nothing wrong with me. At least I'm not a little runt like Nikov here. Blood's good for you. It makes you strong. It gives your sperm vitality. I'd back my little swimmers any day to outrace Drudjer semen. Ever think of that my lad? The human race is won by having stronger sperm.'

I coughed. I forced a morsel of black pudding to my lips.

'You stated on the Friday of last week,' said Nikov, speaking rapidly, as if time's sands were spilling out, 'that the demand for water in the Kennels was beginning to exceed capacity to the extent that rationing would be at best a temporary stopgap. Furthermore, supplies of food were well below the levels needed to … I think the phrase you used in your report was 'to sustain the population in a state of health'. Shall we be blunt? You thought that we were starving them.'

'Let's call a spade a shovel,' said the Boss. 'I hope it's not too peppery.'

'I didn't ...' I protested.

'Is this not your work?' demanded Nikov.

'But ...'

'Would you like a little mustard? I love mustard. But it has to be the yellow stuff. Pure. Uncorrupted. Not polluted like those brown types. Muck.' He used his knife to scoop some mustard from his own plate and he reached across and smeared it on the piece of steak I hadn't eaten yet. He licked his knife's blade with appreciation. Then he gave a sudden sneeze.

'Achoo. A bloody choo.' He chuckled. 'Better out than in.'

I took a sliver of my mustard-painted steak, and laid it gingerly upon my tongue. It stung.

'Know how to make a Drudjer cry? Rub yellow mustard in his eyes. Or crush his bollocks,' he reflected. 'That would work as well. But only for the bullyboys. It's best to stick to mustard for the heifers.'

'Did you think that we were starving Drudjers?' Nikov asked.

I shook my head. I shifted in my seat. My thighs were damp with perspiration and my lips were parched. I mumbled that my job was to report the figures, nothing more. I made no judgements.

That was not, perhaps, the wisest word to use.

'He doesn't judge us, Nikov. Aren't you glad?'

The mustard on my tongue was agonising. Was it blistering the inside of my mouth? It felt like acid in an ulcer. 'No. I didn't mean ...'

'You also told us that the use of mobile phones had much increased,' said Nikov, 'well beyond the increase in the number of devices. You concluded that there was a lot of talk. You tracked this traffic and you pinpointed transmission hubs. You had cross-referenced these places with the data from CCTVs. In short, a lot of people went to certain spots and from those places many messages were issued.'

'Did you write all that?'

'That's what the evidence suggested,' I replied.

'You live across the river from the Kennels,' said the Boss.

'He had a grandstand view of what went on last night.'

'I heard some bangs. I saw some flashes.'

'You went out into the street and asked me what was going on.'

'Do you think we should tell him, Nikov?'

'I'm not sure he wants to know.'

'You don't think he can take it? I've been looking forward to this moment.'

I was terrified. What did he mean?

A waiter had produced a silver tray and on the tray there was a silver dish and in this dish was ...

'Liver!' said the Boss. 'I love a bit of liver but it must be pink inside. You have to slice it thin and turn the flame up so the pan is hot. Arrange the slivers side by side - don't let them overlap! - so that they sear. As soon as you see, on the surface, drops of blood like little bubbles coming from the underside you need to turn them over and when the other side is similarly cooked you serve them straight away.' He used his knife and fork to put the liver on his plate and, as before, he cut a piece for me. 'Eat up,' he said, 'while it is fresh.'

'It was,' said Nikov, 'a pre-emptive strike. The evidence of your report suggested that the Drudjers were fermenting a rebellion.'

The Boss paused with a piece of liver, fork-impaled, mid-air. 'We nipped it in the bud.'

'Who would have thought it,' Nikov said. 'Peacemakers. Making peace.'

The Boss stuck out his tongue and reverently licked the liver. 'Juicy,' he approved. He popped it in his mouth.

I thought my liver was still bloody. There appeared to be a tube inside it.

"If the Drudjers had revolted we'd have crushed them. But it would have taken longer and it would have cost a few more lives. Which means whoever warned us is a hero.'

'Who was that?' The Boss looked straight at me.

'It wasn't me,' I said.

'But you wrote the report,' said Nikov.

'I just gave numbers.'

'Did you think we wouldn't read it?' said Nikov.

'Or we wouldn't draw the obvious conclusions?'

'Did you think that we'd do nothing?'

'Or that we'd increase the Drudjer rations?' said the Boss.

'We can't do that,' said Nikov. 'As you know, supplies are short. You've seen the empty supermarket shelves.'

'The whole world's suffering.' The Boss had called for bread and now he used a torn-off chunk to mop the gravy on his plate. 'That is the difference between a Drudjer and a decent man. You might be hungry but you don't revolt. They plan rebellion.'

'You see?' said Nikov. 'It was you. You didn't pull a trigger but the work you published triggered our response. We'd like to honour you.'

To honour me?

I'd heard those screams.

Whatever happened Blossom mustn't know. And that meant keeping it a secret from her brother and from Sodz and even Mr Kapko and from all of them.

'But,' said the Boss.

'But,' echoed Nikov. 'But despite our efforts at containment we were subject to a terrorist attack.'

'I don't like terrorists,' the Boss explained.

'A terrorist is someone who strategically uses violence to stir up fear, because he knows that frightened people can be dominated,' Nikov said.

I nodded.

"Terrorist. A poncy word. Three syllables. I don't like words that long. I won't eat anything as long as that. Asparagus or artichoke, or cauliflower. Namby-pamby sorts of foods. They sound like ballet dancers. Not for me.' He pointed to his plate. 'Beef. Liver. Carrot.'

'What about potatoes?' Nikov asked.

'They're roasties,' roared the Boss. 'They're good old spuds. He glared at me. 'Do you like Brussel Sprouts?'

Was that three syllables, or two, or one? I couldn't tell. I offered: 'I don't know.'

'What sort of answer's that?' He glared at me. 'You'd better get a move on or you won't be finished by the time dessert arrives.' He laughed. 'I like it when you see the food in flames.'

'Last night a tower block was set alight by terrorists,' said Nikov. 'I believe you know the place. It's where you used to work.'

I did my best to act surprised. 'What? Kapko Industries? How did you know I worked there?'

Nikov used his thumb to gesture at the door through which we'd entered. 'It's the archive room,' he said.

Of course, I thought. They'll have a file on everyone. He has been checking up on me.

'Salt?' asked the boss. 'A little pepper?'

As if it wasn't hot enough. I said: 'That's terrible. About the terrorists.'

'We will destroy them,' said the Boss. 'Wherever they are hiding we will root them out.'

'And that's where you come in,' said Nikov.

And I thought: he knows.

He's giving me a final chance.

Or seeking a confession.

'Eye for eye. They want to play with fire. We will burn them back. Eat or be eaten,' said the Boss. He licked his lips.

'But where do I come in? Because I know the building? I was only on the lower floors. I went into the office once or twice. I never saw the penthouse.'

'Penthouse,' said the Boss. He stabbed a sausage with his fork. 'That's where ...'

'The penthouse is where Drudjer terrorists,' said Nikov, 'murdered Memsahib Brise.'

The husband cut his sausage into slices.

'That's where you come in,' repeated Nikov.

'Is there any evidence that they were Drudjers? Or that they were terrorists? It might have been ...' I tried to think of other possibilities. 'It might have been a burglary gone wrong.'

'I don't like sausage,' said the Boss.

'We're not expecting you to play detective.' Nikov seemed bemused. 'We have professionals for that and they are looking for a gang of Drudjer terrorists. We need to catch them. That's where you come in. We want to use you for your special skills.'

'Tomato ketchup swamps the taste of meat. You need a proper gravy.'

'Special skills?'

'Your system warned us that the Drudjers were preparing to attack,' said Nikov. 'We believe your system can be used to hunt them down.'

'My system?'

Nikov nodded. 'System K. Why did you call it that?'

'We named it after its designer, Mr Kapko; at the time he was the chief executive of Kapko Industries.'

'I think,' said Nikov, 'there is something you're not telling us.'

I froze.

Was this a game of cat and mouse? Two good cops, feeding me, before they both became the nasty cops, accusing me of hosting Drudjers, judging me, and executing me.

'We've been informed that you designed the system.'

'Kapko stole it,' said the Boss.

Who told them that?

'We understand that Kapko noticed your potential straight away,' said Nikov.

'Always had an eye for talent. He was never anybody's fool.'

'He had to find a way to keep you for himself. I have no doubt that he found ways to chain you to your work.'

'I worked for him. He owned whatever I created.'

'On paper, yes,' said Nikov. 'Even so, it would have been a gesture to acknowledge you. Not call it System K.'

'For Kapko,' said the Boss. 'And now it seems that this same Kapko is the leader of the terrorists.'

'The message hub your system pinpointed,' said Nikov, 'is where Kapko lived.'

'We haven't found his body yet.'

'We think it possible that he was warned, that he escaped.'

'I've had enough of this.' The Boss threw down his knife and fork and pushed his plate away from him.

'We'll find him,' Nikov said. 'From now on Mr Angelo will work for us. He will report to me. To no one else. We know that System K can be expanded; we've been told that he was working on a System K+1 when Kapko Industries went bankrupt.'

'Who told us that?' the Boss asked.

Nikov looked at him.

'The heifer?' said the Boss. He laughed. 'Eat or be eaten. System

K+1.'

'It isn't just the update,' I protested. 'I would need more data from a wider range of sources.'

'So we understand. But we collect already all the information that you need. The images from Peacemaker CCTVs and body cameras. The downloads from the phone masts. Not just traffic from the phones but individual numbers linked to messages. We'll call it System A.'

'For Angelo,' the Boss explained.

'Your first priority will be to catch the terrorists. You'll help save lives. You'll bring the man who stole the credit for your work to justice. Will you help us?'

'Yes, of course he will,' the Boss said.

'Yes.' Of course I would. I had no other chance.

'You just provide the evidence,' said Nikov. 'Justice isn't your responsibility. We write the music. All you have to do is sing along.'

When they say that you ask: how high.

I told myself that if my System was the way they searched for Sodz and Mr Kapko and the other two, I could control things. I'd make sure they didn't find them. Not, at least, while they were living in my house. But, to be honest, I was flattered to be asked. I was excited. I could prove my System worked. It was a challenge but that added to the thrill. And when it worked I would receive the recognition I deserved. They'd call it System A. Perhaps I would be given a promotion. There weren't many chances to impress if you were not a Peacemaker. In this world you were either predator or prey. A man must take his luck when he discovers it.

Besides. I didn't know. They might be terrorists.

There was a problem, though. I couldn't let them take the Drudjers yet. They had to leave the garage first. So. What to do? I had to make it look as if I'd pulled out all the stops. The Boss and Nikov had to be convinced I could deliver. But. Not. Yet. I had to slow things down.

'It's all too much,' I said. 'It's too much work for one man on his own.'

'We've thought of that,' said Nikov. 'You'll have somebody to work with you.'

'But,' I protested, 'this is not a job that anyone can do. It needs somebody trained in data, to the level of ...'

'She has a doctorate in data science. She briefly worked for Kapko Industries. I'm not sure if she ever worked for you but maybe you encountered her.'

'What is her name?'

'But she's a Drudjer,' said the Boss.

'A Drudjer?'

'Yes. As luck would have it,' Nikov said, 'I captured her last night. All thanks to you. You were the one who spotted her.'

'So she's your Drudjer,' said the Boss.

I was about to say she wasn't mine, to tell them that I hadn't spotted anyone. But then I stopped myself. I had told Nikov I'd seen something, I remembered. I had said there was the shadow of a Drudjer running. But it wasn't true. It was a ruse. I made it up to make him go away so I could smuggle Sodz indoors.

'It's just as well she wasn't killed,' said Nikov.

I'd imagined her. She was a phantom. Somehow she'd solidi-fied.

'Your Drudjer,' said the Boss again. 'To do with as you choose. Eat or be nibbled.'

I had lied to Nikov. She had paid the price.

Was it my fault they'd caught her?

'Shall we pop along the corridor?' said Nikov. 'I will show you your new office and I'll introduce the pair of you.'

'Drink,' said the Boss.

We drank.

CHAPTER SEVEN: XAN

As soon as I was outside in the corridor I got cold feet. 'It might not be that easy,' I told Nikov.

'It's confusing, isn't it?' said Nikov. 'All these twists and turns. It's like a labyrinth. You'll soon get used to it.'

'You can't just add more data and expect your System to make sense of it,' I said.

He stopped so suddenly I almost bumped his back. He turned around. 'You have to do this for me. This is critical. You have to do it quickly and you have to do it right.'

'These things take time.'

'That's why you have the Drudjer to assist you.'

'That won't work. How do I make her help me? She will be betraying her own people.'

Nikov laughed. 'I don't think that will be a problem. Here we are.'

A Peacemaker was standing guard outside a door.

'Am I to be a prisoner?' I asked.

'Of course not. Not if you cooperate.'

What happens if I can't get home tonight? I asked myself.

The room was wide enough to lie across and roughly twice as long. An upright leather chair with metal legs had been abandoned in the middle of the room. There was a desk against the far wall with a laptop on it. That was all the furniture.

I looked at Nikov to protest.

'I find it's best to keep things spartan. Keeps you focussed. Keeps you pure. An easy chair would dissipate your energy.'

'If I'm to have a colleague she will need a laptop of her own, a table, and a chair so she can sit at it.'

'You'll have exactly what you need.' He emphasised the final word. He turned away.

'I'll let you have a look around.' He left. The door was shut. I heard the key turn in the lock.

There was a small half-window high up on the left-hand wall. It wasn't barred but you would need to be as skinny as a snake. I wondered whether Ochre would be pliable enough to squirm in through that window. I would like to see him writhe.

But nothing entered easily, not even light. The glass was covered with a grimy film so that the sunlight seeping through was filtered and devitalized, not golden but a flimsy yellow wash, enfeebled and irresolute.

I moved the chair to stand beneath the window. As I did, I noticed that a leg was loose. I wondered whether it was safe to climb on, so I mounted gingerly. It wobbled but it held.

The window wouldn't open. Peering through the dirty glass I saw the clock upon the steeple of St Jude's, the church across the river. That meant that I was looking north. I must be in the northeast corner of the building.

I dismounted carefully and turned around.

Back of the door there was a poster of a bullfight. It displayed a matador, his red cape swirled behind him, tiptoed, straight, erect. The bull, mid-buck and twisting, forelegs off the ground, was poised to gore. There was a tiny gap between them, nothing really. It appeared that only this small absence stood between the fury of the brute and the taut delicacy of the man. As if anticipating disembowelment, all the background of the painting had been coloured red, in sweeping strokes. It looked as if a scarlet mist had fallen and the world had been reduced to these two, man and monster, trapped together on the circus sand.

It was the only decoration in the room.

Was I surprised when Nikov showed the Drudjer in? Was I surprised he told me that her name was Xan? I hadn't guessed. I should have done. What other Drudjer would have been in my street? Only those who Mr Kapko had invited to my house. The four that had arrived, John Zombie who had died, and Xan.

The one that Ochre fancied.

Should I mention that?

I understood what Ochre saw in her. She was a wide-hipped lass, big-breasted, built for motherhood, as bonny as a baby blown up big. The perfect woman for a skinny boy. She would envelope him.

That thought distracted me a moment.

Right now, though, Xan wasn't dressed to kill. She wore a tracksuit which had once been pewter grey. There was a smear of mud or something worse across her right arm. On the other side a trouser leg was ripped: and through it gleamed her thigh.

Her feet were bare. Her bottom lip was cut, her right eye blacked and swollen and her right cheek grazed. Her jet black hair was tangled; she'd been barbered raggedly. She brought into the room a smell of sweat and slightly putrid meat.

'She's yours. Do what you want with her. There's just one rule. Don't sleep with her. We don't want little half-caste bastards crawling out of her.' So saying, Nikov left the room. The door was closed. Again I heard it being locked.

She wasn't in the least intimidated. Straight away she looked at me. 'You wouldn't dare,' she said. 'You haven't got it in you.'

Was this some sort of set-up? Nikov couldn't really think I could persuade this woman to assist me to track down the other members of her Drudjer gang. Was I supposed to fail?

She'd not stopped staring. 'You are really quite a little man.' She looked away as if, with that, she'd summed me up. I was dismissed. She walked around the room. She touched the chair, the desk, the window. Turning round, she saw the poster on the door. She crouched. She put her hands up to her head as if she had a pair of horns. She made a mooing sound. 'Weren't you the cuckold? I remember that at Kapko Industries the rumour was that Mr K was sleeping with your missus. I have always wondered whether you were unaware of what was going on. Could anybody be that stupid? I decided that you had to be ignoring it. I guess it's difficult when he's your boss.'

I gasped. Time doesn't heal. It doesn't even blunt.

'We laughed at you behind your back. At least it wasn't in your face. That's why you did it, I suppose. Pretended that you didn't know. Is that why you are working for the Peacemakers? Because a Drudjer stole your wife. That's not just sad, it is pathetic. Little man.'

I wondered whether it would always be like this.

'You don't remember me,' she said. 'You were too wrapped up in your work. And then he stole that too. He was a proper bastard, Mr K. I don't know why you let him get away with it.'

She shrugged. I was found wanting. She had weighed me and I didn't measure up. She plonked her plump backside onto the chair and opened up the laptop. 'Time to do some work.'

'I thought that you were one of Mr Kapko's gang.'

'Is that what Nikov said?'

'He didn't really tell me anything.'

'But you assumed that since I was a Drudjer I must therefore be a terrorist. Why not? We can't be innocent or you would have no reason for your hate. Well you are wrong. Again. You must be used to that, a man like you. The log-on. I will need the log-on if I am to work for you.'

'Last night.' I had to get this straight. 'When they attacked the Kennels, you were there. They killed your friends.'

'I don't have friends.'

'But you're a Drudjer.'

'From another town.'

'But you were captured by the Peacemakers. They beat you up.'

She touched the bruise upon her face.

'That was my own fault, really. I was rather slow to work out what they wanted. I suppose it didn't help that they could only see the Drudjer. I was for the chop. It wasn't till they found out where I'd worked. I tell you, Nikov, he's a bright lad. He caught on. We had a good old chat about my role at Kapko Industries. He seemed to know a lot already; it was just a case of joining up the dots. I saw which way the wind was blowing so I told him that I wasn't very keen on Mr K.'

'But you're ...'

'But I'm a Drudjer? Is that all you have to say? You ought to look a little harder. Just because I am a Drudjer doesn't mean to say I must be fond of somebody like Gannerdjalok Kapko. He's a serial philanderer. Your wife was not the first by any means. He even tried it on with me. He seemed to think that just because I worked for him that gave him rights. And things got even worse when we were relocated to the Kennels. I was brought up in another town; I've never lived in somewhere quite so small and stratified as that. I guess that every place is like a social pyramid: a lot of bricks along the bottom, strong enough to hold the others up and at the top a small group looking down upon the rest. But usually there is a little movement up and down. Not in the Kennels. Kapko's at the top and there he means to stay. There is a lot of hardship in the Kennels; hunger never said hello to Mr K. He would tell us time and time again that we were all in this together but he was in charge of who had what and who must do without. He always had the best of motives. Don't they all? He told me that you had to feed your fighters so that when the time came they were strong enough to fight.'

I looked at her.

She laughed. 'You're thinking: she's not skinny. Do you blame me? I will do whatever must be done. I played along. Still didn't let him fuck me but I found a way around that. Hooked his nephew. Even Mr K would not risk so much scandal. For the Drudjers, 'uncle' is an honorable term. But in the end the bastard double-crossed me. Come the moment we were all supposed to stand together he was nowhere to be found.'

She had good reason to resent him. Did that mean she hated him enough to work with me to build a System which would track him down? I asked her.

'System K,' she said. 'I never worked on it directly but it seems ridiculous to use so powerful a System to discover where a single person is.'

'It has potential to do rather more.'

'I'm sure it does. But will it work for this?'

I told her how it had already proved its worth when it had tracked the messages inside the Kennels to the place where Mr Kapko was.

Then it occurred to me that Xan already knew where Mr Kapko was. She had been given my address. They'd been expecting her. She had been captured on the way.

'Of course you're right. There must be better ways to find a man. Interrogate your prisoners, perhaps.' I looked at her.

She met my eyes. She touched the bruise upon her cheek. 'That might be quicker, I suppose, but less reliable. You can't be certain that the person you are questioning is telling you the truth. I would prefer the slower way.'

Of course she would. The longer we could string this out, the longer she would stay alive. That suited me.

There was a noise outside the door. It opened. There were Peacemakers with furniture. They filed into the room. Xan told them where to put it. After they had finished and departed Nikov stood alone.

'Is that sufficient?'

'Yes,' said Xan. 'For now.'

He looked at me.

'I think so. For the moment.'

'Don't forget,' said Xan, 'that this is brain work. We must think creatively. That means that the conditions must be right. You have to give us opportunities to rest, relax, recuperate.'

He didn't answer.

'Xan is right,' I said.

'You will work hard. They're terrorists. We mustn't let them strike again.'

Xan didn't seem to hear him. 'We'll need decent food, not Drudjer rations.'

Nikov looked at her. His eyes were measuring her girth. I thought he would be furious. He smiled. He looked at me. 'Black pudding. Sir? Or salad?'

'And,' said Xan, 'he says he wants you to take me away so I can have a wash.' She raised her arm and sniffed her armpit ostentatiously. 'He says my smell distracts him.'

True. I nodded. 'I'm not sure it's possible to scrub away the stench of Drudjer,' Nikov said, 'but we can try.'

When they were gone and I was left alone, I sat down and I looked around. Two chairs, two tables, and two laptops cluttered up the floor but didn't make the room feel any cosier. The door was still as shut. The walls were still as solid and as straight. The only colour in this cell came from the picture.

I was on the horns of a dilemma. Xan, it seemed, was willing, even keen, to help me modify the System so it tracked down Mr Kapko. But, of course, I couldn't let it go so far. I'd have to twist things so that it appeared I was pursuing leads but really I was following red herrings. Could I fool her? She was bright, astute. I wasn't sure that I could pull the wool across her eyes.

There was one way to sort this out. She said she hated Mr Kapko. He was not the only Drudjer in my garage. There was Ochre, for example. Last night he had been expecting her. He seemed quite keen on her. Was he the nephew she had mentioned? She had told me she had snared him; was she fond of him? Were they in love? That opened up a whole new can of worms. I could persuade her to cooperate with me. To make it seem that we were tracking down the terrorists when really we were buying time. Until I could get rid of them.

But that meant I would have to tell Xan that I had her lover in my garage. Could I trust her? She was ready to betray a fellow Drudjer, one she hated. Would she stick at sacrificing Ochre if it helped her to survive?

CHAPTER EIGHT: PERSPECTIVE

We passed the day rewriting subroutines to make the formats of the different data sets consistent. It was difficult to concentrate. I wondered what the Drudjers might be up to. I had warned them that they mustn't leave the garage and the hallway; Mr Kapko had concurred. I wasn't sure that Sodz would toe the line. I had asked Blossom, when I caught her for a moment on her own, if Sodz was always so mercurial and she said that was just the way he was and blushed from which I gathered that it made Sodz more attractive in her eyes.

The other worry that I had was that I wouldn't be allowed to go back home. I wasn't sure to what extent they had arrested me; my services were requisitioned at the very least. This was an urgent job, they'd said, and so they might expect that I'd stay on the premises till it was finished. But finally, when I was sodden with fatigue, they came. Xan was escorted to her 'specialist accommodation' by the guard and Nikov said he'd see me off the premises.

But he had not allowed me home. Instead we walked together to the tower block where I had worked, where Mr Kapko lived, where Sodz seduced Salome.

'I was struck,' said Nikov said when we stepped into the lift, 'by what you said. Sir. When we were at breakfast with the Boss.'

In such a little space as we were in, the scent of Nikov's medicated soap was powerful. I told myself that it was better than the smell of sweat and hormones that you get from other men. But there was still that sense of claustrophobia, of Nikov's muscled body coming smotheringly close.

I had forgotten what I'd said.

'You asked for evidence. You wondered how we knew the fire was started by a Drudjer.'

How had I known? Because of Sodz. What could I say to Nikov? Nothing. 'Me? I don't know anything.' I spread my hands to show the vastness of my ignorance. 'That sort of thing is better left to the police. They're the specialists.'

'That's what the Boss said. But the problem is that when you are a leader people tend to see the world the way you've told them that it looks. It's easy, when you seek for terrorists, to find them everywhere. I'm sure that the police investigation will confirm what we expect.'

The lift doors opened. Nikov, courteous as ever, gestured: 'after you'. It was a squeeze. I had to brush against him. I apologised but he ignored me.

I gazed around. We had arrived in Mr Kapko's office on the old top floor. I'd not been here since Mr Kapko told me that I was no longer working on the system I'd designed. It was already in the marketplace. No sense in spending money on a seller. If it broke, we'd fix it. But for now, hands off. I'm sure that it made sense in economic terms but System K, whatever it was called, had been my baby and I couldn't just abandon it. I'd made such plans for how I would develop it. How I would see it grow. I had such dreams. And he had dashed them.

Would it not be savagely ironic if this opportunity the Peace-makers were giving me resulted in the capture of my former boss?

Now Nikov asked me whether I had ever been upstairs.

I shook my head. My wife had, I suspected. Never me.

'It smells of smoke.'

It did indeed, the pungency increasing as we climbed the stairs until it felt as if the tender inside of my throat was being scraped with emery. And there was something else: the sickly scent of burning flesh.

'A Peacemaker patrol was on the scene in seconds.'

'Seconds? That was fast.'

He nodded. 'Fast and fortunate. It meant the blaze could be extinguished quickly, saving evidence. The Memsahib had been strangled just a little while before the place was torched. We analysed genetic samples salvaged from the scene. The DNA was typical of Drudjers.'

'You can do a DNA analysis that quickly. I'm impressed.'

He smirked. 'We're Peacemakers. Efficiency's important.' But I knew that wasn't true. The Peacemakers were vigilantes. Amateurs. Irregulars. Ununiformed, untrained, ill-disciplined. United only by their common hatreds, sprouting up from nowhere, growing faster than they could be organised. That's why they were so frightening. They were a many-headed monster: if you faced one set of fangs another mouth attacked.

'Why terrorist?' I asked. 'You said it was a terrorist offence. But Memsahibs are unlikely targets. Could it not have been a jealous husband? Or perhaps it was a simple robbery gone wrong.'

'That's why we're here,' he said.

I had assumed that we were heading for the bedroom so that he could show me where Salome had been strangled but instead we climbed a second set of stairs. These took us to the roof.

I don't like heights. I suffer from an urge to run towards the edge and jump. It is irrational, I understand that, but I feel compelled. This roof was flat and bounded by a little wall no higher than my knees. It was too easy to imagine running, tripping, falling. Or alternatively stepping backwards inadvertently and sitting down by accident and leaning back a bit too far and tumbling, arcing slowly in a backwards somersault to splatter on the ground below. I looked around. On every side there was another way to fall.

It didn't seem to bother Nikov. Heading straight towards the precipice he hopped onto the parapet and strolled along as if it was a walkway rather than the brink of the abyss. 'Look,' he called. He turned to see what I was doing. I was so afraid for him. I was convinced that he would stumble and I wanted to call out to him to be more careful but I didn't dare to make a noise in case it startled him.

Then I remembered that he was my adversary. If he fell ... Perhaps I ought to push him.

It was just a passing whim. I knew I wouldn't get away with it. They'd have CCTV up here. And even if they didn't, they would have it down below. I would have been recorded coming up with Nikov; there'd be questions if I went down on my own. Perhaps I could pretend it was an accident, or suicide, or even self defence. If we were in a court of law. I might get an acquittal on the grounds of reasonable doubts. But it would never get that far, not with the Peacemakers. They don't do justice. They do tit for tat.

I wouldn't get away with it. That was the reason I let Nikov live. That's what I told myself. It wasn't true. To push him I'd have had to go right up to him. And he was on the edge. I didn't dare go there.

He beckoned me. 'Come here and look.' I crept towards him,

tiny step by tiny step. I stood a body's length away. Quite close enough.

'I love it here. The air's so fresh. Up here you get perspective. You can breathe.'

He pointed. 'There's the guardpost on the footbridge near your house.'

I looked. They had their searchlight pointing at the river and I thought how lucky Mr Kapko, Blossom, and her brother were to get across last night. Sodz had, of course, been here.

'And over there ...' He pointed. 'See? The tower of St Jude's. That's where I learned my values. Right and wrong. It's more important than arithmetic. Don't you agree?'

I nodded, though I didn't understand what he was getting at.

'When you're up here it's easier to see what's going on. When you're down there ...' He shrugged. 'I think the problem is there are too many people in the world. Down there we live in crowds. You can't see anything. Whichever way you look there's always someone in the way. Down there. Up here you can see all the way to the horizon.'

As he spoke he waved his arms. I was afraid that he might over-balance but he didn't wobble in the least.

'The problem is that each of us expects to have a say. There are too many people wanting to be heard, all talking at the same time. What a racket. How's a man to hear what he himself is thinking in the middle of a din like that? That's why I like to come up here. The silence. Things make sense up here.'

'And all the stars,' I said. When I looked up towards him it appeared his head was haloed by more stars than I had ever seen before.

'Back then, before the Siege' he said, 'we couldn't see the stars.

I'm sure that's why it all went wrong. Do you remember? It was terribly chaotic then. Out of control. The world was heading for disaster. There was fighting in the streets. Disorder reigned. You can't have that. You need things settled or your systems start collapsing. That's how people die: their organs fail. So we stepped in: somebody needed to. A parent doesn't just sit by: a child needs proper discipline. We gave them boundaries. We made the peace and we brought order to the streets. You can't deny that people nowadays are happier.'

If I said 'no' he might think that I disagreed with him; if I said 'yes' he might suppose I did deny it. There was nothing I could say.

He stepped down from his platform. 'It is all about control. Control's the key. If you cannot control yourself, the whole thing falls apart. But you must see things clearly, as they really are, before you can control yourself. That's why I need to talk to you.'

'To me?' I looked around. A flat-topped roof surrounded by a little wall. A single, narrow staircase leading down. There wasn't anywhere to run to. I was on my own. If he'd decided to dispose of me I didn't have a chance.

'The trouble is,' he said, 'things are beginning to get out of hand. There's little bits and pieces going wrong.'

'I'm sure you'll sort it out.'

'When the police are looking for a Drudjer terrorist,' he said, 'that's what they'll find.'

I was surprised. 'I thought you said ...'

'That we had evidence. We do. But evidence can be misleading. I want you to operate your system free of any preconceptions. Follow where it leads. Report to me. Just me. To no one else. I want to know whatever you discover. Do you understand?

Whatever.'

He turned away from me and stared again into the emptiness. 'I wish that I could stay up here all night,' he said. 'It's so refreshing for the soul.'

He wouldn't say another word. I wondered, when he led me down the stairs into the penthouse, whether he intended me to see the scene of crime. We went straight past it, down the other set of stairs into the spookily abandoned office, then into the lift. He didn't speak as we descended. When we left the tower block I waited while he locked it with his keys. Then we walked down the street. He broke his silence only when we stood between the Town Hall and the arch to my estate.

The Officer was still awake and hanging by his right arm from a pedestal.

> 'A hero's courageous and smart,
> But there's always a hole in his heart
> So he can't beat the gods.
> Lady Luck's fixed the odds.
> And his end is ordained from the start.'

He always made me jump.

He looked a little like the sort of monkey that you used to see on hurdy-gurdies, dressed up in a velvet uniform and shaking pennies in a tin. He'd been a soldier once perhaps: he wore assorted military clothes with ribbons on his chest. He had been trained for violence, seen violence, been violent, perhaps. Whenever I walked underneath the arch, I was afraid.

It was a single span, a pier on either side. In each pier was a room. When it had been the entrance to a factory, these rooms were where the gatemen lodged; one for deliveries and one to count the workmen in and out. These rooms had long been locked. The Officer avoided them. Above the keystone was a hollow parapet: it was in here he lodged. He had a rope he looped around a merlon in the decorative battlements if he should wish to leave or enter this apartment. Mostly he stayed home, perched on the crenellations like a gargoyle, shouting at the people that he saw.

I said to Nikov, angrily: 'Why do you let him stay there?'

'Does he frighten you?'

'He's mad.'

'You can't catch madness.'

He was wrong. I didn't contradict him; you must never tell a Peacemaker he's wrong. But madness is contagious. Look at us, look at our world, and then deny it if you can.

'He has been living in that arch since long before the street was built,' said Nikov, 'and I shouldn't be surprised if he was still there when our houses are demolished.'

'He has lost his mind.'

'You talk as if he has forgotten where he's put it. Does he bother you?'

'It isn't what he says. I don't take any notice of the things he says. He is confused. That's what surprises me: that you're prepared to tolerate the chaos that he causes.'

'That's just you,' he said. 'He doesn't worry me.' He shrugged. 'I'll say goodnight here. I have some unfinished business in the office that I must attend to. There is no rest for the wicked, as they say.' He shook my hand and crossed the silent road to the Town Hall. I walked beneath the arch.

But when I reached my door, I found that I had lost my keys.

I patted every pocket. Please. They must be here. They weren't. Not here, not there. Not anywhere. I couldn't think of anything.

Shit, shit and shit.

I tried again. I plunged my hands as deep as they would go. I turned my pockets inside out. I checked the belt loops of my trousers and the buttons of my shirt. Keys could get caught. I forced myself to stop. Slow down. Think carefully. I couldn't concentrate. What-ifs were dancing through my mind. What if I hadn't lost them? What if somebody had stolen them from me? Xan? Nikov? Why? I sweated. I was cold.

I told myself this didn't help. I told myself to do a thorough search.

I emptied every pocket, fighting panic. I was organised, arranging all the contents on the ground. No keys. I went through every item, even emptying my wallet, though my bulky keys could not have slipped in with the slender paper notes and plastic cards. They were not there. I ran my hands across my body in the way that Peacemakers search Drudjers.

No.

My keys were gone.

If Nikov … No. Why would he? Peacemakers do not need keys. They smash the door down.

So I must have dropped them somewhere.

Where?

I walked back step by step, my gaze glued to the ground. I ducked and bobbed in an attempt to catch a flash of light reflecting from the metal keys. It wasn't easy: nowadays the streets were mostly dark. Before the Siege, the street lamps worked but now, when one by one they failed, there wasn't anybody to replace the bulbs. And so the streets grew darker. Fear increased. And things got worse.

Again I walked beneath the arch. The Officer was still awake.

> *'When you walk with your eyes on the ground*
> *Like a prisoner dogged by a hound*
> *You betray that the cost*
> *Of the soul that you've lost*
> *Is a pearl that can never be found.'*

He was mad, I thought. The whole world, but for Nikov, knew that he was mad.

I kept on looking for my keys. I kept my panic manacled and tried to measure out the pavement pace by pace. If I had dropped them they should still be here, the streets were empty, no one would have picked them up.

If they were not here ...

Why would Nikov take them?

He could search my house while I was out and I would be no wiser.

It was very cold tonight.

He could have watched me from the door of the Town Hall and when he saw me walking back towards the tower block, my eyes fixed downwards, he could sneak beneath the arch; he could be in my house right now.

By now he would have found the Drudjers in my garage.

There was nothing I could do.

I couldn't run. Where could I go? I didn't have a garage I could hide in; nobody would welcome me. I'd be a refugee without a refuge. I'd be caught. I would be executed. That's the way it was.

All I could do was go back home and face whatever music might be playing there.

I trudged again beneath the arch. The Officer gave me advice:

'It is better to live on the street
Than to live by betrayal, to cheat
And to lie. Run away
Or you'll soon have to pay
With your soul. That's a high price to meet.'

Of course! While I was looking for my keys I hadn't heard the Officer. That meant that no one had passed through the arch. If Nikov had, I would have heard a crazy limerick.

It meant that I was safe, for now.

I walked back home to knock on my own door.

'It's me,' I whispered through the letterbox. 'Please let me in. I haven't got my keys.'

I gazed round surreptitiously. The windows of the houses in the close stared blindly back.

The door unlocked. Swung open. Ochre stood there in the hall. The sacrifice. Behind him, crouched beside the kitchen door, was Mr Kapko.

Mr Kapko had a gun. He pointed it at me.

CHAPTER NINE: THE ERRAND BOY

I blinked. I shied. 'What's that?' I asked. 'Please don't. Please point it somewhere else. Please tell me that it isn't loaded.'

Ochre had been staring past me, out into the night. 'He is alone.' He beckoned me inside.

I hesitated. It is difficult to walk towards a gun. The small black circle at the barrel's end seems huge as if it is the focus of the universe. Time's pivot. Big enough to swallow all your thoughts.

'Now, Ochre,' Mr Kapko barked and Ochre, startled, grabbed me, dragging me inside. He shut, and locked the door.

I looked at Mr Kapko. There were questions surging in my mind but all that I could say was, stupidly: 'You have a gun.'

Of course he had a gun.

But how? How does a man like Mr Kapko have a gun? He was the owner of an electronics company.

He was a terrorist.

'The backpack,' I remembered.

He agreed. 'I hid it underneath the picture of my wife.'

I shivered. I recalled how Nikov had picked up the bag; how I had lied and said it was my son's.

Thank goodness Nikov hadn't looked inside. Because if I knew anything, I knew that Mr Kapko, shivering and hiding in my garage, would have done nothing to prevent me being taken out and shot. Shot with the gun that Nikov would have found. Shot with the gun that Mr Kapko brought into my house.

'Are you all right?' asked Ochre. 'Take a seat.'

I sat down, shakily, upon the stairs.

'I should have known,' I said. 'They're calling you a terrorist. They say you are the leader of a gang of terrorists.' I looked at Ochre. 'You as well? You have a gun? And Sodz? And Blossom? Thought I was your host. It seems I am your hostage.'

Ochre splayed the fingers of his hands in protest. 'No, of course we don't. Just him.'

'Just me and yes, it's loaded,' Mr Kapko said. 'I think that puts me fair and square in charge.'

'But we're not terrorists,' said Blossom, coming from the garage out into the hall. 'My brother studies medicine.'

'I told him,' Ochre said, 'that guns are pointless. How can he outshoot the Peacemakers?'

'There are a lot of things a gun can do.' So saying, Mr Kapko gestured to the garage door. 'Go in.'

'It's my house.' I was angry.

'But I have the gun. You see?'

I didn't want to do it but I did. I had no other choice. I stumbled to my feer and bowed my head and let him herd me like a stick-shy bullock. In my head I told myself that I would be revenged: give me the chance and I'd be even. Couldn't see it, though.

And then I saw the garage. It had been divided into four. Each of the Drudjers occupied a section of the floor. The borders of each territory had been marked; they'd used whatever they could find: a book, a piece of string, a bundle of stale clothes. They had allotted Blossom the prime patch; she governed access to the shelves where we had stacked some cans of soup, a jar of peanut butter, and some packets of dried pasta, porridge oats and rice. Was this because they trusted her the most? She was the girl; perhaps they felt that if push came to shove she'd be the weakest, she would be the one whose quarter could be overrun most easily. Beside the door, the smallest area was that of Ochre. He had no more room than he would need for sleep. They'd made a little corridor between him and his sister; this gave access to the door for Sodz and Mr Kapko. They lived in the most distant corners of the garage and their realms were more or less of equal size. Sodz sat on Blossom's side while Mr Kapko's sector pushed against and into Ochre's.

'You have been arranging things.' My things, I thought. 'You might have asked me first.'

'You still don't get it.' Mr Kapko waved the gun again.

'This is my floor, my room, my garage in my house. I bought it with my money.'

'The money came from me,' said Mr Kapko. 'I gave you a job.'

I was wide-eyed. Astonished. Open-mouthed. 'I worked for it.'

'The world has changed. Things aren't the same, not any more. They took my company away from me. They took my home. They called it confiscation but it wasn't lawful. It was theft. They wanted it and they had guns and that was all they needed. New rules now. Might's right. Out there they are the bosses but, in here, I have the gun. You understand?'

I nodded. It was all that I could do.

I understood. I understood too well. It meant that they expected to be here far longer than I wanted them.

I mumbled that it must have taken ages. So much work.

Sodz, sitting, legs crossed, in the corner of his kingdom, rolled his eyes. 'We have sufficient time, old pal, old buddy, droog, mon vieux, my old satsuma, we have lots and lots of time.'

'We've been discussing things,' said Mr Kapko in a tone that told me that I wouldn't like what he'd decided. 'We will have to stay a little longer than we'd planned.'

'You might have asked me first.' It was a feeble protest.

He just shrugged. He didn't even bother to reply. I should have known. That wasn't how he did things. Ask? He didn't ask when he was my employer. He had told me he had given me a job. As if it was a gift. He'd paid me. Like I hadn't worked for it. Why should he ask when he had rights?

Employ. It is a synonym for use.

'Why must you stay? Is it because of him?' I mustered up a weary flare of anger. 'It's because of Sodz. Because he killed Salome.'

'I was framed.'

'It would be madness to attempt to break out now,' said Mr Kapko. 'We must wait till things are calmer.'

That made sense. But while they lingered in my garage they were putting me at risk.

I somehow had to summon up sufficient energy to fight. I couldn't quite remember what it was that I was fighting for.

'The Peacemakers are angry. They are saying you are terrorists. That changes everything.'

'It changes nothing, not for us. We're Drudjers. They can only shoot us once.'

I shook my head. I knew that I was being lied to but I couldn't figure out the lie.

What could I do?

Some rice, some pasta and some cans of soup. 'You can't stay here,' I said. 'I don't have any food.'

'We've made a list,' said Blossom, 'of the things we need.'

'The shops are shut,' I told her. 'If they're open they have empty shelves. You have to queue for everything. It isn't only in the Kennels things are hard.'

'We know all this,' said Sodz. 'We're not expecting you to go to shops, as such.'

'And there'd be questions asked. It's all recorded, everything. How much each household buys. How many toilet rolls they use. Their water use, their gas and electricity. All this data is collated and examined, scanned for patterns and anomalies. It's funny if you think it through.' I looked at Mr Kapko. 'System K.' He had been hoisted by his petard.

I stopped. All of those words had emptied me.

All that I really want to do right now, I thought, is fall asleep.

But there was something not quite right. I had hung pictures on the garage wall when we'd had it converted. The photo of my wife and sons was hanging slightly skewed. They must have touched it. That was wrong. It angered me. But there was nothing I could do. I didn't even have the strength to reach across and nudge it into place.

'We won't use shops,' said Sodz. 'We'll use the market noir.'

'Black market? But I can't. I have no contacts.'

'I am at your service.' Sodz performed an ostentatious bow. 'Delighted to assist. I aim to please. Call me the middleman, the go between, the matchmaker, the broker. Semi-licit goods and contraband, beneath the counter stuff: this is, as you might say, my area of expertise, my specialité. I'd be delighted if you were to favour me with your most estimable patronage and custom, sir.'

I didn't even have the energy to laugh at him. It was preposterous. 'You're asking me to break the law.'

'It's not the law,' said Mr Kapko, 'it is just a Peacemakers' Decree.'

'I'm not involved. I won't.'

'You can't just let us starve,' said Ochre.

'Hungry men,' said Mr Kapko, showing me his gun.

'And it was hunger made us flee the Kennels,' Blossom said.

That was true, I thought. If they were hungry they might leave to look for food. They might be followed back. Or captured. Tortured. They would tell them where we were.

But really, what did they expect?

'The last thing that you want to happen here is somebody to starve to death,' said Sodz, 'and little Ochre is already very thin. Live Drudjers might be difficult; a corpse would be impossible. Unless we ate him. Not much meat. I'm sure he'd disagree with me.'

I made a show of scanning Blossom's list. 'I haven't got the money. I can't get these things.'

'I don't do hats and rabbits but,' said Sodz. 'Abraca-what's-it, open sesame and all of that.' He feigned surprise. 'Well look at this!' He held between his index finger and his thumb, another pearl. 'Give me a tongue of toad and I will conjure up the devil.

Mr Kapko smirked. 'We Drudjers pay our way.'

'I can't do this,' I told them. 'I'm no good at cloak and dagger stuff. I don't know what to do; I won't know what to say.' I thought of people wearing hats and secret microphones; carnations in their buttonholes. 'I know my limitations. I will get it wrong.' I looked around.

'Don't tell me that you're scared.' Sodz smiled. His mouth was wide. He showed a lot of teeth. 'I don't think angels can be frightened. 'Ochre would be, he is just a boy, but Ed's a big, brave, mucho macho, valiant coraggioso, masculino, virile, plucky, daring and intrepid grown up man.'

'I'm not a boy,' said Ochre.

'I don't do this sort of thing.'

'It's easy. All you need to do,' said Sodz, 'is go to the *Enchanted Isle*.'

'That's not a shop,' I told him, 'it's a night club. No one goes there now. It's full of Peacemakers. Besides, I don't know where it is.'

'It's off the High Street. Do you know the derelict department store? The one that shut down in the Siege?'

I nodded. It was on a crossroads in the centre of the town. The heart of retail, at the time. It had a cafe where the grannies went for tea and cakes and gossip. Where had all the grannies gone? These days you never saw old people.

I felt old enough to take their place.

'There is a burnt-out bank, the far side of the street from there.'

There was. There'd been a spate of torching banks before the Peacemakers appeared and put a stop to all that sort of thing.

'There is an alley down the right side of the bank. The club's half way along. Its entrance is a shabby door framed by a pointed gothic arch. There is a picture of St Peter on the panels of the door, although it's rather faded and the paint is flaking off. He's lost his keys. But still, it's him. You'll recognise him. Well, I think you will. It's not a very well-lit alley and it's late. But anyway, St Peter, San Pierre, Don Pedro, Holy Pete. Knock on his door. Be bold. You sometimes have to hammer loud enough to wake the dead. If someone tries to tell you that they're full, just say that Simon sent you. When you get inside, you have to walk across the dance floor to the right hand corner of the room. Then find the stairs. Go up, not down, not ever, never, not for all the jalapenos in Peru, should you go down. Go up. There is a small reception room upstairs. Some tables, mostly Poker. On the far side there's a bar. Ask for Madame. Then say: 'The Shark is swimming in strange seas'.'

'This is ridiculous,' I said. 'Grown men and women playing silly games.'

'It works.' He gave that long, slow smile of his. Again he showed a wide expanse of teeth. The shark, I thought.

'I can't go through the streets at night,' I told them, 'with a pearl. If I get stopped by a Patrol, what happens then?'

'There's not a curfew,' Mr Kapko said. 'That's only in the Kennels.'

'I am sick of this,' I said. 'It's always 'Drudjer worse' and 'Kennels worse'. It isn't so much better for the rest of us. Out here. The 'normal' world. There may not be a curfew but you can't just stroll along the streets at night. I will be stopped. By men with guns. And, like you said, a gun is all you need to make the rules.' I knew exactly what would happen if I went out there. I would be stopped. Asked questions. It was likely they would want to know my name, why I was out so late, where I was going. I would have to answer. But I wouldn't know which answers were acceptable. That all depended on the Peacemaker Patrol. He made his mind up on the spot and let you pass, or turned you round, or marched you under escort to a check-point for a more intense interrogation. If you were allowed to go, perhaps you'd meet another Peacemaker and once again be subject to the same routine. Except that it was not the same. This was another man and he might think the answer that was good enough before was not the one he wanted.

'Stick to the shadows,' Sodz advised. 'Avoid Patrols.'

'I can't. I'll have to cross the river. Not the footbridge leading to the Kennels; I will have to use the road bridge by the tower block. There is a checkpoint there; they man it night and day.'

'His name is Tomas,' Sodz replied. 'Just tell him you are Simon's friend. And pay the toll.'

'The toll?'

'He likes a drink.'

'You mean a bribe.'

'No, not at all. Don't think of it like that. It is a tip, a little lubrication for a thirsty throat, a recognition of the dedication shown by all the noble Peacemakers who, let us not forget, are volunteers and working solely for the public good; it is un pourboire, a gratuity, an honorarium. He likes tequila, god knows why, but you can't get tequila at this time of night and if you're carrying a bottle you'll attract Patrols like turds draw dogs so take a banknote folded very small and slip him that.'

'And if he wants to search me and he finds the pearl?'

'If I were you, I'd pop that in my pants. He won't look there. And even if he had a rummage he would only think that you were lucky to be polyorchid. I know Tomas. He will be impressed.'

I shook my head. They had the answers, all of them.

'I'll go,' I said, 'but later. Not right now. I'm knackered. Let me have a little sleep.'

Sodz said that he was sorry but the nightclub closed at midnight.

'If this is a trap,' I swore, 'if you are trying to ensnare me.'

'Why?' asked Mr Kapko. 'What would be the point of that? We're all in this together.'

But that wasn't true.

CHAPTER TEN: AT THE ENCHANTED ISLE

I didn't want to wake the Officer by going through the arch and so I took the track along the riverbank. It used to be well-trodden but, like so much, it had been neglected since the Siege. Now it was overgrown with thorns which were as tangled as a barbed wire fence. It kept the Drudjers out: a swimmer didn't have a place to come ashore, a boat could not be landed on this bit of bank. But just a little further from the river there was still the vestige of a path. Most times I kept away. This was the sort of badland where a man might meet a nightmare. Once I had been searching for my sons' lost ball when I had come across a cache of magazines; so pornographic were their images that I was shocked and this was in the days back then when we were tolerant of so much filth. I can't forget those pictures even now. The faces of the children: their fragility; the cynical destruction of their innocence. I felt contaminated after seeing them. I had to wash myself.

One thing I'll say for them: the Peacemakers had put an end to things like that.

This time I travelled in between the brambles and the nettles with no greater damage than some scratches and a sting or two. I couldn't go too quickly; even though there was a little moonlight it was difficult to see my way. I stumbled once and wrenched my ankle so I had to limp a few steps but the pain had eased before I reached the fence. There was a gap here in the railings which I scrambled through unscathed. I crossed the empty car park. In the past there would have been some lorries here, their drivers overnighting in their cabs; from time to time a gathering of campervans. Now even travellers avoided us.

Once I had reached the road, I paused to catch my breath and look around. In front of me: the office block that had been Kapko Industries. I scrutinised the penthouse; I could see no signs of smoke. If I turned right I would be facing south, towards the coast. The farms and villages down there had bred the Peacemakers. If I went left across the bridge and up the High Street and kept going past the suburbs and the warehouses until I reached the hills beyond, I'd find the army. Rumour said that they were coming from the north. They seemed no closer than a month ago.

I started walking north, across the bridge.

The checkpoint was abandoned.

I was relieved despite the reassurances of Sodz. I'd never tried to bribe a Peacemaker before. I didn't know the etiquette.

But I was worried. There had always been a guardpost here; it was the first place that the Peacemakers secured when they had commandeered the town. I felt destabilised.

Perhaps the Army were much closer than I'd thought, perhaps the Peacemakers had fled.

Was I the last man left?

There wasn't anybody on the High Street. That was ominous. Although so many shops had closed, I'd never been alone here. It was late and these days most of those of us who had not left the town stayed home at night, but I had never seen this street deserted. There was always someone. But not now. Not even Peacemakers.

Had something happened? Surely I'd have heard.

It was as silent as an empty tomb.

I couldn't help but look from side to side as I walked down the road. What was I so afraid of? Monsters hiding in the doorways? Yes, perhaps.

I reached the desolate department store, the sooty cinders of the bank. These were the landmarks Sodz had given me. I found the alley and the door to the *Enchanted Isle*. I tapped on it. Knock loudly, Sodz had said; enough to wake the dead. I thought I'd rather let them sleep.

The door swung open and I was assaulted by a cloud of vapour, smoke and alcoholic fumes, of human sweat and inexpensive perfumes and the jabber jabber of half-sober conversation. Shrieking jazz. It was a pandemonium. I'd found them. All of them, or so it seemed. They'd gathered for one massive party. They were here and there and all around. They lined the walls. They squatted in the corners. They had curdled into little mobs which spread across the dance floor like the blots on jelly in a Petri dish. There was, of course, a scrum around the bar. The noise was diabolical. They called and cheered and shouted. They were celebrating their success: the raid last night. It was as if I'd poked my nose into a nest of wasps. I would be lucky if I wasn't stung.

I'd not been here for years. I'd come while I was courting, once or twice. A nightclub's not the natural habitat when you're a young geek seeking sex. I need a lot of help from alcohol to dance; I didn't like the prices at the bar; I'm not that keen on crowds. Yet here I was. I felt the same way as I had back then: a flimsy, not so subtle, fake.

As Sodz had told me to, I dodged my way across the dance

floor to the corner of the room. There was a little band upon a tiny stage in front of which some girls were dancing jaggedly before a restless audience of staring Peacemakers. It looked like everyone was waiting for an auction to begin. I found the staircase though it was half-hidden round a corner. Then I hesitated for a moment. Up or down?

He'd said I should on no account go down.

I wondered why.

If I went up I was an errand boy obeying my instructions. Going down was disobedient; it would be brave. I didn't know what I would have to face if I went down. Things might be worse. At least, right now and for the moment, while I was of use to my four Drudjer masters, I was safe.

But on the other hand, if Drudjers said I should go up it might be more to my advantage to descend. If I've learned anything it is that when a man like Mr Kapko gives advice for free you'll pay a price if you accept it.

But it wasn't Mr Kapko, it was Sodz. Did I trust Sodz? He was a murderer according to the Boss; he was a terrorist. And yet the story that 'The Shark' had told had been so honest in its details. There had been so much he didn't need to say.

But - would there ever be an end to buts? - Sodz was a hustler. Honesty is what a conman uses when he wants to scam you. He will fill you up with truth so you won't notice when you swallow down the little lie.

I took my first step going down and then I hesitated.

Mr Kapko hated Sodz.

I climbed the stairs. Went through a doorway. Found a mostly empty room. There were, as Sodz had said, a few square tables, chair-surrounded, strewn across the floor. The largest one, the only one that was rectangular, had three men sitting at it, playing cards. Not Poker, though. Pontoon, perhaps.

They were all Peacemakers, of course, conforming to the look. All men, well-muscled and clean shaven with their hair cut short and wearing deep-blue denim jeans and plain white teeshirts.

'Hit me.' One of them was asking for another card.

I walked towards the bar. There was a woman standing there who checked me out as if she was recording me in all my ways: exactly how my knees were bent, to what extent I swung my arms, how much I stooped, the awkward angle that my feet made with straight forwardness. She would most certainly be able to describe me if they asked. At least she had been blatant in her scrutiny. The players watched me from the corners of their lidded eyes.

I knew I was completely out of place, as blatant as a streaker at a passing-out parade. Downstairs it hadn't seemed to matter: there had been a crowd to hide me, there was noise and movement, and musicians playing jazz. But it was not like that within this silent room. I was the only one (except for her and barmaids never really count) who wasn't one of them. I might as well have walked in here with a big label perched above my head that said I was a Drudjer-lover, that I had four Drudjers hiding in my house. I might as well have had a target on my back.

I perched upon a barstool and she asked me what I wanted and I croaked 'The Shark' and then my throat closed up. How could I speak that stupid line in front of witnesses? That they were listening was obvious. Why should they not be?

'Ice with that?' the barmaid asked. She had a badge upon her breast. It told me that her name was Hope.

'The Bank has Blackjack,' said the man who had his back to me. He gathered up his winnings.

'Not again. It looks as if I used up all my luck last night,' one of the losers said.

'What happened, Malc?' the banker asked.

'They're fucking Drudjers, Gary. What do you expect?' said Malc. 'Half-decent people would have fought. Not them. They fucking screamed. They ran in all directions.'

'Doesn't sound that dangerous,' the other player said.

Malc spat. 'That shows you don't know anything. At times of chaos, Tomas, that's when things are at their worst. It wasn't proper. When I hit one Drudjer, suddenly another Drudjer head popped out from somewhere else. That's not the fucking way to fucking fight.' He took an angry drink as if he blamed the beer.

There were four Drudjers hiding in my garage, nowhere else to go. Hemmed in by death. Trapped. On edge. And Mr Kapko has a gun so I'm the one in danger. That's the way it goes. The more things slide, the closer comes the crunch.

The barmaid handed me a cocktail glass. The liquid was an oily shade of green. She must have thought I said chartreuse. I whispered: 'Shark, swim, sea.'

'You're welcome,' she replied. She must have thought I'd thanked her.

Malc described the battle in the Kennels. He admitted, with a deprecating laugh, that he'd been nervous just before the start. 'But once you're in the thick of things, you know, you just react.' The other boys were hanging on his words. He played the hero, eating up the admiration in their glances, swelling, pushing out his chest and spreading out his arms, as if he knew that he deserved to take more space, to breathe more air, than other men. He told them how he'd slaughtered. 'Saw this fuck-ing Drudjer running straight towards me, fucking murder in his eyes, and in his hands a sword, a fucking sword, I swear, long as my arm and sharp and shiny, curved; I knew that if he reached me I'd be fucking carved like turkey. It was him or me, I thought. I took the stance and aimed and all the time that he was coming at me he was screaming and I thought I've got a shot, one single fucking shot, and if I miss I'm fucked. I pressed the trigger and the fucking pistol kicked like it would catapult itself away from me but I held on, my ears were clanging from the fucking noise and I was peering forward through the smoke to see where he had got to and he wasn't there and I was thinking fuck me where's he got to? Thought I'd fucking missed him. Fucking knew that I was finished then. Already felt the metal slicing me. And then I looked again and he was fucking twenty yards away, contorted, limbs akimbo and his belly almost chopped in half; I tell you that those fucking bullets we were using did the fucking trick.'

I wondered how I ought to sit? I didn't want to look like I was listening. Should I sprawl back to make them think I was at ease? I doubted I could make that seem convincing. Should I perch upon my stool: cocked, upright, stiff? The gamblers slumped, at ease. They'd think that I was on parade. I tried to tap my fingers on the table to the rhythm of the music from downstairs but I could only vaguely hear it and the syncopations caught me out. I wondered where I ought to look. Not at the Peacemakers, for heaven's sake. And not towards the barmaid; she might think my mumbles were attempts to chat her up. I stared into the distance till I glimpsed myself reflected in the looking glass behind the bar. I saw a clown.

'I was in action too,' said Gary, as he dealt another hand.

'Whatever.' Malc was openly contemptuous. 'You're on the fucking staff. They kept you in reserve.'

I wondered whether I should sip my drink or down it in a single gulp.

'It's just as well they did. They needed us. I had to storm the tower block when it was set alight. It isn't easy going up the stairs into a burning building. Such a lot of smoke. I've spent the whole day hacking. And you couldn't see. And it was hot.'

He caught me half-way through a swallow and a little liquid went into my windpipe but I didn't dare to cough. I held my breath. The spirit burnt my throat. My eyes began to weep.

'Can you imagine? So much smoke, I couldn't see a thing. And all the men in my patrol were churning up the place and blundering about. One even cannoned into me.'

'You lost two men,' said Malc. 'That's what I heard. And he escaped. I'll stick on that.'

'Twist,' Tomas said.

'The five of hearts. We didn't lose two men, you're wrong there, Malc. Sam sucked up smoke but he'll be fine and Billy's is a flesh wound.'

'Friendly fire is what I heard,' said Malc.

'Twist,' Tomas said again.

Malc muttered: 'Fucking idiot.'

'The Queen of Spades. Bad luck. It could have been the Drudjer; he could easily have had a gun; you know what they are like. It was all flames and whirling smoke. The visibility was dreadful. When I held my gun in front of me it disappeared, that is how thick it was. It was like breathing hair except it stung like buggery.'

Malc asked: 'How do you know that being buggered hurts?'

'I'm bust,' said Tomas, throwing in his cards.

'Bank pays nineteen,' said Gary, reaching out to take their stakes. 'Another hand?'

'You have the devil's luck,' said Malc, 'or is it something else?'

'It's something else,' said Gary. 'It's the way I play my cards. I use my brain.' He tapped his head.

'Don't think I'm thick,' said Malc. 'I'm not a fucking fool. I know you, Gary Mead, I've got you figured out.'

They stared at one another for a moment.

Tomas said: 'I saw you taking up your places, Gary.'

'What?'

'I saw you from the checkpoint on the bridge. I watched you running down the road from the Town Hall. You and your men. To take up your positions round the tower block.'

'Not marching? Fucking running?' Malc's disdain was palpable.

'Last minute thing,' said Gary. 'There we were, expecting action in the Kennels, all prepared, and then the Boss walks in. You should have seen him. Like he'd seen a ghost. I asked him what had happened and he told me he'd just had a call. From her. The Memsahib. Tells me we must go there straight away. He said that someone was attacking her.'

'I can't believe that anybody could attack a fucking Memsahib.' Malc was furious. 'The fucking Drudjers are inhuman. Even animals don't act like that.'

'How was the Boss?' asked Tomas. 'I'd have been in shock.'

'He's not like that,' said Gary. 'You don't know him. Like, a thing like that, he gets pumped up. It gets him mad. And then he gets decisive. That's the way he is. I guess that's why he is the Boss.'

'He had a plan?' asked Malc.

"A pincer movement. I would take my men and we'd surround

the entrance to the offices. The Boss would wait outside the private entrance to the penthouse. Both holes blocked. His only other chance to get away was jumping off the roof.'

'I need another bloody beer,' said Malc. 'Where is she? Girl!' He held three fingers up. 'And make it fast.'

'But he escaped,' said Tomas.

Gary shrugged. 'I don't know how. At first, I thought perhaps he'd fled before we got there. But it can't have been. We must have waited in position twenty minutes. Then I phoned the Boss to check he was okay and he said he'd just seen the Drudjer poke his head across the balcony. That's when he told me he was going in. He said he'd flush him out. He'd go up in the private lift and chase the Drudjer down the stairs so if we waited where we were we'd snaffle him red-handed. I'd have argued that he shouldn't go up there alone except I didn't have the time to think. In any case, he'd not have listened. There are some things that you can't say to the Boss. It's just the way he is. Impulsive, bull at gate, he leaps before he looks, that sort of thing.'

'The Boss was sure he saw him?' Tomas asked.

'The Drudjer set the place alight. That's how we know for sure that he was there. And it was then we saw the smoke. I tried to warn the Boss. I phoned. He didn't get the call. He must have been already in the lift.'

I watched the barmaid's buttocks as she walked up to the table. I admired the way she swayed. I glimpsed her breasts in profile as she turned. Warmth in my belly. Tightness in my pants.

And then she turned and started walking back towards the bar and she was coming straight towards me and she almost brushed me as she passed. 'You mentioned sharks?' she murmured.

'Yes,' I said. I couldn't think. What was the line? That somebody was swimming in the sea? Or had Sodz said the river?

'And that was when you fucked it up,' said Malc. He raised his glass. 'Let's have a toast. To proper soldiers and the fucking staff. To discipline.'

I wondered if they were about to fight.

But Gary only said: 'That's where you're wrong Malc. What you muscle boys don't understand is there are things we know you don't. As soon as I saw smoke I knew we had a choice: to catch the Drudjer or to fight the fire. We had to go in: there was half a chance the Memsahib was alive; we had to try to rescue her. Besides, we might have caught the Drudjer too. But most of all we had to get up to the roof because ...' He looked at me. Looked straight at me. He changed his mind. 'There was a reason and I'll tell you what it was but not right now.'

'The Boss said fucking wait but you went charging in,' said Malc. 'And then you lost the Drudjer. You were going up the stairs and he was going down. And he slipped through your fucking fingers like he'd greased your palm.'

Whenever men are playing cards there's menace hanging in the air but at that moment Mel had gone too far. As Gary spluttered and began to stand, the barmaid intervened. 'Now boys.' She tipped her head towards the door.

Malc turned around. 'It's Mister Pure.' He sounded disappointed.

'Hello lads. Malc, Tomas, Gary.' Nikov walked into the room. 'And Mr Angelo. It isn't often that we see you here. I hope you'll have a drink on me. My usual, Faith, and get this gentleman another of whatever he is having. It looks ... colourful. And beers for our three heroes.'

As he reached the bar he put a flyer on it. 'I would like the pair of you to take a look at this.'

It was a CCTV photograph. A man dressed in a suit, his face caught in the act of turning from the camera so he was in half-profile, from the right. It had been massively enlarged: the details had been lost. But it was Sodz. I recognised his clothes, if not his face. He had been snapped last night, I guessed, when he was visiting Salome. What was in the background? That was badly blurred. It might have been the river but that would have been a guess.

I shook my head. 'I don't know any Drudjers.' I was pleased to find that I could lie so easily. I raised my glass to show my nonchalance.

'Good looking lad,' the barmaid said. 'He's been in here.'

I had to put my glass back down. I didn't want to spill it. Felt a little sick. I didn't want to draw attention to myself.

'Last night?'

'He might have been downstairs. It's not like he's a regular.'

'His name is Sodz,' said Nikov.

I couldn't help myself. I gasped. They turned to me. I coughed. 'This drink is strong!' I said. 'Just what I needed.' Good response, I told myself. They looked away. I'd got away with it.

'Name doesn't ring a bell,' the barmaid said. 'Your drink.' She handed him a glass of orange juice.

'Perhaps he used an alias,' said Nikov. 'You will tell me if you see him.'

'Yes, of course,' I said. It wasn't till the barmaid said she'd keep an eye out that I understood that Nikov hadn't been addressing me.

He didn't notice anything. He wasn't much cop as a cop, I

thought. No wonder that the Boss had asked me to assist.

He wasn't much cop as a cop. That made me want to giggle. That was good. He was not much cop ...

The barmaid moved my drink away from me. She gave the sort of look that teachers give you when they disapprove of something you have done but they don't want to tell you off in front of all the others in the class. 'I'm fine,' I told her and I moved my glass a little closer.

Nikov had already wandered over to the card game, sitting in the empty chair by Gary. 'Tomas. Have you ever let this man across the bridge?'

'Is he the one?' asked Malc. 'The dirty Drudjer. He should stick to fucking his own fucking kind.'

'What do you mean?' asked Nikov.

'Fucking nothing,' Mel replied. 'I know that Memsahibs never do that kind of thing.'

'What kind of thing?' asked Nikov.

'Nothing. Tomas knows. He's always letting blokes like this across his bridge.' Malc made the universal sign for money with his fingers and his thumb.

'I do my duty,' Tomas said. He sat more upright than he had before.

'But this describes him perfectly,' said Malc. 'His fucking height, his build, the clothes that he was wearing and the fucking colour of his hair. I've seen you say hello to him.'

'It isn't him,' said Tomas. 'Here it says that he is elegantly dressed. I wouldn't call him elegant. More like a bird, you know, that bird with all the colours. Starts with p.'

'A peacock?' Nikov offered. 'Parrot? Bird of paradise?'

'That doesn't start with p,' said Tomas.

'Parakeet?'

'No! No. Hang on a sec. A popinjay!'

'Don't be an idiot; that's not a bird,' objected Malc.

'It is; a jay's a type of bird,' said Tomas.

'You're a fucking fool,' said Malc.

'The point is that the man was not a Drudjer. I can tell.'

'You can't,' said Malc.

'Of course I can. The Drudjers can't afford those sort of clothes. And they wear ethnic stuff. You know, those funny under-pants.'

'You checked?' asked Malc. 'You asked the man to take his trousers off? You fucking fairy.'

'No. It wasn't him,' insisted Tomas. 'The man you're thinking of, the man who comes in here, he's not the man you're looking for.'

'I've fucking seen you here with him,' said Malc. 'He buys you drinks.'

'You see,' said Tomas. 'Drudjers aren't allowed in here.'

'And they don't drink,' said Gary.

'But I didn't say he did,' said Malc. 'I said that he buys them for Tomas.'

There was silence for a moment as a tribute to Malc's triumph. Tomas, sulking, said, again: 'I do my duty.'

'Yeah,' said Malc. 'You did it well last night. You did it fucking properly. You let a fucking Drudjer terrorist across the fucking bridge so he could kill the Memsahib. What's that worth? It must be worth at least a fucking bottle of champagne.'

'He's not a Drudjer,' Tomas said. His eyes looked all around the room.

'Why aren't you at your post tonight?' asked Nikov.

'He's been sacked,' said Malc.

'It's my night off,' said Tomas.

'His reward,' said Malc, 'for having fucking Drudjer mates.'

'He's not a Drudjer,' Tomas shrieked.

'But did you let him cross the bridge last night?' asked Nikov. 'This man, whoever he might be. The man that you have drinks with. Did you let him cross?'

'Of course I did,' said Tomas. 'Like I always do. I follow orders.'

'Orders?'

'Orders. Gary, back me up. There is a list of people who can cross the bridge. A Drudjer can't. This man, his name is on the list.'

'His name?' asked Nikov.

'Simon Shark.'

I squeaked. I couldn't help myself.

'You know the name?' asked Nikov, turning round and staring.

'No.' I shook my head from side to side so fast my cheeks were wobbling. 'No. It just sounds such a silly name.'

'It's not a Drudjer name,' said Tomas, eagerly.

'It sounds made up to me,' said Nikov.

'But it can't be him,' said Tomas, 'if his name was on the list.'

'This list,' said Nikov. 'Where do you ...?'

'From Gary.'

'Me? I'm just the messenger,' said Gary. 'It's the Boss who writes the list.'

'But you're the Boss's fucking boy,' said Malc.

'That Gary,' said a whisper in my ear. It startled me; I jumped. I turned and saw the barmaid's scarlet lips a fraction from my face. 'He has more fiddles than an orchestra.'

I used the corner of my mouth to whisper back: 'Sharks, swim, strange, seas.'

'One thing was strange last night,' said Tomas. 'He was on there twice. The first time on the normal list, the people who can always cross the bridge, the ones who live on one side of the river and who work the other side. But he was also on the extra list, the ones who have been added specially, for just that day. We had a laugh about it. I suggested that he'd have to come back later, cross the bridge again. But he said once a night was quite enough.'

'The dirty dog,' said Malc.

'I didn't know there was a special list,' said Nikov.

'But I'm telling you it wasn't him,' said Tomas. 'He came afterwards.'

'What do you mean?' asked Nikov. 'After what?

'He's only saying this,' said Gary, 'so that he can get away with it. The truth is that he let the Memsahib's killer cross the bridge. If Simon Shark was really on the list I guess we can't blame Tomas. How would Tomas know? He checks their papers, checks their names against a list; if they check out he lets them go. That's why it's called a checkpoint. This is not a job that needs a lot of brains.'

'That's just as well,' said Malc.

'There's more to it than that,' said Tomas. 'For a start you have to be observant. Notice things. I notice when they're nervous.' For a moment I was sure that he was looking straight at me. 'I caught a smuggler yesterday like that. She was so scared she shook.'

'Caught her,' said Malc. 'You didn't catch the Drudjer terrorist.' He snorted. 'Simon fucking Shark!'

'It wasn't him,' said Tomas. 'Check it out. I keep a log. It's all in there. The time he crossed the bridge. It proves that it was afterwards.'

'What was it after?' Nikov asked again.

'The trouble is, they keep me in the dark,' said Tomas. 'No one told me yesterday that they were going to invade the Kennels. They just think because I'm sitting on a bridge in town I won't be part of it. There might have been some Drudjers trying to escape. I should have been alerted.'

'After what?' asked Nikov. 'You keep telling us this man, this Simon Shark, came afterwards, but what you don't say ...'

'After Gary's lot,' said Tomas. 'Like I said, I saw them heading for the tower block and it was after that he crossed the bridge.'

'The Drudjer? Sodz?' asked Nikov.

'He is not a Drudjer,' Tomas said.

'Madame,' the barmaid said, and she spoke softer than a sigh, 'will see you now.'

I couldn't walk out now. They'd all be watching me.

'The Gents,' she said aloud, as if I'd asked, 'is through that door.'

I took the hint.

CHAPTER ELEVEN: MADAME AND FAITH

I didn't really need to use the gents but I decided that I ought to try so I unzipped and stood at the urinal trying to convince my bladder to discharge. It isn't always easy to get going. Then I thought about the pearl that I had hidden in my underpants. I squeezed my thighs together so it would stay safe. That made it even harder to achieve a flow. At last, a trickle started.

She'd followed me. I hadn't noticed her. I was distracted. I was concentrating somewhere else. Then I became aware she was behind me. 'Well,' she said and in a single word she packaged sentences and paragraphs of mockery. 'You weren't supposed to … When you've finished don't forget to wash your hands. And after that you choose the middle cubicle.'

It's often easier to start than stop.

At last, my bladder emptied and, the final droplets shaken off, tucked in, zipped up, hands rinsed, I found the middle cubicle engaged. Its door was closed. I tapped on it. No answer. Did I dare? I pushed. The door resisted. I pushed harder and it opened.

I was glad that it was empty. There was no one there, nor was there any toilet, nor a wall. It was a two-step passageway. I took those steps and as I did I heard the door behind me close and click. Some sort of automatic locking, I supposed. No going back. I took a further step into the room beyond.

It was an office. On the far side was a window that extended, floor to ceiling, almost all the way across the wall. In front of that there was a table with a black glass top and sturdy metal legs with high-backed chairs around it. There was a woman sitting at the table. She was short and stout. Her cheeks were powdered and her hair was tightly curled. Her face was round, her eyes like currants in a bun, her little mouth a crimson pucker of reproach. She wore a necklace made of gaudy-coloured fragments of ceramic: flat-faced, angular and crooked-cornered, like the shards exploding when you shatter brittle toffee with a hammer.

She gestured. I should sit. She pointed. Opposite. I sat.

'Are you Madame?' I asked.

She turned towards the window. I turned too. Looked through. Looked down onto the dance floor. I could see the band. The dancing girls. The Peacemakers. I saw them but I couldn't hear a thing. Without the music, as they wavered back and forth, and turned and lurched and jiggled, they looked uncoordinated and ridiculous. I glanced at her. Was I supposed to laugh? She didn't look amused. I understood. It was a warning. It was not the chaos she was showing me. It was the multitude. I might be in her office now but I was on my own.

The barmaid was beside me suddenly. She handed me a can of cola and a half-pint glass. 'No alcohol,' she said. 'I think you've had enough.' She put a brandy bottle and two cognac glasses on the table, then she sat beside the other woman. 'My name's Faith,' she said.

I was confused. 'Your badge says Hope.'

'My twin. We like to swap from time to time to catch the boys out.'

'Nikov called you Faith. That means he knows you well?'

'From school,' she said, 'and from St Jude's. Such stories I could tell.'

'And you know Sodz. The Shark.'

'He is a customer.'

The other woman looked at me. She raised her eyebrows, pursed her tiny lips and tipped her head a little to one side.

'Madame would like to know your name.'

'What for?'

'You came to us,' said Faith.

'My name is Smith. John Smith.'

Faith stood. 'I think that our discussion is concluded, Mr Smith.'

'What's wrong?'

'We operate by word of mouth. We only work with people whom we know, to whom we have been introduced, whom we have been informed of. What we do is based on trust.'

'My name is Edward Angelo.'

Madame reached out and gripped her brandy glass and swirled the liquid in it once and tipped it down her throat. The glass replaced, she nodded.

Faith refilled the empty glass and added brandy to her own, untouched, one.

'What do you want from us?' asked Faith.

'I have a list of groceries we need.'

Madame looked up. She held her hand out.

'We?' asked Faith.

I could have kicked myself. She was a barmaid. I had a degree. I fumbled in my pocket and I found the shopping list. I handed it to Faith. She laid it on the table and she smoothed it out. It was a little crumpled, I suppose. Faith passed it to Madame who started to peruse it line by line, her index finger pointing to each word, as if she found it difficult to read.

'I recognise the handwriting,' said Faith. 'You're not a very honest person, Mr Angelo. Not only did you lie about your name to us; you said to Nikov that you'd not seen Sodz. Where is he, Mr Angelo? You know he's wanted for the murder of Salome Brise.'

'He didn't do it.'

He is very charming isn't he?'

Madame was pointing to an item on the list. She shook her head. She showed the list to Faith.

'We can supply the groceries but not the pharmaceuticals,' said Faith. 'I trust you have some means to pay. We don't take credit, I'm afraid.'

'I have a pearl.'

She asked me to produce it.

I began to stand. Madame's hand slapped upon the table. If a look could kill, I would have been impaled against the wall. I blushed. I stuttered. 'Um. I have to. Um. I've hidden it. It's in my pants.'

Faith nodded and I stood. I felt indecent. These two women, one so young and pretty, one so old and damaged, watching. Faith was grinning but Madame tracked every movement of my hand with fierce intensity, as if she hated me, as if she thought that I was reaching for a weapon. First I had to slacken off my belt and open up my fly a little way. I slid my hand inside my underpants and round my penis. 'Do you have to stare?' I asked. I realised I should have turned around but now it was too late: this rubbernecking pair would mock my modesty. They looked at me like falcons focusing on meat. I groped around my testicles. It wasn't there. I hoped it hadn't fallen out. I felt a little further back. I found it. Careful now. I didn't want to push it backwards, rolling down my perineum till it popped into my anus.

'Would you like a hand with that?' asked Faith.

'I need to concentrate,' I snapped.

I had it, then I lost it, then I had it pincered in between my longest fingers, like a scrap of pork held by a pair of chopsticks. I focussed. Inch by inch I drew it forwards, underneath my bollocks, taking care I didn't nudge my penis out into the open air. At last I had it safe, cupped in my hand, displayed to them.

Madame reached out to take it but I closed my fist on it.

'Don't be ridiculous,' said Faith. 'We need to check if it is genuine.'

I passed my treasure to Madame. She put it on the table, poking it to make it roll. It wobbled slightly, curving in its path. She picked it up and placed it in her palm. She nodded.

'Pearls feel cold,' said Faith, 'like bare feet on a marble bathroom floor. A pearl takes time to warm up. I know men like that.' She looked in my direction, at my groin. 'Perhaps you'd like to tuck yourself back in. Zip up.'

Madame produced a magnifying glass with which she scrutinised the pearl.

'It has been bored for stringing on a necklace,' Faith explained. 'In an artificial pearl the entrance to the hole has rounded edges. Also, in a true pearl, you can often see a line inside it in between the nacre and the nucleus.'

Madame was shrugging. Not good news, I thought.

She tucked her magnifying glass away and put the pearl between her lips.

'What is she doing? Tasting it?'

'An artificial pearl is smooth; with a real pearl you can sense the imperfections on its surface if you rub it side to side along your teeth,' said Faith.

Madame put down the pearl. She looked at Faith. She gave the slightest nod.

'Let's talk about delivery,' said Faith.

'Delivery?'

'It's food for five. You didn't think that you were walking out of here with all that in your pockets?'

Just like that. She made me feel so stupid. Thought that she was someone special, I supposed. She wasn't. She was just a girl. Good-looking, though.

'What's your address?' she asked.

I froze. Of course. I understood. The whole thing had been leading up to this.

'We can't deliver if you're not prepared to tell us your address.'

So this is how it feels to be betrayed. I was a fool. I came in here and said those stupid words about the Shark and handed her the paper and she recognised the handwriting of Sodz and now she has the pearl, she knows I know him, she's deduced that I am hiding Drudjers, all she needs is my address and she can go out there and blab to Nikov and I'm dead, I'm dead, dead, dead.

'I thought he was your friend,' I said. 'He was the one who recommended you. I can't believe you'd turn him in. Is it because you think he killed her? You're prepared to trade a little on the black but murder, that's another game. Sodz made things just a bit too hot for you. He was your friend but you're prepared to turn him in for that. That isn't nice. You'll learn. You will regret it. Sodz is innocent.'

'I know he is.'

'Is it because Salome was your friend? You're angry she is dead. It's okay to be angry.'

'Thank you very much.'

'It doesn't mean he did it. Sodz may be a lot of things but he's no killer.'

'Hah!' The single syllable escaped Madame.

Hang on a moment.

Stop.

It makes no sense, I told myself.

'You knew my name already. Nikov greeted me by name when he came to the bar. You didn't need to ask me who I was.'

It must have been some sort of test.

Like this?

She didn't need to ask me where I lived. If she was in cahoots with Nikov, he already knew.

Madame now nodded. She could read my thoughts from the expressions on my face. I bet she was a poker genius. I guessed that, in her day, she had excelled in what she did.

Faith said, again: 'We work on trust.

I told her where I lived.

'Tonight,' said Faith. 'No time like now. Where is the best place for the van to park?'

I wondered whether Sodz had thought this through. I hadn't. 'Nikov lives across the road.'

'That's why we have to do it now,' said Faith, 'while he's downstairs.'

'It isn't possible,' I said. 'There's nowhere you can park.' I started trying to explain about the searchlights. 'And you can't drive through the arch: it's just a footpath and in any case you'd wake the Officer. He's mad,' I told her: 'Who can trust a lunatic?' She asked about the access to my street and I admitted that there was a road along the river bank 'but you would be in full view of the guardpost on the footbridge.' But was there nowhere she could park the van along that road where it could not be seen? I shook my head. There must be somewhere, she insisted. 'Just the building site.'

She pounced on that as if she was a kitten with a tangled skein of wool. She teased it with her pretty paws and slowly, somehow, she untangled it. Before the Siege they'd planned apartment blocks along the river. They had cleared the site and put up boards so children couldn't play there. Then came all our troubles. They abandoned it, another relic of our past prosperity.

The van could park beside these boards; it would be hidden from the footbridge. It would still be overlooked by houses on the other side but some of these had been abandoned. 'At night,' Faith said, 'most people draw their curtains. No one wants to look outside. Not since the Siege. Not now the Peacemakers patrol the streets. Nobody wants to see things that they shouldn't see.'

The plan was: Faith would park the van and then unload it box by box and, box by box, she'd ferry them along the road. She'd dodge the searchlight from the footbridge; if it swung her way she'd hide inside the nearest shadow. Once she reached my garden she would loiter, hiding in the hedge, until the Town Hall searchlight passed. Then she would quickly knock upon the door and hurry back to get another box while I dashed out to grab the one she'd stashed.

'It's all about the timing,' Faith reminded me. I'd have to wait inside my door and open it the instant that she knocked.

I asked her what about the van? She said that usually her sister, Hope, would drive. 'That's how we work. If things go wrong the driver leaves the scene; the evidence goes with them. But Faith, of course, is otherwise engaged seducing Nikov. Some girls always seem to land the fun jobs. But that means I'm short a driver. No, Madame, I can't use Mr Angelo. You don't choose greenhorns for a tricky job like this. Besides, he doesn't have the documents. If someone stops the van we'll need to have the paperwork in order. No, Madame, it can't be you. I know you're not too old. You're not decrepit, but … I know that all the driver has to do is sit there, but … I know you wouldn't offer if you thought you'd prove a liability, but … OK. You win. You're right.'

Madame would drive.

Faith turned to me. 'No one should ever underestimate Madame.'

So all was sorted. Faith would go downstairs at once, brief Hope, and load the van. How soon would she be ready? Twenty, thirty minutes at the most. I had to get back home at once, as quickly as I could. I must be ready, waiting for the knock.

CHAPTER TWELVE: YOU'RE OFFAL

Of course it all went wrong.

I left the club at once. The sky had clouded over. I decided not to use the river path. Without the moonlight I would find it hard to see my way. I would be slow, might get delayed, might not be there for Faith. So I decided I would risk the road. The streets I had found empty when I came; the party at the night club showed no signs of faltering. I hoped that all the Peace-makers in town were celebrating.

As they were. Except for one. I crossed the bridge unchallenged and I turned right at the tower block. From there I took the route I'd walked with Nikov; it seemed that had been weeks ago but it was earlier tonight. Then it occurred to me that I might find the keys I'd lost. I didn't have the time to search so I walked swiftly, with a jerky gait, my eyes turned down to scan the ground. Perhaps, if I had looked ahead ... But I had almost reached the arch when I bumped into him.

The Boss.

'I've been with Nikov,' I explained before he had the chance to ask. 'At the *Enchanted Isle*.'

He said that he was going home. He had been working late. 'I kept the chef behind. No Memsahib now to cook for me when I get home.'

I mumbled I was sorry for his loss.

'A bit late now.'

I asked if he was sleeping in the flat.

'I'm not afraid of ghosts. Vague, insubstantial things. Won't have much chance against this too, too, solid flesh.' He tapped his chest. 'The Memsahib never troubled me when she was living so I don't suppose she will now she is dead.'

'But hasn't it been damaged by the fire?'

He sighed. 'That stupid Drudjer. He did me a favour, I suppose. Burnt all her stuff. You need to catch him soon. They say revenge is best served cold but I can't wait for that. I'll have his bollocks on a plate. First peel away the membrane. Fry in butter with some onion and a little garlic, chopped. Then roast: ten minutes at two hundred. Let it rest, and serve with mashed potato, peas and gravy. Claret, warmed.'

I thought I was about to vomit. It was more than forty hours since I had slept. I'd eaten nothing since my meaty breakfast with the Boss. I had been drinking cocktails on an empty stomach. I had nothing left. I wanted to lie down, there, on the pavement, and curl up into a ball, and sleep. If he would let me sleep.

I couldn't. I must get back home. I had to get away from him and fast.

'I understand your feelings,' said the Boss. 'You have had Drudjer friends.'

'No,' I protested.

'You have worked with them.'

'But they were colleagues, never friends.'

He made a gesture which suggested such distinctions should

be swept away. 'I think that what you fail to understand is that the Drudjers are, far more than us, the products of the way they are prepared. When treated nicely, anyone will grow up nice. But life's not kind. At times like these, when things are harsh, you can't kid-glove the weaklings. They can't cope with that. They feel frustrated. They get nasty. Drudjers, as a breed, are likely to be vicious brutes. They have to be controlled. How many Memsahibs will it take before you understand?'

'It wasn't Sodz,' I said.

'Not who?' He made a masticating motion with his jaw. 'How do you know his name?'

I told him. Nikov. The Enchanted Isle. The Peacemakers. The evidence of Tomas. 'So you see,' I said, 'it can't have been this Drudjer. Memsahib phoned to say he was attacking her and you went over there at once, with Gary. It was only after that, says Tomas, that the Drudjer crossed the bridge.'

He looked at me. His stare was like a skewer. It kebabbed me.

'Nikov tells me you are smart. Too clever by three-quarters, so I've heard. But being intellectual doesn't cut the mustard, not with me. I need a man who does what he is told to do, not more, not less. I'll be the judge. You catch him, bring him in, and I'll take it from there.'

I nodded. Swallowed. Nodded.

'You look like you have been boned and butterflied and blanched,' he said. 'You need a long, slow, stew in your own juices overnight so that tomorrow we will see you fully spiced. And know your place: you're offal, not a prime cut. If you can't even make that grade, tell Nikov. We will have you filling sausages.'

I swallowed. Nodded. Gulped.

'Be in by breakfast,' and he smiled and let me go and ambled off towards the tower block.

By then I was already late. I walked beneath the arch. Of course the Officer was still awake.

> *When your lifeline is tangled and tied*
> *In a knot and your dreams start to slide*
> *Down the slippery slope,*
> *Then abandon all hope.*
> *Go to hell. Have some fun on the ride.*

I wondered whether he spent all his time composing doggerel or whether he performed ad lib.

One thing I knew was that he would be watching. Had he seen me earlier tonight when I had knocked upon my own front door?

As soon as I was back inside, as soon as I had closed the outside door, I was interrogated.

'Did you see Madame?' asked Sodz.

'Where is it?' Mr Kapko asked.

'Are you all right?' asked Blossom.

'Did you get it all?' asked Ochre.

I explained that Faith was coming with the groceries, that she might be arriving any moment, that we had to listen out for her. At which point Mr Kapko took control. I'd pop outside to get the packages and Sodz and Ochre would be waiting in the hall to pass them down to Blossom in the garage who would put them all away.

'He needs to rest,' said Ochre. 'He is not as young as we are.'

We were scarcely ready when the knock came on the door.

I opened it.

Thank goodness that, just at that moment, no one else was in the hall.

It wasn't Faith but Nikov.

'Sir. I'm glad you're still awake. May I come in? I'd like a coffee if you have one and I need to pick your brains.'

What could I do? I took him to the kitchen, ushering him past the opened door into the garage. They had turned the lights off. I supposed that they were hiding in the corners. I imagined Mr Kapko had his gun out.

'Don't you have a kettle?' I was boiling water in a saucepan.

'No,' I lied. 'It broke.'

I didn't offer him a seat. I wanted him to go.

My senses were on full alert. He'd claimed he could smell Drudjers. Even if he couldn't I was painfully aware that those four bodies in the garage had a ripened pungency.

'I was surprised to see you at the nightclub.'

'It has been a long day. I've been working hard.'

It was not, of course, an answer. If anything, you'd have expected it to be the other way around. But Nikov nodded. There was something on his mind.

'He could be lying. Tomas could be lying.'

'Why would Tomas lie?' I asked him.

'People do.'

Four Drudjers in my garage. Any one of them at any time could cough or sneeze or move and make a sound. What could I do? Would it be best to chatter, hoping that I'd drown out any noise that they might make? Or should I be as rudely taciturn as possible so he would take the hint and go?

'The world,' he said, 'is all fucked up. There's right and there is wrong and no one seems to care.'

I'd left the jar of instant coffee granules in the garage for the Drudjers. I suspected that they might have finished it. 'I've just remembered that I'm out of coffee.'

'Tea will do.'

It wouldn't. I had left the caddy … But I'd bought an extra pack of tea bags just the other day. I seen them and I'd bought them: that was how we shopped then, doing what we could to keep the cupboards stocked. 'I'll have to open a fresh packet,' I explained. 'Excuse me for a moment. I must fetch it from the garage.'

'I can go,' he offered, standing up.

'You don't know where it's kept. I'll only be a moment.'

They were standing in a line against the furthest wall. The crushed against it. Did they think it might dissolve and let them through? Or did they think that if they put an extra centimetre in between themselves and Nikov it would make a difference?

I found the tea bags and returned. At least I had the chance to close the garage door.

I felt a little safer now. Not safe enough.

'They all take bribes,' he said. 'They think that I don't know. They laugh at me behind my back. They call me Mister Purity.'

He's in confession mode, I thought. He must be drunk. The best that I can do is give him tea and get him out of here before he hears the Drudjers.

And before Faith knocks upon my door.

I froze. I had forgotten that.

I asked him how he took his tea. 'I don't have any milk. Or lemon. And I'm out of sugar.'

'That's OK. I like it black.' He laughed. 'Peacemaker Pure.'

'I reckon we could both do with a good night's sleep. Why don't we just call it a night? Things always look more rosy in the morning.'

'It's important, isn't it? to do what's right. When something's wrong you have to change it. You must knock things down and clear the site before you can begin to build.'

'Why don't we sleep on it?'

'The problem is the people.'

'Many times I find that if I sleep on problems I'll have solved them by the morning.'

That was when Faith knocked.

I froze.

But Nikov didn't. His reaction was immediate. It was as if he was expecting this to happen. 'I'll get that,' he said. I didn't have the chance to disagree. He marched along the hall to the front door and opened it.

'Hello,' he said. 'Well, well,' he said. 'So that's the game,' he said. 'I'm not surprised. Perhaps a little. Mr Angelo. Who would have thought it? Now you're here you'd better come inside.'

He ushered Faith into the house. They walked along the corridor. He was behind her all the way. 'Sit down,' he told her. 'We're just having tea. Perhaps you'd like a cup.'

I couldn't think of anything to say except: 'I haven't any milk.'

'So this is why,' said Nikov, merrily, 'you have been trying to get rid of me.'

'I wasn't,' I protested.

'Yes you were. All of those hints about a good night's sleep. That isn't what you're after: good night, yes; sleep, no. I'm just surprised at you Faith. I would not have said he was your sort.'

'Well you know me,' she said. 'I'm nothing if not versatile. I like experiments. Besides, I think he's cute. Do you have any sugar?'

'You, my dear, are sweet enough,' he told her.

It began to dawn on me that Nikov thought that Faith was here to spend the night with me. That would be fun. If I could play my cards right, maybe she would have to stay.

And I deserved it, didn't I? There were four Drudjers hiding in my garage; I was risking all for them. At any moment I might be discovered. It was only fair that I should take some pleasure when I had the chance.

She was a lovely looking girl. I liked the way her thighs were sheathed in denim. She would be an unexpected present it would be a pleasure to unwrap.

'I'd like to run a few things past the pair of you,' said Nikov, 'if I might. I know your time is precious but I won't be long.' He winked at me. 'Some things are worth the wait.'

'No problem.' Faith seemed utterly relaxed. It made no sense to me: she must have known that there were Drudjers hiding in this house. If they were found, how could she possibly explain herself. Unless ...

Unless she had betrayed me. Why had Nikov suddenly appeared? The plan had been that Hope would keep him busy. Faith had lingered after knocking on the door, she must have done. Was that for Nikov's sake?

I'd been set up. I doubted that Madame was outside, sitting in the van. This whole thing was a play they'd made to catch me.

It had worked.

What were they waiting for?

For reinforcements. Yes, that must be it. Their plan was that they'd keep me chatting till the others came.

I could provoke a showdown. I could shout that we had been betrayed. Then Mr Kapko would come running in here with his gun. There would be shooting. People would be hurt. There was a rotten chance that I'd be one of them.

And maybe my assessment of this situation was inaccurate. Perhaps Faith was for real. If I just played along I would discover that. Then Nikov, once we'd talked, would go back home and Faith would have to come upstairs with me.

'It seems to me,' said Nikov, sitting at the breakfast bar, inviting Faith to sit beside him, 'that the Drudjer could have crossed the bridge when Tomas says and still have killed the memsahib.'

'How?' asked Faith. 'I heard what Tomas said.'

'There is a private entrance and a lift up to the penthouse.'

'But,' she said, 'I thought the Boss was waiting there.'

'One thing that I don't get ...' I interrupted. Faith put up her hand, the palm towards me. Stop, it said.

'You weren't there when the conversation started, Nikov. Ed and I heard all of it. The Boss said he would stake the private entrance out.'

'Perhaps he couldn't get there straight away,' said Nikov. 'Perhaps the Drudjer sneaked in when his back was turned.'

'What I don't understand,' I said, 'is why ...'

'They waited twenty minutes,' Faith said. 'Gary said his men were in position long before they saw the smoke.'

'I don't suppose,' said Nikov, 'I could have another cup of tea.'

'It's getting late,' I said.

He nodded. 'Yes. Of course. It's just that I won't get a wink of sleep until I've got this sorted in my mind.'

I wondered whether I would sleep at all. I filled the saucepan from the tap and set it on the cooker top. I couldn't think what else to do.

'You need to turn the heat on,' Nikov said.

I did what I was told to do.

'It all depends,' said Faith, 'if you believe what Gary said.'

'I know what Gary's like,' said Nikov.

'*In vino veritas*,' said Faith. 'He'd had a few. Right at the start he told us that the Boss received a phone call from his wife. She said that someone was attacking her. What did the Boss do then?'

She seemed to be addressing me. I couldn't think. I shook my head.

'You would have thought,' said Faith, 'that he'd have hurried home to rescue her. You would have thought he'd storm in there to save her. He's a man - what was the phrase that Gary used? - a man who doesn't look before he leaps.' She looked at Nikov. 'Is that right? Is that how you'd describe the Boss?'

He nodded.

'But instead he makes a plan to catch the killer. It's as if he knows that it's too late; as if he knows his wife's already dead.'

I took the boiling water from the stove.

'And when his men are all around the tower block,' said Faith, 'he makes them wait. Is that because he knows there is no harm in waiting?'

Carefully, I poured the boiling water on the tea in Nikov's mug.

'Or does he have to wait,' asked Faith, 'because he knows the Drudjer isn't there yet?'

'Not the Boss,' said Nikov. 'Not the Boss.'

Faith's gone too far, I thought. You can't say things like that to Peacemakers and get away with it.

'I know you're loyal, Nikov, but I know you're honest too.'

'Sometimes you take advantage of our friendship, Faith.'

I hoped he wouldn't shoot her here. Not in my house.

He stood. 'It's time to go,' he said. 'I have outstayed my welcome. I will leave the two of you. Have fun.'

He tucked his chair back neatly in its place and turned and left the house without another word.

I seemed to have forgotten how to breathe.

'Poor boy,' said Faith. 'It's tearing him apart.'

'But he's a Peacemaker.'

'That doesn't mean he's happy.'

'I should check ...' I said. I stopped.

I wasn't sure if Faith knew there were Drudjers here. She knew, so I supposed, about the Shark. She might have worked out from the quantities of food that we had ordered that he wasn't on his own. But guessing isn't knowing. Many people hated Drudjers. Many people hated men with guns.

I had a sudden thought. 'Madame.'

Faith shook her head. 'She will have gone by now. We have a

rule. Don't hang about. Drive off.'

This might just turn into my lucky night, I thought. 'You can't go yet. He thinks you're here to stay the night.'

'I'll have that cup of tea he didn't drink,' she said.

She never got it. I had picked it up. I was about to put it in her hand. Then someone knocked upon the door. I froze. They didn't wait. The front door opened and I dropped the cup. It shattered. Nikov walked in through the doorway. Tea splashed up at me. I stared at him.

'It's only me,' he said. 'Were you aware that someone's left a box of tins of chopped tomatoes underneath your hedge.'

I couldn't think of anything to say.

'Beneath the hedge?' Faith giggled.

'In the garden.'

'Like a foundling baby. Darling. Is there anything that I should know?'

How could she treat it like a joke?

'It's probably the Officer,' I said. It was a lie. It was the only thing that I could think of. I explained that sometimes people left him gifts, though normally they left them underneath the arch. Perhaps someone had got the wrong address.

Faith looked at me in what I hoped was admiration. Nikov looked at me in what I'm sure was disbelief. And yet he didn't challenge me. He said he must be off.

This time I followed him along the hall and once he'd gone I locked the door.

'I don't like canned tomatoes anyway,' I said.

Faith laughed.

The garage door came open slowly. Sodz stepped out. He looked from side to side.

Faith ran to him and threw her arms around his neck and clung to him and kissed him on the lips. He put his hands around her waist - his fingers almost met - and kissed her in return.

If anyone was having sex tonight, I thought, it wasn't me. Again.

Thank goodness. I felt so fatigued the thought of even climbing up the stairs to bed enfeebled me. My eyes kept closing; it required an act of will to open them.

Sodz asked her, when he had the opportunity: 'Do you believe me? That I didn't do it?'

'I am sure of it,' said Faith. 'You had no motive. It's a 'jealous husband' crime. I think that he, the Boss, discovered that his wife was having an affair. I don't know how, but I suspect he knew she was expecting you last night. He knew exactly when you would arrive.'

That sounded right. He'd boasted of his punctuality.

'I don't know if he meant to kill her but I'm certain that he did. I don't know if he had already planned to frame you. I'm not sure it matters. After she was dead he went back to his office. Gary said the Boss received a phone call from his wife but I think that was just an act the Boss put on. It gave him quite an alibi. He sent off Gary to the office entrance of the tower block because he knew that you would use the private lift. Perhaps he timed his own arrival there till after you had entered, or perhaps he hid and watched you going in. Then, once you were inside ...'

'It was a trap,' said Sodz. 'She was the bait. Salome hated to be used. She hated cobwebs and she hated sweetcorn and she hated stinginess. And she loved me. She said he wasn't jealous.

They'd been living separate lives for years. She said he had his women; it was only fair if she had men.'

'Perhaps,' said Faith, as gently as she could, 'it was because you were a Drudjer. He could share his wife with men.'

CHAPTER THIRTEEN: THE KEY TO THE ESCAPE

And after Faith had gone?

'A box of cans of chopped tomatoes,' Mr Kapko said. 'We spent a pearl for that.'

'You can't blame Sodz,' said Blossom.

'No?'

'It's not Faith's fault,' said Sodz.

'You can't pin this on me,' I added.

'Well,' said Mr Kapko tetchily. 'I see that this is my responsibility. Because I brought along a clown whose only value is the people that he knows.'

'Speak softly,' Blossom said.

'Hush,' added Ochre.

'After all I've done for you,' said Sodz.

'You've done for me,' said Mr Kapko. 'Yes indeed, you've done for me. You've brought me here.'

He looked around the garage, seeing, I supposed, the walls. Four people stuffed into a space that once had served to keep a car. Four people trapped. Four people who, till Nikov had departed, had been standing silent, barely breathing, throbbing-hearted, swollen-bladdered, prickle-haired, skins stinging with the nettle-fire of fear. Four people who might just as well have been in prison.

'Faith said that she would try again tomorrow.' Sodz was trying to conciliate.

'I should have known that boys like you know girls like her,' said Mr Kapko. 'Why am I surprised? I should have realised that when you reach into the sewers you get shit.'

The garage was a mess. There was a dented soup can, kicked into the corner; next to it, a scorched, encrusted saucepan.

'We've never had a problem with supply before,' protested Sodz. 'You can't expect perfection nowadays.'

'Not when you delegate to idiots,' said Mr Kapko.

'Uncle, hush,' said Blossom. 'Not so loud.'

'Your operation has experienced a glitch or two,' said Sodz. He looked around the garage. 'I don't see John Zombie here.'

'Nor Xan,' said Ochre, drooping.

I could see, a greasy thumbprint blemishing the whiteness of its rim, a broken plate. It had been mine. Who broke it?

'I achieved,' said Mr Kapko, puffing slightly, speaking like his words were being squeezed between his teeth, 'the rescue of four people from the Kennels in the middle of a battle.' Here, he paused to take a breath. And then another, Then a third. 'Including you.'

'John Zombie's dead,' said Sodz. 'At least nobody's dead because of me.'

'Except Salome,' Mr Kapko said.

'That wasn't me,' said Sodz. 'I thought that you were listening to Faith. She said it was the Boss, her husband.'

Had I turned the stove off? Had I put the saucepan somewhere safe? I'd wash it up tomorrow.

Mr Kapko, sweating, even though the the night was chilly, said to Sodz: 'You killed her. It was you as certainly as if you put your hands around her throat yourself. You heard what Faith said. She was killed because she screwed a lowlife. Did you give her a disease? Did she contaminate her husband? Is that how he discovered that his wife had been debased?'

I couldn't think. Fatigue had damaged me.

'Perhaps the Boss discovered that his wife was having an affair with me because somebody told him.'

I was sure the back door would be locked; I hadn't opened it today.

'Are you suggesting I did?' Mr Kapko's voice was calm but cold with animosity.

'You were always thick as thieves,' said Sodz.

My thoughts were moving sluggishly inside my brain as if the sea in which they swam was clotting.

All I wanted was to fall asleep.

'You scum,' said Mr Kapko, breathing heavily.

'Are you all right?' asked Ochre.

'Uncle?' Blossom asked.

'You tell that ... lowlife ... Drudjer,' Mr Kapko said. His voice was scraping through his teeth. His words were hollowed out. He looked depleted.

I was wondering how long I had been sleepless but I couldn't do the sums.

I turned to leave. 'Where ... do you think ... you're going?' Mr Kapko asked.

'I'm off to bed.'

He shook his head. 'We're all in this together.'

But we weren't. They were the Drudjers but I was the one who fetched and carried, who provided, who gave up oblivion for labour. They were spending all their days enjoying doing nothing.

'Take it easy,' Ochre urged his uncle. 'You're unwell. One of your turns.'

'I'm fine,' said Mister Kapko though the way that he was panting gave the lie to what he said. He shuddered with the effort of command. I would be sleeping in the hall, he said, upon the floor, across the door, so I would trip them up should Peacemakers come bursting in. I would be watched all night: Sodz first, then Ochre next. The guard - here Mr Kapko had to stop to catch his breath - must sit upon the bottom two steps of the stairs, must keep their eyes on me. He would provide them with a torch but they must only - and he paused to rally - use it if they needed to, in case the light showed through the door. As for himself, he wheezed, he would be sleeping with his pistol underneath his pillow. At the slightest - did they understand? - the slightest, whiff of trouble they should wake him up.

'I don't see why I have to stay awake when you're the one who wants to keep an eye on him,' said Sodz.

'Let's do as Uncle says,' urged Ochre.

But I didn't even have a pillow or a blanket, I protested. Sodz said he would lend me his. He wouldn't need them. 'For the first half of the night I'll be awake and watching you and in the second half I'll be awake and making jazz with Blossom while her little brother's sitting in the hall and old man Kapko's snoring.'

'You touch my sister,' Ochre warned.

I didn't care. I could have slept still standing. It was hard to differentiate between my thoughts and chaos but there seemed to be a part of me that was content I didn't have to climb the stairs. I trudged to my appointed place and lay down, fully clothed, upon the floor.

The carpet's coldness sucked the warmth out of my blood; its unforgiving hardness cramped the comfort from my arms and legs. From time to time the searchlight on the footbridge passed across the window and projected on the wall a monstrous shadow-silhouette of Sodz. But I was weary to the point of senselessness. I fell asleep at once.

At once, or so it seemed, Sodz woke me up. 'Are you awake?' he asked. 'I need to talk with you.'

I don't wake well. 'What what?' I said and he said hush.

Sometimes it's worse to sleep a little and be woken than to stay awake.

'Not yet,' I mumbled. If I opened one eye only would that make the morning go away?

My half-peek coincided with the searchlight and revealed a bare-skinned body overtopping me and shrouding me.

I growled and tried to swat it.

What on earth?

I sat up suddenly. Too suddenly. My skull, it seemed, was shrinking and my brain was being squeezed as if it was a sponge.

I tried, reluctantly, another peep. The light had passed across and so the hall was full of night again but there was something in the darkness. Something solid, smelling sharp and stale and sourly masculine. Light from the footbridge flashed again and I saw Sodz, stripped to his skin.

I panicked, pushing him away, my splayed-out fingers sticky on his sweat-greased chest.

'Calm down,' he said, 'shut up. We need to talk.'

I gulped. 'You're naked.'

'I've been doing exercises. Push-ups. Crunchies.'

'Nude?'

'It is important to keep fit. And anyway, I'm wearing underpants.'

His lower body was illuminated by the torch. A firm, flat belly and a pair of hairy thighs. And in between …

'That's not a pair of Drudjer shorts,' I said. It was a posing pouch.

He filled it well.

'You have some very fixed beliefs,' said Sodz. The torch went off.

I thought, in darkness, that the world had changed. These days the Drudjers weren't like Drudjers ought to be.

'What time is it?'

'I've let you sleep,' he said. 'My shift is nearly done.'

'Why did you have to wake me up?'

'We need to make him tell us where we're going next.'

I didn't understand. I'm slow when I am sleepy.

Sodz explained. 'Phase one was coming here. I always thought it was a stupid move. I pointed out that you lived on the wrong side of the river from the Kennels. If the army was approaching from the north we should be going that way, not down south. They're even stronger in the south. But he insisted that he had a plan.'

I itched. Must be the carpet. I supposed it was infested with a swarm of horrid crawling things, like mites or tiny spiders, hiding in the fibres, lurking, till I offered them my skin and they thought 'food and lebensraum' and they invaded me. I itched because they bit me and they scratched me and they reproduced on me and laid their eggs and shat on me and died on me. I itched because they had infected me. I tried to scratch but there were itches that I couldn't reach.

'He said he brought me,' Sodz says, 'but it's obvious he doesn't want me.'

'Who?'

'He said that I was worthless, that he only wanted me because of my connections with Madame.'

Oh. Mr Kapko. 'So he knew about Madame and Faith before.'

'Of course. He was my biggest customer.' Sodz bobbed his head, ebullient again. 'I am the CEO, head honcho, principale, don, el capitan, el jefe of the biggest, most reliable and best logistics operation in the Kennels. I delivered. He distributed. Of course he wanted me. He had it planned.'

I heard a rustle and the shadows moved. 'What are you doing now?'

'I'm dressing. It is getting rather chilly. I don't want to catch a cold.'

I heard, relieved, the fastening of a zip.

'He thinks he doesn't need me anymore,' said Sodz. 'Tonight

was just a hiccough. Faith will try again. But once we have some food, I'm surplus to requirements. I'm redundant. I'm superfluous and that means I'm expendable.'

I nodded though he couldn't see me. 'That's the way he works.'

'I know. That's why I have to learn how we are getting out of here. He has a plan, I'm sure of that. And that is why you have to help me. Once we're gone, you're safe. But not if he leaves me behind.'

That would be typical of Mr Kapko. He was always looking to the future and he never thought about the past.

'So your job was to feed them?'

'Yes.'

'And Ochre's? Blossom's?'

'I don't know. They're family. His brother's kids.'

'But what about the others? Xan and John.'

'I think he had a thing for Xan. She'd worked for him. John Zombie, though.' He shrugged.

'He's really called John Zombie?'

'No. He's a politico. It is an alias, a pseudonym, a nom de guerre. It's his resistance moniker. I've lost my socks.'

'That's me,' I growled. His questing fingers brushed my leg.

'I'm sure I put them somewhere. Here they are.' There was a little silence. Then he said: 'It's time to wake young Ochre up. So do you promise you will help me?'

'Yes.' If Mr Kapko had a plan - and I had never known him when he wasn't planning something - we would all be safer if we knew it.

Sodz had finished dressing. He was standing at the door into the garage, looking in. He turned the torch on. Then he laughed. 'The little chico: El Hotissimo.'

I went to see what he was looking at.

The torchlight played on Ochre. He was lying on his side, still sleeping, with a smile upon his face. His running shorts were straining to contain a breathtaking erection.

'Happy dreams,' said Sodz.

The dreamer snorted, groaned, rolled on his back and opened up his eyes. He stared. There was an uncomposed look on his face. And then he focussed. 'Um,' he said. 'Hello.' He paused and looked around. 'What are you staring at? Oh shit. Fuck off.' He rolled onto his front.

'Don't break it,' sniggered Sodz. 'It doesn't look like it can bend.'

'Give it a rest,' I said.

'It don't need rest,' said Sodz, 'it needs some exercise.'

'Shut up,' I told him. 'Just shut up. Shut up, shut up.'

He looked at me, a curious expression on his face. He shone the torch around the garage. Blossom gently snored and Mr Kapko, tangled in his twisted dreams, was groaning. Ochre, shrunk back down to normal size, rolled to his knees, stood up and stretched his arms above his head.

'Still stiff?' asked Sodz. 'Your sister's fast asleep. I wonder if she's happy?'

Ochre took the torch. 'Your place is over there.' He pointed to the furthest corner of the garage. 'I'll keep watch and pop in here from time to time and if I find that you have moved an inch towards my sister ...'

'What?' asked Sodz. 'What do you think a little lad like you could do?'

'Sleep tight,' said Ochre. 'Pleasant dreams. Feel free to use my bedclothes.' And he waited, watching, while Sodz walked across the garage to the corner he'd been given; waited, watching, while Sodz settled down to sleep.

He came into the hall and switched the torch off.

'Ochre?'

'Yes.'

'What happens next?'

'What do you mean?'

'Sodz says stage one was fleeing from the Kennels, coming here. You can't stay here forever. What's the next step of your journey?'

'Uncle has a plan.'

'And has he told you what it is?'

'Not yet. He will do, when we need to know.'

He was so trusting. He annoyed me. So I said that Sodz had told me Xan was only here so Mr Kapko had a woman to make pregnant so that he could spawn a tribe of little Drudjers.

'I am Uncle's heir,' said Ochre. 'Sodz is wrong. I am the one that wanted Xan along. That was the deal: I told him I would come if Xan and Blossom could as well.'

I was amazed. 'You told him? Mr Kapko?'

'I insisted.'

No. That wasn't how it worked with Mr Kapko. I should know. I'd worked for him. He did exactly what he wanted. If you begged he might throw you a crumb but if you stood your ground you lost your job. Unless he needed you.

He must have needed me. Perhaps I should have been a bit more firm with him.

'John Zombie too?' I asked.

'He wasn't anything to do with me,' said Ochre. 'We were never mates.'

'You seemed upset when he was shot.'

'Of course I was. He died in front of me. I wish I could have saved him.'

'Was John Zombie special friends with Mr Kapko?'

'John!' I heard him chuckle. 'Chalk and cheese. John's a musician, lately into protest songs, and Uncle is a businessman. He used to say John was degenerate. He said that it was men like John who let the Peacemakers portray us as amoral, villainous and tainted.'

Mr Kapko wasn't stupid. He'd have always known there was a chance that he might have to hide. That isn't easy at the best of times but it is twice as hard if you don't even like the others in your hiding space. I'd seen how much he hated Sodz but he'd have told himself he must put up with him so Sodz would use his contacts to supply them all with food. And therefore, by analogy, if Mr Kapko didn't like John Zombie but still offered him a place among this team of fugitives it must have been because John would provide them all with … what?

Stage Two, I thought. The second part of the escape.

John Zombie, Sodz had said, was a political musician. He'd have contacts. There must be resistance groups across the land. Perhaps there was an underground. John Zombie was the key to the escape.

And he was dead.

So what did they do now?

I heard a movement. Ochre's footsteps. There was light. I watched as Ochre shone the torch and peered into the garage. He was checking. Sodz and Blossom. Brotherly concern? Or something more?

The light went off and as it did the searchlight from the footbridge filled the darkness for a moment. Then the night.

'In any case we have to wait for Xan,' he said. 'You want to know the truth? It's my fault we're still here. I told my uncle that we had to wait. There's still a chance that she might find her way to us.'

'No chance,' I told him and I wished it wasn't quite so dark so I could see his face change when I told him. 'Xan's been caught. She is a prisoner. I've seen her. I have talked to her.'

'Xan?' That was all. Then he was silent. If I listened closely I could hear him breathe.

Then Ochre asked: 'And you have seen her? Is she ... hurt?'

I wished I hadn't mentioned her.

'She is in prison?' Ochre asked.

'She's locked away in the Town Hall,' I said.

'Then you can help us get her out of there.'

That wasn't what I wanted, not at all. It wasn't. It was madness. 'Get her out of there? Escape? You must be joking? It's impossible. It's much too dangerous. She's in the basement. Locked away. It can't be done.'

'I would do anything,' he said. I felt him coming close to me. He clutched my arm. 'You name your price.'

And that was when I wondered whether I was wrong. That it

was not John Zombie who was crucial to my getting rid of my unwanted guests. What was he? A musician! He would be disorganised and scatter-brained like all of those who strum and tootle for a living. He was probably a pacifist. He'd be a dreamer, not a fighter with the underground.

But somebody like Xan. She would be perfect.

She'd told me she was from another town.

She was the answer. She was how I'd clear the Drudjers from my garage.

I would have to prise the secret out of her.

CHAPTER FOURTEEN: A PROPOSITION FROM XAN

'That sounds like thunder.'

'You should know,' Xan grumbled. 'I don't get to see the sky.'

'Do you do anything but moan?'

'Oh, pardon me. I'm sure that I have nothing to complain about. I ought to count my blessings. I'm allowed to work. I should be joyful I can see a little patch of sunlight. Lucky me.'

The atmosphere was tighter than a rubber band can stretch before it snaps and slaps you in the face.

Another crash, another rumble from outside. 'That doesn't sound like thunder,' Xan announced.

'It must be.' Though, when I had walked to work today, the sky was cloudless.

'No. I overheard the guards. They're getting jumpy. There are rumours that the army's coming from the north.'

If that was cannon fire, I thought, the guns were several sizes bigger than whatever had been used against the Kennels.

'It would be ironic,' Xan observed, 'if I survive the Kennels to be killed in here.'

I hadn't thought of that. The army would be aiming at the Peacemakers' headquarters. Here. 'Perhaps they're still too far away.' I hoped.

Xan was a prisoner but I was trapped as well.

I might have promised Ochre I'd do anything I could to get Xan out of here but, truly, there was nothing I could do. It's only in a story that a hero gets to choose the path to take. Here in the real world, life is like a corridor. Most doors are locked. You cannot stop, you can't go back, you cannot see around the corners. If you have a map it has been drawn by someone walking on another path.

Last night I'd slept but not enough. This morning it was hard to concentrate. At least we'd moved on from the work of yesterday which had been dull, routine, not difficult but needing detailed care; the sort of work in which it's easy to make simple slips from tiredness. Now, today, we had begun to model, searching for parameters. It was a lot less boring: it required creative thought. Which, when you've slept perhaps four hours in forty-eight, is difficult to generate.

Xan kept on glancing over. 'Heavy night, last night?' She didn't put the question in a sympathetic tone.

'Cold room,' I said, 'hard bed.' I didn't want to tell her I'd been sleeping on the floor. She might have wondered why.

'I know,' she said. 'I had the same. But my elite accommodation benefited also from a chorus of complaints and cries from all the other cells along my corridor. The good news is I had some pretty wicked dreams. I dreamed that I was growing wings and all my teeth were falling out. I think I must have been a chicken: when I tried to fly I couldn't, even though I wanted to. Do chickens cry? The feathers on my cheeks were quite bedraggled with my tears. I don't remember any eggs though. Maybe they'd been stolen, maybe that was why I wept. At least

I had my plumage. All the other chickens had been plucked. It made them look much smaller and it made them all the same. What made it even harder was that all my fellow hens had been decapitated. Even so, they kept on running up and down.'

These people who insist on telling you their dreams. They're boring. Anyway, they're only boasting. I don't dream.

They say I do, they say we all do, but I don't. They tell me that I'm wrong: I do dream but forget my dreams the moment that I wake.

But that's the same. You are what you remember. I don't dream. I never dream.

And if I dreamt I wouldn't dream of chickens. If I could, I'd like to dream of Xan. In bed. With Ochre. That would be a thing to see! The whippet with his woman.

If she was. Last night the boy had told me he'd do anything for her. But was his love reciprocated? Did she love him back? It could be useful if she did.

Should I tell Xan that Ochre was alive?

She'd ask me how I knew.

Some things are best kept secret. Could I trust her? She'd already made one bargain with the devil: she would help me with my work on System A if Nikov let her live. If she knew I was hiding Drudjers she might seek to trade that information for her liberty. Presuming that she didn't care for Ochre.

What would Nikov do, I wondered. Shoot me? He had not shot Xan. He wanted something from her so, while she was useful, she could live. Perhaps he'd do the same for me.

But then I'd be locked up like Xan.

That might be better than the floor at home, a servant to four Drudjers.

Maybe he would lock me up with Xan. I wondered whether there were bunk beds; if there were, who'd be on top?

Another thudding boom. That sounded closer.

Should I tell Xan? I shook my head. It wasn't worth the risk.

But if I kept my silence how was I to ask her where the Drudjers should be going when they left my garage?

If she knew.

Xan was a puzzle. Why had she agreed to help me with the System? Surely she was bright enough to understand it would be used against the Drudjers. She had said she'd done a deal to save her skin but someone in a situation such as that would not have worked as willingly as she did. They would have done the least they could. So why did Xan work harder? She might say she hated Mr Kapko but that surely wouldn't give the sort of motivation that was needed when you are, once you have stripped away the rhetoric, betraying your own people.

Was she buying time?

By now we'd spent all morning working on the System. We were hoping we could run a simulation by tonight. The problem that we had was that the System seemed to teeter on a precipice: one value on the wrong side triggered a cascade. It didn't seem to matter what we did. We tried to nudge the tipping point to stable equilibrium but somehow it migrated, of its own accord it seemed, back to the edge of chaos.

Xan said: 'Is it that reality itself is permanently on the edge?'

She had a trick of gnawing at her fingers when she thought. She didn't bite her nails. Instead she nibbled at the knuckle. It was usually her thumb, perhaps the index finger. Once I saw her little finger being chewed.

'If we could stop the System at the very moment it begins to oscillate,' she said.

'We'd have a chance of seeing what corrections it might need.'

She nodded.

'We could try,' I said.

She scrutinised the teeth marks on her fingers. 'Why?' she asked. 'Why are we doing this? We're cracking nuts with sledgehammers. I don't believe that's all they want. This System's powerful; there's so much it can do. It is ridiculous to use it just to find the killer of the Memsahib.'

'You've said this before.' She had.

'Which leads to the conclusion that there's more to this than meets the eye. They want this System up and running for another purpose.' She stopped looking at her thumb and stared at me directly. 'In the cells they're saying it was you who told them to attack the Kennels.'

'No. Not me. I only write reports. I didn't even say that. What I told them was that there were shortages of food and stuff like that.'

'And they attacked. Our blood is on your hands.'

It seemed she was a Drudjer after all.

'They didn't have to. There were other things they might have done. Increase the rations, maybe.'

Xan was laughing mockingly.

'They could have,' I insisted. 'Anyway, what I predicted didn't happen did it? So my System doesn't work.'

'What do you mean?'

'I forecast that the Drudjers might rebel but now they won't.

They can't. They're dead. The Peacemakers pre-empted my prediction. Now it can't come true.'

'You're saying you foretold the future but it was a different future from the one that happened.'

'Yes. It's all to do with feedback loops.'

'And that is how you're able to excuse yourself. Your get-out clause. That's how you tell yourself you're not responsible for all that Drudjer suffering.'

'I'm not to blame,' I told her.

It was hot in here. We were too close. I was exhausted.

'That would mean,' she said, 'Cassandra was the only prophetess who ever saw her prophecies fulfilled.'

'Cassandra who?'

'She was a Trojan princess. She foretold the future and she always got it right but she was cursed: no one believed a word she said. So when she told the Trojans that the Greeks were hiding in the Trojan horse they laughed at her. But she was right and that was how the town was captured. If they had they believed her it would not have happened. Then her prophecy would not have come to pass.'

She started chewing on her thumb again.

The door burst open. It was Nikov. I supposed we weren't as high in his priorities this morning if it really was artillery that we could hear. I wasn't clear what Nikov did; the Peacemakers had improvised themselves as a response to what they saw as civil war; their jobs and offices were often ill-defined. So far he'd played policeman but, when you are being shelled, I guess a man like Nikov does what he perceives needs doing.

'I have not got long,' he told us. 'Any news?'

'We've made a lot of progress,' I replied.

'I've had a thought,' he said. 'Last night, when we were talking, Faith said that the Boss received a phone call from the Memsahib.'

'Gary told us that.'

'Your system traces phone calls.'

Xan was sitting at her laptop, fingers poised above the keys. 'I need the number that was called.'

He looked at her.

I rushed to reassure him. 'We can only get a list of numbers calling and the time duration of the call, not what is said.'

'The Boss has lots of calls. Some come from numbers that might be politically sensitive.'

'Xan won't say anything.'

He looked at me. 'She can't. She's stuck in here.'

'There is another way that we can do this,' Xan explained that she could use the number of the phone that called the Boss.

I didn't like it. It was wrong. He shouldn't speak to her. He ought to work through me.

He winked at her. He knew the number of the Memsahib's phone. Xan typed it in.

'What time was this?' she asked.

'The evening. Seven-thirty give or take.'

But when she heard, she shook her head. 'The last call from that phone was 5.15 PM.' She pointed to the number on her screen. 'Is that the Boss?'

'No,' Nikov said.

'Hang on,' said Xan. She pressed some keys. 'That number's registered to Simon Shark.'

My heart dropped.

'Sodz,' said Nikov.

'Sodz?' asked Xan. As if she didn't know him. But she must. Like him, she had been given my address.

'That proves it,' Nikov said. 'He was involved.'

'You don't know why she called him, though,' I said. 'She might have been arranging that he come and see her. Giving him the time and place. She knows her husband will be at the office late, perhaps she knows the Kennels are about to be attacked. She's making an appointment with her gigolo.' Of course, I thought, it fits. She knew about the Kennels. She told Sodz. He passed the information on to Mr Kapko. That was why he came to me that evening, just before it started.

Nikov asked: 'Is Sodz a gigolo?'

That was the way he said it: calm and curt. It should have warned me but I was excited.

'Yes,' I said.

'Last night you told me that you didn't recognise his photograph but now it seems you know him.'

'I've been told.' I couldn't not say anything.

'Who told you?'

'Faith,' I said. I had to give him someone's name. When you are in a hole the only thing that you can do is dig. I had to tell him someone, someone that I might have seen last night, between the time I saw the photograph and now.

'I wonder how she knows a thing like that.'

'She is a barmaid.'

'Do you think she turns a trick or two herself? Was that why I discovered her with you last night? I was embarrassed that I interrupted a romantic rendezvous but now I learn it was more trade than tryst.'

'I only meant that in a night club you must meet all sorts.'

'I went to school with Faith,' he said.

Xan interrupted. 'I've been studying the data as you've talked. Last week she made a lot of calls to Mr Shark but not as often as she called this number here.' She pointed to her screen. 'Who's that? Her husband?'

'That's the Boss.'

Xan said: 'I've checked the calls that he received and on that evening no one called from six till eight o'clock.'

'What? Nothing from that number?'

'Nothing. Not one call from any number.'

'Gary said the Boss received a call.'

'Then Gary lied,' said Xan. She didn't say this spitefully or mockingly. She didn't sound triumphant or embittered. She simply stated it. She told a Peacemaker his colleague was a liar. She, a Drudjer. She, a prisoner. She, completely at the mercy of this man, told him that Gary lied.

So, selflessly, I tried to save the situation. 'Xan, you're wrong. What Gary said was that the Boss had told him that the Mem-sahib called.'

'I see,' said Nikov and his voice was like a heated wire that slices ice. 'What Mr Angelo is saying is that Gary told the truth.

It was the Boss who lied.'

I couldn't move. I couldn't breath. I felt as if I was a prisoner in court, awaiting sentence. Xan had been forgotten. All of Nikov's wrath would now be aimed at me.

Light flashed in through the tiny window that looked out upon St Jude's. That's when I knew that I was right. As Faith had said, this was a jealous husband thing. The Boss had lied about the phone call. Why? Because he knew his wife was dead.

There was a booming crash. The floor vibrated and the building shook. I wondered what it must be like upstairs. At least, down in the basement, we were bunkered.

At least they wouldn't need to bury us. They only had to knock the building down and we would be entombed, an instant cairn, prefabricated to remember us.

'That doesn't sound like thunder,' Xan observed. 'That's heavy guns. The army's getting closer.'

She was an ungrateful bitch. I'd saved her from the tiger. Now he was about to pounce on me, she took the opportunity to pull his tail.

'I understand,' said Nikov, 'that I told you on the roof that you were to report whatever you discovered but ...' He paused. I waited and I waited and my spirits sank.

'But now we're in the basement.' I could not believe that Xan was telling jokes.

'It's not your fault. You've scarcely met the Boss. I know him. He's not capable of lying. He is blunter than brutality. The others pull their punches, not the Boss. That's why I wouldn't work for anybody else. That's why you're wrong. That's why it has to be the Drudjer. Like I said before: it's not your place to play detective. Use your System. Find him. We'll decide what must be done with him.'

He turned. He left the room.

Another flash. Another bang. Another rumble. And the sound of screaming in my ears.

'I saved you there,' said Xan.

'What do you mean?' I yelled at her. 'You saved me? You? I tried to help you and you nearly got me killed.' I went to grab her. I don't know. I didn't have a plan. I wanted to attack her. I suppose that I was aiming for her face. Perhaps her throat. Perhaps a little bit below. I meant to push her. Maybe slap her. Just a bit. I didn't mean to really hurt her. I was angry. She deserved some punishment.

I never got the chance.

I found that I was lying on the floor and staring upwards at her face, my body crushed against the ground, her heavy knee upon my chest, her squeezing hand around my throat.

'Don't make a sound,' she snarled.

I tried to blink away my tears.

And then ... then nothing. Then a pause. Like we were in a tableau, posing for the sculptor of a statue symbolising subjugation.

Xan was counting, not aloud, but I could see her moving lips.

A minute passed.

Then she released me. She stood up. She helped me struggle to my feet. She put a finger on my lips to tell me to stay silent. I obeyed. My back was aching where the ground had bruised my shoulders and my chest was hurting where her knee had pinned me down. My head was throbbing. I was angry. I would get her back for this.

'I thought they might have bugged this room,' she said, 'but, since they didn't come to save you, we can work on the hypothesis they haven't. If you want to call the guards you'll have to shout.'

'I ought to have you whipped for that.'

'That would be quite ungrateful.'

'Me? Ungrateful? Me?'

'Since I have saved your bacon.'

'Saved my bacon? How?'

'Not quite so loud,' she said. 'Just now, with Nikov. I was looking up those phone calls and I saw that Simon Shark had used his phone today.'

Sodz used his phone. I didn't know he had a phone. Not on him.

'So I used the system and it gave me an address. From where he called. Just now.'

He'd used his phone while he was in my garage.

'It was no surprise,' she said. 'I recognised it straight away. It was the same address as I'd been heading for when Nikov intercepted me.'

My garage.

'Then I had a thought. The other database, the one we haven't integrated yet. The list of those who pay the tax on property. Who owns that house?' She looked at me. 'Who lives at that address?' She smiled; she showed her teeth. 'I hadn't known. He never told me; Gannerdjalok Kapko never said your name. I just assumed it was an empty property, ex-Drudjer probably; I'd thought that it was no more than a place to rendezvous. He didn't even tell me who I would be meeting there, just: if I wanted to escape this was the place to head for.'

What I had to do, I told myself, is to be calm.

'I've saved your skin,' she said, 'so what's that worth?'

The thing to do, I told myself, is to negotiate. Accept whatever price she wants to charge. For now. She has a hold on me. For now. But not for always. I must play along, for now, but when my chance comes I must seize it. Somehow I will have to silence her.

She walked across the room and filled the kettle we'd been given from the jug of water next to it. She crossed the room again, picked up our mugs from where they waited, side by side, upon the desk, and took them to the kettle. Then she switched the kettle on. 'The trouble is, it puts temptation in my way. Whatever were you thinking of? Would you like tea?'

I shook my head.

She spooned some grains of instant coffee into both the cups and placed her hand upon the kettle's handle, waiting, watching it. 'For information of this magnitude I reckon I could get a ticket out of here. Do you suppose there won't be a reward?'

'He won't play ball.'

'Of course he will.'

'You don't know Nikov.'

'Nikov? No. I don't suppose that Nikov will cooperate. The Boss will though.'

'The Boss?'

'It must have been the Boss. He lied about the phone call. Why? Because he killed his wife. That's why he wants Sodz caught. He needs a scapegoat; someone who can take the blame. Who better than a Drudjer?'

'He will promise you the earth; he won't deliver it.'

'Don't want the earth. I only want my freedom. That's a decent deal.'

'He will renege on it.'

'It's worth the risk.'

It wasn't worth the risk to me. Was she so stupid that she didn't understand? If Sodz was found in my house, I'd be shot.

'Is Gannerdjalok Kapko there as well?' she asked.

Dread's like a river. It will turn your guts to water. I was frightened I'd disgrace myself. She said she hated him. If I said he was there she would be twice as motivated to betray us.

But.

Perhaps.

She hadn't said she hated Ochre.

She had said she'd 'hooked' him. That implied that she was using him. He fancied her all right. Perhaps she'd started to reciprocate. It didn't need to be a full-blown love. Affection, that might be enough.

I might as well. I hadn't anything to lose.

'I never dreamed that you were helping us,' said Xan. 'Why would you want to? He'd two-timed you. I'd have thought you hated him.'

'It's not just them,' I said. 'It's Blossom and it's Ochre too.'

She stood there, staring at her coffee cup. 'You know, life's simpler when you are a prisoner.' She blew into the liquid. Vapour, like a dragon's breath, bloomed from the surface. 'Eat the food they give you, shit according to their schedule, sleep and wake when you are told. The less you can control, the easier it is to lie back and accept your fate.' The steam condensed. 'But now,

I have to make a choice. I must decide. I must weigh up the pros and cons. Life isn't simple anymore.'

'He wants me to attempt to rescue you,' I said.

'Who? Ochre? Well, of course. Not Gannerdjalok. Not a chance. He'd sell me in a second. Ochre though. He's very sweet.'

Did that mean that she loved him?

'Ochre, Blossom, Sodz and Kapko. Any more?' she asked.

I told her that they needed her to tell them how they could get out of there. She didn't seem to understand. The second stage, I said. I told her how I'd worked it out, that she had the connections. It was the reason she'd been given my address, so she could help them finish their escape. I offered her my services. I said I had already been to the *Enchanted Isle* for Sodz. I pointed out that I was trusting her to keep that information secret. I explained that I would keep her secrets if she told me how she planned to help the getaway. I'd take a message to the Drudjers in the garage. I'd do what was needed to assist them.

I even promised I would spring her from this prison, I would help her to escape. I mentioned Ochre, what he'd asked, and I pretended that I had a plan.

She looked at me.

She said I didn't seem the sort to be a hero.

'Well,' I said. 'That's where you're wrong.'

She raised her eyebrows. 'Truly?'

'Yes!'

'Okay. Let's start with little things. Things we can do today. Because it might be harder than you think to get me out of here.'

I understood. She wouldn't tell me anything about the others moving on until she joined them. Mr Kapko wouldn't wait. As soon as she had shared her information with him he'd have gone.

So first I must facilitate her breakout from this place. And I had lied when I had said I'd made a plan. I didn't have a clue.

'So. First,' she said. 'There's something we can do today. If you are sure you want to help us. If you really are heroic.'

'What?'

'Let's call it System A Plan B.'

'Plan B?'

'In fact, we have already started fighting back.'

I shook my head.

'Here's how it works. They want to use your System to find Sodz,' she said. 'We could have given him that information but we didn't. We said something else. Fought back. Suggested that the Boss might be a murderer. That is the sort of information that might sabotage a man like Nikov.'

'You, not we.'

'That is beside the point. Why don't you drink your coffee?'

'It's gone cold,' I said.

She tutted. 'You and I both know your System is a lot more powerful than simply catching dissidents. The question is: does Nikov understand this? Does the Boss?'

'I think so.'

'What you said a little earlier was that your System is designed to prophesy the future.'

'In a sense. It's like the weather. If you know it's raining here today and that the wind is blowing that way you can guess it will rain there tomorrow. Of course there's rather more to it than that. As we said earlier. There's feedback. People don't behave like clouds. But it is more or less the same.'

'But what's the point? If you could tell me who will win tomorrow's horse race, that would be a useful trick.'

'It's not as glamorous as that but if I can predict demand for services like electricity, I can make sure I have enough supply to meet demand.'

'Or you can put the price up.'

'If I did that my price hike might reduce demand and cancel out the increase I expected.'

'That's a feedback loop.'

I nodded.

'Or,' she said, 'it's your escape clause. You say that A will happen. They do B. A doesn't happen. You blame them. It is ingenious.'

'It's not like that. You're making out that I'm some sort of charlatan.'

'I'll drink it cold,' she said. 'Your coffee. If you're leaving it.'

I passed it over.

'What it means,' she said, 'is that you cannot lose. You make a forecast. If you're right you get the kudos. If you're wrong, providing they have acted on the information, you can tell them they've forestalled whatever you predicted.'

I felt fatigued. I should have had that drink.

'Providing that they act, we're safe,' she mused. 'In theory it wouldn't matter what we say, if they believe us. If we played it right, they'd even start depending on us. That would make us indispensable. No: 'she's a Drudjer, we can take her out and shoot her any time we want to'. Indisposable.'

I really didn't want to spend the afternoon like this.

'Why not?' she said.

I answered: 'Why not what?'

'Let's run the System backwards. Find out how to make it forecast what we want to see. Then build a story for the Boss. Let him decide to intervene. We need to guide him there. The point is this: his interventions will accomplish what we want.'

'What do we want?' I asked her.

'Their defeat,' she said.

I wasn't certain if I understood. 'You mean we make the System lie?'

'You could say that.'

'We tell them if they want to win they must take Option A when Option B will give them victory and Option A will bring defeat.'

'That's it. We give them false advice to bring them to destruction.'

'No.' I shook my head. 'It wouldn't work.'

'I think it will.'

'They'll smell a rat.'

'We can outsmart them. They are only Peacemakers. That doesn't make them clever. Bigots never are.'

'To lie is easy; lying well is hard.'

'We only have to twist parameters. We only have to tweak a value here and there.' She tapped the nail of her left index finger on her two front teeth. 'We guide them to the precipice and even when they're falling they will still believe that we were honest guides.'

My System. It had taken half my life. I'd worked on it at University. I had developed it at Kapko Industries. So I could keep on working on my System I had kept my mouth closed when he'd had my wife. So I could keep on working on my System I'd been silent when he put his name on it. And even after I was made redundant, when I could have found a better job, more lucrative, I'd come to work at the Town Hall so I could operate my System; so that I could keep improving it.

This was my chance to show the world what System A could do.

She wanted me to make it tell a lie.

Of course I had to play along. I understood this was her price. I'd let her wreck my System. Then I would assist her to get out of here. And after that, when she was at the garage, she would lead them all to freedom. Only then would I be safe.

I had to sabotage my System. System A. My life's work. I must help Xan to destroy it.

Or. If I could get away with it. To make her think that I was turning System A into a lie.

To make her think she had escaped.

To get them all out of my garage. Did I care what happened to them after that?

CHAPTER FIFTEEN: SOMEBODY ALWAYS HAS TO BE IN CHARGE

'What do you think you're playing at?' I hissed at Sodz as soon as I got home.

He wasn't where he should be. He was in the hall. That made me even madder.

'Things aren't good in there,' he said. He pointed to the garage.

'Things aren't good in here.' That was the moment when I could have hit him. That, perhaps, I should have done. I should have pushed my fist into his handsome face. I wanted to. 'I can't believe you'd be so stupid as to use a fucking phone.'

'Hang on,' said Sodz. He backed away. 'That wasn't me. Ease up. I told him not to. It was Ochre. Clever, clever Ochre. He can pass exams but in the big wide world he doesn't have a gram of common sense.'

At which point Ochre, hearing, I supposed, his name, came from the garage.

I asked him if he'd used a phone.

'I had to. I was really quick. They wouldn't have the time to trace the call.'

He'd seen too many films. 'You just don't get it, do you? What you've done. You've put a noose around my neck.'

He didn't understand me. I explained. How, at the moment that a call was made, the number calling and the number called, the date, the time, and the location were recorded.

'The location data?' Sodz said. 'Do you mean...?'

'They know your phone was active here.' I pointed to the ground.

Sodz walked along the hall and up to Ochre, standing in the doorway to the garage. 'I told you not to make the call.' He pushed him. Ochre staggered back into the garage. Sodz went after him. I followed.

'They know we're here,' said Sodz. 'We have to move. You have to tell us where we're going next, old man.'

The garage stank of unwashed flesh. Had they grown used to it? The floor was littered with their rubbish. They had dimmed the lights but I could still see that the plastic water bottles I had filled before I went to work had been exhausted and discarded, that an empty box of tissues had been torn to shreds, and that a pack of playing cards lay scattered on the floor as if a card-house had collapsed. It was a mess.

Down at the far end of the garage, Blossom knelt by Mr Kapko. He was sitting propped against the wall: his body slightly slanted, slightly twisted; both his knees bent, slightly splayed.

'He's still not well?' I asked.

Sodz walked straight up to Mr Kapko, looking down on him. 'Ed says they know we're here. It's time to share with us the next stage of your plan.'

'Please Sodz,' said Blossom. 'Please don't talk to him like that. He's ill.'

'He talked to me that way and worse. He called me clown. He said that I was worthless.'

'Two ... times ... right,' said Mr Kapko, blowing hard.

'His problem is,' said Sodz, 'is that he always has to be the best, the awesomest, the Mr Wonderful, the top tycoon, the richest Drudjer in the town. He can't admit he's fucked it up. It might make him seem normal. He would rather bugger up our chances.'

'That's not fair,' said Blossom. 'Uncle's ill. He'll tell us when he's better. Then we'll all move on.'

I pointed out that even if they left, I'd still be for the high jump. The recording would be in the archives.

'Can't you just delete it?' Ochre asked.

'I don't have access to protected files. The details will be there forever. It's an unexploded bomb. Until some snooper stumbles on the evidence that I have sheltered Drudjers in my house. And then ...' I raised my hands.

'It detonates,' said Blossom.

Ochre said that he was sorry but he had to make that phone call.

'If it hadn't been for Xan, ...' I said.

'Xan?' Ochre asked.

I wished I hadn't mentioned her. 'Xan was the one who saw the record of the phone call on the database.' I told them how it happened.

'Well done, Xan,' said Ochre. He had missed the point.

'So she was in your office,' Blossom said. 'I thought you told us they had locked her in the cells.'

'They let her out to work with me.'

'So Xan is … prison … labour,' Mr Kapko puffed.

'What does she do?' asked Blossom.

'Is she like your slave?' asked Sodz. 'Is she in chains? Your penal bitch, your bottom, your submissive? You into bondage? Spare a thought for subby little Ochre.'

'You can shut your filthy mouth,' said Ochre. 'Xan is not that sort of person.'

Well, I thought, why not? Perhaps she was. Perhaps we all are, in the circumstances. She's a prisoner. That's what they do. It's all about survival. If I asked, perhaps she would. Why shouldn't I? We're all like that. Top dog today, cock-licking cur the next.

It's turn and turn again. And it's my turn.

'It really isn't anything like that,' I said.

'You see?' said Mr Kapko. He was difficult to hear: his voice a cross between a mumble and a groan. 'They're all the same.'

'Hush, Uncle,' Blossom said.

'Non-Drudjers!' Mr Kapko said.

'You need to rest,' said Ochre.

Mr Kapko raised his finger, pointing it at me. 'Whoever … works for them is … not … our friend. Our enemy. You will … be judged.' He had to stop to breathe and breathe, and breathe, and breathe again. 'Collaborator. If … there is one … Drudjer left when all of this is … over. You'll be judged.'

I looked at him. He was a sick old man. 'Will I be stood against a wall and shot? Or would you rather watch me hang?'

'That's not what Uncle means,' said Blossom. But it was.

It wasn't fair. He was the one who'd started this and even now he threatened me. But he was ill and weak and on the ground in front of me and I could kick him if I wanted to and so she pitied him. He had her sympathy. I was the one she blamed.

For what?

I couldn't win. Whatever happened I was fucked. If Nikov walked in here right now he'd take me out and shoot me. I'd be shot if anybody ever found the record of the phone call Ochre made. And even if the Peacemakers were toppled and the Drudjers were triumphant I'd be shot, so Mr Kapko said, for being a collaborator.

More than anything, I longed to stamp on him. I don't know how I stopped myself.

Instead, inadequately, all I did was taunt him. 'We are using System K. Except it's not your System any more, not that it ever was. It's mine. Again. You never even understood it. We've improved it. System A, we're calling it.'

He'd always used his power. Might makes right, he'd tell me. I had worked for him and he had thieved from me. Now he was at my feet. And might makes right.

'And Xan ... She tells me that she hates you. Did you know she hates you? She is willing, she is happy, she's delighted to be working on the System. On my System. System A.'

That's when I found myself decided. 'Do you know the most amusing thing about my System? System A? We're using it to trick them. So don't tell me you will stand me up against a wall accused of working for the enemy. I'll probably do more to help defeat the Peacemakers than any Drudjer ever will.' I didn't tell them Xan had thought this up. 'We're going to dupe them.' I explained how it would work.

'Ed. Please. You promised,' Ochre said. 'Help Xan escape.'

'You'd spoil our game?' I asked.

Then Mr Kapko groaned and twisted. He contorted and he moaned and panted and his forehead bloomed with sweat.

Sodz backed away and whimpered.

Ochre kneeled beside his uncle.

'What is wrong with him?' asked Sodz. He made the sign to ward off evil demons.

Ochre turned and looked at me across his shoulder, asking me if I had any aspirin.

'There's some paracetamol upstairs.'

'He doesn't have a headache,' Ochre snapped. 'It must be aspirin. For his heart.'

'I don't like sickness,' Sodz said.

'No one's asking you to like it,' Ochre said. 'We are expecting you to cope.'

I watched the boy and Blossom. Now they were both kneeling on the floor. They faced each other. He was bending like a figure two and she reflected him, her buttocks round and powerful. Her face was only inches from his lips, her breasts as near to touching him as kittens cuddling. My stomach lurched.

'We really ought to have some GTN,' said Ochre.

'What?'

'Some glyceryl trinitrate. For angina. That is what he was prescribed but then we were all moved into the Kennels and there's been no GTN there for a month.'

He looked at me. 'That's why I made the phone call. I phoned Faith. We put it on the shopping list but I was worried that she wouldn't understand how much we needed it.' He looked abashed. 'I made an error there. I thought she might face difficulties finding it and so I told her that its other name was nitroglycerin.'

'That's an explosive.' Sodz was mocking. Even at a time like this he couldn't miss a chance to be derisive. 'Do you plan to detonate your uncle?'

'It's explosive?' I was horrified.

Sodz said: 'If only I had known. He called me a loose cannon; all the while his drugs were dynamite.'

'The quantities we use in medicine are safe,' said Ochre.

'That's why Faith said no,' said Sodz. 'She doesn't hold with violence. She works for charity.'

A charity, I thought, that traded pearls for cans of chopped tomatoes.

'Yes,' said Ochre. He was wretched. 'I suppose that's why she put the phone down.'

In the silence Mr Kapko's breathing sounded heavy, ragged, forced.

'Are you a doctor?' I asked Ochre but he shook his head.

'He is,' said Blossom, 'or he should be. He was training. He'd have qualified by now. But he's a Drudjer so he had to leave the hospital.'

'I don't see why they won't let Drudjers learn,' said Ochre.

'What is wrong with Mr Kapko?' I enquired.

'He's suffering from CVD.'

'What's that?'

'Cardio-vascular disease. In his case coronary heart disease.'

'A heart attack?'

'In laymen's terms.'

'A heart attack?' I said again.

'It doesn't work like people think. It isn't always Wallop and you're on the floor and needing CPR. In Uncle's case right now it is angina. Chest pain. Chronic, not acute. Angina's nothing but a symptom but it tells us he needs treatment. It's a warning sign. There is a chance that it might be more serious. But in the Kennels there was nothing I could do. He needs to get to hospital. He needs a specialist, a proper diagnosis so we know what treatment we should give him.'

Suddenly, things started making sense to me. I looked around the garage, at the scattered cards. 'He's had this for some time.'

He nodded. 'For a little while.'

'He knew that he was ill before he left the Kennels.'

'Well it wasn't like we had to make a declaration or we would invalidate our holiday insurance,' Ochre said. 'We had to leave. We didn't have a choice.'

'That's why you're here,' I said.

'Of course. We're here because we couldn't stay. We'd have been rounded up and shot.'

That wasn't what I'd meant. 'It is why you are here. You. Ochre. You.'

Just put the cards in order. Mr Kapko knew. I don't know how he knew. He must have known the Kennels were about to be attacked. And so he put together an escape plan. It was just for him, of course. 'That's how he thinks,' I told them. 'He is first, he's last, from start to finish he's the only one who matters. All the rest of us are tools for him to pick up, use, and throw away.'

Sodz nodded. Blossom froze.

'He's always been a master of the details. He has got a goal but to accomplish it he has to break it down; he has to plan it step by step.' I started pacing round the garage. 'One!' I checked the smallest finger on my hand. 'He knows that when he gets across the river he will need a place to hide. He knows my house; he's been here with my wife. It's perfectly positioned. He's forgotten, or he's not aware, that you can see the foot-bridge from the stairs. I guess that when he went upstairs with her he never stopped to look out of the window.'

From my stomach then, there came a squirt of bitter liquid forcing me to pause. I clamped my lips. I swallowed and the acid burnt my throat. It hurt.

'The second step.' Next finger. This one used to have a ring on it. Not any more. 'He cannot guarantee I'll have sufficient food for him. So he brings Sodz along. Sodz has connections. Sodz can get supplies.'

That brought us up to where we were. What next? 'He doesn't mean to stay here longer than a day or two. The Peacemakers might search the house.' I touch my middle finger. 'He will need another place to go to. That is John Zombie's job. Or Xan's, perhaps. I'm not quite sure. It's one of them. It might be both. It's somebody who knows a safe place somewhere else. He needs them with him, so he tells them where to rendez-vous. It's turning into quite a crowd.'

'You're … clever,' Mr Kapko croaked. As if he'd only just dis-covered that.

'The fourth step.' Index finger. 'He's been told he has a problem with his heart and so he needs a doctor to attend him. Ochre is invited to escape. And Blossom? Maybe he's decided she will be his bride. Or maybe that was Xan's job. Maybe both. He's always liked the ladies.'

'No,' said Ochre. 'That was me. I said to Uncle I would only come if Xan and Blossom were allowed to come as well.'

'That's not the way it worked,' said Blossom.

'Yes it was,' her brother answered. 'I refused ...'

'It was the other way around.' She stopped, her mouth still open. 'But ...' Her face seemed darker than the shadows that surrounded her.

Sodz said: 'John Zombie. Must have been. A music man makes many friends. And now he's dead. And so we're finished. We are never getting out of here.'

'The army's coming,' Blossom said. She looked at me. She had big eyes. I liked to see her on her knees, those big eyes slanting up at me. 'If we can just stay in the garage till they get here.'

'I,' said Mr Kapko, grinning like he'd won the first prize of a feather at his funeral, 'can get you ... out of here.' He paused to catch his breath. 'John ... Zombie ... told me ... where to go and ... who ... to contact.' Then he coughed. It hurt. He put an old hand to his chest. He beckoned. Sodz bent over him to listen. 'You won't ... take me ... if ... I tell you.'

Sodz was nodding. 'Yes. We will. I promise you. You have my covenant, my guarantee, my pledge, my bond; I swear it.'

Mr Kapko tried to laugh. 'The word ... of honour ... of a gigolo.' He flapped his hand as if to shoo them all away. Sodz shuffled backwards. Ochre stood. And Blossom sat back on her heavy haunches.

'Uncle needs to rest,' said Ochre. 'Ed, you have to go to the *Enchanted Isle*. See Faith in person and explain.'

I didn't want to risk it. I was well aware I had been lucky last time. Luck runs out.

In any case, there was no point. 'The last time I was there she said 'no pharmaceuticals'. I didn't understand but now I do. She must have been referring to the GTN.' I looked at Sodz. 'Perhaps she thought that you were after drugs, you know, for fun.' He was half-crouched and leaning on the wall. 'You're looking floppy, like you need Viagra.'

Sodz was like a puffer fish that swells and bristles when you poke it, or a porcupine. 'Not macho chico here.'

'Of course,' said Ochre. 'Yes. I should have thought of that. There is another way.' He sounded coy, reluctant. 'Amyl nitrite.'

Sodz, uncurling from the wall to stand straight up, began to smile. I watched the grin grow as it spread across his face. His teeth appeared. The puffer fish became the shark.

'So. Ochre. Poppers? Is there something you would like to tell us?'

Ochre answered carefully, enunciating every word, as if he were a teacher and his pupil, Sodz, stood at the bottom of the class. 'They are vaso-dilators. Uncle's problem is that, in his heart, the blood vessels are narrowing. As a result it is more difficult to pump the blood that keeps the heart alive. Some drugs expand the veins and arteries: the one most widely used is glyceryl trinitrate which is nitroglycerin; before that, way back in the eighteen hundreds, amyl nitrite was the medicine of choice.'

'And amyl nitrite is contained in Poppers.' Sodz was prodding Ochre in the chest, delighted.

'Yes. In Poppers which are used by some because the side-effect of sniffing amyl nitrite is a sudden rush, a brief euphoria.'

'And muscle relaxation,' Sodz contributed.

'You know a lot about it,' Ochre said. 'And muscle relaxation. This helps homosexual men have anal sex more easily, less painfully.' He glared at Sodz. 'It is a nightclub. I suspect that Faith might find it relatively easy to acquire some Poppers.'

'Let me get this straight,' I said. 'You're asking me to go to the *Enchanted Isle* to purchase drugs that buggers use. For him. So Mr Kapko doesn't die. It's funny when you think of it like that.'

I went to him. Stooped over him. Looked in his face. His eyes were shut. He must have sensed me standing there. He started smiling. Whispered something that I couldn't catch. I bent a little closer.

'If ... I die ... they won't know where ... to go.'

I let my gaze sweep down his stricken body, showing him how I disdained him. He was sitting on his pillow. I could see the handle of his gun protruding. I reached down for it. His eyes were closed, he couldn't see what I was doing, but he somehow had a sense of it. He put his hand down by his bum to intercept me. He was old and he was sick; he was too slow, he was too late. I grasped the gun and tugged. It slid from underneath him and I picked it up and held it in my hands. His eyes were open now. I saw the hate in them. He'd never liked me, I supposed. I thought: now I can shoot him. Now I had the gun. I didn't like the way that he was watching me. I wasn't underneath him any more. It was the other way around. I had his gun.

I turned around. I showed them that I had the gun. They saw that things were not the way they had been. Not at all. 'I'll go to the *Enchanted Isle*. But first, I think I'll have a shower. Pop upstairs. I'll change my clothes. I take it nobody objects.'

I looked from face to face. First Blossom, then at Sodz, and Ochre last. I didn't look at Kapko. I was over asking him.

Somebody had to be in charge.

Somebody always has to be in charge.

CHAPTER SIXTEEN: THE MAN WITH THE GUN

It felt so good to have a gun. Now tides and tables had been turned. I was elated as I climbed the stairs. Luck has its ups and downs. I was on top again.

I walked into my bedroom. Opposite the door there was a full-length mirror. Crouching, feet spread, knees bent, torso angled slightly forward, arms straight, elbows soft, wrists locked, hands caressing grip, right index finger on the trigger, sighting down the barrel. Looking good.

Then I stood straight, arms folded, left hand in the crook of my right elbow, with the pistol slanting up and to the left. A classic stance.

And then I aimed the gun towards the ceiling, holding it beside the chin and cheek and temple on the right side of my face, my left hand underneath and cupping to support my right arm's elbow. That was not so cool until I turned to face the mirror in three-quarters pose and set the muscles of my face, with just the slightest frown, grim-lipped, so I looked confident and deadly. That's the pose.

The man in charge. The man who has the gun.

I put the gun down gently on the chest of drawers. It lay beside the photo of my wife, the one in her bikini, snapped on holiday, before she had the boys.

I stripped. I stood before the mirror naked. I reviewed myself. My face was old; my body wasn't bad. I wasn't perfect, that was sure. But this was how it was. I stood there, in reflection, bare, myself and I decided I could live with that.

My fingers itched.

I picked the gun up, holding it beside my penis and I felt the coldness of the metal chill my balls. I started stroking. Getting hard. I pushed the handle of the pistol back against my pubis so my phallus and the barrel were in parallel. The gun, of course, was harder and its shaft was slightly longer. Not as thick though. Not as satisfiable.

My penis twitched and I decided to stop rubbing it. I didn't want to shoot. Not yet. I'd save myself for later. Soon.

I held the gun before my eyes. Inspected it. I had known guns before; I'd been, at university, a member of a shooting club; I knew enough. The magazine was in the grip; I found the catch. It should have held ten bullets; when I emptied it I only counted six. I wondered what had happened to the other four. I hid the bullets in my bathroom cabinet behind some out-of-shelf-life indigestion powders. Emptied guns can still be deadly if the target doesn't know. I buried it beneath the knickers in the dressing table of my wife. I felt its ominous black metal functionality would be a perfect counterpoint to the frivolity of lacy thongs.

I missed my wife.

How would she feel when Kapko died? I hoped she'd mourn him; it would serve her right to be bereaved. I didn't think she'd grieve for me. She'd made it plain she liked him more than me. When you betray the man you've married it's a statement: he's worth less. You've relegated him, demoted him, degraded him, made him a little smaller.

Who laughs last laughs loudest.

How I wished that she could see him dying in the squalor on the garage floor.

I wouldn't miss her. She could stay away. I didn't want her back.

She had so many pairs of knickers. Red and black and white, some lace, some satin, nothing sensible, some thongs, some boy-cut, some bikini style. I thought about the way her knickers reached across her buttocks, how they cupped her cunt. I took a random pair of panties from the drawer and sniffed them; touching them against my lips. I kissed them. Then I put them on.

This wasn't right. They weren't designed to hold a cock and balls. Not when the cock had grown as stiff as mine.

I stood and watched my image in the mirror. It was time to think.

Now he was ill, perhaps about to die, somebody else would have to take the helm. Not Ochre. Don't be foolish. Ochre was a wimp. I did admit that I had been impressed about how calm he'd been with Kapko, maybe, dying but that wasn't leadership; it was his training as a medic. Sodz had been the opposite: he'd acted as if heart disease was a contagion he could catch. Sodz wasn't management material; he was too up and down to take control: one moment whimpering, the next ebullient. In any case, they'd neither of them listen to the other.

Therefore, since there had to be a leader then it must be me. I was the oldest and the Drudj respect their elders. They were living in my garage. I protected them. I had the gun.

If I was in command some things would have to change. They'd have to clean their mess up for a start. Perhaps they thought it didn't matter: they were moving on. For me it was important. When they went I'd have to blitz the place so not a scrap of evidence was left to say they'd stayed.

There wasn't anything that I could do about that phone call. I would make them pay for that.

I scrutinised my image in the mirror. Winced. Eyes growing shadows. Puffiness. The bones retreating underneath the paling skin. Beneath my ear, above the jugular, a nasty spot.

If I was going to be a hero, shouldn't I get something out of it? Look at the legends: Lancelot and Guinevere, Napoleon and Josephine, James Bond and girl, girl, girl, girl, girl.

So why not me?

Because of Ochre. Brother. Boyfriend. Obstacle.

A hero overcomes.

I'd have to find a way of getting rid of Ochre.

I'd have to do it so that Blossom wouldn't hate me. So that, bereft of brother, she would turn to me for comfort. She'd be crying on my shoulder; my strong arms protecting her. One thing becomes another: solace, sex.

I dressed in fresh, clean clothes - she'd like that - and I went downstairs. I noticed, looking through the window, that the guard post on the bridge had been abandoned. I decided that I wouldn't mention it. They mustn't know. They'd want to move upstairs. It suited me to keep my Drudjers staying in the garage.

All at once there was a flash and straight away a loud explosion and I saw the window bulge and dimple and the air was puffed and sucked and I was buffeted. The whole house swayed. I thought the stairs were tilting and I had to clutch the banister.

I met a frightened Ochre at the bottom of the stairs.

'How close was that?' I acted cooler than a cucumber, my *sang* so bloody *froid* that icebergs drifted through my veins. If I was to be leader, I would have to play the part.

'You have to help me get her out of there,' he said.

'The garage is the safest place to be right now. No windows means no glass.'

'I don't mean Blossom. Xan. If those explosions mean the army's coming, we can just sit tight. But Xan's in danger.'

'She is in the basement. That is almost like a bunker.'

'What will happen when the Peacemakers evacuate. You think they'll take her with them?' He was restless, pacing up and down. 'They certainly won't leave her. She was in the Kennels. She's a witness. They will want to silence her.'

'If she gets caught attempting to escape ...' I left unvoiced the second section of my thought: If she gets caught they'd kill the men who helped her.

'Don't you see? It's like an illness; it's like when you get the antibodies flooding in to fight the germs. That's when you get a fever, for example. There's a crisis point. And that's the point when you can lose control. When things go wrong.' His hands were linked together, each one clutching at the fingers of the other, knuckles squeezed. 'Things happen that you don't expect. Chaotic things. And that's where Xan is now. She's at their mercy. Things can happen very fast. It's better if we get her out of there as soon as possible.'

'We? You said 'we'?'

He nodded. 'Please. We have to try. I have a plan.'

Of course he did. In here he would have nothing else to do but dream up plans.

It couldn't be more simple, Ochre said. I went to work with Kapko's gun, collected Xan and walked her out of there.

He seemed to think my speechlessness meant I agreed with him.

At last I stuttered: 'No, no, no and no.'

'Why not?'

'Because they'll kill us. There are guards with guns. The moment that my back is turned they'll shoot me down.'

'Then make them put their guns down.'

'How?'

'You need a hostage. If you had the Boss at gunpoint, they would have to do exactly as you told them.'

'No.' I shook my head in emphasis.

'Why not?' he asked again.

'Because I couldn't get a gun into the building. Do you think they wouldn't search me? In the foyer there's an archway: you get scanned and it detects if you are carrying a metal object like a pistol or a knife.' This was totally untrue. I made it up. I lied to him. The Peacemakers weren't that sophisticated. Their security was lax. It was the way they were: men with a mission, self-proclaimed, disorganised. But Ochre wouldn't know that.

'Then we have to get the gun to you another way. Is there a window to your office?' Ochre asked.

I nodded. I was wary. 'But the window's shut.'

'Tomorrow then, as soon as you arrive, you open it. And then I'll sneak around the building with the gun and drop it through the window.'

'You?'

'I'm little and I'm nimble. I am like a ninja. Yah!' To prove his point he raised a leg to kick the sky.

I shook my head. 'The window doesn't open.'

'I could smash the glass.'

'Suppose you did. Suppose they didn't hear. Suppose I got the gun and marched along the corridors and found the Boss and took him hostage and went back for Xan and we went through the entrance and the guards threw down their guns. Where do we go? They'll follow us, you can be sure of that. We can't come here. Where do we go? And what am I supposed to do about the Boss? Just shoot him on the roadside? No,' I said. 'Forget it. Don't be crazy. It won't work. It's suicide.'

Which made me think.

Perhaps.

If someone had to die.

I had to make it seem that he'd come up with it. That I had tried to talk him out of it. So, afterwards, they'd see me as a hero. One who'd failed, perhaps, but one who'd tried. Who'd done his best.

The whole world loves a tragedy.

He said, and he was snivelling, 'I'm trying hard to come up with suggestions. All you do is shoot them down. It sounds as if you want Xan for yourself.'

Was I so obvious? 'Why ever would I want her for myself?'

'To help you with your precious System A.'

I breathed again. 'Of course I want Xan to escape. It's just that I've a better plan.' I put my finger to my lips. I tiptoed to the garage door; I opened it a crack to peep inside. Sodz squatted in his corner with a book and Blossom knelt by Kapko. Carefully I closed the door, crept back to Ochre. Lowering my voice , I said: 'Tomorrow morning you sneak out of here and take the gun. You shoot at the Town Hall. They'll panic. That's the way they are. That is what happened when Sodz set the tower block alight. And he escaped. We'll do the same. You stage a terrorist attack. And then you flee. You run off down the road. You draw the guards. They'll follow you. And in the chaos and confusion you have caused I'll guide Xan through the corridors and up the stairs and if you've done your job there will be no one in the entrance hall so she can just walk through the doorway and escape.'

'I've never shot a gun,' he said.

'I'll show you how.'

'I couldn't shoot a person.'

'And you wouldn't have to. Shoot into the air. You only have to make them think they're being shot at. Scare them. Then you let them chase you.'

'I can run,' he said. 'I'm fast.'

I had a vision of him in his bright blue shorts. A target that they couldn't miss.

'Where should I go?' he asked.

I couldn't say I doubted it would matter. I couldn't tell him I expected he would never reach a hiding place. So I suggested he should run towards the hospital. 'There must be someone who will help you there or somewhere you can hide.'

He nodded. He was buzzing with excitement. 'Will it work?' he whispered to himself and then he answered his own query: 'Who can tell? The thing is that I have to try.'

I knew that it would prove a failure. Yesterday the Town Hall had been shelled. There'd been no panicking. The guards had stayed beside their posts.

I didn't tell him it was hopeless and I didn't say I wouldn't even try to navigate the basement labyrinth with Xan.

I said I thought we had a fighting chance. I told him we must get the timing right. Eleven in the morning. Xan and I would be prepared. We'd listen out for gunfire.

'We had better keep this secret, just between ourselves,' I told him and he nodded. She would try to talk him out of it, he said. It suited me. If Blossom didn't know I could convince her that I hadn't either.

It was sad how much he trusted me.

I walked into the garage. There was still a part I had to play before tomorrow's drama. A single pearl, I told Sodz, wouldn't be enough for Poppers. Two would be more difficult to hide, he said, but I explained that I was confident I'd not be searched by Tomas.

'You'll try to keep one for yourself,' he said.

'I'm doing this for him.' I jerked my thumb at Kapko.'Ever since you turned up at my house' - I emphasised the 'my' - I have been looking after you. I thought you promised me a pearl to pay the rent.'

He turned his back to me and when he faced me once again he held a pearl in either hand. He liked his prestidigitation. Were they up his sleeve or had he also hidden them inside his underpants? Before I handed him to Nikov I would need to make him strip so I could find what else he'd hidden.

But for now I nodded, took the pearls, and put them in my pocket.

'And, before I go, this garage is a shambles. Pigs are tidier. While I am out, you'll clean it, tidy it. I want it spotless. Do you understand?'

They nodded. They'd obey.

CHAPTER SEVENTEEN: OF PEARLS AND POPPERS

I never got to the *Enchanted Isle*.

Equipped with pearls I left my house and walked beneath the arch.

'If power's your ultimate goal
Then the demons you need to control
Are the ones that you keep
Buried deep. Let them sleep
Or like Faustus you'll sell your own soul.'

The Officer might be articulate, I thought, but he was out of touch. If he knew anything he wouldn't be a down and out. He'd be successful, not a hobo living on an arch.

Just look at me.

There is, I thought as I was walking down the street, a tide in the affairs of men and I was surfing it. Old fickle fortune comes in fits and starts. I'd had a run of rotten luck so I was owed a break.

Consider: Mr Kapko, Kapko, had been in my house for scarcely any time at all when my new neighbour Nikov came to call.

Then, later on, as Sodz arrived, bad penny Nikov had again turned up. And last night, Nikov, jinx-like, had been there when Faith arrived. They say that these things run in threes. By now I should be rid of Nikovs.

Nikov was my nemesis. Or was I his? It would appear that on the face of it he was a formidable foe. But was he? Looking at the facts, I started counting up all of the chances he had missed. He'd picked up Kapko's backpack ... and then put it down although there was a heavy gun in it and maybe gold as well. When Sodz was hiding in my hedge, I'd easily diverted Nikov by pretending I had seen a running Drudjer. All he'd had to do today was look at Xan's computer screen to see that Ochre had been calling from my garage. But he hadn't. Nikov was a man who didn't make the most of opportunity. He must be rather stupid.

And if he was not that bright then what about the rest of them? The Boss had killed his wife; his cover-up had more holes than a pair of fish-net stockings. I had spotted he was lying straight away. And as for Tomas: his evasions, when he'd tried to justify allowing Sodz to cross the bridge, had been pathetic.

Xan had said it would be easy to outwit them, for the Peace-makers were idiots. It looked like she was right.

I wondered whether we would even need to make my System lie. We could tell Nikov and the Boss whatever we decided. They'd believe it.

I began to snigger to myself as I remembered how I had trans-formed myself from, in the eyes of Kapko, villain who'd ex-ploited Xan to serve the enemy, to hero saboteur. I'd fooled him; I had fooled them all. Now both sides treasured me.

I smirked. I'd made it. Both the Boss and Nikov thought I was a genius. But I'd transcend them. Right across the world, in all societies, there's always someone at the top. The people must be organised. And System A would help the leader do it. So, whoever was in power, I would be the navigator of the ship of state.

The Peacemakers were here today and might be gone tomorrow. I'd arrived today and in the future System A might spread across the world.

But first I had to sort a few things out at home. My guests had stayed beyond their welcome; it was time for them to go. But now, with Kapko seriously ill, it looked unlikely they would willingly continue on their exodus. I wasn't sure if I believed him when he said he knew John Zombie's plans but, even if he did, he'd made it clear that, if he had to, he would take the secret with him to the grave. They were as stuck as I was. It was up to me to move them on.

It would be awkward, I supposed, if Kapko died. In all the books it's the disposal of the corpse that poses the most problems for a killer. I was slightly squeamish when it came to mess. Dismembered, I could stuff him the freezer. We could even roast him if the food ran out. Suppose they searched the house, though? Found his flesh. They would conclude I was a murderer. And they would think the same if they dug up his body. Not that I could bury him. Where would I do it? In the garden? It was overlooked by flats. Perhaps the best thing I could do would be to cart the corpse out in the dead of night - the dead, the dead, the dead, I thought - and just abandon it. Or I could tip it in the river now the footbridge was deserted. From all the dramas on TV that I had watched, I guessed forensics would find evidence the body had been moved, but they could never say from where. And there would be no marks of violence upon it: he'd have had a heart attack if I let nature take its course.

My best plan was to fail to bring him any drugs. I'd have to make it look as though I'd tried. But if I went back empty-handed, what could Ochre do? Take him to hospital? They wouldn't treat a Drudjer.

He would die in pain. And that would serve him right.

Then there was Sodz and Ochre. Sodz was easiest. He was a wanted criminal. Xan thought the Boss would do a deal. If I could only find a way to bypass Nikov and to hand Sodz over to the Boss, no questions asked. He'd not go quietly. Sodz was the opposite of silence. He would blab about the others. It was crucial that he wasn't heard. Would that be possible? The Boss would want his day in court. if Sodz was tried with all due process and convicted, then the world would have to say the Boss was innocent. But, at the moment anyway, the justice system was still independent of the Peacemakers. The punishments the vigilante Peacemakers imposed were extra-legal lynchings.

Maybe, if they tortured Sodz ... He'd not stand up to torture. Could they force him to confess to something that he hadn't done? There'd have to be a quid pro quo; he'd want to trade. 'If you confess you get a life in prison; if you don't, the noose.' He'd take that, wouldn't he? Then, once they'd schooled him in the details, they would make a film of him confessing. They'd upload it. That was how they would exonerate the Boss.

I needed an appointment to discuss this. Not with Nikov. Xan was right. He was too honest. He would say: 'You're harbouring a murderer, a Drudjer.' He would shoot me. Why not? once he'd got his hands on Sodz.

Sodz was a problem. Ochre, I suspected, would be easier.

He'd do it to himself: my plan, our plan, his plan to set Xan free was little better than a fancy form of suicide. He'd shoot the single bullet I would give him and he'd run away and they would chase. He might be killed attempting to escape. He might be caught. I could be confident he wouldn't tell them anything. He'd die attempting to protect his sister; that would mean protecting me.

And really, was it anything to do with me? The whole escape thing had been his idea. You couldn't blame me if I changed my mind, if I decided not to get involved.

It was a shame that Ochre was determined to destroy himself. I rather liked the little lad. But he was in the way.

I'd have to tell Xan Ochre died to set her free. The news would break her heart. I'd have to mend it. As I dried her tears I'd mutter that I'd risked my own life in a futile but heroic rescue operation. She would sob: at least I'd tried. We would embrace. I'd woo her with her gratitude. She'd melt.

It wasn't like she had a lot of choice. Apart from me, who did she have? The other prisoners? The Peacemakers? For goodness sake. I was her intellectual equal, only me. That is important, afterwards.

It might be slightly trickier with Blossom. She'd be harder to convince. She would be angry that I'd let her brother sacrifice himself. I'd have to plead: I couldn't stop him. Would that be enough? It might appease her but it wouldn't make her want me. There would have to be a little more than that. Another rescue effort? That was it. First, Ochre had to leave the garage while I was at work so that I was unable to prevent him. Next I'd get back home and Blossom would be frantic. Where was Ochre? Missing. I would comfort her. That's how it starts. I'd have my arms around her. I would cuddle her, my chest against her tits. She'd want to kiss me. I would pull away: 'Not now; I have to go and look for him.' She would be scared; I would be brave. A touching parting. Lots of touching. Not too much. I'd leave. When I returned I'd shake my head. More weeping and more comfort. This time, more.

It was convenient that one was at my workplace and the other one at home. With any luck - and I was more and more a lucky man - I could have both. Not only that but also there was no chance they would ever meet.

That's what I had been thinking as I walked along the street, so deep in thought I hadn't noticed the increasing noise. But then, as I concluded that my plan was good, I raised my head and looked around.

There was a melee round the bridgehead. Not just Peace-makers; I recognised the owner of the pizza takeaway along the High Street. I was surprised to see him here. I'd heard that he'd had difficulties with supplies: the Siege and the ensuing civil war had led to shortages of basics such as flour which, with the fighting in between the army and the Peacemakers, were unresolved. But on the other hand he'd never had so many customers. The Peacemakers loved pizza, he had said. He ought to be at work right now.

Why was he here?

It was a little daunting, weaving in between so many people when my purpose was to source a dodgy drug a Drudjer needed. It was not like I could push and shove; I didn't want to start a fuss. I didn't want to draw attention to myself. More-over, I was moving in the wrong direction. I was going north; I was the only one. The tide was flowing south.

At last I reached the front. My path was blocked by Tomas.

'Can I cross the bridge? I want to get to the *Enchanted Isle*.'

He shook his head.

Behind me was a rumpus and I heard a voice I recognised. 'Move. Get a fucking shift on. Out the fucking way. We're coming through.'

I turned around and there was Malc. He'd almost reached me. He, together with two other Peacemakers, pushed through the throng. 'Come on. Fuck out of it.'

I stood aside. They passed me. Tomas let them through his makeshift barrier. They charged across the bridge. I tried to follow them but Tomas barred my way.

'You know me, Tomas. I'm at the Town Hall. I work for Nikov and I need to get across.'

He shook his head. 'The Bridge is closed.'

I indicated Malc and mates. 'You let them over.'

'They are on the list.'

'Why don't you check the list again? If I'm not on it then I ought to be. Ask Nikov.'

'Ask him for yourself,' said Tomas, nodding to the right. I looked in that direction. Nikov was engaged in conversation with a person in the crowd. He was gesticulating.

'No. He's far too busy. Don't you see how angry he will be if I have got to bring him over here to make you let me cross the bridge.'

'I have my orders.'

'Nikov doesn't want to get involved. He mustn't be involved. Because … It's all about the Memsahib. You remember what you said last night. In the *Enchanted Isle*. About the Drudjer. It was on this bridge. And that … that's evidence. And we need witnesses. To what you said.'

'Why can't you talk to me?'

'Good question, Tomas. But … the thing is …'

'You were there,' he said. 'There's Nikov. There is Gary. They all heard me. Malc as well.'

'I know.' I knew. My story was as thin as skin and twice as full of holes. 'But they are Peacemakers. And as for me I am a public servant and we're not allowed to testify in court.' I gambled that he wouldn't spot that I'd just made that up. 'We need an independent witness. Like the barmaid. She was there. I don't remember what her name was.'

'Faith?'

'Was that it? Maybe it was Hope?'

'No. It was Faith. They're not so similar that I can't tell.'

'That's why I need to get to the *Enchanted Isle*.'

'You can't,' he said.

I had anticipated Tomas might expect a bribe. That's why I'd brought two pearls.

But how was I to do this? I was in the middle of a milling throng. Who knows who's watching in a crowd?

'I don't suppose ... we could continue our discussion in a more secluded place?'

'Secluded?' Tomas looked from side to side. I guessed he was as much aware as I that crowds have eyes and ears.

'Somewhere that's a bit more private. What I have to say is sensitive. You understand.'

He shook his head.

I had no choice. I pushed my hand into my pocket. I was glad I hadn't put them in my pants. My fingers found the pearls. I only wanted one. I rolled a single pearl along the fabric on the inside of my pocket till it fell into my open palm. I closed my fist to cuddle it. I took it from my pocket. I presented it to Tomas. Carefully, as slowly as a flower blossoms, I uncurled my fingers, I was watching Tomas all the time, my gaze fixed to his face. He saw the pearl. I watched his eyes grow wide. I'd hooked my fish,

He put it in his pocket faster than a Drudjer with a penny.

'Stay,' he said. 'Don't move.'

He hadn't understood. 'I need to cross the bridge.'

'But I've already told you that you can't. You haven't noticed all these people coming south? The bridge is closed for going north.'

I pointed up the High Street at the backs of Malc and his companions. 'They are going north.'

'Except for Peacemakers. For military purposes. Stay where you are. Don't move an inch.'

He took my pearl. He took it and he walked across to Nikov.

'Ed? Ed! Whatever are you doing here?'

I glanced. I didn't want to look. I wanted to keep Tomas in my sights. What was he saying? I could run, I thought. My legs were ready; they were telling me to run. Where to? There wasn't anywhere that Nikov wouldn't know.

'What do you want?'

'It's nice to see a friendly face,' Faith said.

Sarcastic bitch. 'You have no call to be like that,' I told her.

'Well at least my face is friendly,' she retorted.

I had missed my chance. 'They've gone,' I told her. 'Nikov. Tomas. They have disappeared. Where have they gone to? Did you see them go?'

She shook her head.

'He took my pearl,' I said.

'Another pearl?'

'I need some Poppers.' I explained to her why I had come.

She said the club was closed. The Peacemakers had forced them to evacuate. 'We had to leave just as we were. I tried to talk to them. They wouldn't listen. They were saying that the army was approaching. Do you think that's true?'

They had been herded from the club and down the High Street. 'All our friends were there, the cafe owners and the shop-keepers. But no one knows what's going on.'

'You cannot get me any Poppers?'

'We can't even bring the food we promised. When we left, we had to leave the van.'

I thought: that's played into my hands. I knew that I was on a lucky streak. No Poppers. I could keep the pearl. What's more, it meant that Kapko would continue suffering and maybe die. Plus: when I went back home and told them that I couldn't get him Poppers, I'd be telling them the truth.

And just to add the cherry to the cake, there was no food. They'd have to leave the garage soon or starve to death.

Unless the army rescued them in time.

I wouldn't tell them anything about the army. They might think their liberation was at hand. I wanted them to leave. Except for Blossom. She could stay. I hoped she would. Who'd know she was a Drudjer? I could say she was my wife.

But if the army were about to cross the river I would have to expedite my plans. I had already talked to Ochre. We were all set for tomorrow. As for Sodz. I needed to discuss him with the Boss as soon as possible. Then, Kapko dying in the garage, I'd be left with Blossom. We could go upstairs. They wouldn't see her now the footbridge was unmanned.

The footbridge.

If the army was approaching, why ...?

It was an ambush.

They could try to swim the racing river; otherwise the army only had two ways to get across it. They could fight their way along the High Street, shop by shop, until they reached this bridge. It would be bloody. That was why the Peacemakers had emptied all the shops and restaurants; they would fill them with themselves. They'd fight for every inch. And, if the army got that far, the bridge would be defended. Snipers in the windows of the tower block would have a perfect field of view.

But there was always an alternative. The army could pass through the devastation that had been the Kennels, come across the undefended footbridge by my house and go in a straight line along my street, beneath the arch, to the Town Hall. The prime objective. The Headquarters of the Boss. You catch the king, it's checkmate.

Nikov would have thought of this. He lived along the street.

Two rows of terraced houses. It was like a man-made canyon. They would occupy the houses. All those windows, each one with a gunman. That's a lot of death.

There would be gunmen stationed in my house.

And Nikov knew that someone sitting on my stairs could see the footbridge. That would be the perfect place to put a sentry. He'd see the army coming, spread the word. Then they would wait in silence till the soldiers were between the houses. That was when they'd spring their trap.

I had to get back home at once. They might be coming even

now. I had to get the Drudjers out of there.

I turned my back upon the bridge and started walking south.

That's when I noticed Nikov was approaching me.

I stopped. I turned around again. Perhaps I ought to run across the bridge and flee along the High Street.

'No,' said Faith. She grabbed me by the arm. 'There's loads of them up there,' she told me. 'You'd have zero chance.'

I stood irresolute. And Nikov, dodging through the crowd, was closing in. It was the pearl, I thought. He spoke to Tomas and he's seen the pearl and he's put two and two together. This was deadly. If he caught me with another pearl, he'd think …

For just a moment Nikov disappeared behind the back of Mr Pizza-man.

I passed the other pearl to Faith. 'Hang on to this,' I told her.

Nikov said: 'Good evening Mr Angelo. I'd like a word. Please come with me.'

'What's this about?' asked Faith.

'You stay with Tomas,' Nikov told her as he took me by the elbow, turned me, and began to walk me down the road.

'Where are we going?'

Nikov opened up his other hand. He had the pearl from Tomas.

'It is not just me,' I said. 'The whole world knows that he takes bribes.'

'There is a little more to this than bribing Tomas,' Nikov said. 'This way. Please. Sir.' His grip upon my arm was stronger than politeness. He began to walk me up towards the entrance to the tower block.

'I thought that we were going to the Boss.'

'It's a little late for that.'

'Where are you taking me?'

He urged me up the steps towards the doors to what had once been Kapko Industries. We went inside. In better times we'd used this wide reception hall for Kapko's boasts: displays which charted how the firm had grown from one man to a multitude; exhibits of the latest products; charts to show our sales around the world. It was a little like the arch the Officer was living on: the solid celebration of a dream. I wondered whether it, in turn, was fated to be colonised by derelicts.

Right now the place was full of Peacemakers. A team were bringing office desks and chairs downstairs to put them into piles. I thought that they were making bonfires. Nikov contradicted me. 'We're building barricades. The army's nearly on us. Should they reach the bridge we'll station men upstairs to hold them off.' I understood why he was telling me. He didn't mind the army knowing that the road bridge would be heavily defended. He wanted them to choose the footbridge. Maybe at this very moment there were Peacemakers outside my door, about to force an entrance so they could prepare their trap.

'We'll take the stairs. Sir. After you.'

So saying he released my arm and for a moment I considered running up the stairs and through the penthouse, up the other flight of stairs onto the roof and then … Then I was trapped. Unless I jumped. He knew I wouldn't jump. He knew that I was scared of heights.

'Where are we going?'

'To the roof.'

'Why?'

He wouldn't say.

We'd reached the landing for the first floor of the offices. We had to pause a moment while a pair of Peacemakers manoeuvred a computer desk around the corner, taking it downstairs.

'You've changed your tune. You told me it was not my place to play detective.'

'I have changed my mind. You have convinced me. You were right. The killer wasn't Sodz. He has the perfect alibi. He hadn't crossed the bridge before the Boss received that phone call. Come along.'

We started up another flight of stairs. 'So you agree with me?' I asked him.

We had reached another landing. 'I've accepted that the killer must be someone else.'

'The Boss.'

'The Memsahib wore a string of pearls. We found it. It had broken. I suppose it broke when she was strangled.'

We were at the penthouse. Nikov held the door ajar and ushered me inside. 'Sir. After you.'

I didn't want to enter. Emanating from the door was a disgusting smell: a mixture of burnt toast and roasted beef and dirty water, grease and coal and charring hair.

'Forensics tell me, Sir, that, even with the fire and the incompetence with which it was extinguished, there is still a lot of evidence. As if we needed evidence. We know who killed the Memsahib, don't we? Sir.'

'So you agree it was the Boss.'

'I've my suspicions. Sir. I've had them for a while. And then, today, I have received a crucial piece of evidence.'

I looked around. I saw the wine stain Sodz had mentioned: red on white like blood on virtue.

'Come along,' said Nikov, urging me towards the stairs that led up to the rooftop.

'Other evidence. What other evidence?'

'The roof's the place to have this out. It's just a few more steps, Sir. That's the way.'

I stumbled up towards the door. I opened it. I stepped onto the roof. He was behind me, pushing. Though I didn't want to move, I had to, going from the safety of the stairwell doorway just a little way towards the edge.

'The evidence,' said Nikov. 'Tomas handed me a pearl.' He held it up between his index finger and his thumb. 'It's from the necklace of the murdered Memsahib. Now explain to me: how did it come to be in your possession?'

'No,' I said. 'Don't be ridiculous. It wasn't me.'

CHAPTER EIGHTEEN: THE PATRON SAINT OF HOPELESS CAUSES

Again, I found myself in Nikov's best-loved place. A rooftop: flat and featureless, save for the box-like turret of the stairwell from whose safety I had just been forced. Across the blackened desert of the blistered surface, little cube-shaped metal boxes had been scattered; ventilation, I supposed, though to my fearful mind they seemed like opportunities to stumble. It was only twenty paces from the stairwell doorway to the less-than-knee-height wall around the edge. I wondered which would take more time: to run those twenty steps or plunge five storeys to the ground below.

I huddled in the shelter of the red-brick belvedere while Nikov, arms spread wide, strode to the edge and stood, embracing open air.

I didn't understand what he could find to love about this roof. It felt to me as if I had been served up on a plate to some almighty giant. There was nowhere I could hide.

And it was blowing hard enough to scoop me up and carry me across the precipice. The wind is stronger when you're higher.

Nikov looked across his shoulder at me. 'Come!' He beckoned.

Did I have a choice? He was a madman but he had a gun. I dragged myself across the black-top to his side.

'I love it here,' he shouted at the wind. 'It's wonderful. Look at that sky. It seems to spread forever. Limitless. When I'm up here I feel that there are endless possibilities.'

He's young, I thought, immortal. I had never felt so old.

He pointed down towards the river, to the people milling round the bridge. I didn't want to look. I kept imagining what would befall me if I tumbled: how I'd flap my legs and arms as if I thought that I could swim across the sky. There would be terror. Helplessness. A crushing, pulping impact. Overwhelming pain. And after that ...

'It's getting dark,' I told him.

'First things first,' he said. He pushed me to my knees, the little wall against my quadriceps. He knelt beside me. 'Do you ever think that up beyond the clouds and further, out beyond the blue, beyond the atmosphere, you could go on forever?'

I was scared. 'I'm cold.'

'You're shaking. What's the matter? Can you feel a spirit dancing on your grave?'

I told him that it wasn't me; I hadn't killed the Memsahib.

'But I didn't say you did.'

'That's what you think.'

He laughed. He looked at me as if I hadn't understood. My God, I thought. That's why we're here. I gazed down at the tower of St Jude's, beyond the bridge. He'd told me that was where he'd learned morality. That's why we're kneeling side by side. It's a confessional. He is expecting me to spill the beans.

'You did a great job of convincing me it wasn't Mister Shark.'

'I have an alibi as well,' I said.

'Of course you do.'

'You saw me. I was in my house. At home.'

'But that was later. You had time enough before then.'

'No. I was at home.'

'Alone?'

'No. Yes. Yes. Yes, I was alone.' Because the only person who could vouch for me was Kapko and I might as well be hung for having Drudjers in my garage as for murdering the Memsahib.

'Wouldn't you feel better if you told the truth?'

I doubted it. In my experience that never works. You tell your wife that some young girl you've just passed in the street is pretty and your soul might feel unburdened for an instant but you will begin a punishment of snide remarks and fond but obdurate restrictions on your movements that will last eternally.

I pointed out I didn't have a motive but he laughed at that. He said we all have motives. Sir.

I kept my eyes horizon-fixed. I wasn't falling for his tricks. 'It wasn't me.'

'Who was it then?'

'You're sure it wasn't Sodz.'

'You heard what Tomas said.'

'Perhaps he lied. To save his skin. You know that he takes bribes.'

'They all do. He can't help it. It's expected. Gary wants his cut. I think that Tomas told the truth. In fact, I'd stake my life on it.

You saw the way he was the other night: how he'd prevaricate; how he would answer any question other than the one that he was asked. But he refused to lie. I'm not sure that he can. Which means Sodz has an alibi. So let's go back to starters, Sir. How did you come to have this pearl?'

This is the way with silence: it crescendoes. Quickly. Soon the 'no one's saying anything' is roaring in your ears. Then you'll find anything to fill the gap.

'I must have found it.'

'Must you?'

'Yes. I did. I found it.'

'Where?'

'I can't remember.'

'That's convenient.'

'Down on the river bank.'

'Perhaps you could be, Sir, a little more precise.'

I shook my head.

'Down there?' He pointed.

'I can't look. I don't like heights.'

That was a stupid thing to say. The hand that had been resting on my shoulder gripped my neck. He forced me downwards, outwards, so my upper body curved as if I was a figure two. Some sort of stupid swan. I had to grab the balustrade to stop him tipping me across the edge.

'What are you … Nikov … no.'

'If I were you,' he said, 'I wouldn't close my eyes. You might as well enjoy the view while you still can.'

'I think I'm going to be sick.'

'I doubt that landing in a pool of vomit will reduce the impact very much,' he said.

'Please, Nikov, please.'

'If you fell now, Sir, do you think you'd somersault?'

'Don't Nikov.'

'Would you rather land upon your feet or on your head? Or on your front perhaps? Spread out? I don't suppose that it would matter much.'

I heard somebody whimper. It was me. My fingers squeezed the wall so hard I thought that it might crumble.

'When you hit the ground your bones will shatter and the splinters pierce your organs like a self-impaled souvlakia. I think the Boss must have a recipe for that. At least he wouldn't need to tenderise the flesh.'

That's when my stomach jumped and plunged; that's when I heaved. I watched the contents of my stomach drop.

'You've made a mess,' he said, 'but not as much mess as there would be if I ...' Here he made a movement and he tipped me forward for a moment and I thought that I was over and I shrieked and then he grabbed me and he held me there, kept in this world by nothing other than his strong young arms and I was hanging, staring downwards at my death, and then he rocked me back. 'You would be pulped. There'd be a lot of blood. Your skull would be cracked open like a rotten egg. And what would happen to your sense of self, I wonder, as your brains were splattered on the ground? A blob here smeared across the grass and over there another dribble mangled with the mud. I wonder if you'd have sufficient momentary con- sciousness to feel yourself fragmented. Plural Sirs. Or would experience be drowned in pain? You finished puking yet?'

No, no, no, no, no, no. 'No, Nikov, please, I'll tell you anything. No, Nikov, please, I got the pearl from Faith.'

'You see? It's always better when you tell.' He let me go.

There was a moment when I didn't move. I thought I was a gargoyle, turned to stone, forever spewing. Then I jerked myself back upright, then I scrabbled backwards from the wall, then I was grovelling upon the scratchy blackened asphalt of the roof and sprawling like a turtle flipped onto its back.

He stood. He looked at me as if he really was a god and I was something he did not quite understand and couldn't care for. Then he stepped across to me and placed his foot upon my unprotected genitals. I tensed.

'Did Faith explain to you how she came by the Memsahib's pearls?'

'Please Nikov, don't. She said she got the pearls from Sodz.'

'I thought we had decided that he wasn't here.'

'He wasn't. Yes he was. He was but that was afterwards. He didn't kill the Memsahib. Truly. Please don't hurt me. He was there but later. By the time he reached her flat she was already dead. She was, I promise. He just found her body, that was all.'

'The pearls?'

'The pearls were rolling all around the floor. He picked them up.'

'He told you all of this?'

That was a trap. I was surprised that I was still aware enough to notice traps. My breath must stink, I thought. My body ached. My hands were shaking and my testicles were trying to retreat behind my pubis. I felt dreadful. 'This is what he said to Faith. He told her that he crossed the bridge and caught the private lift up to the penthouse but that when he saw her she was dead.'

'How dead?'

'Already dead.'

'As dead as you will be if I discover you are lying?'

'Nikov, I am telling you the truth, I promise. Sodz just stole the pearls. And then he heard the Peacemakers and so he set the flat on fire and used the chaos to escape.'

He wagged his foot. A gentle tap upon my testicles. That's when I nearly wet myself. 'It's what Faith told me, Nikov, honestly. I swear.'

He took his foot away. My balls were safe. For now. And then he said: 'Let's see what she says, shall we?' And he called her. 'Faith!'

The door that led onto the stairwell opened. Faith stepped out.

She must have heard me drop her in it but she didn't seem at all annoyed with me. She must have known she was in trouble but she didn't seem at all abashed. She stepped out on that rooftop like a tourist on a lookout point. She wandered from the stairwell doorway to the edge - she had to step across my body on the way - and peered down at the river. 'What a view,' she called. My stomach started squirming even watching her. She turned around and crossed the roof to gaze down from the other side. 'This would be a fantastic place to hold a herd of Drudjers. Block the stairs and then the only way they can escape is if they jump.'

She walked straight up to Nikov. 'But you wouldn't, would you? It's your special place. Why is that Nikov?'

He was tolerant. 'I like it here.'

'No,' she said. 'It must be more than that.' She turned to me. I was still flattened to the surface. 'Why on earth are you down there?' She sniffed. 'Whatever is that smell?'

I could have told her that it was the scent of terror. It was urine. I had only leaked a drop or two. I'd sweated buckets though.

I closed my legs and turned so I was lying on my side away from her.

'You must remember, Ed,' said Faith, 'last night when Gary, in the bar, was telling us that when he led his men into the Tower Block he took them straight up to the roof. Then he stopped talking and he looked at us. There must be something secret on this roof. What is it: buried treasure? Have you found it yet?'

She wandered over to one of those little metal boxes sprouting from the roof that I'd assumed were ventilation shafts. She crouched beside it and inspected it. She poked inside it with her finger. 'It would be a splendid place. Most people think you bury treasure underground, not high up in the air, but dragons fly and hoard their treasure in the mountains and a building such as this is really just an artificial mountain, isn't it?'

'There isn't any treasure,' Nikov said.

'Don't tell me that you haven't looked. I won't believe you. But. No. I suppose I would. You always were the sort who wanted what nor rust nor moth destroyeth.'

You won't joke, I thought, when he is holding you above the drop so that the only thing preventing you from falling to your death is Nikov thinking you have given honest answers to his questions.

'Sometimes,' Nikov said to Faith, 'I think you know me better than I know myself.'

That's typical, I thought. It's who you know that counts. The pair of them were friends.

So he was going to believe her, wasn't he?

Then I'd be for the high jump.

How I wished I'd not thought that.

'We'd better get to business,' Nikov said. 'You've heard what Mr Angelo has said. How he accused you. Was he telling me the truth?'

She raised her eyebrows. 'Once upon a time,' she said, 'there was a little lad. We called him Nicky, to be friendly, but I'm not sure that he ever fitted in.'

'Time passes, people change,' said Nikov.

'As you would expect,' she said, 'Madame is just the same as she has always been.'

'She must have made a fortune in the last few months.'

'You've made a lot of work for us,' acknowledged Faith, 'but, as you know, the profits are donated to St Jude's. We will receive our just reward when we are brought before our maker. As will you.'

'Right now,' he said, 'I'm judge. So tell me. Do you have a pearl?'

'What you would really like to do,' said Faith, 'is search me. You have always wanted an excuse for that. Do you remember when we got to grips as kids? You were a fumbler. Now you're hoping for a second chance. You know that Ed won't stop you. He's the sort who tuts and walks on by while watching from the corner of his eye. Come on then, Nikov. Shall I take my bra off first?'

I looked at her as Nikov said: 'Why don't you save us all the trouble and produce the pearl?'

She looked at him. She looked at me. I nodded. But she turned her back on both of us and wandered over to the edge. She pointed. 'Look at that. It's always there. That never changes. It's eternal and immutable and … I could never understand why you forsook St Jude.'

'St Jude,' said Nikov, 'is the patron saint of hopeless causes.'

'Nicky was an altar boy. He had the most angelic voice. I always thought that when he was a man he'd either be a singer or a priest. Where did it all go wrong?'

'I grew up and it broke. There are some things that even good old Jude can't fix.'

'Do you remember Father Kerrigan?' she asked. 'He was a character!'

'He was a drunkard,' Nikov said.

'Poor Father Kerrigan. Try not to be too hard on him,' said Faith. 'We all have weaknesses.'

'He brought disgrace upon himself. A man who can't control himself should never be a priest. He set the worst example to the rest of us.'

'But you'd have made a good priest,' Faith replied.

They called him Mister Purity, I thought.

'Your trouble is,' she told him, 'that you always tried too hard.' She turned to me. 'When Nicky was a little boy he was the lad who stood outside the circle looking in.'

'My name is Nikov.'

'Just like that,' said Faith. 'He wanted to be one of us but never quite enough. We knew that; kids can always tell. We would have welcomed him as Nicky.'

'It's a silly name.'

'What's wrong with it? It's just informal. It's a way of saying we'll accept you in your socks with holes in and your shirt that is a size too big.'

'It's a diminutive,' said Nikov. 'You were trying to belittle me.'

'Perhaps we were,' admitted Faith. 'But sometimes you must make yourself a little smaller if you want to fit.'

I couldn't understand what she was doing. Playing, I supposed, for time, but why? Deflecting Nikov's anger to herself from me. But why? Attempting to convert him? You can't turn a wolf into a dog.

'Let's talk about this pearl,' said Nikov.

'Did you know that Nicky had a secret? He was so ashamed. He thought it was a secret but it wasn't. No one ever had a secret at St Jude's. We shared. We gossiped. We condemned and we forgave. It wasn't even Nicky's fault. His father gambled. So? It's not a sin. It isn't even mentioned in the Bible. Nicky's father gambled. That was all it was.'

'It was enough,' said Nikov. 'I want to know about the pearl.'

'Some say that Nicky's mother threw his father out and others that his father went off with another woman. Anyway, they split and somewhere down the line there was adultery involved.'

He looked at her. He didn't glance down at his watch or tap his foot. He waited, and he waited patiently. But there was something dangerous about the pursing of his lips.

'But then, and this was sad, his mummy died and so he had to leave St Jude's and go to live with daddy and with daddy's whore.'

'She was a lovely lady.'

'But she was a Drudjer.'

'So she was.'

'And she replaced your mother.'

'So she did and tried her very best to do the step-mum thing, which isn't easy at the best of times.'

'Then you became a Peacemaker.'

'I did.'

'A Drudjer hater.'

'No. I've never hated Drudjers.'

'But you hunt them.'

'Rules are rules.' He shrugged. 'This is a poor attempt to ana-lyse my psyche, Faith. It's very crude. But I suppose it's not a genuine attempt to help me - what's the phrase? - to under-stand myself. You're really only trying to distract me. We are straying from the point. I have been told by Mr Angelo that you possess a pearl. I'd like to see it please.'

'I thought you'd never ask,' said Faith, producing it.

He told her where it came from. 'Yes,' she said. 'I know.'

'How did you come to own it?' Nikov asked.

Faith looked at me.

I stared into the twilight. What had Nikov said? Beyond the clouds ... My body felt so soft against the roughness of the sur-face of the roof.

'You heard him. He says you have talked to Sodz, and he implies that Sodz,' said Nikov, 'passed them on to you.'

Faith nodded.

'But that makes no sense since Sir attempted to bribe Tomas with a pearl. If Sodz gave Faith the pearls how is it Mr Angelo possesses one? There are two possibilities. The first is that you paid a pearl to him for services he's rendered. I've been thinking hard and I cannot come up with anything that Mr Angelo could do for you. So I eliminate the other possibility. There's only one thing left. Sodz gave the pearls to Mr Angelo and he's been paying you.'

He might as well have kicked me in the guts. I squirmed and as I did I scraped my wrist against the asphalt. As I struggled up I bruised my hip and as I scrambled to my feet my knee was wrenched. The bastard. He was playing me along. For him, perhaps, it was a game. 'That isn't how it was.'

'How was it?'

When you're bluffing and your bluff is called you either have to throw your hand in or to double down. I chose to lie. 'She bribed me. Last night, when I went to the *Enchanted Isle*, I told her that I knew that she had talked to Sodz. She begged me for my silence.'

Nikov shook his head.

'Then she came round that night. You saw her, you were there. That's when she handed me the pearl.'

He tutted. 'Honestly! And then you gave that pearl to Tomas so he'd let you cross the bridge to go to the *Enchanted Isle*?'

'You have to speculate. Invest. I thought, if there was one pearl, there would be a whole lot more.'

He shook his head. 'So you are an extortionist. That's your defence.'

'At least I'm not a murderer.'

'For goodness sake,' said Nikov. 'Tell the truth.'

When you're accused of something, faking outrage sometimes halts an adversary in their tracks. 'In what way am I lying?' I demanded.

'For a start,' said Nikov, 'you are hiding Drudjers in your garage.'

CHAPTER NINETEEN: WHAT NIKOV WANTS

My mouth was opening and closing but my brain had given it no words to say.

He knew.

I looked up to the fading sky. No help from that direction. I was on my own. And Nikov knew.

But if he knew then why ...? Why wasn't I already dead? Why hadn't Nikov shot me that first night? He could have done. He could have tipped me from this rooftop. Nearly did. He hadn't. Why?

It was a bluff.

He was a little liar.

Anger freed my tongue. 'What do you mean: I'm hiding Drudjers? No I'm not.'

He looked at me.

'Who says I am?' I asked.

He looked at me as if he'd tasted something nasty.

'Was it Faith? It can't be Faith. It was Faith, wasn't it? I might have known. You and your little Nicky. Father Kerrigan. St Jude's. Was that what happened when you left me? You just couldn't wait to hop across the road to tell your little choir boy lover from the past that I had Drudjers in my house. I should have known. You're just a girl who will do anything for pearls.'

She shook her head. 'You are an idiot.'

'Or was it Xan? She told me she would tell. I should have listened, shouldn't I? She said you'd set her free if she could give you Sodz.'

'I told you that I had a nose for Drudjers,' Nikov said. 'My step-mum was a Drudjer. I could smell them from the start.'

I forced a laugh. I told him not to be ridiculous.

'It's over, Ed,' said Faith. 'You've more or less admitted it.'

'You're such a hypocrite,' said Nikov, 'telling me that Tomas lies. You wouldn't know the truth if you were swimming in the stuff.'

'You have no proof. You can't prove anything. Come on. Let's go there now. You'll look a little silly when there's no one there.'

When you are drowning, clutch at anything. Why not? My brain was waterfalling thoughts. Suppose he took me up on it; suppose we went back home right now. Who knows what might have happened? All the Drudjers might have left. John Zombie might have organised their getaway despite his death; a zombie can. Or, or ... or even if they were still there, they had a gun. Except they hadn't. I had given it to Ochre. Maybe, maybe, maybe he'd escaped pursuit and had returned. But I had only given him a single bullet so the gun was empty now. Think! Nikov didn't know that. Let's imagine Ochre points the gun at Nikov. Nikov puts his hands up. I take Nikov's gun. You see? Accumulate sufficient straws and you can build a raft.

I told him that I'd tumbled to his little game. 'You've tried to frighten me, you've tried to bully me and now you want to trick me into making a confession. But I know you don't know anything. If you had known you would have raided us, you would have captured them.'

'Why should I clutter up the Town Hall cells when you have locked the Drudjers up on our behalf? Why should I bother to feed prisoners when you would? Why should we waste our resources guarding them when you have kept them safe for us for free?'

Smug little bastard had an answer for whatever.

Faith asked: 'What about the search for Sodz?'

Good question. All that fuss that Nikov made about the murder. Coming to the office, asking Xan to trace the call. If he knew Sodz was sitting in my garage, what was that about?

'I knew he wasn't guilty. If we had arrested him we'd have extracted a confession. We'd stop looking. Then the real murderer would get away.'

It was beginning to grow dusky, I suppose, because, just at that moment, all at once, all round the roof, a set of solar-activated lights I hadn't previously noticed, sunk into the corner where the roof met wall, lit up. They made it look like we were standing in a silver sea. Our heads were still in darkness, though, as if we wore the opposite of haloes.

What had Nikov said? He knew Sodz wasn't guilty? But ... 'How do you know he isn't guilty?' I demanded. 'Just because he has a stupid alibi?'

'There is a little more to it than that. You dropped the hint. I told you that we had a sample of his DNA. You were impressed how speedily we had it analysed. I checked. The sample had been sent off to the lab two days before the killing. As you said, it didn't prove the Drudjer was the killer; all it meant was that he had been in the flat some time before the killing.'

Such a lot had happened on the floor below. I wondered if Salome's spirit, still to be avenged, was trapped beneath us.

'I presume,' said Nikov, 'that the Boss suspected that the Memsahib was unfaithful; that he harvested the DNA so that he could identify her lover. At the very least it gives the Boss a motive.'

'We've been telling you,' said Faith,' he was the killer.'

'Yes. It looks as if he was.'

The sky had reached that depth of blue which is the darkest it can be before the stars come out.

'There isn't any proof,' said Nikov.

'Father Kerrigan,' said Faith.

'A rubbish bin of empty bottles, new ones every day,' said Nikov. 'That's sufficient proof for me.'

'I don't mean that,' said Faith. 'I mean that no one's perfect.'

Nikov snorted. 'Father Kerrigan was very far from perfect.'

'Nicky thought he was. Poor Nicky. First his dad, then Father Kerrigan, and now the Boss.'

'That's not the issue.' Nikov shook his head. 'The problem is how I can set it right. There is corruption from the bottom to the top. They say I am obsessed with purity. What's wrong with that? We're dirty. I just want us to be clean.'

She touched him on the shoulder. 'You don't have to. You can walk away and save yourself.'

He shook his head. He took his phone out of his holster. 'Tomas? Faith is coming down. When she gets down there, let her go. She needs to find Madame.'

'What will you do with Ed,' asked Faith, 'now that you know

he's innocent?'

'He isn't innocent,' said Nikov. 'He is hiding Drudjers in his garage.'

'But,' I said.

'But,' echoed Faith.

But Nikov was insistent she should go. He held the door ajar and watched her going down the stairs. He waited.

I was apprehensive. What would happen now? Why did he want me on my own? Just now he'd held me half across the drop; I had been terrified. Then Faith had come and Nikov had been charming and polite. I dreaded the return of nasty Nikov once the witness had been sent away.

There wasn't anywhere that I could run to, nowhere I could hide.

He knew about the Drudjers.

Tomas called to say that Faith had left the building.

Nikov cut the call.

'I really didn't have a choice,' I told him. 'Kapko just walked through my door. I couldn't stop him. Anyway, he had a gun. He threatened me. And then the others came. Four onto one. I never stood a chance. It's been a nightmare.'

'I don't care about the Drudjers,' Nikov said.

'They've not been there for long. And Kapko's dying. And I have been planning how I can get rid of Sodz without you finding out that I am breaking Peacemaker pronouncements in a technical and minor sort of way.'

'I wouldn't call it 'technical and minor',' Nikov said. 'I'd say your life is in my hands. Come on.' He beckoned me to follow him. He walked towards the edge.

'Where are we going.'

'Don't you understand? I'm giving you a chance.'

He stood beside the little parapet that separated roof from sky. I stood beside him but a half-step further back, behind his shoulder, so that if he thought to push me he would have to turn and scoop me from my place.

'Look over there.' He pointed north towards a line of lights which wandered through the growing gloom, as if a constellation, plunging from the sky, had landed and its stars, freed from their places by the crash, could not stop moving but did not know where to go.

'Is it the army?'

'Yes.'

'They're getting closer.'

'They'll be at the river by tomorrow night.'

Was this the chance that he was giving me: to clear the garage of my guests before the Peacemakers arrived to lay their trap?

'That's why the footbridge is unguarded, isn't it?'

He asked me what I meant. I said I thought he planned to lure the army down our street and then to ambush them. 'The Town Hall is your bait.'

He laughed at that. 'It's rather obvious. I don't think that the army generals will fall for that. We took the footbridge guards away because we didn't need them once we'd cleared the Drudjers from the Kennels. In any case, the army cannot reach the footbridge without going through the Kennels.'

Here he stopped, as if he'd said too much. I understood. 'You've booby-trapped the Kennels.'

But he wouldn't say. 'I doubt the Boss would like a battle on his doorstep. What we want to do is keep the army on the north side of the river. That's the plan. It won't be easy. I would say that makes a problem of four Drudjers insignificant. Would you agree?'

Of course I would. Not only did I never disagree with men with guns - or anyone when I was on a roof - but also I was starting to believe my little Drudjer problem would be overlooked.

Although it really rather pissed me off that Nikov had been stringing me along. Last night, for instance, when he had pretended Faith had popped in for a one night stand. How he had laughed at my discomfort, even coming back because of the tomatoes. He had put me through it, laughing up his sleeve. And when he brought the number of the phone that Sodz had used (no, it was Ochre); Xan had processed it and Nikov had not even glanced towards her screen to see if she was telling him the truth. He didn't need to. He had known. He'd always bloody known. He had been playing me as if I was a puppet, jerking at my strings, to make me dance a jig that he'd composed. I was exhausted. I had been to hell and back. And Nikov knew.

'The army's close enough to cuddle,' Nikov told me, 'but the Boss can't think of anything but how to pin the murder of the Memsahib on a Drudjer. Don't you see? It isn't just that he's corrupt. It clouds his judgement. He's incompetent.'

'Perhaps he's done a deal,' I said. 'Perhaps they've bought him. Maybe he instructed you to search for Sodz so you would be distracted while he parleyed with the army.'

'Not the Boss. That's not his way. He was a founder of the Peacemakers; one of the men who saw what needed to be done and did it. He is honest, he's straightforward, he's a dreamer.

He's the Boss.'

I understood what Faith was getting at. 'Your dad,' I said to Nikov. 'Father Kerrigan.'

'Perhaps.'

The wind was gusting. It was even colder now.

'What can I do?' asked Nikov.

This is what I should have told him. Keep your head down. Keep your mouth shut till they start to sing their hymns; then synchronise your lips and make it seem as though you're joining in. Don't rock the boat. Don't stand out from the crowd. Stay underneath the radar. Do as I do.

He had asked an expert.

Following my own advice, I didn't say a word. I shook my head and sighed to show I sympathised.

'The only thing that I can do is to replace him,' Nikov said. 'You see that, don't you?'

What?

'Yes. Yes, of course. I understand.'

'It is the only thing that I can do to save the Peacemakers,' he said.

This is the trouble with a man like that. His father wasn't perfect: no one's is, mine wasn't. I'd inferred, from what Faith said, that Father Kerrigan had let him down. And now the Boss. He might have stopped believing in St Jude; he still believed in miracles. He still put all his trust into a person in authority and they would have to let him down and let him down and let him down again before his faith was wobbled.

It was madness, of a sort. And I was on a roof with him.

How do you soothe a lunatic? Use cliches to placate them. I agreed he had to do what he must do.

'The question is not what, but how.'

'That's certainly the question. Shall we step a little further back?'

'Assassination?' Nikov said.

'Assass ... assass ... assass,' I stammered.

'I would have to keep my hands clean. That's essential. When I take his place, I have to be untainted. If the others think I toppled him, they will be seeking ways to topple me. That won't be good.'

I wondered whether Tomas would believe me if I went back down alone and told him Nikov had been raving mad and talking treason; that he had been suicidal; that he'd jumped.

Would anyone believe me?

Nikov said: 'It's not that I'd be fearful for myself but it would undermine morale. We're volunteers. The day we stop believing is the day the Peacemakers are finished.'

I was hoping that he wouldn't notice if I took another step away from that damn drop but as I tried to shuffle backwards he reached out and grabbed my arm.

'I hope you understand,' he said, 'why I can't kill the Boss myself.'

I nodded till I thought my head might come loose from my neck and fling itself into the void. I nodded till I realised that he wasn't looking at me and he couldn't see me nod. And still I nodded, while he stared like any wish-full dreamer into empty space.

Protect me from idealists, I thought.

'That's why you have to do it for me.'

No.

I hadn't heard him properly.

He didn't say what I just thought he said.

He didn't mean it.

But he did.

I should have seen it coming

Men like him are always very keen on martyrdom. But not for them. For someone else.

'I can't assassinate the Boss,' I said.

'Why not?'

Because it would be suicide, I thought. I said: 'Because I haven't got a gun.'

'I thought you told me that the Drudjer had a gun.'

Would Kapko do it? Yes, I thought, he would. He had sufficient hate. He'd have no moral hesitation: might is right means guns do good. But Kapko wouldn't do it if he couldn't get away. Survival of the Kapko was his ultimate commandment.

Then again, I thought, he's dying anyway. Perhaps he would. Perhaps he'd do it. That would get me off the hook.

And then I thought of Kapko lying in the garage, slumped against the wall, and then I knew it wouldn't work.

'He isn't well enough.'

'I'm not suggesting that the Drudjer does it,' Nikov said, 'but you could use his gun. And then ballistics couldn't trace it back to me.'

'You can't be serious,' I said.

'You have sufficient access to the Boss.'

'You haven't heard me: I'm not doing it.'

'You have to.'

'No I don't. I won't. Whoever tried to kill the Boss would need to have a death-wish. This is mad. He's guarded. An assassin would be shot and killed before he ever reached him. Even if he managed it, he would be captured afterwards. And put to death. Unpleasantly.'

'You overestimate how well we can protect the Boss. You underestimate the possibilities. You'd have a chance. Once you've fulfilled your mission, if you get across the river to the army, you'll be safe.'

I shook my head.

'You have a better chance of living if you will agree to my proposal.'

'Better chance than what?' I asked suspiciously.

'A better chance than if I shoot you now. I can, you know. You're hiding Drudjers in your garage.'

'But you said you didn't care about the Drudjers.'

'That's because I don't,' said Nikov, 'if you'll do what I am asking you to do.'

There should be laws, I thought, against idealists. But then again, we're all fanatics when we're young. A youngster sees the world has wrongs and wants to right them. When you're young, you reckon that not only your beliefs are true beliefs but also that it's possible you can convince the rest of us. By words. Or deeds. It doesn't really matter when you're young.

'There is a better way,' I said. I couldn't think of one.

'Such as?' he asked.

'Assassination has to be the last resort,' I told him, nodding sagely, like he hadn't thought of that already.

Kapko couldn't. Ochre wouldn't. Sodz?

'The Peacemakers have been contaminated by corruption,' Nikov said. 'It's up to me to make them clean. I cannot take the problem to the top. I have to purge the system by decapitating it. There's no alternative.'

'You're right,' I said, 'of course, you're right.' A man who has a gun is always right, I told myself. 'The Boss must be removed. That doesn't mean you have to kill him.'

Nikov said he didn't see what else was possible.

It seemed that it was up to me. As always.

Kapko couldn't. Ochre wouldn't. Sodz.

Why not?

If nothing else he could be bait.

The Peacemakers, like pirates in the old days, chose their leaders by acclaim. Once someone was selected to command they had supreme authority; they could demand the ultimate in loyalty. But like the alpha in a wolf pack, Bosses only ruled while their subordinates consented to be ruled.

This meant they could be ousted.

We'd have to set the whole thing up. Persuade him to participate. There was a whole damn box of dominoes that could go wrong. And if it all exploded in our faces? By the time that death arrived we'd welcome its oblivion.

But this was probably the only chance I had.

'There is a way to knock him off his perch,' I said to Nikov, 'by exposing him. We tell the Peacemakers that he has killed his wife. They only need a small excuse to boot him out: they are already losing to the army.'

'They won't believe us,' Nikov said. 'He's told them it's a Drudjer. Drudjers are the enemy. He is the Boss. They'll stick with what they know.'

'They'd have to be convinced if he admitted it himself.'

'He won't do that.'

'It won't be easy,' I agreed. 'We'll have to trick him into a confession.'

'How?'

'The Boss wants Sodz, in shackles, standing in a dock, in public, charged, convicted, sentenced. Sodz found guilty means the Boss is innocent. It's his big chance to move on from the murder of the Memsahib. Imagine that the trial is broadcast live. There will be a tidal wave of sympathy towards the Boss: his wife killed by a Drudjer. All the Peacemakers will rally round. They'll forget the loss of so much territory to the army. He'll be reaffirmed and his position will be incontestable.'

I looked around. This was as good a stage as any. Right above the place the murder was committed. We'd have cameras, or course. A live-stream which would need to be unbreakable.

'That's what we have to make the Boss think,' I explained.

'You have a plan?' asked Nikov.

'Yes.'

CHAPTER TWENTY: WHAT WILL WE DO WHEN WE GET OUT OF HERE?

When I got home I told my Drudjers that the food delivery had been delayed. Not cancelled. There was no sense scaring them. If they began to panic they'd be unpredictable. They might stampede. I needed to control a situation which was on the edge. The bargain I had reached with Nikov was dependent on my handing over Sodz.

I therefore painted them a picture of the world outside. The army was approaching. That was true. The Peacemakers were getting jumpy. That was not a lie. They'd put on more patrols. I didn't know that for a fact but it seemed likely. I concluded that it would be extra dangerous to try to leave right now.

It helped that Kapko was asleep. Without him they were fragments. Sodz, suspicious, said he was surprised that I was saying they should stay; it was a first: till now I had been urging them to go. But Blossom pointed out they couldn't leave till Uncle had recovered.

They were three scared children in a box, their faces turned towards me. Blossom squatting, sitting on her heels, eyes round and blank with trust, and Sodz, crouched on the far side of the room, uncertain, staring at me, wanting to believe me.

Ochre, on his knees beside his Uncle, looking up and back, across his shoulder, asked: 'What did you do about the Poppers?'

I regarded Kapko, lying propped against the wall. His eyes were closed. There was a film of sweat upon his face. His breaths were shallow.

I said that I had done what I could. 'Faith knows we need them. If she can she'll bring them with the food.' And that was not untrue.

I told them I had talked to Nikov. 'He expects the army will be at the river by the day after tomorrow.' That was honest. And it gave them hope.

I said it was a bit like being in a lifeboat following a shipwreck. 'Yes, we're hungry now, but if we pull together, we can make it. It's incredible how often people do, against the odds. It's not as if we're in the middle of the ocean. We are nearly there, a few days from the shore. It's not much longer. We can do it.'

'We?' said Sodz. 'Since when did you become a shipmate, pal?'

'I'm not sure Uncle ...' Ochre started.

I wasn't having Kapko wreck my plans, put me in danger; not again. 'Do you think we can move him? Look at him. You want to try to smuggle him through Peacemaker patrols? You think you'll have a chance to dodge their bullets carrying a dying man? You want to make a run for it then go, go now, don't hang around. You might just make it. On your own. But not with him.'

'It's not too bad,' urged Blossom, 'no worse than a fast. We're Drudjers. It's the spirit of the Drudj: to face your hardships, to endure, to triumph. We'll get through this if it's only for a few more days.'

Sodz grumpily agreed.

'When I get out of here,' said Blossom, 'and as soon as I am somewhere safe, I'm going to buy a bar of chocolate and I'll eat it very slowly, square by square.'

That made me think of how I'd like to watch her fingers, slightly stickied, pop a chunk of chocolate in between her tongue-stroked lips. Her teeth would pulp it. Goo would swim into the caverns of her mouth and slide with her lubricious spittle down the inside of her cheeks. The lucky chocolate would be licked to dissolution in her tongue's enfolding clutch. Her tastebuds would be overwhelmed as flavour gurgled over them.

'And what will you do, brother?' Blossom asked.

He shook his head. I realised he couldn't think beyond tomorrow. That was just as well perhaps. There might not be 'beyond tomorrow' for the boy.

Sodz tilted forwards, drawn into the game. 'It's difficult,' he said, 'to choose between an ice-cold lager and a glass of blood-warm claret. First things first? The lager, in a sauna, and then after, a massage.'

'You'd better have a shower first,' said Ochre. 'No masseuse would want to touch you at the moment.'

'You will learn, if you are lucky, when you're older, that the ladies love a man who has been marinated in his own secretions for a day or two.'

I noticed Blossom made a face.

'I'd take a shower,' Ochre said, 'but first I'd run. I'd run and run and run.'

'Where would you go?' asked Blossom.

Ochre shrugged. 'It doesn't really matter where. It could be round and round a meadow. Just so long as I am in the open air.' He looked from wall to wall. 'So long as I can move my arms and legs.'

'And then? What next?' asked Blossom. 'When we have escaped from here what would you like to do? I don't mean straight away but not the sort of thing you have to plan for. In the middle distance. Not right now, but soon.'

'Hang on,' said Ochre. 'Uncle hasn't had a chance.'

Sodz looked at Kapko from the far side of the room. He kept his distance from the dying man. 'The only thing he needs to say is where we're going next. 'Cause if he doesn't tell us, all these suppositions and hypotheses, perchances and peut-etres, what-ifs, maybes, haplys and potentialities, are only let's pretend and make believe. And anyway, he is asleep.'

'Not ... sleeping,' Kapko said. He pulled a face. He mumbled.

Blossom leaned across so he could whisper in her ear. 'No, Uncle, no.' She looked unhappy.

'Tell them,' he commanded and he raised his hand as if in blessing. But the effort was too much. His hand fell back. He scowled and coughed and winced.

'It isn't really in the spirit of the game,' said Blossom. 'Uncle says the first thing he will do when he gets out of here is ...' She looked down at the floor as if she thought that if she told her feet she wouldn't feel embarrassed. 'Uncle says that we should carry on the fight.'

I laughed at that, a sort of bitter cackle, quickly cut. The others looked at me as if I had been telling dirty jokes in church. 'I'm sorry but he isn't. When was he a fighter? Him? The only cause he's ever fought for was himself.'

Which was the truth.

But he was Drudjer. They were Drudjer. I was not.

There was an empty plastic bag upon the floor. The wrapper for some peanuts. They'd been eating those two days ago. Two days this litter had been on the floor. They must have walked around it, sat beside it, looked at it, but never picked it up.

'And after that,' said Sodz, 'when I've been rubbed and yes, OK, when I have had a shower, I am going to the airport and I'm flying off to somewhere with a beach.' He pointed at the poster that depicted, through a trompe l'oeil circle broken through the wall, a palm tree. 'Sun and sand and surf. Shark's in the sea. I'll strip down to my shorts; I'll soak up smiles from all the swimsuit sweethearts strolling up and down the shore. I'll lie there like a spider in the centre of his web ...'

'You have the hairy legs already,' Blossom muttered. She had noticed.

'... and I'll wait for one of them to come a little bit too close and then I'll pounce. All summer Sodz will have a shagathon and when he isn't having sex he will be eating lobster, drinking champers, smoking long and blessed spliffs stuffed full of sacred skunk and sleeping.'

'All of that? You must be hiding quite a few more pearls,' said Ochre, 'to afford all that.'

'You think Sodz has to pay for pleasure? Boy, you need an education. Love, for Sodz, is free.'

'The lobsters aren't.'

'They buy the lobsters.'

'Sounds exploitative,' said Blossom.

'That's a sourface thing to say. This is being happy, girl. Don't you like giving? Happiness is giving gifts. We all like being generous. Sodz gives himself to girls, for free, no stinting now, and in return, should they make little presents, if that's how they show their love, if that's what makes them happy. What? You think I should say no, no, no, it is exploitative which is abusive which is predatory which is selfish which is being used. Who's being used: the she or me? To give: it is a part of loving. It's the best. And if it makes them happy, why should I refuse?'

He reached into the air in front of him as if to pluck invisibility out of the atmosphere.

'It's just as well I know you,' Blossom said. 'It's just as well I know when you are chatting garbage.'

Somehow Sodz looked dignified and hurt at once.

'I'd like to go abroad as well,' said Blossom. 'Backpack round the world. I didn't dare before. There's no way Mum and Dad would have allowed me. They'd have worried. They'd have said it wasn't safe. That seems so stupid now.' She spread her arms to show that she could nearly reach the wall on either side. 'Who would have thought that I'd be safer climbing mountains, crossing deserts, hitching lifts and waitressing in foreign bars than I am now, here, hiding in a garage in the town where I grew up.'

'Sounds nice. Can I come with you?' Ochre asked.

'Of course not. My big brother? I am doing this alone. All by myself. I want the chance to take my own decisions, make my own mistakes. I had enough of you three snoring all last night. '

'Won't you be lonely?' Ochre asked.

'He thinks you're selfish,' Sodz said suddenly. 'He thinks that sisters ought to stay at home.'

'We've all been taught to think of others; that's the Drudjer way,' said Ochre. 'Mum and Dad ...'

'They're dead,' said Blossom, 'like the rest of them. The way they brought me up? The Drudjer life? It hasn't got me anywhere.' She looked around. 'It brought me here.'

The thing about an empty chamber like the garage, as with any hollow cavity, is this: when you have silence you can hear it echoing between the walls.

'I want to finish off my training,' Ochre said. 'First chance I get. I want to be a doctor to save lives and cure diseases. Single-handed.'

'And I'd like to go to college,' Blossom said. 'Once I've survived the world. What I'd do next. I want to go to college.'

'Mum and Dad ...' Her brother stopped himself. He looked away. I saw his Adam's apple bobbing as he swallowed.

'Mum and Dad,' he said. 'It isn't decent for a Drudjer girl to look at naked bodies.'

From the way that Blossom rolled her eyes I knew this was a conversation one-way street they'd travelled down before.

'But I don't look at them. I've told you. They're just models and I see them as the elements within a photograph,' she said. 'And aren't you being just a trifle hypocritical? You look at naked bodies all day long.'

'That's different. You know it is. I am a doctor.'

'Wannabe,' said Sodz.

I don't think Ochre heard. 'The bodies that I look at are diseased or damaged. They are not attractive, not like yours. I don't mean yours, your body' he said quickly, but I think he did. 'I mean your models' bodies. They are always pretty. Beautiful. Of course they are. That's what you do. That's what a photo's for. To make seductive images. To make the viewer fall in love. With bodies.'

'Blossom, if you want to practise,' Sodz said, 'I will take my clothes off for you anytime.'

'You'd better not,' said Ochre.

Three of them: the boy, his sister, and the stud. The gigolo, the siblings. Not the usual triangle. The young outsider and the girl who wanted to be independent. And the brother who was trying to protect her by preventing her.

It was a garage. It was meant to store a car with fifty litres of inflammability. I doubted whether it could hold these Drudjers.

'I'd like to play the game,' I said, although I knew I couldn't tell them what I really wanted. Blossom. By herself. 'What I would like to do when all of this is over …'

'No,' said Kapko.

'You can't play,' said Sodz. 'It's not your game.'

'It's not the same,' said Ochre. 'You can leave here any time you want to leave.'

You see? They stick together, Drudjers.

'What I would do,' I said, insisting, 'is that I would turn off the alarm and close my eyes and when I woke I'd lie there all day long instead of running errands for a bunch of parasitic Drudjers. All day long and half the bloody night. I'm like your servant. Fetch me this and fetch me that.'

'You haven't fetched us anything,' Sodz pointed out.

'I tried. I got myself arrested …' I had said too much. I saw it in their faces. Blossom's was concerned. She was a nice girl. Kapko's face displayed suspicion. He was thinking: if he was arrested, how's he here?

'It was all right,' I said. 'They let me go.' I shrugged. 'As you can see. I talked them out of keeping me.' Another stupid thing to say. It frightened them. I saw Sodz look alarmed. 'I didn't tell them anything they didn't know already.' That was true enough. He'd known from the beginning, Nikov had. He let me suffer all that stress. It was a form of torture. He had made me suffer. Was that how he got his kicks?

'It's not the worst thing in the world, you know, to sit in here. You might be bored; at least you're safe. Out there,' I flung my arm towards the outside wall, like I was pointing at the palm tree, 'things are difficult. I can't just come and go. You think I'm free? I am the most tied down of all of you. And why should I put up with it? When all is said and done, you're in my house. My house. My bloody house.'

'It's not … your house,' said Kapko.

'What?' I hadn't heard him right.

'He said …'

'What do you mean, it's not my house?'

'I … paid for it,' said Kapko. Now, it seemed, he was a little stronger, of a sudden. Bastard thrived on nastiness.

'The money's mine,' said Kapko. 'Came from me. I paid.'

'You paid? You paid because I worked for you,' I told him. What was this that he was playing at?

'You're sounding like John Zombie, Uncle,' Blossom said. 'He says all property is theft. He used to say …'

But Kapko wasn't saying that. What he was saying was my house was his. That's not the same.

'Gave you … a job.'

I was astonished. 'Gave me? You have never given anything to anyone. I worked for you. Have you forgotten? System K? You paid me but you never paid enough. Not for all that. All that you took.' My work, I thought, my wife. 'You own my house? I think you'll find that it's the other way around. I think you'll find I paid for you. Your flat. Your precious penthouse. There's a bit of that apartment should be mine by rights. I'm glad you've lost it. Glad the Peacemakers have taken it. I'm glad they got the pennies that you pocketed from others. That's a sort of justice. Serves you right.'

He groaned. I grinned.

'Glass houses,' Sodz said, 'Pot and kettle, mote and beam. The mother crab says to her kids: 'Walk straight'.'

'Not me,' I said. 'I've always worked for others. Like I'm doing now for all of you. For free.' I didn't even have a pearl to show for it.

'It is because you're not a Drudjer,' Sodz insisted. 'If you were, you wouldn't think like that. You haven't got a clue how lucky you have been. You think we want to hide here in this garage?' He looked up towards the ceiling like he thought that any moment it might fall on top of him. He looked from side to side, as if the walls might come together, squeezing him between them. 'Do you think it makes us feel like lords and ladies, dons and donnas, caballeros and contessas to be sitting here in this dark, stinking, freezing hole; to wait for you to bring whatever leavings you can scrape together from the table of the hijos of puttanas who have robbed us? That's the way you people are. You always have been. Hanging on to what you have. The Drudjers have been persecuted through the centuries. So many times your people have attempted to eradicate us, to annihilate us, to exterminate us. Will there never be an end to pogroms, hecatombs and holocausts? We have been starved, we have been butchered, we've been driven over cliffs or put in pens and burned alive. But most of all we've been exploited. We have been in bondage, burdened, forced to labour and to sweat and drudge and slave so you can live your easy lives, so you can work while sitting down, so you can have your leisure and your entertainments. Then, just once, it goes a little way the other way and you're aggrieved? You say it isn't fair, it isn't right, it isn't just? It isn't. Any Drudjer could have told you that. For us, it's rite of passage stuff. We call it growing up. So don't you winge that you have been hard done by. Count how many Drudjers wept so you can own a house.'

I made a promise to myself. He'd pay for that. I'd make him pay.

'I will grow roses,' Ochre said. 'If I get out of here I'm going to find a patch of land and make a garden.'

There was silence. We had lost our appetite for games.

But Ochre was determined. 'I grew roses back at home. My Mum,' his voice broke slightly and he paused, regrouped, found strength, continued, 'she encouraged me.'

'What sort of roses?' Sodz asked.

'Do you really want to know? She tells me,' Ochre jerked his head at Blossom, 'that I'm boring when I talk of roses. I like Floribunda best. It's like a shaggy dog. Unkempt. Like Beethoven.' He blushed. 'You'll think it stupid, I suppose,' he muttered.

'No.' Sodz shook his head. 'Good on you, Ochre. Roses. Beautiful.'

There was a pause, then Blossom said: 'We won't get out of here until they drag us from this garage to the gallows.'

'No,' I said. 'Let's hope it doesn't come to that.'

'Hey, Sis,' said Ochre, 'don't look down; there's always hope. We haven't been discovered yet. Ed's helping us. You will still help us, won't you Ed, despite what Sodz ...?'

'Of course I will.'

He looked at me. I knew what he was thinking. Xan. Tomorrow. It was do or die.

'It's nice you have your brother to look after you,' I said to Blossom. Then I looked at Ochre and I nodded. 'If he can't then I will. Understand?'

CHAPTER TWENTY ONE: THE RESCUE

The gun was loaded with a single bullet. What's the point in wasting ammunition? Even though the chances were that I would lose the gun I might as well retain the extra bullets. You can never tell.

It was a shame about the gun. I didn't want to let it go. But, after I'd got rid of Ochre, Sodz and Blossom wouldn't know I'd lost it. They would still do as I told them if I bluffed.

And Sodz was only here for one more day.

I left my room. At least I'd had a full night's sleep, though warped and peppered-through with shards of broken dreams. Downstairs, I looked in through the garage doorway. Sodz was still asleep, it seemed, and Blossom sat cross-legged on her furrowed bedclothes, reading. I had given her The Count of Monte Cristo. Ochre knelt by Kapko with his fingers on the old man's wrist.

'How is he?' I asked Blossom.

'Uncle? Not so good.'

'He's not revealed the secrets of his buried treasure yet?'

She shook her head.

I beckoned Ochre over when he'd finished taking Kapko's pulse. 'I need a word in private. I would like to show you …

something.' This was what we had agreed.

He played his part as if he was a puppet made of wood. Some people never learn to act. 'You understand that I'm not quali-fied. You ought to see a proper doctor.'

'Little chance of that,' I said. 'They got rid of the Drudjer docs and others left. Now it takes weeks for an appointment. Shall we use the downstairs loo?'

It's never easy fitting two men in a toilet but we managed and I showed him how to cock my gun and told him to be firm but gentle with the trigger. 'Once you've shot it off,' I said, 'keep hold of it. I'd like it back if possible.'

He nodded. 'And you'll rescue Xan.'

I promised. I can promise anything. I've practised and per-fected promising.

I put the safety catch back on and hid the gun down on the floor behind the toilet brush. I straightened up, unlocked the door, walked out into the corridor.

Straight into Sodz.

I hoped he'd not heard anything.

'I'll show you mine if you will show me yours? I didn't think this little runt would be your type. His backside's far too skinny and I wouldn't trust his mouth.' Sodz showed his teeth.

'It wasn't anything like that,' I said. 'It was a consultation.'

'I will show you mine and you can keep your skimpy little shorts on? Takes all sorts.'

'Shut up, for goodness sake,' said Ochre.

'I won't report you to the ethical authorities if you will let me take your sister in there.'

'Don't be stupid, Sodz,' I said as quickly as I could. I didn't want the boy to back out now. If Ochre thought his sister wasn't safe while he was rescuing his damsel in distress, he might decide to call the whole thing off.

I wanted Blossom for myself.

The street was silent as I left the house. I wondered whether Nikov had already gone to work. He'd said he had a busy day today; that's why he had postponed arresting Sodz.

As I walked underneath the arch, the Officer recited:
> 'Earth to earth, ash to ash, dust to dust
> Greed for greed, hate for hate, lust for lust.
> If there's someone you'd save
> Then you have to be brave
> But it's fools who give hustlers their trust.'

It made me jump.

But he was always talking nonsense. Anyway, he'd got that wrong, completely wrong. I wasn't saving anyone.

Outside the Town Hall I could see more Peacemakers than usual. Should I call this whole thing off? I didn't want him getting hurt. I liked him. It was such a shame. If he was not her brother … But there's never any point in thinking things like that. You have to journey in the world: if there are mountains then you have to climb, if there are lakes you have to swim, if there are forests you will need to bring an axe.

The entrance area was crowded. I saw Nikov standing by the desk. He seemed to be deploying people: as I watched he spoke to somebody and pointed; after they'd gone trotting off he started talking to another. 'Mr Angelo,' he called out when he saw me. 'Just the man. The Boss wants you for breakfast. Do you know the way? Don't worry. You will see your Drudjer later. I am sure she'll keep.' That raised a raucous laugh.

'She isn't going anywhere,' I answered. When you're being laughed at, laugh along. It's safer on the inside of the flock.

I walked downstairs and through the corridors. I went into the archive room and threaded in between the shelves of secrets. When I reached the door that led into the dining room and office of the Boss, I found it closed. I hesitated. He had sent for me. What did he want? And, more importantly, what did he know?

'Come in,' he roared before I had a chance to knock. I turned the handle, opened up the door, and poked my head inside, preparing to withdraw.

The breakfast had been cleared away; the table too. The centre of the room was dominated by a punchbag, hanging from a pyramid of chains hooked to a metal ring set in the ceiling. He stood beside it. He was wearing bright blue boxing shorts - his belly overflowed - and matching gloves. He stood, his feet a little way apart, on hulking legs. His chest was bigger than a barrel, bigger than a hogshead, bigger than a butt. His breasts were slabs of steak, the nipples sharp, protruding from a forest, thickly furred. His upper arms were thicker than my thighs.

He was so sweaty that his body shone.

'Come in,' he said and punched the bag as hard as hell. It swung towards me, thumping into me, surprising me. I stumbled, nearly tumbled, shocked.

'You want to know the secret? Never hold your breath. Punch while you're breathing out.' He slammed again into the bag. This time I dodged.

'A boxer throws his punches swiftly,' said the Boss, 'like this: left, right, then left.' He matched his actions to his words. 'And then, as soon as you've attacked, defend.' He crouched, his fists beside his head, protecting it.

'Keep balanced,' he explained. 'Don't overpunch. The force should come not from your shoulders but your heart. I think of all the bastards I have ever known. And then ...' his arm shot out to catch the bag as it was swinging back; it shuddered to a stop. 'You have a choice: to eat or to be eaten. That's the way that fellow saw the world. Survival of the ...' - and he sent the punch bag swinging with a roundhouse - '... fittest.'

Then he stood and faced me, gloved hands on his hips. 'Three minutes, then a minute to recover. It's a smashing way to exorcise your ghosts.'

I thought about the Memsahib.

'Would you like a go?' he offered. 'I should think that you have lists and lists of bastards you would like to punch.'

I shook my head.

'I bet you have. We all have bastards hiding in the corners of our memory. This is the way to set them free and punish them. Come on,' he urged. 'I'll tell you mine if you will tell me yours.'

I nodded. I felt terrible. I didn't want to do this but I didn't dare say no. If I refused, I thought that I might end up as his punch bag. If I played along, I might betray my secrets. I was scared.

'My father was a stupid bastard,' said the Boss. 'He taught me all he knew, and that was mostly how to use my fists.' He turned and whacked the bag. 'When he was drunk he thought he was the ruler of the world. He couldn't even rule his wife.' Another jab. 'He thought he was so clever but a pair of Drudjer con men took him for a ride. He hadn't got a clue.' A one-two combination. 'He had been so big before that happened; afterwards he seemed so small.' He moved a little closer to the bag and threw a hook. 'Last time I saw him, he was on his way. Good riddance to bad rubbish.' And he hit the bag again: an uppercut. 'He let me down. I hate a man who lets me down.' Another hook. 'I hate a man who tries to cheat me; no one cheats me twice.' He moved a little further back and jabbed and jabbed and jabbed. 'I hate a traitor more than anything.'

He knows, I thought. How? No one knew except for Nikov and myself. Had Nikov told him? Had the whole performance on that rooftop been a lure to make me implicate myself? I watched the Boss assault the punch bag. I imagined I was swinging there, my wrists above my head, my body dangling from a hook. I thought about the bruises I would have, the broken bones, my kidneys ruptured and my liver mashed.

He paused, his gloved fists on his knees, stooped, panting. 'You,' he said.

'My wife,' I said, unthinkingly, 'betrayed me with my boss.' I stopped. What had I said? He was the Boss. His wife had been betraying him. With Sodz. For which he murdered her. My stupid mouth. He'll think I know. He'll think that I suspect him.

'Ancient news.' He shook his head. 'If I were you and I met Kapko in the street I'd batter him to death.' He threw himself upon the punch bag. One, two, three, four, five. But this was not a frenzy. You could see it in the contours of his face. He knew what he was doing. He was viciousness controlled.

At least he didn't know about the Drudjers. Nikov hadn't told him. That was something.

'On the other hand, if you were me.' He shook his head. 'I dread to think. You are the sort to turn the other cheek. It isn't manly.' One last time, he thumped the punch bag. Suddenly he stopped. He turned and faced me. Sweat was steaming from his body and the spicy odour of his body scratched the inside of my nose. 'Imagine you are walking down the street. You meet a Drudjer heifer in her filthy rags. She's begging. How do you react?'

I knew the answer he expected. 'Cross the road.'

'And you'll feel guilty, won't you? All those years you have been told it's nice if you are nice. Well let me tell you why you're wrong. So you can stop pretending. First, they lie. They're not as badly off as they would make you think. A lot of beggars have a bank account. They don't pay tax. They beg because they're lazy. Secondly, they want to make you think you're in the wrong. They want you to apologise. Because they're poor. Well, pardon me. Imagine if your wife suggested it was your fault she was having sex with other men. How's that? What did you do? Were you the one to strip her naked? Was it you who strapped her to the bed? Did you procure the Drudjer man to cover her? When I find Sodz, I'll make him squeak; he won't be singing basso any more. Before I've finished with him he'll be begging me to let him die. I'll caponise him, stuff a carrot up his arse, truss him with twine, insert a slice of lemon underneath his skin and barbecue him slowly on a spit.'

Now he was panting. He had lost his place. 'Where was I?'

'Begging Drudjers.'

'Yes, I know, I know, I have been telling you about those Drudjer beggars. We had done the first two? Yes, I know. We're up to number three. So, thirdly, if you featherbed the Drudjers you are harming all of us. Our species must evolve progressively; if you protect the weaklings you will let them reproduce and that allows their weak, decrepit DNA,' - he did a little, limping dance as if he was a sissy which, for someone of his bulk, looked like a travesty- 'to taint and to pollute the gene pool. One, two, three.' He counted on his fingers. 'Fourthly, most importantly, your softness undermines the Peacemakers. You think you're being generous. But ask yourself why they are hungry, why they're thirsty, why they're outcasts, why their clothes are torn and poorly-fitting, why they're ill, why they are on the wrong side of the law? You have to ask yourself these questions. Why? They'll tell you it's because they have been persecuted by the Peacemakers. It's nonsense. Let me tell you that's a load of bull. Dig down a little further. Use your head. Why would we waste our efforts and our time if there was any other way to run society? Tell me that. You can't. We keep the peace, that's why we're called the Peacemakers. It's in the name. The answers on the label, stupid. This is what we do. We keep the peace. They threaten it. It's not our fault that they're in such a state. They're poor because they are inadequate. And if you help them all you're doing is condoning their deficiencies.

Now there were little bits of spittle flying from his mouth. I let them hit me, trying not to flinch. I didn't want to draw attention to a weakness. That would anger him. He was already in a rage.

'I'm telling you: be wary of your Drudjer. If you reach a hand out she will bite it off. That's what they're like. You give a little money and they ask for more. You take them home and they take over and, before you know it, they are living there like Lord and Lady Mucky Pup and you're their bloody servant.'

I'd have liked to swallow but I couldn't. Had he guessed? Did he know Xan's proposal; that we ought to sabotage the System? Did he know I had a garage full of Drudjers, each one telling me what I should do?

'You see?' As if to show that he was in a playful mood, he punched me on the shoulder and it hurt. 'I know.' My mouth was dry. 'I know exactly what you're like. But stick with me and I will teach you how to toughen up. I'll make you strong.'

He clapped his boxing-gloved hand on my shoulder and I shook. He turned me till his mouth was close enough to bite my ear off if he chose. 'But don't betray me. I hate traitors worse than anything.'

It was nearly time, I thought, for Ochre to attack.

CHAPTER TWENTY TWO: XAN'S SECRET

When I got to the office I was shaking.

What had Nikov told the Boss? About the Drudjers? Maybe, yes, perhaps. But not about the coup. He couldn't have. He wouldn't. He'd be dead by now. And so would I.

Unless the Boss was fishing. Maybe he had spotted something in the current. Was he using me as bait? To catch a shark you pour a little blood into the water. Any blood. It doesn't matter where you get the blood from. No one cares. It's only bait.

Could he be using me to snare his second in command? We planned to use the trial of Sodz to turn the tables on the Boss. Did he intend a further twist?

But this was paranoia. Nobody could know about our plan: just Nikov and myself. I'd not said anything to anyone. So why would Nikov?

But.

When Nikov spoke to me last night he had attempted to recruit me to a plot he had already thought about: assassination. Maybe I was not the first. Why should I be? Perhaps he had already sounded others out and been rejected. Maybe one of them had spoken to the Boss.

Was that what this was all about? Was this the Boss recruiting me to spy on Nikov?

No, I didn't think so. Not like this. The Boss, if he was to enlist me as a sleuth, would offer me two options: you inform on Nikov or the next time that we meet for breakfast you'll be on the table; I will carve. That's how he'd do it. Not by dropping hints. He'd be as blunt as buttocks.

And, besides, I couldn't tell on Nikov. Nikov knew about the Drudjers. I was stuck.

'What's eating you?' asked Xan. She sat there, lolling, hands behind her head, and watched me think. She hadn't even logged into the System yet.

'What are you doing?' I demanded. 'You should be at work by now.'

'No. Not today. I thought I'd have a holiday.'

The Boss was right, I thought. You give a Drudjer half an inch, they take the piss.

I wondered whether Xan had told the Boss about the Drudjers in my garage. She had said she might. 'Get back to work right now,' I yelled at her. To think that Ochre was about to risk his life for her and she was happy to betray him in exchange for her release. The Boss was right again. You couldn't trust a Drudjer.

'What is wrong with you?' she asked. She sounded grumpy but she turned round and started logging in. The Boss was right a third time: you can only motivate a Drudjer heifer if you bully her.

I walked across so I was standing over her, so, when she looked at me, she must look up. 'Have you been talking to the Boss?' I watched her closely. I was sure she would deny it. But I couldn't tell. She was inscrutable. Our faces, born of our habitual honesty, grow hot, or else our eyes grow shifty when we lie. But Drudjers, being practised fibbers, have been trained to keep their features utterly impassive as the untruths bubble from their lips.

'Don't be so stupid, Ed. Would I be here right now if that had happened? Where would you be?'

In the kitchen, I imagined, being plucked and gutted, cleaned and trussed and popped into the oven. If they had one big enough.

'Get back to work,' I said. 'I need to think.'

Xan said: 'A trouble shared?'

I shook my head.

She said: 'Why don't you ask your System?'

'That's ridiculous.'

'You're worried. That's because you don't know what the future holds. That's what the System's for. You could try tea leaves, I suppose, But seriously, if you want to take decisions, you must start with what you know.'

I knew that Nikov knew about the Drudjers and was prepared to overlook them. I might hope that, if and when the Boss found out, he'd be as tolerant, but I didn't know that. Not for sure. It was a risk.

So I was stuck with Nikov.

So I was committed to the plan. At least it wasn't murder. But the trouble was that it was happening tomorrow and I wasn't ready. There was such a lot to think about.

I swallowed. If I had to do what must be done it would be better if I did it perfectly. I had to get it right. But last night I had tried to think about our plans and, when at last I fell asleep, I started having dreams of all the things that might go wrong.

I'd dreamed that Nikov, Sodz and I were kneeling on the little wall that rimmed the roof above the Tower Block. The Boss, dressed in a judge's robes, a black silk handkerchief perched on his wig, had been set up above us: he was standing, feet apart, upon the entrance to the stairs, as if he was a statue and the rest of us, comparatively little men, must creep beneath his legs to leave the stage. I dreamed that Sodz had been reluctant to perform his part, which I could understand, for if he got his lines wrong he'd be murdered for the murder of the Memsahib. I had dreamed that when we tried to turn the tables on the Boss, accusing him, he laughed and mentioned something we had overlooked, a crucial piece of evidence. I dreamed that then the roof began to tilt. I felt my knees against the parapet begin to slide. As I slipped off I tried to clutch the wall but it was smooth and handholdless. I tried to scrabble for a purchase with my toes but all that happened was I scraped skin from my feet. I started falling.

That was when I woke. My heart was palpitating. I was water-logged with sweat. And I was on the floor; I'd tumbled from the bed.

I lay among the tangled bedclothes which had slithered off with me. I tried unravelling the message of the dream. What was that vital evidence we'd overlooked?

This is the trouble with a dream. Some parts are vivid and exact and other moments fluid and obscured. I knew, as certain as I know I am, that there was something that I didn't know. I felt it had to do with Faith.

She had been hunting treasure on the roof.

It was absurd to think that anyone would bury treasure on a roof.

What had I missed?

If there were secrets on that roof then why had Nikov taken me up there? So he could frighten me; because he knew I was afraid of heights? But not the first time. He had not known then. That time he'd let me think that we were going to the Tower Block so I could see the crime scene but we'd scarcely hesitated there. We'd gone straight up.

I had assumed it was his special place, his source, his Sinai, his Parnassus. But there was another, more prosaic, possibility.

When Nikov took me there the first time, I'd assumed it was because there were no cameras or microphones upon the roof, so he could speak to me as plainly as he wished. And yesterday when he had frankly talked about his plan to kill the Boss, he must have known that he would not be overheard. But maybe I was wrong.

Was someone staking out the roof?

I'd not seen anything but that proved nothing. I had only noticed there were lights when they turned on.

I thought I knew of all the covert electronic systems that kept tabs on people in the town. I thought I knew them all because they'd be a part of System A. But would they?

'Xan, do we have any System inputs on the Tower Block?'

Of course we didn't, that would be preposterous, she pointed out. The Boss would have been spying on himself. He lived up there.

Unless he didn't know.

'Is it not possible,' I said, 'that there's another System parallel to ours?'

'Of course it's possible but what would be the point?'

'To guard the guards. To spy upon the spies.'

She shrugged. 'How would we know?'

The Tower Block was built by Kapko Industries, a company

who built their fortune on a System that collected data to be used for more effective management. What made more sense than that the System should be turned upon itself to help him run his company?

Suppose that Nikov had discovered this. That would explain why he'd been so determined that the trial of Sodz should be conducted on the rooftop. With some skill and quite a lot of luck he could manipulate the angles of the hidden cameras, the cameras that nobody but him knew anything about, to stream proceedings to the Peacemakers, to make the Boss appear as somebody corrupt, so utterly corrupt he killed his wife, so totally and irredeemably corrupt that he'd attempted to frame someone else as murderer.

It was a plan, a clever plan. It might just work.

But if there was a System keeping tabs upon the roof, then why was Nikov unafraid of being overheard when he was up there urging the extermination of the Boss?

He had been standing on the little parapet around the edge. I had assumed it was bravado. Now I realised he must have known that he was out of sight of cameras and out of range of microphones.

You don't, I thought, get cleverer than that. The good news was that if he was as bright as that, I reckoned we might have a chance.

I got no further in my thinking. Malc walked in. He held a pair of handcuffs. Straight away I knew I was in trouble.

'Nikov wants you. Better get a fucking move on, mate.'

'N ... Nikov?' But if Nikov wanted me he wouldn't send a man like Malc. Must be the Boss. This was a stupid game of cat and mouse. The Boss had let me go; now he was hauling me back in again. It's how you break a paper clip: by bending it this way and that until it comes apart.

Malc walked to Xan. She held her hands up and he locked the manacles around her wrists. 'His orders. Drudjer heifer's coming too.'

'What's going on?'

And then I knew. With chilling sure-as-sunset certainty, I knew. This was the work of Ochre. What an idiot. It's what he'd said that he would do. I thought I'd talked him out of it. He'd planned to seize a hostage. He had dreamed that Xan would be released as quid pro quo. I'd told him that it wouldn't work.

He would be killed. For goodness sake, he only had a single bullet in his gun.

There'd be a gunfight; Ochre would be shot. And Xan. And anyone who happened to be closer than they ought to be. Like me if I was there.

'Not me,' I said to Malc. 'You don't want me. Just Xan.'

'He fucking said he wants the fucking pair of you and I'll be fucked if I will fucking let him down.'

I went in front, Xan in the middle, Malc behind. These days I seemed to spend my life in corridors and one-way streets. And never going where I wanted. Always setting my direction in the way that someone else was pointing.

I was sick of it.

I listened to our footsteps as we climbed the stairs. Three pairs of feet. We seemed to synchronise. A Drudjer and a Peacemaker and me. In time. That wasn't very likely. Step and step and step and each step closer to the end. The top. I was in front; I'd be the first. I braced myself.

There wasn't anybody in reception. That was odd. I'd never

seen it empty.

'Been a fucking terrorist attack,' said Malc. 'Some fucking crazy shooting at the guards.'

Instinctively, I ducked.

He laughed. 'Don't worry Mr Dataman. You're safe with Malc. The little fucker ran away.'

'Where are the guards?'

'They're after him. Like fucking blood-dogs. Little fucker doesn't stand a chance.'

We walked outside into the courtyard. There was no suggestion of disruption. Ochre's shot had mattered less than snowflakes on a mountainside.

Two Peacemakers were sitting at a table playing chess. 'You can't do that,' objected one. 'A bishop only moves along diagonals. Why don't you take my pawn? It's all alone. Just waiting to be captured. That's the way. You're sure. Okay. I'll take your bishop with my knight. You didn't see that coming, did you? Got to watch for that when you play chess. It's what we call a sacrifice.' He sat back, satisfied, his predatory fingers interlocked across his stomach. Then he glanced at us. 'Is that the data cruncher and his Drudjer?'

'Yes. Seen Nikov?' Malc replied.

'He couldn't wait. He left his keys. He said you had to take them to his house.'

Malc swore. 'But I'm on fucking duty. I can't leave the premises.'

'He said the data guy could take her.'

'Him?' Malc looked disgusted.

'Me?' I was appalled.

'He said you knew exactly where he lived.'

'That's where we're going?'

'Fucking dataman? You can't trust him. He'll let her run away. These fucking number crunchers couldn't hold onto their bollocks if they weren't attached to them.'

'He said that' - here the chess-man started speaking in a made-up voice that tried but failed to mimic Nikov - 'Mr Angelo would comprehend the consequences if the Drudjer fled. He talked about a fall from grace. - You sure you want to move your castle there? Well, if you're certain. There. I think that's check. - The question that you have to ask is why does Nikov want the heifer taken to his home?'

Malc's laugh was too high-pitched to be a dirty chuckle; higher even than a snigger, more a giggle. 'Nikov doesn't want a witness. Mister Fucking Purity. I always knew it was a fucking front. He always fucking acted like he was too good to stoop to fucking Drudjers but I knew that sometime soon ...'

'He would succumb?' the chess-man asked, his finger on the bonnet of his queen.

'Suck what?' said Malc.

'Succumb. Surrender to her charms. Capitulate.'

Malc made a face. 'The fucker wants to fucking fuck her, if that's what you mean.'

I glanced at Xan. She stared into the distance, eyes like shards of crystal in a cliff-face.

'I suppose the question is - no, you can't move there, that's check too - the question must be why he wanted data-nerd to take her.'

'No,' said Malc. 'He wouldn't. You are not suggesting Mister fucking Purity likes fucking fucking men.'

'Did I say that?' the chess-man asked. 'Might be a threesome?'

Malc seemed reassured.

'And then again,' said chess-man, 'number-cruncher might be Nikov's proxy.'

'What?' asked Malc.

'His proxy for the doxy,' said the chess-man. 'Proxy. Stand-in. Substitute. So Nikov doesn't have to do the dirty for himself.'

'His fucking substitute? But where's the fucking fun in that?'

'Some people,' said the chess-man, 'like to watch.'

From Malc's reaction it appeared he was so far from understanding voyeurism that when he himself was having sex it must be always in a darkened room and even then he'd keep his eyes tight shut.

This was - it had to be, I hoped it was - no more than dirty talk, the sort of banter beta men indulge in when they're jealous of the rutting opportunities of someone else. But what were the alternatives? Why else would Nikov have arranged for me to take her to his home?

I held my breath and let my thoughts explore the possibilities. I'd been too long without. Without the touch. Without the skin on skin. Without the rising and the raising and the swelling of the pressure and the build up and the boosting and the surge.

It would be pleasure, ripping off her clothes.

One to give, one to take, one to view.
Who is she? Who am I? Who are you?
Even naked we're masked;

And the question unasked
Is why I'm left alone in the queue.

'What?' asked Xan, 'is wrong with him?'

'The man is crazy,' I explained.

We walked beneath the arch. She didn't seem reluctant. She was striding out in front of me. I had to jog a step or two to catch her. Then she stopped.

The pair of us were standing in the middle of my street with Nikov's house exactly on our right and my house just a little further on, upon the left.

She said: 'You could just let me go.'

'I can't do that.'

'Take me to Ochre,' she commanded.

'No.'

'Why not?'

'They're watching us.'

She turned around. 'From here,' she said, 'you cannot see the Town Hall courtyard.' She kept turning to complete the circle. 'There is no one here except that funny little fellow on the arch. We're out of sight. This is our chance.'

'I can't.' It was a test. The bitch was tempting me. She knew I couldn't. 'Nikov might be watching from a window.'

'He isn't. Ed, please, listen; this might be my only chance. You heard them, what they said just now. He wants to rape me.'

'No,' I said, 'he doesn't. No. He wouldn't. Nikov's not like that.'

'He is a man,' she said, her heavy eyes downcast towards my waist.

She angered me with her assumptions. What she said. I'd like to punish her. In my mind's eye I saw her underneath me. I'd make her apologise. 'We're not all rapists,' I replied. 'Is Ochre?'

'Take me to him,' she replied.

'I can't.'

'Why not?'

Because he isn't there, I thought. I couldn't tell her that.

The door of Nikov's house was opened. Nikov stood there in the doorway, like a standing portrait in a frame that is too cheap for it. He beckoned and I gestured: Xan should go ahead. We walked to Nikov and he let us in.

The houses were identical except, as he had said, in his house there was no internal door into the garage.

'Shall we go upstairs?' he said.

We started climbing. I went first, Xan in between us, Nikov at the back. Because his house was in the middle of the terrace, Nikov had no window running up the stairs. It made the place seem darker.

As in my house, Nikov's lounge was on the middle floor. I hoped that's where we would be going. Xan was wrong, I thought. It wasn't rape. It couldn't be if I was forced to do it too.

We reached the middle landing. Faith was waiting for us there.

'Faith? What on earth?' I said. 'Whatever are you doing? Why are you here? What's all this about?'

Faith led the way into the lounge. She gestured at a sofa. 'There,' she said. 'Sit down.'

She acted like she owned the place. I knew that she and Nikov had been friends at school but maybe there was more to it than that.

Faith. Would she watch me too? I wasn't sure that I could handle that.

The couch was a two-seater, open-ended. Xan sat down. I didn't want to get too close, I perched as far away as I was able to: one buttock on the cushion of the sofa and the other hanging in the air. It wasn't easy.

On the wall behind me a colossal mirror had been hung. I knew this since it was reflected in another mirror on the far side of the room. I watched the images of Xan and me, perpetuated, bouncing back and forth till they were focussed in a tiny far-off point.

Two leather swivel office chairs had been positioned on the far side of the room. In front of one there was a leather footstool. On the footstool was a laptop, linked by cables to a camera lodged on a tripod. Facing us.

Not just for Nikov. This was not some solipsistic solitary voyeuristic masturbatory delight.

I couldn't. Not while being filmed.

This is the trouble with the Peacemakers: they're hypocrites. The warning had been unequivocal: don't mate with Drudjers, Nikov said. Besides, it was forbidden by decree. And now all this. Did he intend to force me to have sex with her so he had evidence against me, just in case the plans we had agreed last night went wrong?

Faith picked the laptop up and sat down with it on her knees. Then Nikov, standing just behind her, leaning so that he could see the laptop's screen across her shoulder, asked if we were comfy.

Xan held up her wrists.

'I think you'd better wear the manacles for now. When we start filming they'll contribute to the ambience. Perhaps it might be prudent if I kept the key.' He walked across to me and stretched his hand out and I fished it from my pocket and I placed it in his palm. He closed his fist on it.

'The thing is,' Nikov said, 'that I am really quite annoyed. You've angered me. In fact, I'm hurt. Your lack of trust has wounded me. You should have told me. In my ignorance I might have made a serious mistake.'

I said that there was nothing that I hadn't told him. Well, what else was I to say? It might be true. It was the Drudjers' fault. Since they'd arrived I'd had so many secrets I was finding it impossible to keep abreast of who knew what. 'There isn't anything that you don't know,' I said.

'I don't mean you.' He looked at Xan.

My heart descended faster than a body falling from a Tower Block.

Xan had suggested that we misreported System A to try to con the Peacemakers so they would take decisions which would damage them. She'd said it. That had not been me.

This set up with the camera was not about me having sex with Xan for Nikov's pleasure. It was not to make a sex tape so that afterwards he had an opportunity to blackmail me. It wasn't sex at all. It was interrogation. I was there so Nikov could pretend to Xan that I would rape her if she didn't spill the beans.

And if she called his bluff then Mister Purity would make me do it so that he could keep his hands clean. If he was to be the next Boss he could not afford to have his reputation sullied. So he'd stay behind the camera. So that by filming me he'd have the evidence that he was not involved. It bought my silence too. It would ensure my loyalty. I'd never dare do anything to damage him. If he released the pictures I would be destroyed.

'We'd better get this over with,' he said.

Faith reached a hand out to the camera and turned it slightly. Then she nodded.

'What's your name?' asked Nikov.

'Xan.'

'Xan what?'

She looked at him and shook her head. 'You're getting nothing from me, not while he's here.'

She meant me.

'Okay,' he said. He looked at me. 'Go home,' he said. 'You've played your part. Go home but, Mr Angelo, make sure you stay there. Later on I'll send for you. You must be at your home where I can find you when I want you. Go home now.'

'What's going on?' He didn't want me? That confused me.

'Go back home.'

I buggered off.

CHAPTER TWENTY THREE: BLOSSOMING

You know how, when you're taken to the edge and then let down, it's so much worse than never going anywhere at all.

I had a squirmy feeling in my gut, like hyper-sensitivity, like I was dancing and I couldn't stop, bare-footed, stumbling on a floor of shattered glass, like I was halfway here and halfway there and halfway somewhere else, and being pulled and prodded from all sides, and being summoned and repelled. Desire and desperation, badly mixed.

I crossed the road. I faced my own front door. This was my home. It didn't feel like it. Inside, I should be safe and snug and warm and cosy. It should be my refuge. It should be where I belong. But now the Drudjers were inside. I'd given sanctuary to them and lost it for myself. I felt estranged.

I had to force myself to put my key into the lock and turn it and to push the door and go inside. It took determination. And the last thing that I needed, then and there, was Blossom. Blossom in a storm.

'Where's Ochre, where's my brother, what, where is he, what's become of him?'

Some women look unsightly when they're scared or in a rage. Not Blossom. She was one of those who blushed, whose lips went pouty, who began to strut. She moved more. She was less protected. She'd been weeping, which she tried to hide but I could see it peeping from her angry words and attitudes. She was a little tiger. I'd enjoy the wrestle. She'd be putty to my moulding.

'Ochre's gone,' said Sodz.

I couldn't concentrate on him. She was the one I focussed on. His chatter was distracting. Something stupid about 'looking after Mr K' and 'going to the toilet' and 'the front door closed' and 'it was all that I could do to make her stay behind.'

She looked so hurt and haveable.

I faked surprise: 'He's left the house?'

Sodz, always Sodz, as irritating as an insect, buzzed, 'The runty little pipsqueak is obsessed with Xan.'

I tried to swat away the sting. I should be focussing on her. I wanted to.

'You have to go and look for him,' begged Blossom. 'You must go and find him now.'

She had enormous eyes when she was begging. I would make her beg. She had been crying. I would make her cry. I'd taste her salty weeping on my tongue. I'd taste her salt. I'd taste her.

'Did you know?' asked Sodz. 'Did he confide in you?'

'Please, Ed,' said Blossom and she placed the soft tips of her fingers on my arm. I shivered. Goose-bumped. Tingled. Flushed.

I muttered something. Ochre on a rescue mission. Thought I'd talked him out of it.

Each time she looked at me, I stalled. I couldn't speak. My tongue seemed swollen, too fat for my mouth. My lips seemed numb. My throat was parched.

'The idiot, el tonto, lo stupido, the dumb dipstick ...' Sodz was going on and on.

But Blossom seemed to be decided. She was calm. 'Please Ed, I'm begging you, go out and look for him.'

She looked at me. I wondered if she knew.

Her lips were firm, her face aware, her body was unbending but she turned and faced me and she put her arms down by her sides and let me fill my eyes. Her body seemed too delicate for what I wanted it to hold. Her stomach seemed too slender to accommodate what I desired. Her breasts, her hips, her buttocks…

'After Ochre left,' said Sodz, 'we heard what sounded like a gunshot.'

Blossom's features warped. I thought how close the look of grief was to the look of anger, to the look of lust. I tried to speak. All I could manage was to croak: 'Just one?'

Sodz nodded. 'But, you know, one is enough.'

'Please Ed, please go and look for him,' said Blossom. 'Find him. Bring him home.' She reached her hand towards me. 'I'll do anything.'

I swallowed.

'I'd do anything for Ochre,' Blossom said.

Sodz knew what we were saying. 'No.' He understood.

'Suppose he was your brother?' Blossom said.

'This isn't right,' said Sodz.

She said: 'Please don't tell Ochre.'

'Blossom …' Sodz began.

I interrupted. 'Go upstairs.'

She said: 'Please Sodz. This is the only thing that I can do for him.'

He said: 'He wouldn't want this.'

Time! I couldn't wait. I grabbed her by the arm. I tugged her to the bottom of the stairs.

She worried she'd be seen. I told her Sodz would stay with Kapko. What about the Peacemakers? she asked. What Peacemakers? I said. My mind was full, there was no room for Peacemakers. The bridge, she said. I roared at her to fucking climb the stairs. She scurried like a startled rabbit fleeing from a fox. She hesitated at the middle floor. Keep climbing. We would do it in my bedroom, on the double bed.

'He's out there,' I reminded her. 'The sooner that we get this over with, the sooner I can go and look for him.'

She scampered up the second flight of stairs. I had to hurry to keep up with her.

'You see?' I said. 'You want it too.'

She shook her head but she meant yes. She'd better.

'Take your clothes off. Let me see your skin.'

'You promise me that if I let you ... if we .... you will ...'

'Yes, yes, yes.'

'You have to promise.'

'Yes,' I yelled.

She started to undo the buttons of her blouse but I was too impatient so I grabbed the fabric and I ripped it open and she gasped. She tried to take it off but she'd forgotten it was buttoned at the cuffs and she was tangled in it. I was angry. I was shedding clothes. If I could strip why couldn't she? I was already naked and my cock was bigger, harder, stiffer than it had been for a long long time. I took it in my hand and stroked it, stroke, stroke, stroked it, while I watched her struggle with the blouse. For fuck's sake get a move on. Come on. Get a fucking move on. Hurry up.

At last her blouse could be discarded and she reached around, unfastening her bra. Her breasts were big, they tumbled out of it. Her areolae were enormous, haloing her nipples. She's so young, I thought. I reached out, touched a nipple. I was being gentle but she shuddered at my touch.

The bitch.

I opened up my paw and placed it on her pap and squeezed. She yelped.

'Behave yourself,' I said.

Her eyes were fixed upon my cock.

I ordered her to take her other clothes off. 'Naked. Now.'

She kicked her shoes off and unhooked her skirt, stepped out of it. She stood there in her panties. Navy blue. Plain panties. Not exactly sexy.

'Take them off.'

She didn't move.

I stepped towards her. She stepped back.

'Don't play around with me,' I said and slapped her on the cheek. Her head snapped round. She stumbled and she fell.

'Get up, get up,' She lay there on the ground. I reached down, grabbed her shoulders, hauled her to her feet. She tried to get away from me. I grabbed her knickers, pulled. Her bum was big; her hips spread wide. I tugged the knickers down below her knees. She was exposed.

My cock was bursting. With my right hand I reached down and cupped her crotch and with my left I touched her tit. She squirmed and writhed. She tried to push me backwards with her hands. She seemed to want to get away from her. I wasn't having that, not now, not just as things were hotting up. I took my fingers from her fanny and I grabbed a handful of her hair. She yelped. I pulled her downwards.

'Get down on your knees,' I told her. She obeyed. She didn't have a lot of choice. I put her in position so that she could suck me off. My cock felt like a tree trunk, rooted, gnarled. It touched her lips.

'No teeth,' I said. 'Be good. I'll only go and look for Ochre if you're nice to me.'

She wasn't very good at it. She hadn't had the practice, I supposed. Too young. She'd learn. I'd teach her.

'Make it good and wet,' I told her. 'You might be a little dry inside.'

She looked at me. I'd dreamed that I would see her looking up at me like this. Her eyes were wide, as I had hoped. But they were apprehensive. She was scared of me. I didn't like it. 'Close your eyes,' I yelled. I took my cock out of her mouth and then I pushed her over.

She was sprawling on the floor. I grabbed her knees. I yanked her legs apart. I lay on top of her. It was a fumble finding where to go. She wasn't ready. I was. More than. So I pushed and pushed and entered her.

She gasped.

I reassured her. 'You'll get used to it.'

I started moving, slowly, in and out.

But in the end I couldn't do it in the normal way. I couldn't look into her face. I couldn't bear to see her face. It wasn't right. It wasn't how a woman should behave. She should at least pretend.

I turned her round. I made her get down on her hands and knees. I took her from behind, as if we were a pair of mating dogs. I treated her just like the Drudjer that she was. I fucked her. Hard and fast.

She didn't make a sound. She should have made an effort. I was not expecting moans and squeals and yes, yes, yes, oh yes but something. All the music that accompanied my making love to her came from the ragged rasping of my breath and from the slapping of my thighs on hers and at the end my groan.

I came. I needed the release. I grabbed her hips, I dug my fingers into her soft body and I pulled her onto me and spurted semen into her. I held her for a moment as I shrivelled then I pushed her down, face down onto the bed, and rolled away from her.

A thought occurred to me. I touched my sticky dick. I brought my fingers close up to my face, examined them. No blood. 'I'm not your first,' I said.

I thought, I should be angry, I should feel betrayed. I sat up, looked at her still kneeling with her ass up in the air. I pushed her so she rolled onto her back. I grabbed her face and squeezed it. 'Look at me! I'm not your first.'

I saw her staring back with frightened eyes. 'You are a slut,' I said. 'How many have you had?'

She had that dumb look Drudjer women sometimes get, the sullen, obstinate, pig-headed look. 'I need to know,' I told her. 'Have you given me the pox?' They said all Drudjers were diseased. 'Are you some kind of prostitute?'

'Just one,' she muttered.

'Who?' I asked. 'A Drudjer, I suppose. Not him, not Sodz?'

She shook her head.

'Then who?'

She shook her head again. She angered me. I grabbed her throat. I squeezed. I saw her eyes go wide. 'Tell me his name,' I said. She couldn't breathe. I saw her frightened face. 'Tell me his name,' and I relaxed my grip. She choked. 'Tell me his name or I will strangle you.'

'My Uncle.'

'Kapko?'

'Yes.' She nodded. In her eyes were tears.

CHAPTER TWENTY FOUR: THE CHASE

So much for good old Uncle Kapko. He'd persuaded Ochre to accompany him, when he fled the Kennels, with promises that Blossom would be saved as well. Then he had gone to Blossom with a proposition: if she let him fuck her he would bring her with him on his great escape … and he'd let Ochre come as well. He'd played them both. His brother's kids. So much for family.

He'd had my wife. I'd had his niece. I guess that made us even.

I decided I was owed another fuck with Blossom. That would put me one ahead.

We went downstairs in silence. Sodz was in the hall. He sniffed. He said to me: 'You look like you're the cat who has devoured the cream.' He turned to her: 'And you look like you've been well licked.'

'Ochre mustn't know,' she said. 'Please Sodz. He mustn't know.'

'For his sake,' Sodz replied.

Now she demanded that I search for Ochre. My side of the bargain. But how could I? I'd been told by Nikov that I had to stay at home. I didn't tell her that. I told her I would start the hunt at once. I went outside. I closed the door. She wouldn't know.

By standing on my doorstep I was following instructions.

Nikov hadn't said I had to wait inside.

And here was just as good a place as any to find Ochre. If I wandered round the streets there was a chance that I would miss him, but if I stood still, stayed here, then soon, or if not soon then later, he would come to me. If he was still alive.

So I was watching from across the street when Faith came out of Nikov's house. She closed the door behind her and she waited for a moment. As she looked around. I ducked behind the hedge. I don't know why. It was because she looked so surreptitious.

Something wasn't right. I didn't understand her. When she spoke she sounded genuine, except that didn't jigsaw with the way she acted. Selling her black market goods was one thing, being friends with Nikov was another. It was not her fault that she had gone to school with him but filming Xan while Nikov was ... whatever he was doing; that was unacceptable.

And all that crap she talked about the church.

I watched her as she checked the coast was clear. A long slow sweeping scan across the houses in the street. A concentrated scrutinising stare towards the archway; could she see the Officer? She sniffed the air. She nodded. Then she turned.

She must have called to Nikov. In a moment Xan came out, still handcuffed. Nikov followed. They began to walk towards the river. I crouched down so that they couldn't see me, so that I was hidden by the hedge. I had sporadic glimpses of them through the branches as they passed my house. 'We'll leave him there, for now,' said Nikov. 'I can pick him up when I return.'

What did he want with me?

I ached. It wasn't good to squat. My thighs were shrieking and my back began to throb. I was afraid I'd topple over. Had they passed? I couldn't see them at the moment but my view was limited by leaves. I couldn't hear them. Was it safe to take a peek? I couldn't bear it any longer, but it wasn't easy, even once I'd made my mind up. I tried to stand. The pins and needles in my calves were agony. Thank goodness they were out of sight because I had to hop from foot to foot to help restore the blood flow. Then I wasted precious seconds rubbing as my muscles stung and burned. So, by the time I had the chance to take a look, they'd disappeared.

This was all, I thought, because of bloody Ochre. Malc had come with manacles for Xan a short time after Ochre fired his shot. They must have captured him; they must have made him talk. He would have squealed at once. He'd have been proud to tell them that he did it all for Xan. That would have puzzled them: they weren't the sort to understand the concept of self-sacrifice. They would have reckoned there was something dodgy going on. Some secret Xan possessed, perhaps. That's why they'd taken her to Nikov's house to be interrogated. That was why …

But why did Nikov want to speak with me? And how was Faith involved?

I had to know the answers to these questions.

They'd been heading for the river. If they went straight on they'd reach the footbridge. Now it was unguarded they could cross it to the north bank and continue on into the Kennels. Hadn't Nikov said the Kennels had been booby-trapped? I doubted even he would risk a minefield.

So they hadn't gone across the bridge.

There were alternatives. They might have stayed on the south bank and turned along the path to town. I didn't doubt that Nikov knew it; he'd grown up round here. But if he'd wanted to go that way, why not use the road? A Peacemaker like Nikov doesn't need to hide.

The other possibility was if they had turned left before the footbridge, and continued down the road Madame had parked in when she'd brought those cans of chopped tomatoes. That would take them to the hospital. It must be that. That was where Ochre had intended to seek refuge; he had worked there; he had known where he could hide; perhaps a cupboard where the catheters were kept and where a trainee doctor could enjoy a spot of rest and procreation with a nurse. So I assumed that he'd been caught and Nikov had been sent for.

Perhaps they thought that maybe if Xan saw her lover injured, bleeding in the gutter, maybe if they offered her the chance to save him if she gave them what they wanted, maybe then she'd give the game away.

I knew she had a secret: she'd refused to talk to Nikov while I sat beside her on the sofa. I deduced her secret must concern myself. What did she have on me?

The only thing that I could think about was the proposal she had made to use my System to beguile the Peacemakers. But that was her idea. I'd only ever half agreed so she'd keep working. I supposed that she might twist it all around and claim it had been my suggestion. In the end it all boiled down to who you would believe. She was a Drudjer.

So it wasn't that; it couldn't be.

The only other thing she knew was that I hosted Drudjers. Why would Nikov want her telling him what he already knew?

So not that either.

Which meant that there must be something else. Involving me and yet ... A secret that I didn't know about. What could it be?

My blood ran cold. Could there be something wrong with System A?

Xan must have worked on it at Kapko Industries. Or Kapko told her something. I'd been taken off it. I'd invented it but I had been assigned to other projects. Kapko must have interfered with it. Perhaps he added malware like a virus or a Trojan. That was just the sort of thing he'd do; he'd see it as a safeguard for his intellectual property. My System. He'd have taken Xan into his confidence because she was a Drudjer. Drudjers stick together. Keep us out. They would have laughed at me.

I don't like being laughed at.

Somehow Nikov had become aware that there was something wrong; he'd learned that Xan might have the answers. That was why he'd said that he was coming back for me. Once Xan divulged the details he'd be asking me to put things right.

Or else he'd blame me.

Xan could fib. What if she were to say to Nikov the malicious software was a part of my design? He might believe her. Then I'd be in trouble.

It was crucial that I found out what she said. I had to follow them.

But I had reached the parting of the ways and still there was no sign of Nikov, Faith and Xan. Where had they gone? Across the footbridge? Left? Or right? I stood there, lost, uncertain.

Then I saw the half-glimpse of the murmur of a movement from across the river, not direct but to the right. It must be them. Perhaps it was a duck. It couldn't be.

There was a path along the bank but it led nowhere. No one went that way. There wasn't anywhere that you could get to on that path. Except the church. St Jude's. Where Faith heard Nikov singing in the choir.

Why were they going there?

St Jude's was decommissioned and abandoned when the Drudjers were migrated to the Kennels. It was on the margin of the ghetto, and the Peacemakers believed, and probably correctly, that its graveyard offered hiding-places for escaping Drudjers. On the other hand, they couldn't let the Drudjers have a church, not even after it had been deconsecrated. Somehow there seemed something blasphemous about polluting previously sacred places. So the church and churchyard were surrounded with a fence which was electrified and topped with razors. No-man's land. Not even God's. Not any more.

I caught another glimpse of movement and I knew. It was them. I just didn't understand.

Unless it was a decoy. That would be a clever trick. You go across the footbridge. Your pursuer thinks you must be going to the Kennels; nowhere else makes sense. He doesn't know about the booby-traps. The predator becomes the trophy. Nikov isn't stupid. That's a cunning way to shake your tail.

I waited till I was quite sure that they were out of sight and then I followed, scampering across the bridge and plunging down the footpath. That bit wasn't easy. There were places where the thorny branches arched out of their parent knots to pluck at me, to scratch at me, to claw my face or try to trip me up as I walked past. That slowed me down. I didn't dare to make a sound. But on the other hand I didn't want to catch them up. For all I knew they had been halted by the fence. And even, as seemed probable, if Nikov had a key or knew a secret gateway, it might take him time to pass into the churchyard. So I stumbled onwards, making patchy progress, and I paid the price with stings and scrapes and scars.

I had been right. There was a gate into the churchyard. It was open when I reached it. No one was in sight.

Was this a trap?

I lingered for a moment, hiding in the foliage. Then I saw movement from the corner of my eye. I snapped my head around to stare ... into the river. Here there was an underwater obstacle. The water whirled around to form an eddy which had trapped some rubbish that was being carried by the current. Sticks and polystyrene food containers, cardboard cups and condoms, chased each other, churning endlessly.

They must have gone into the church.

To follow I would have to leave my cover, I would have to walk across the graveyard in full view of anyone who cared to have a peek. If Nikov saw me, how would I explain myself? Would he believe me if I said I was a fan of sacred architecture?

I was no believer. Though I'd lived in town for years I'd hardly ever popped in to this church. The last time I had visited, it was because they had a book fair held to raise some funds to help look after refugees. But I'd found nothing there to float my boat so I had wandered round the pillars, goggled at the roof, deciphered the inscriptions on a tomb or two, admired a stained glass window and gone home.

What I remembered was the sense of being out of place or rather, maybe, out of time. The building and its contents seemed to clash. It was as if it was an echo of a long-gone world, an echo that had been distorted, silenced, reimagined, amplified and turned around. St Jude's, I had discovered, had been founded in the age of plagues and superstition, trashed by the puritans and torched in the Enlightenment, and then rebuilt by people who enriched themselves from coal (or rather who had been enriched by those who sweated underground). The pits were now exhausted, empty hollows. St Jude's too had served its purpose. Barricaded by the Peacemakers. Dehallowed. Dead and emptied. Filled with nothing but its tombs.

I ran. I fled across the graveyard to the entrance of the church. I scuttled up the seven steps into the shelter of the porch. I stopped. I had to think. The wooden door was not quite closed. It wasn't really open. It was, just, ajar; a gap no wider than my hand. I could see nothing, only darkness. I could hear no sound. I pressed my palm against the door. It moved. It opened up a little. Nothing. So I pushed again until the opening was wide enough to squeeze through. Once again I listened. Not a murmur. Breath abated, I stepped through the crack into the emptiness.

If they were looking, they would see me now. I knew that I was silhouetted in the daylight streaming through the door. I closed it carefully. Dark fell, as black as blindness. That's the thing about the door into a church. It might be noon in summer on a sunny day, the light outside might be alive and brilliant, but past the porch you enter silence, darkness, gloom. It's always cold inside a church. It's always sombre.

Nervously, I waited for my eyes to grow accustomed to the wretched twilight.

Just inside the door there was a stoup of holy water. Squatting on the far side of the basin was a grinning monumental demon. I crouched down behind its arrow-headed tail and glanced around.

Still there was only soundlessness.

With all those flat, stone surfaces. I should have heard at least an echo.

Why, if they were in the church, could I not hear them? If they weren't in here, where had they gone?

In films and games and books a hunter flits, as if an acrobat, from hiding place to hiding place. I hurried to a column, squashed myself against it, looked around. I saw a painting, oil on canvas, gilt-framed, fastened to the wall. A saint and martyr was depicted, twice as large as life and mostly naked, lying on a grid above a pit of glowing coals, as if he was the main course in a barbecue. He must be sore, I thought.

I scuttled to another column, passing an immense St Stephen being stoned by someone whose determined stare, directed at the viewer, challenged me to grab a rock and cast it too.

Was that a mumble? It was something like the sound of distant voices but this echo chamber jumbled and distorted them so I could hear them but I couldn't understand what they were saying. Given how the sounds were bounced around the walls I couldn't even guess in which direction they were coming from.

I lurched a little further down the nave. I stumbled on a loosened flagstone. Half the floor was carved with names and dates and in memoriams and RIPs. This is another thing with churches. They are warehouses for skeletons.

So I progressed, in fits and stops, towards the transept, seeing saints. A picture of Saint Lucy being blinded with a quill, a martyrdom the painter must have dreaded. Saint Bartholomew, the top half of his body flayed, his skin draped toga-like across the raw flesh of his shoulder, stared at me. Next came Saint Joan of Arc, still chatting to her angels as she burned, Saint Benjamin impaled upon a stake, and Saint Sebastian, transfixed with arrows to his tree.

I wondered whether little Nicky had been schooled by Father Kerrigan. Cook, stone, blind, flay, burn, saw, impale and pierce. Was that why Nikov was the way he was?

I was surprised the Peacemakers had not removed the paintings from the walls. Would not these images of sanctified brutality suit bedroom walls for someone like the Boss? Or they could sell them. Letting them stay here inside a church whose neighbour was a ghetto full of Drudjers was, you would have thought, condemning them to being looted or defaced.

At last I reached an over-ornamented rood screen. Peeping through the archway I could see the choir stalls and the altar. Were they hiding there? But then I heard more muttering and I realised that it was coming from my left. There was a little doorway there. Some steps led downwards. They were underneath me, in the crypt. I moved on tiptoes, passing wooden carvings: sinners, twisted and grotesque, encircled by a gang of pitchforked devils, being driven down to hell. The portal to the undercroft had been adorned with images of what appeared to be a kitchen, with a butcher's board and cooking pots and skewered meat above a flowering of flame. But all the flesh was human. Well, I thought, you can't say that I've not been well and truly warned.

Against the wall, or rather peeling from it, was a piece of laminated paper: underneath an arrow pointing down, someone had scrawled the words: 'One way'.

I hesitated for a moment. I could hear the voices well enough to know where they were coming from. But, echoed and re-echoed by the walls and steps and ceiling of the passage down into the vault, the sounds were still too indistinct for me to understand what they were saying. I would have to get a little closer.

I went downwards hesitantly: one step at a time and putting both feet on each step before attempting to descend the next. I used a hand against the wall to guide me. I supposed, belatedly, when I was nearly half way, that I might be entering a trap. If I was spotted, if I had to get away, I couldn't climb these steps, not quickly; I'd be caught. My best chance was to find a hiding place inside the crypt.

The air down here felt greasy. It slid oozily into my nostrils. I could feel it smearing in my mouth. There was a nasty, acrid smell. I tasted something gritty in between my teeth.

'Ah, here he is,' I heard Faith say.

I ducked into a shady corner of the undercroft.

It was a lengthy vault, divided into two parts by a waist, so that in plan it would have seemed a little like a figure eight. My end was dominated by a cuboid tomb on which two knights in effigy lay, side by side, as if they were a married couple on a double bed, but fully armoured rather than in their pyjamas. One of them was holding, in his marble hand, his sword; it pointed to the ceiling as if he saluted heaven, or expected danger from the skies.

The other section of the vault was where I'd heard Faith speaking from. It seemed that somebody had entered there. That meant there was another way down to this underworld.

'I hope I haven't kept you waiting,' I heard someone say. The voice was deep with undernotes of fruit but dry and incompletely clipped.

Faith's voice said: 'This is Major Whitstable.' She waited for a moment. 'Major, may I introduce you.? This is Nikov Fujimoro.'

Major? Wasn't that an army rank? That puzzled me. I couldn't work out what was going on.

This section of the undercroft was lighted by a bright electric lamp which dangled from the ceiling, swinging slightly like a pendulum. This single source of light created monstrous shadows in the nooks and niches round the walls: a plethora of hideaways. Against the wall, the knight's sword cast the shadow of a cross held upside-down above an altar.

There was no love between the army and the Peacemakers. The soldiers thought their enemy ill-disciplined and badly organised, worth nothing as professional opponents, but as adversaries to be dreaded. Amateurs. Fanatics. Rabid dogs embracing martyrdom but dying hard. Stone crazy. Terrible. You can't surrender to a zealot.

The soldiers thought the Peacemakers were not just enemies but devils. Why was someone from the army here?

And what was Nikov playing at?

CHAPTER TWENTY FIVE: BETRAYAL

I didn't dare move any further forward. That would put the light behind me. I might shine my shade into their section of these catacombs.

Then I heard Nikov say: 'This is Xan Madjtik.'

Madjtik.

Surely not, I thought. That must be a coincidence. For all I knew it was a common Drudjer name.

Compared to Madjtik Enterprises, Kapko Industries was like a porpoise with a great white shark: a relative, to some extent, but mostly seen, if noticed, as a tasty bite.

'Indeed,' the new voice said, the soldier, Major Whitstable. 'The video convinced the mother. But you will excuse me if I make some tests. There have been cases of imposture. We must satisfy ourselves that we are not deceived. Forgive me if you are Miss Madjtik. You are certainly her living image.'

Mrs Madjtik wasn't just a Drudjer, she was Drudjer royalty. She'd turned a data distillation app into a company that had a larger income than a dozen nations.

Xan? Her daughter? Don't be daft. She was a prison labourer assigned to me.

I heard the Major asking lots of questions. Filling in the gaps, he said it was. Where she had lived. Where she had been at school. The name of her first pet. Xan knew the answers. Then the questions grew more intimate. Still Xan was fluent. I discovered that the decoration on the inside of the downstairs toilet in the house that she had lived in as a little girl had been the lifesize terracotta statue of a woman they'd called Floss; she had a damaged nose. I learned that Xan had once been sick from gorging on ice cream; it was the first time she had tried pistachio so now she couldn't stand the taste of it. The first time she had smoked a cigarette it had been stolen from her father; as a consequence her mother made him quit.

She was a Madjtik.

It was little wonder Kapko wanted her to be his wife. No wonder she had spurned him.

If she was indeed the daughter of the Madjtik family, and from her answers it appeared she was, it all made sense. I understood her doctorate in datanomics and her job at Kapko Industries. His wooing her: it wasn't love, it was a merger.

Or a takeover. Had Xan been planted into Kapko Industries as a fifth columnist?

I heard the slight scrape of the turning of a key, the click as it unlocked Xan's manacles. I huddled closer to the confines of my corner. I would wear the chains if Nikov caught me now.

He'd had me fooled! I had believed in Mister Purity. And now I learned he was the same as all the rest of them, except that Nikov played for higher stakes.

Xan Madjtik's ransom would be worth a fortune.

When you have a name like Madjtik you defy the ordinary rules and even if you don't want to defy them you will have a mummy or a daddy or a personal assistant who'll defy the rules on your behalf. When you are Mrs Madjtik and your

Drudjer daughter has been captured by the Peacemakers you have the clout to tell a Major in the army that your daughter's freedom must be his priority.

That was when I understood what this was all about.

It was betrayal.

You can't grow as rich as Mrs Madjtik if you ransom daughters. This was not a case of finer feelings. This was theft. Good, solid, business-sense-based theft.

Xan had been using System A. My System. System A for Angelo. She knew its secrets. This was typical of Drudjers; it was how they worked. This was the theft of intellectual property, my property, my System, how it worked, its structure, all of it. What was the betting that, in three months time, they would be selling System X for Xan or System M for Madjtik?

Didn't Nikov know? Did he not understand that this was suicide? Look what was happening. The Peacemakers were being driven back; the Army was defeating them. I was the one advantage that they had. My System, System A, enabled them to manage and administer a town like ours without the need for lots of lawmen; they could redeploy the extras into battle.

But I couldn't work the System on my own. I needed Xan.

I had to stop them.

There was nothing I could do.

If I revealed myself they'd think that I was spying.

Nikov was a traitor. Nikov was corrupt. I saw it now. This was the chance to line his pockets. This was evidence that I could take before the Boss. He'd told me just this morning how he hated traitors, Nikov would be finished, put to death.

Nikov knew that I was hiding Drudjers. Dead men cannot tell their secrets. I'd be safe.

Unless he found me hiding here. Apart from Faith I was the only witness. If Nikov knew that I was watching ... He could not afford to let me live. Dead men can't blab. He'd silence me.

I tried to crush myself still closer to the wall.

'So I accept,' said Major Whitstable, 'Miss Madjtik as a token of your good intentions. On this basis we can now proceed.'

'To peace?' asked Faith.

The trouble was, the niche that I was hiding in was rather small. I had to squash myself against its surfaces. These were of marble. Marble soaks up heat. The crypt was underground. The far side of the wall was buried in the earth. All of these factors added to the chill. I was as cold as corpses. But I dared not move.

'I have authority,' said Major Whitstable, 'confirmed upon me by the Army High Command, to sign a temporary ceasefire on the basis that we have discussed and subject to the terms we have agreed.'

Now I remembered Nikov on the rooftop. He had said he only had a day to stop the army. So today he'd neutralize the threat posed by the army and tomorrow he'd remove the Boss.

'I also,' Nikov said, 'have been invested by the Boss with all the powers I might need to act on his behalf.'

He said this and the echoes mocked him. I have lived with lies for long enough to know what sounds like truth. This wasn't it. I wondered if the Major heard it too: the false foundation underpinning Nikov's claims. The Boss knew nothing of this secret meeting in a crypt.

It was a gamble. I had not seen Nikov as a betting man but here he was: he'd borrowed from the bank and he was putting all his chips on making peace. Tomorrow, if he was successful in his bid to oust the Boss, he'd have no problem. If he failed …

And I myself, Ed Angelo, was crucial to his plans.

The Major said: 'Why should I trust you?'

'Why indeed?' asked Nikov. 'Faith?'

Faith said: 'Because you trust Madame.'

'She's an old friend,' agreed the Major.

'Quite,' said Faith. 'And she will vouch for me and I will vouch for Nikov. We want peace. It's horrid seeing people being killed. Besides, the fighting isn't good for business now that the *Enchanted Isle* is closed and, to be honest, the Black Market never really paid its way. There, Major, is that frank enough for you?'

'So we're agreed?' asked Nikov.

'No more fighting after midnight,' said the Major. 'But you must withdraw across the river.'

'That will be completed by tomorrow night. From then, you will have full possession of the north bank; we will have the south.'

'And what about the Drudjers?' Faith enquired.

'We've cleansed the Kennels,' Nikov said.

'You weren't exactly thorough,' said the Major, 'judging from the flood of refugees who swarmed across our lines.'

'We thought that they might slow you down,' said Nikov.

'You were right. They did. We don't want any more.'

'Miss Madjtik is a Drudjer.'

'I'm aware of that. It's not the same. She isn't poor. If you have any more half-naked, dirty, smelly Drudjers begging to be fed then you can keep them.'

'Yes,' said Nikov. 'That's agreed as well.'

'The boundary will be the river. No one is to cross it.'

I lived on the south side of the river. That would be the territory of the Peacemakers. The army were not coming to set free the Drudjers in my garage. Blossom, Kapko, Sodz and I, and Ochre too if he returned, were stuck. Till Nikov, knowing we were there, decided that it would be more convenient to wipe us out.

I'd have to pray that Ochre had been caught. That Kapko died, That after Sodz had testified tomorrow Nikov would decide to silence him. Then it would just be me and Blossom. I could have her time and time again. What could she do? She couldn't run away.

'Hang on,' said Xan. How could I not have known that tone? She was a Madjtik through and through. The moment that she had a thought she spoke and she expected all the rest of us to listen. She had talked to me like that when she had been my slave. Now she was telling Nikov what to do. He'd captured her, for goodness sake.

'One moment, please,' said Xan. 'If I might be allowed to speak. I'm very grateful to be rescued, Major Whitstable. But what about the others?'

'No,' said Nikov. 'This is not the time to be discussing amnesties.'

'No.' Major Whitstable was adamant. 'Your mother mentioned only you.'

'I know it's difficult,' said Faith, 'but we cannot afford to let our personal beliefs dislodge the fragile balance of the peace negotiations.'

'You're a special case,' said Major Whitstable.

'We have already mentioned this,' said Nikov. 'Both sides have agreed to keep their own.'

'We don't want hordes of Drudjers overwhelming us,' said Major Whitstable.

Xan pointed out she was a Drudjer. Major Whistable replied that she was not a horde.

'I don't want hordes,' said Xan. 'Just one. I won't go anywhere without him. You might as well re-handcuff me. I will not be a pawn in your negotiations. I'll stay where I am if I can't be with Ochre.'

Bloody Ochre.

'Who?' said Nikov. 'Doesn't ring a bell. Not one of ours.'

'He is in hiding,' Xan explained.

You see? She was and always was a Madjtik, through and through. She wouldn't sacrifice herself for Drudjer rights. She wasn't interested in the masses. There has only ever been a single Drudjer any Madjtik's ever cared for. Xan loved Xan. And if she wanted Ochre she would have him, even if it meant betraying me.

I know, I know, I know that Nikov knew about my Drudjers. But knowing secretly, deniably, unevidenced, is not that same as being told in front of witnesses. Xan was putting Nikov in a corner. That was dangerous. It might be dangerous for me.

'If he's in hiding then we don't know where he is,' said Nikov.

'I know where he's hiding,' Xan replied.

You don't, I thought. He isn't there.

'No,' Nikov said. 'I am afraid, Miss Madjtik, that you're not in a position to demand. The Major and myself have more important things to think about. The Major will agree that I've fulfilled my promise. If you wish to stay here, in this church, then that is up to you. Should you decide to try and make your way across the river then I ought to warn you that my men know nothing of your parentage; their orders are to clear the streets of Drujders. Go or stay, it's up to you; it is of no concern to me. But once this treaty is concluded, should your mother wish to ransom any other Drudjer I am more than happy to discuss it.'

How the fates enjoy their games: like cats with mice. While Nikov told Xan this my hopes began to rise again.

'But on the other hand,' the Major said, 'and since it doesn't really matter one way or the other, maybe Nikov will agree to this. You come with me right now, Miss Madjtik and tomorrow night we implement the amnesty. That done, we look for … what's his name?'

Xan answered: 'Ochre.'

'Yes, of course. We look for Ochre. Nikov looks for Ochre. When he finds him, we'll agree to swap him for a Peacemaker that we have captured. One for one. And just your boyfriend. Not a Drudjer more.'

That suited me, I thought triumphantly. I'd be keeping Blossom. And there was the added benefit that any search for Ochre would begin tomorrow night, not earlier.

If only Nikov would agree.

'We'd have to keep this covert,' Nikov said. 'And all that I'm agreeing to is looking for this special Drudjer; I can't guarantee success in finding him.'

'But I know where …' Xan started.

'No,' said Nikov. 'This is something I don't want to know. Not now. Not till tomorrow night. Why don't you whisper what you know to Faith? Then she can put me in the picture at the proper time.'

It was agreed. There was a moment's silence. I supposed the men were shaking hands.

'Goodbye then, Major,' Nikov said. 'Miss Madjtik. If there is a next time let us hope it is in better circumstances. I can promise that you will enjoy a higher standard of accommodation. We cannot be held responsible if we don't know who you are. I would be grateful if you would tell Faith where we can find your sweetheart. Faith is leaving with you now so you can chat. She will get word to me tomorrow night. Then I will do my best, Miss Madjtik, you can rest assured.'

I heard them leaving. It was time for me to make my way back through the church, back down the path, and back along the river. Back to Blossom.

But, before I had a chance to move, the lights went out.

CHAPTER TWENTY SIX: BLESSED ARE THE PEACEMAKERS

I thought, for one despairing time-stopped moment that seemed longer than a lifetime, that all four of them had left and shut the door and locked it, and that I would be stuck here, down here, in this mausoleum, buried down here with the dead, sealed in this dungeon and forgotten, left to starve, to die, to rot, to be discovered as a skeleton endeavouring to claw a tunnel from his tomb.

Then I heard Nikov speaking.

'Don't you feel at all responsible? I'm sure we'd all think more of you if you admitted it. You mucked it up. There was so much potential to this place. But what a mess you've made of it. The squalor and the hatred and the ignorance. Why did you let it happen? You're all-powerful; it wouldn't be exactly difficult for you to sort it out. But no, you thought it would be better if you let us run it for ourselves. And you were wrong.'

That's when I should have guessed. I didn't.

Nikov started up again. 'So now I have to do your work for you. And, to be honest, I'm a bit fatigued. I am exhausted. Don't you think that maybe you have asked too much of me?'

He must be on a phone call. That was why I could hear only his half of the conversation. Who, I wondered, was he phoning?

'Don't you understand what I am up against? Of course you do: you've seen the men I'm working with. They're weak, they're stupid, they're contemptible. Just one good man, that's all I ask. Someone I could rely on. But there's no one. I must take the burden on myself. And we all know what happens then. One man against the world? I'm doomed to failure. You have always known it, well, of course you have, you wrote the screenplay. I have been a fool to think I might have had a chance. I'll keep on trying, that's the best that I can do. But now I know it's hopeless.'

That was when I understood that Nikov talked to God.

That's when I knew that I was in the dark, beneath the earth, trapped in a crypt, and my companion was a lunatic.

I didn't know if I should be as silent as the grave and stay in hiding or if I should try to make a run for it. But it was blacker than the black of Hell and I was sightless. Blind. Completely blind. The only way that I was getting out of here was if I groped my way. And could I do that soundlessly?

I tried to reconstruct my route. There'd been the stairs, then I'd turned left and then a few steps forward to my hiding place. As far as I remembered. But I wasn't certain. Fearing I was lost, I shrunk still further down into my recess.

And that was when I saw the light.

I was so spooked by then that I imagined it was God Himself come down in all His glory for a chat to Nikov. Maybe He'd been chastened by the things He'd heard. Perhaps He thought He could explain Himself. But then I saw the light was dodging here and there. I didn't think that God would dance. It must be Nikov, with a torch.

And he was heading straight for me.

I tried to shrink. The beam of light was vacillating as he

walked. I guessed that he was using it to guide his steps. There was a chance it wouldn't shine on me.

Short of a miracle, I thought, or possibly a geophysical catastrophe, the earth was not about to open up and swallow me and if it did I wasn't sure that I'd be any better off.

I did the only thing that I could think of.

Closed my eyes.

They say that if you can't see them they can't see you.

It didn't work.

I heard an exclamation. It was Nikov. 'Mr Angelo?'

I knew his torch was shining straight into my face because its brightness filtered through my eyelids.

'Whatever are you doing there?' he asked.

I couldn't think of anything to say.

'I thought I told you that you had to stay at home,' he said.

I opened one eye cautiously but, dazzled, shut it rapidly.

'Instead you're here. Have you been spying on me?'

'No. I'm not a spy.'

'You don't look very comfy. Why don't you step forward. What are you afraid of? Do I bite?'

I took a step towards him. 'Take away the torch,' I said, 'so I can see.'

'I'll put it over here,' he said.

The pinkness, so like sunrise, faded. Carefully, I looked towards him. He was smiling, standing just a little way in front of me, and holding up before my face Xan's handcuffs.

'First things first,' he said. 'We want to make sure you are safe and sound. If you would be so good as to hold out your hands.'

He must have mesmerised me. I obeyed. I didn't really have a choice. He had a half-sized mocking grin upon his lips; he touched his free hand to the handle of his holstered gun. I let him snap a handcuff on the wrist of my right hand. I watched him do it. There was nothing I could do to stop him. Silently, I raised my gaze. I looked him in the eye. He nodded in approval. Then he beckoned and I meekly followed him towards the tomb, the box that held the body of the knight and his companion, that was adorned with their stone likenesses. When Nikov raised the hand that held the other bracelet of the cuffs my arm was forced to follow. Then he walked around the far side of the tomb. And then he stooped. The movement was so swift it caught me by surprise. My handcuffed hand was dragged into a swooping out-and-downwards arc. Of course it couldn't leave my arm behind. My shoulder too was forced in line; that dragged my torso after it. Like the derailment of a train, whose carriages jump from the track because they can't stop following their locomotive, so my body leapt and plunged. Before I knew it, I discovered I was jack-knifed at the waist, the upper portion of my body sprawled across the effigies. I felt the studs and bosses that protruded from the sculptures prodding into me. That was the moment when I heard a click. The handcuffs. Locked. I'd been attached. In a ridiculous position. I was spread across a dead knight who was sleeping for eternity beside his fellow man of arms. It must have looked as if I was engaged in some bizarre form of submission, with a sculpted navel squashed into my face, as if I was attempting to perform fellatio upon a statue. With my bottom staring starwards (if the barrel vaulting of the ceiling was removed) I was defenceless. Someone watching must have thought that I was worshipping the couple on the tomb: a deviant example of the adoration of an idol. Maybe I was begging, maybe I was warped and maybe I was offering myself.

I was outraged. 'You have no right,' I told him. 'Let me go.'

'I told you that you had to stay at home.' He moved behind me. 'Don't you ever listen? Stay ... at ... home, I said.'

'I'll go. Release me and I'll go back now. I'll do it straight away.'

'Too late for that. I warned you. But you never listen.'

'No. I'll change. I have changed.'

As he spoke I felt him put his hands beneath my waist, his fingers reaching for the buckle of my belt.

I reached back with my free hand, pushing him away. 'What do you think you're doing?'

He grabbed me - two hands onto one, I didn't stand a chance - and bent my flailing arm behind my back and wrenched it savagely so that my shoulder screamed with pain.

'You haven't left me any other choice,' he said. 'You have to learn that there are consequences. If you sin, you suffer. That's the way it is.'

I kicked. Connected. Heard him yelp. I was released.

I told him that he was a traitor. Said he didn't have a clue. I yelled that he was stupid, that he didn't know what damage he had done, that Xan was nothing but a pirate, that she'd copy System A, that she would call it System X, that I'd been robbed, that he had thrown away a pearl that was a damn sight more important than the Peacemakers.

He didn't answer. Not a word. I couldn't even hear him breathing.

So I bellowed that I'd tell the Boss, that I had spoken with the Boss, the Boss was asking me to name the traitors, I'd name Nikov, Nikov didn't stand a chance, if Nikov thought that he would be the leader of the Peacemakers tomorrow then he ought to think again, this peace would never happen.

'Don't you want a ceasefire?' Nikov asked. He wandered round the tomb so that I didn't have to look across my shoulder; I could see him easily. 'I thought we all did.'

I said he had lied. 'You told the Major that you have been delegated by the Boss to parley, to negotiate a truce. It isn't true.'

He laughed. 'If anyone can recognise a lie, it would be you. I don't know how you do it: tell so many lies. Don't you lose track of what you've said?'

He scratched his head. 'But aren't there lies and lies? I think mine was a rather minor stretching of the truth? A little lie. Perhaps not white, not quite, but pretty pallid. After all, it will be true tomorrow, so it's nearly true, it's just a little premature.'

He frowned. 'That's if you're still prepared to help me. I suppose you're scared; you're worried what will happen if it all goes wrong. What can I say? There's always hope.'

'It's still a lie.'

'Your trouble is that my lies are so tiny when compared with your enormous fibs.'

'My trouble is that you tell lies when you're supposed to be the paradigm of purity.'

'Don't be misled by nicknames. Look, I lied. So what? It happens. It was for the best.'

'The end can never justify the means.'

'Of course it can. Don't be so innocent. My end is peace, my means a teeny tiny lie. I think that's justified.'

He picked his torch up and he shone its beam upon a picture

hanging on the wall. 'Look over there. You see it?'

I could see the picture of a young man, bearded, dressed in robes of white, with sandals on his feet, his right hand raised in blessing.

'There. That's it. The sermon on the mount. You must have heard of it. He blesses people. Quite a scattergun approach. The poor, the meek, the hungry, those who weep. But here's the best bit. Blessed are the Peacemakers. The Peacemakers. God's children, that is what he calls us. We're the kids of God. That's rather nice, I think.'

I looked at him. 'You're kidding me.'

He told me that he didn't understand.

He thought he was the son of God.

'I am a Peacemaker,' he said, 'I have been making peace.'

He was a bloody madman.

'Anyway,' I said. 'You have yourself admitted it won't work.'

'What won't?'

'This thing about the Boss.'

'This thing tomorrow? Overthrowing him? I never said that wouldn't work.'

'You did. I heard you. In your monologue just now. I heard you saying it. You said, when you were standing in the dark, you couldn't do it, that it wasn't going to work.'

'I did say that.' He nodded.

'So you think we'll fail. We'll try to overthrow the Boss and it will all go wrong. What happens then?'

'I'm confident that we'll succeed.'

'That wasn't what you said just now.'

'It wasn't what I said. It's what I heard.'

I ran the conversation over in my mind. It had been Nikov talking. No one else.

He said: 'I know it's difficult to understand. You're right of course. I can't be certain of success. Not with the Boss. It's just the same when you are going into battle. You can never know the outcome, not for sure. It always helps to have a little chat before you start. To talk things over. It's important that you find a place to do it. You have almost always got to be alone. And somewhere special. As you know, I like it on the roof. But here, down in the darkness, that works too. Of course it doesn't matter where for him. He's everywhere. He'll listen in the middle of a crowded street. But I get too distracted. All those others. All that noise. It makes it difficult to concentrate. But in a place like this, when you're alone; that's when the signal comes through loud and clear. That's how I can be confident. I promise. You'll be fine providing that you stick with me.'

He didn't only talk to God. He thought God answered back. And God had reassured him.

But, as you'd expect, God hadn't said a word to me.

Tomorrow we would meet the Boss. We'd try to overthrow him. By tomorrow night we would be dead. Perhaps Plan A, assassination, would have been a safer course.

I had to stop this lunatic. He wanted self-destruction but I didn't see why I should share his flames.

'I'll stop you.'

'You?' He laughed. 'Don't be so silly. You can't stop me.'

He was smug, so bloody smug. He thought he had it all sewn

up. I'd show him.

'Ochre.'

'Ochre?'

'Ochre.'

'Isn't he the Drudjer drone that Xan is keen on?'

'Yes,' I said. 'You've promised her you'll find him. Well, you won't. You think he's hiding in my garage. Well, he isn't. Ochre ran away. You see? That's put a spoke in it. Imagine Mrs Madjtik when she learns you can't deliver on the promise that you made her daughter. There'll be hell to pay.'

He looked at me as if I was a wounded animal, like he was wondering if it was fair to let me suffer any longer. He shook his head. 'You cannot really think the fate of one pathetic Drudjer matters. Major Whitstable likes Drudjers even less than we do.'

I was cross. I couldn't stand him being so superior. I'd make him snigger on the far side of his face. 'I'll tell the Boss.'

'Oh no you won't. You've got too much to lose.'

'He'll overlook the Drudjers. He'll be grateful.'

Nikov's face showed incredulity. 'You think you can replace me? You? As his lieutenant? You?'

I nodded.

''But he'll never trust you,' Nikov said. 'I know the way he thinks. He'll look at you and think: a traitor once, a traitor twice; a leopard doesn't change his spots; a Judas keeps on kissing.'

'I will have performed a service for him.'

Nikov's mocking laughter bounced from wall to wall. 'You

know he killed his wife. You'll always be a threat to him. What, did you think that you could tell him you'd forget it? Don't be stupid. Not a chance. I would be frightened, very frightened, of the Boss, if I were you.'

The trouble is that sometimes these self-satisfied conceited jokers who pretend that they have all the aces, really do. He wasn't bluffing. In my heart of hearts I knew it. Maybe Nikov was a knave but he was holding all the court cards in his hand.

He said: 'Why would you want to stop me anyway? I'll bring us peace; I'll purge corruption from the Peacemakers. I'm on your side.'

'Okay,' I said.

'You play your cards right, you can be my right hand man.'

'I said okay,' I told him. There are times the only way you can survive is to submit. Surrender. Let them think they've won. Then go to ground, and hang around until another chance turns up.

'So that's agreed,' he said. 'There's nothing left to do except get ready for tomorrow. Got to get it right. It won't be easy. First we have to sort out Sodz and then we turn the spotlight on the Boss. There's quite a lot to think about. So if you will excuse me, I'll pop off back home and make the necessary preparations.'

'But,' I said.

'Have I forgotten something?'

'Me,' I said. 'I'm handcuffed to this tomb.'

'Indeed. You are. I was about to punish you for spying. Well remembered. I presume that you are ready now to be chastised.'

'Just let me go,' I yelled at him.

'It doesn't work like that. I can't have my lieutenant thinking he can get away with being insubordinate. You can't move on until you pay the penalty.'

'It wasn't my fault I was hiding here when you decided that you'd have a little chat with God.'

'God says the only way you can achieve redemption is through suffering.'

I thought about the paintings in the church. I wish I knew what Father Kerrigan had done.

'If you are ready I will pull your trousers down,' said Nikov, 'and I'll flog you on your bare behind.'

'You're joking. No. That is disgusting. It's perverted.'

'It's punishment. It's meant to hurt. It's meant to be degrading.'

'You're a …' But I stopped myself. He meant to punish me. I couldn't stop him. All in all, it might be better if I didn't wind him up. Submit. Surrender. Live to see another day. 'Just get it over with.'

Again he stepped behind me and again his arms went round my waist. I felt his fingers fumble. He undid the belt and carefully, meticulously, drew it from the belt loops.

'Don't worry,' Nikov said. 'I'll use the belt tip, not the buckle end. I wouldn't want to scar you.'

I had hoped that he would spank me with his hand. But leather! This would hurt. I felt my trousers being tugged away and down my thighs and past my knees to pool around my ankles. Then I felt the sharp sting of the cold air of the crypt against the bare skin of my buttocks as he peeled away my underpants.

There didn't seem much point in praying. God? Down here? With me? If He was anybody's, He was Nikov's. He'd forsaken me.

I hoped I wouldn't wet myself.

At least those martyrs, in their portraits, in the church, above, had, most of them, been draped. They hadn't been humiliated. I was painfully aware that I looked ludicrous.

I jerked. I yelled. I jolted. Burning, smarting, piercing pain. I hiccoughed, howled and fought for breath. Again he lashed me and I bellowed and I arched my back. The third time I was almost ready and I heard the whistle of the leather through the air but this time as it smacked into my blushing flesh the pointed end tip of the belt snaked round my thighs and tapped my testicles. My stomach heaved. I couldn't breathe. My body burned.

I whimpered.

'Good,' said Nikov. 'That's sufficient. I'll assume you've learned your lesson. There need never be another time. If you behave yourself. It's over.'

I could scarcely think for sobbing. What had happened? Why was I so sore? Was that me, snivelling? And what was Nikov saying now?

'We'll meet tomorrow.'

He was leaving me.

'Please stay,' I pleaded. 'Please don't go.'

'The purpose of chastisement,' Nikov sermonised, 'is to provoke reflection. You need time to think.'

'Don't leave me. Please, I begged him. 'Not like this. It's dark. It's cold. I'm on my own.' I didn't want to be alone.

'You'll be all right.'

'Suppose I need to use the toilet.'

'Try to hold it in.'

I begged, implored, entreated and beseeched. I would have promised anything. I would have knelt. I would have prayed to him. 'You can't abandon me. Please, Nikov. Please forgive me. Don't be stupid. Please. You've had your joke.'

'You told me you would tell the Boss. I hope I've talked you out of that. It would be catastrophic for yourself. But sometimes people act perversely. I'd be foolish if I gave you even half a chance. You're stopping here tonight.'

'Please Nikov, take me somewhere else, not here, surrounded by the dead.'

He laughed at that. 'Do you believe in monsters?'

'Rats,' I told him.

'Rats?' He seemed to find that funny. 'Rats? You have a free hand; you can brush them off. And you can kick.'

'Please Nikov.'

'I'll be back tomorrow morning. You'll survive till then.'

He took the torch.

I begged. 'Don't leave me in the dark.'

The light receded as he climbed the stairs.

CHAPTER TWENTY SEVEN: EXHUMED

I'd hardly slept.

The first thing I had done was curse. I swore at Nikov and I swore at God. I swore at Xan and Mrs Madjtik and the Major and I swore at Kapko who had got me into all this trouble in the first place and I swore at Ochre for his doomed heroics and I swore at Blossom and I swore at Sodz. I blamed the Drudjers: but for them there would have been no need for Peacemakers. I didn't mince my words. I don't suppose the church had ever heard so much profanity. Obscenities bounced round and round the crypt. They kept me company.

It wasn't fair. It hadn't been my fault. I had done nothing. It was them: the big boys. That had been the story of my life. I was too easy-going. I had been exploited and abused. Derided. What a story Nikov would be telling in the mess. The data-fellow: stripped and spanked and shackled, shut up with the dead. I was a laughing-stock. They'd snigger to each other: Have you heard the one about the data-guy? I couldn't ever look them in the face again.

Not that I ever had. It wasn't safe. You meet their gaze; they think you're insolent.

I was exhausted. Cursing takes it out of you. I'd used my thoughts up, wasted them, and now my brain was drained. Just when I needed it. To think. To reason. To be sensible.

I wasn't a believer. I have seen men killed; I know a corpse is empty. When we're finished, that's the end of it. No soul and so no afterlife. No afterlife and so no judgement, no eternal punishment and, sure as hell, no everlasting bliss. Which means no ghosts.

That's how I reasoned. But it's one thing to be logical and sensible and rational when you are young. It's easy to be sure you're right when you are young. But when you're helpless, in the dark, alone, and slumped across a box of bodies, terrors spread like an infection through your mind. In the dark, the slightest noise becomes a threat. In darkness, the imagination breeds more monsters than whole libraries of gothic fantasies. Perhaps tonight, you tell yourself in whispers so you can't be overheard, you'll learn what you don't want to learn: what lies beyond the grave.

I had to urinate.

I didn't want to wet myself but, with my trousers puddled round my ankles, it looked likely that I would. I had to pull them up. Besides, I knew I would feel safer fully clothed. I'd never heard of anybody being buggered by a demon but it isn't wise to put temptation in a devil's way.

My right arm was attached to something on the far side of the tomb. My left was free. It just wasn't long enough. I tried to reach my ankles but I couldn't. Nowhere near. I'd always found it difficult to touch my toes unless I cheated.

That was it, I thought. I had to bend my knees to move my feet to meet my hand. That was a little harder than I had expected. I was scared my feet would slip out of the trouser cuffs. And it was painful: sculpted tomb tops, I discovered, have a lot of knobs and nodules and, each time I shifted my position, one of them, it seemed, found pleasure jabbing into me. But, inch by inch, I semi-crawled and semi-climbed onto the tomb.

It wasn't easy, even after I was lying on my back, my still-bare buttocks chilling on the knight's companion's marbled hand. There seems to be a scientific law that causes clothing to be inside out by preference. And, in the dark, I had to grope for labels to distinguish what was meant to be the inside. It was quite a struggle but I squirmed and wriggled and contorted. In the end, so far as I could tell by touching, I was dressed.

I couldn't zip my flies up: I was operating single handed. So I made the most of things. I knelt and aimed a stream of piss into the darkness; I could hear it splatter on the floor. There, I thought. If anything's a desecration, that is. This would be the moment that, according to the laws that govern horror stories, by my actions I'd have opened up a portal to the nether world of nightmares.

Get a grip, I told myself. Ghosts, zombies, vampires, bogeymen: they don't exist. They are the stuff of fiction; fiction by its very definition is untrue. But …

But. I was in total darkness. That's the best material for shaping into horrors.

I was much too tense to fall asleep. I dreaded dreaming. In a dream imagination is reality.

I was too scared to make a sound. This place turned echoes into groans.

I tried to think of something else. I thought of Kapko. Then I thought his soul might even at this moment be evaporating from his corpse. He was malevolent. If ever any shadow had been doomed to haunt the earth it would be his. He had bedevilled me in life, so why not after he was dead?

And Ochre? I have heard that spirits haunt the guilty.

But you can't blame me. He'd been determined to destroy himself. The whole plan was a silly game of ring and run, like knocking on a granny's door and skipping off, except in Ochre's case he'd shot a bullet at the Town Hall guards and bolted. What a fool. What was it but a dressed-up sort of suicide?

It wasn't my fault. All I'd done was not to try and talk him out of it. Not that he would have listened.

And what about his sister? She'd not haunt me: she was very much alive. I wondered what the little tart was doing now. She would be doing Sodz. Trust him and trust that whore to get together at the moment that my back was turned. By now - what time was it? - he would have had her. She'd be lying underneath him, arching up to meet his thrusts, her grunts and his crescendoing into a shrieking climax. Bloody typical. It wasn't fair. I don't have anything to call my own. Can't even keep a woman. She was lucky to have had me! She was lying in my bed, wrapped up in sweaty sheets and Sodz, and I was lying in this hellhole. And they say that God is just! He's never given me what I deserved.

My handcuffed arm was throbbing. Any way I turned it ached.

Perhaps I dozed. I don't think I was fully conscious all the time. I know that I kept waking, jerking upright. But I couldn't tell what time it was. Your mind plays tricks on you in darkness. Time moves sluggishly and then leaps forward. Dreams invade your waking thoughts.

I thought I heard the sound of footsteps coming down the stairs. I thought that it might be the priest, resplendent in his loincloth, helmeted with horns, the rubies on the pommel of his sacrificial dagger shining even though this place of death was blacker than the ace of spades.

Just get it over with, I thought. If I was to be immolated to appease whatever demons Nikov and his cronies conjured up, I prayed it would be when I wasn't ready. I didn't want to be prepared. I didn't want the chance to think about what was to come. That's all I asked. That it was painless. Sudden. Unperceived.

And then I saw that it was Ochre.

That was when I knew. I knew that he was dead. I knew that this was Ochre's ghost. I knew that this was Ochre's vengeance. Then it all made sense. If there were ghosts there was an afterlife, there was a hell, there was a judgement and there was a judge.

And then, just like in dreams, the spirit reached for me. And, as in dreams, I cringed away. And that was when he touched me.

I'd have woken then if it had been a dream. I didn't, so I hadn't been asleep.

'Are you awake?' he asked.

His hand was warm.

'Are you all right?' he asked.

The world, I thought, has gone awry. I was a damsel in distress, chained to a knight in polished marble armour, waiting nervously for an encounter with a dragon, for a fate of death or worse, and I was to be rescued by a Drudjer. It was a humiliation.

'Don't worry. I'll soon get you out of here.'

He squatted down, released me from the handcuffs. Sniffed. He must have smelt my urine, spilled upon the stones. 'You must have had a horrid night of it.'

I rubbed my wrist. My arm was numb. It felt as if the flesh belonged to someone else. I tried to do my fly up but my fingers wouldn't do as I demanded.

'Can I help? But only if you'd like me to. Don't worry, I'm a doctor. Trainee doctor anyway. I've seen it all before.'

My muscles were so cramped it felt as if I'd been assembled out of aches. He had to help me slide down off the tomb. He put my arm around his shoulders to support me as I staggered to the stairs. I was so slow and so uncertain on my feet that anybody might have thought I'd done the Rip van Winkle thing and been asleep for fifty-seven years.

And I felt dirty. Through the frozen night I'd sweated out of terror. Now my skin was covered in a salted crust, my nose and cheeks were greasy, and my armpits, one of which was wrapped round Ochre's neck, pumped out the smell of milk gone rotten.

We hobbled through an atmosphere so thick with pungency it felt that we were wading through half-clotted jellied urine.

Ochre, in his slender, youthful beauty, didn't say a single word. He didn't have to. I knew what he felt. I was disgusting. Old men are. He understood. He pitied me. I hated him.

I told myself I'd pay him back for this.

We started toiling, step by step, towards the surface.

Suddenly I stopped. 'How did you know that I was down there?'

'Nikov told me.'

'Nikov?'

'He's a Peacemaker.'

'I know who Nikov is. He told you?'

'I was lucky Nikov found me. Just imagine it was one of those who shoot before they ask a question. I have seen that happen, seen it in the street, a Drudjer and a Peacemaker.' He shuddered. 'Makes me sick to think about it. Like John Zombie. Horrid. Watching. When I'm in the hospital it's different. At least I've tried. I've done my best. But in the street. When you're just watching. When there's nothing you can do. Not even comfort them. Not even ease the pain.'

He looked at me. His eyes were beautiful. 'Come on,' he said. 'Let's see if you can manage one more step.'

'But why did Nikov tell you where I was?'

'Oh yes,' he said. 'Of course it wasn't easy. When he caught me, I thought that was it. That he would shoot me. When he didn't, I began to worry even more. You know. You must have heard the stories. What goes on down in the Town Hall basement. I'm not a brave lad. I don't think that I could stand it if they tortured me.'

I saw that he was shivering. It suited him. I told myself that I would make him shake.

'And then he told me Xan had been released. Can you imagine how I felt? I could have kissed him. Nearly did. That would have been embarrassing. Imagine it: a Peacemaker, embraced by me.'

He was a skinny little insubstantial piece of fluff and Nikov was so solid.

'Then he said that I could go and be with her, and Blossom too, and that tomorrow there'd be peace. It was the best thing in the world. So when he asked me if I minded finding you and setting you at liberty ... well, by then I would have sold my soul to him and if he wanted buy one get one free he could have had my body too.'

'And Blossom too? I'm not sure Major Whitstable ...'

'Of course! I told him: I'm not going anywhere without my sister. And I asked about the others and he said that he would set them free as well but not right now because there were a few formalities that had to be completed. I suppose it's paper work. You'd be surprised but even as a doctor you are always facing unfilled forms.'

I stopped.

He tried to urge me on. 'You take your time. Am I too fast? I don't suppose you slept a wink last night.'

It wasn't that. I was exhausted, that was true. But Ochre's chatter sounded like the weather forecast for an ice age. Nikov this and Nikov that, like Nikov was his new best friend. I had a premonition. 'Ochre, where is Nikov now?'

'He's waiting for us in the church. He said he wasn't in a hurry. Well, he is, but he was very understanding; he expected you'd be slow. He told me he has planned a busy day.'

'Did Nikov give the key to you?'

'The key that locks the handcuffs? Yes, of course he did. How else would I have got it?'

'He's using you,' I told him. Sometimes he seemed so naive.

'I know he is. He told me that himself. He's told me all about today. I'm quite excited. Do you think it's possible? What do you think the biggest problem is? Apart from Sodz. Another step?'

He gripped my arm. His hand was strong.

'He said I had to help you there.'

As if the little Drudjer hadn't helped me quite enough.

'It won't be easy,' Ochre said.

We'd reached a little landing on the stairs, adorned with pictures of the devil's kitchen and the arrow pointing down. And I was going upwards. That seemed typical of life, life these last few days.

That was when I had another thought. I grabbed at Nikov. 'Where's the gun?' I hissed.

'It's safe,' he said. 'He didn't search me?'

'Do you mean that you still have it?'

'In my pocket.'

'Let me have it. Give it to me now.'

'I thought it might be better if I kept it. For the moment. Don't you think it would be safer? Nikov didn't search me, maybe he forgot, and maybe he believes he frisked me when he caught me. But he might search you. Suppose he caught you with a gun. You'd be in trouble.'

'That's a chance I'll have to take. Give me the gun.'

'You know I shot the only bullet?'

'Yes. I want it anyway.'

I knew he was reluctant from the way he handed me the gun, as if he didn't want to part with it, as if he'd like to hold it just a moment longer. This is how a gun is like a woman: by possessing one you tell the world you are a man, in possessing one you feel more masculine. I wouldn't let a little faggot such as Ochre hold my gun a minute longer than he needed to.

I thrust it in my pocket.

Then the pair of us emerged into the body of the church. And there, indeed, was Nikov, hands on hips a great fat greasy smirk across his lips.

'I hope you had a pleasant night,' the grinning sadist said to me.

CHAPTER TWENTY EIGHT: WE'RE ALL FUCKED NOW

I stood a little to one side, ignored, while Blossom billed and cooed and scolded Ochre. How she carried on. You would have thought she was in love with him. Not loved him like a sister loves a brother. Not like that. *In* love with him, like she would be in love with me.

I had to put up with a whole first act of 'Ochre this' and 'Ochre that' and 'why were you so stupid?' and 'do you remember when you were a kid?' and 'I thought I had lost you' and 'don't ever ever ever do a thing like that again'.

I took the chance to slip upstairs. Reload the gun. I didn't want to have to use it. I was hoping Sodz would be persuaded to surrender. Hoping. Not expecting. So the gun might be the back-up that I needed.

Nikov was outside. He'd given Ochre and myself till eight o'clock. It wasn't long; a little more than fifteen minutes. I suspected it would not be long enough.

Why can't you just walk in the house and grab him? I had asked. I thought I knew the answer. It would not be easy: Nikov was alone and one of him and five of us were odds he didn't fancy. But of course he didn't say that, not to me. He had explained he needed Sodz to trust him. What he meant was that he wanted us to do the dirty work. It was a good-cop-bad-cop play with Nikov as the nice guy. This is how that works: the angrier Sodz gets with us, the easier for Nikov, picking up the pieces, to convince him that his best chance for survival was to act out Nikov's script.

Downstairs again and Blossom was still giving it the mother-to-the-max routine. I was acknowledged, briefly, with a glance flung off in my direction and a word of thanks. Then we were back to Ochres.

But she didn't tell him what she'd done to get him back.

Perhaps that's why she had both arms around her brother, that was why she crushed her breasts on Ochre and cold-shouldered me.

I'd turned her on.

'We haven't time for all of this,' I told them. Blossom wasn't hearing. Ochre couldn't get a word in sideways. Sodz was staring, looking lost.

I told them Nikov knew.

Half-propped up by a pair of pillows and the wall, contorted, pain perspiring through his pores, uneasy, Kapko was the only one who paid attention. 'Nikov knows?' he muttered, speaking like his lips and teeth and tongue could scarcely shape the syllables.

I nodded. 'Nikov knows you're here.'

'Who?' Kapko asked.

I hadn't thought of that. 'Well, you, for one, and Sodz, and Ochre and, of course, myself. I don't know if he knows that Blossom's here.'

'How do you know he knows?' demanded Sodz.

'He's outside now,' I said.

Sodz shied, as if I'd chucked a stick at him, like he was dodging it.

'What are you doing?'

'Got to get away,' he panted.

'Don't be stupid. Don't you think the house has been surrounded?' I could not afford to let him make a run for it.

'Who told him?' Kapko grunted.

'If,' said Sodz, 'the whole place is surrounded, how did you get in?' He glared at me.

'He brought me back,' said Ochre. We'd agreed our story. Nikov would tell Blossom I had rescued him but afterwards, as we were coming home, we had been caught by Nikov.

'He let you go,' said Sodz, 'and in return you told him I was bloody here.'

'I didn't.'

'No, he didn't.' I backed Ochre up. We were a team. 'We neither of us told him. He already knew.'

'The good news is,' said Ochre, 'Xan has been released.'

'Xan?' Blossom asked.

'How did he know?' asked Sodz and as he spoke I saw dawn breaking in his eyes. He had been frowning with his bushy eyebrows lowered so his eyes had been the shape of pea-pods more than peas. But, now he understood, his face was opened like a flower in the morning and he looked more devilishly beautiful. He glanced at me. 'That fucking phone call. That was it? The call that Ochre made to Faith for Kapko's pills. The poppers. On my phone. I told the little runt he shouldn't use it.'

That suited me. It got me off the hook.

'The good news is,' repeated Ochre, 'Xan's been freed.'

The others seemed to be as shocked as I had been to learn Xan was a Madjtik. Only Kapko, coughing in the corner, didn't seem surprised. 'And Nikov has agreed,' said Ochre, 'we can go as well.'

'What, all of us?' asked Sodz.

'Not yet,' said Ochre. 'Me and Blossom first.'

'But Nikov says,' I said to Sodz as quickly as I could, 'that you can earn your place.'

'Earn my place?'

'Sodz, please' urged Ochre. 'If we give him what he wants …'

'Give Nikov? What does Nikov want?'

'There's something you can do for him,' I said.

'You bargained me against your freedom?'

'No,' I said. 'That wasn't how it was.'

'I might have guessed,' said Sodz. 'It's just the same as it has always been. The Kapkos and the others.'

'Nikov promises you'll be all right,' I said.

'Don't make me chortle. Uncle, niece and nephew. Pretty little group. So cute, so loving, so incestuous.' Sodz looked at me, a sideways glance, sly, full of cunning. He was desperate. 'I only need to say one word and I can blow it all apart.'

I told him that he had to listen. 'Nikov needs you.'

'Nikov needs me like I need a bullet in my brain.'

'Please listen. Nikov knows you didn't kill the Memsahib. He wants you to go to court and testify, so you can be acquitted, so the proper culprit can be caught.'

'You're joking. What a fucking fairy tale,' said Sodz.

'And Nikov swears that if you help him he will set you free.'

Sodz looked around the garage. 'Aren't I free right now?'

I shook my head.

Sodz mimicked me. 'He'll set me free. But first I must be taken into custody, detained, incarcerated in a dungeon, softened up and forced to do whatever Nikov wants me to and after that, and only if I've pleased him, Nikov might agree to let me go.'

I nodded.

'What a cocked-up, crazed compendium of cock-and-bull.'

'No,' I said. 'You have to listen. Yes, I understand it is a risk. Of course it is. But I trust Nikov.'

'You must think I am el stupido, stolto, tonto, brain-dead, dafter than a brush without a bristle and not half so handy.'

'Sodz,' I said, 'you don't have any other choice. He knows you're here.'

'Why's he not coming in to get me then?'

'He's giving you a chance.'

'Come quietly?' Sodz shouted out. 'If you surrender, Sodz, you'll save us so much fuss. Just be a good boy, Sodz, behave yourself, to make it easier for us to slaughter you.'

'He won't do that,' I said. 'He promised.'

'Promises,' said Sodz, 'from Peacemakers.' He started pacing up and down. 'Where is the gun? Where's Papa Kapko's gun?

You took it. You must have it.'

'No,' I said.

'Give him the gun,' said Kapko.

'No,' I said. 'What would you do with it?'

'If I must die,' said Sodz, 'I don't intend to go alone.'

'A blaze of glory,' Kapko moaned, excitedly, as ever, urging others to take risks he wouldn't dream of facing.

'That's just stupid,' I retorted. 'Sodz, you've got it wrong whichever way you look at it. I promise you that Nikov said that if you do the things he asks, you won't get hurt. But if you try a shoot-out, you'll be killed. And maybe all the rest of us. If we survive the cross-fire they might shoot us just for failing to persuade you to capitulate.'

'I lost the gun,' said Ochre.

That surprised me. That was smart.

'I stole the gun to use when I was trying to help Xan escape and when I had to run away I dropped it.'

'Stupid little fool,' said Sodz.

'It's time to make your mind up. Here's the deal,' I said. 'It's either you go out there and surrender or he comes in here and takes us all.'

'So I'm to be some sort of sacrifice?' said Sodz.

'You could say that.'

'You are putting all of us in danger, Sodz,' said Ochre.

'Sodz stays here.' He stamped his foot upon the ground.

That was the moment Blossom intervened. She turned from Ochre and she reached for Sodz and took his hand. She put their palms together like a pair of bellies and she let her fingers interlink with his as if their limbs were twined.

'You can't let them do this to me,' said Sodz.

She looked at him.

'Please Blossom.' Sodz was whispering.

She moved towards him and she kissed him on the cheek.

'It isn't fair. I didn't kill Salome.'

'No,' she said. 'You wouldn't.'

'I have never hurt a fly.'

'I don't know anyone more gentle.'

'She said that. Salome.'

'Yes. She must have loved you very much.'

'I think she did. I miss her.'

'Here's your chance,' I intervened, 'to get Salome her revenge. It's what we want, what Nikov wants. To catch Salome's killer. To make sure he faces justice. She'd have wanted that.'

'But just suppose it all goes wrong?' He touched his throat. He swallowed and his Adam's Apple moved. 'They'll hang me.' He was looking far away. 'They'll put a rope around my throat. Pull tight. Can't breathe. Lips swollen, tongue ... Eyes going dark ... Sodz dead. I can't be dead. What would I do? No more punani? No more beauty? No more me? You can't ask that of me. Sodz dead? The light gone out? Sodz cramped inside a coffin, in the dark.'

'Please Sodz,' said Blossom.

'Please?' His lips exploded with the word. 'For you? Why should I die for you? What have you ever done for me? You and your fucking family. Oh yes, you stick together. You, your brother and your uncle and, guess what, you have a lover now. I should have fucked you when I had the chance!'

He kicked the rubbish bag. It split. Its contents spilled across the floor.

'What does he mean?' asked Ochre, staring upwards, not addressing anybody in particular, not meeting anybody's gaze.

'What did you think would happen when you wandered off to play the knight in shining armour for your damsel in distress?' Sodz sneered. 'What did you think your slutslag of a sister would be doing once her little brother was away? When you were hiding in your hospital she went upstairs with him.'

He looked at me, and Ochre looked at me. I didn't bother to deny it. What would be the point? I wouldn't be believed.

Sodz stood there twitching with defiance.

Ochre froze.

Sodz said: 'Why don't you ask your sister?'

'Ed?' said Ochre.

'Ed,' said Sodz.

She opened up her lovely mouth as if to speak and then she shut it. Then she opened it again.

'Fuck off,' squeaked Ochre in a strangled voice.

'I think we're all fucked now,' said Sodz.

'Tell me it isn't true.'

I felt detached. It was as if I was outside myself, a dirty mark upon the wall, a member of the audience.

'It's not as bad as that,' she said. 'I never wanted to.'

'It's no big deal,' said Sodz. 'It's only sex.' He made it sound as if it was a massive deal.

'She was my sister.'

'She still is,' I said.

'Not now,' he said. 'Not any more.'

He was so young, I thought. His muscles tight, his body poised, he balanced on the edge of chaos, on the brink. One way lay anger and the other tears. He hurt. I stared at him. He was magnificent. I couldn't take my eyes from him.

'I did it,' Blossom said, 'for you.'

'For me?'

'To make him go and look for you. To bring you home. So that you would be safe.'

They made a pretty pair.

'He forced me to,' she said.

'That isn't true.' I couldn't let that stand. 'It was a deal. I did what you demanded. I have paid. I've paid and paid and paid. I've paid for you, ten times I've paid for you.'

'So you're a whore,' said Ochre and he raised his hand to hit her but she stared right back at him. They were so beautiful, I thought, the pair of them, eyes wide, lips parted, chins thrust out, cheeks hollowed. Bodies set to fight or flee or fuck. My heart was dancing a flamenco.

'But it was for you,' she pleaded.

'Like the other time,' I said.

They froze.

Sometimes the words escape before you have a chance to think.

'What do you mean?' asked Ochre. He turned round to stare at me. His eyes were blank. They filled his face.

I looked at him.

'Did she say that?' he asked.

I nodded. 'I was not her first,' I said. 'She told me. Kapko was. She said she did it so he'd bring you here instead of leaving you behind.'

Sodz started laughing. 'Papa K!' he said. 'Oh, Papa K. He knew what he was doing. He tells Ochre he'll let Blossom come if Ochre does the doctoring, then he tells Blossom he'll let Ochre come if she will sleep with him. I wish I'd thought of that!'

'Whore,' Ochre whispered. There was nothing left. He had no voice, he had no colour in his cheeks. He had been punctured. All his rage had poured away. It left him like a burst balloon, a limp, a lifeless thing, an empty scrap of rubber that had been discarded on the floor.

She said: 'Don't cry. Please, brother. Please don't cry. I am so sorry. Please be strong.'

She reached for him, embraced him, kissed him on the cheek. She'd started crying now. I watched a fat tear rolling down her cheek and thought that if I could have her again I'd cover her with pearls.

'It's why he helped us,' she explained. 'He said that he would give me the address of someone who'd look after us if I would sleep with him. I said I'd only do it if you could come too.'

His lips were parted and his mouth was open but he couldn't speak.

They clung to one another.

'You have to see the funny side of it,' said Sodz. He poked a hand at Ochre's back. 'You were so frightened for your sister with the Shark. All of that time. You were so scared. You knew she fancied me. It turns out you were looking in the wrong direction, boy. Sodz was the only one who never got to shag her!'

'This doesn't change a thing,' I said. 'You have to go with Nikov.'

'You think I want to help this fucked up family?' said Sodz. 'I'm staying here.'

I pulled the gun out of my pocket and I pointed it at him.

His face was puzzled. 'But I thought you said ...' he said to Ochre. 'Yes of course. You lie like all the other Kapkos. What a tribe.'

I clicked the safety catch.

'What do you think you're playing at?' he asked.

'I'll count to five,' I said. 'One...' and I wondered if the other two would let me do this.

Sodz said: 'But I thought you liked me' and he stooped and picked a book up from the floor and hurled it at me but it missed and landed, broken-backed, its pages spilled.

'Two.'

'If you go now, you have a chance,' said Blossom. 'Please. I know you'll do it and I know you will be safe. And afterwards, I'll come and see you on your beach.'

'We'll meet in hell,' he snarled.

'Three.' Sodz just stared at me. What was he thinking? Would he call my bluff?

'Go.' Mr Kapko said.

'He promised, Nikov promised,' I explained. 'He knows you're innocent. He only wants you so he can confront the Boss.'

Sodz laughed. 'What happens to me after that?'

'Four.' Now the tension squeezed my temples. I would have a headache after this.

'OK,' he said. 'I'll go.'

He walked around the garage. I just watched. He stepped into the hall. I followed. Blossom and her brother would have followed too. I waved them back. Stay in the garage. Make no sound. I closed the garage door behind me.

CHAPTER TWENTY NINE: BROTHER AND SISTER

As Sodz walked from the house, I stood well back so Nikov couldn't see my gun. He didn't know I had it. Never let them know your strengths. He'd take it from me.

Anyway, I'd rather Nikov thought I had persuaded Sodz through words and with the power of my personality.

The doorway framed them like a double portrait. Sodz was in the foreground with his hands behind his back and staring straight towards me like the painting of a nude whose unrelenting eyes demand an explanation. Nikov, on the other hand, stooped slightly, looking downwards, fixing handcuffs to his prisoner, looked like a servant.

'Where are all the rest of them?' asked Sodz. 'I thought the house had been surrounded.'

No one answered.

'Shit. You're kidding me.'

A scrawny bird, crouched like a gargoyle on the roof ridge of the terraced houses opposite, pronounced a strident squawk, then overbalanced, skidding from its perch to slither down the slates, its great wings clapping at the air in an abortive bid to fly, its talons scratching at the slope to slow its downfall.

'Nine o'clock,' said Nikov, 'at the entrance to the Tower Block. As we arranged.'

'I've not forgotten.'

Sodz, his eyes wide open, seeing, not believing, shook his head from side to side as if that would dislodge reality.

I closed the door as Nikov started leading him away.

I had a little more than thirty minutes. Time enough.

I walked into the garage. There was something stagnant in the air. A brother and a sister: standing still as statues, staring carefully away from anything that mattered. Their uncle: crumbled, floppy, sunken, lying on the nasty floor. The mess: an empty jar that had held jam, a teacup tilted on its saucer, and the corner of a crust of bread, abandoned to the fuzzy tentacles of mould.

'You can't just let him lie there,' Blossom said.

'Why not?'

'There must be something you can do.'

'There are a lot of things that I could do but most of them have been forbidden by my Hippocratic oath,' said Ochre. 'What I want to do is see him suffer. I would like to watch him die. I wish he would, and quickly.'

Kapko groaned and grunted.

'But the trouble is, I don't believe him anymore. He's lied so much: how do I know that if he screams he's really feeling it? Perhaps it's just another act. I wish I could be sure that he was really ill. Then I'd be happy.'

'Don't say that.' His sister reached out, tried to grab his hand. He batted her away.

'Don't be like that,' I told him. 'She's your sister so you should be nice to her.'

'You mean like you were?'

I ignored the taunt.

'I did my best for her,' said Ochre. 'Him as well. And look at my repayment.'

Kapko's face was blanker than the white face of a clown. He had a hand upon his chest as if, by pushing, he could press away the pain; as if he thought that if he made an effort he could mend his petrifying heart.

'Why don't you tell me where it hurts?' asked Ochre, 'and I'll find another place to hurt you.'

'Is he dying?' I asked Blossom.

But her brother answered: 'Bit by bit. Too slowly.'

'Can I help?'

'There isn't anything that anyone can do,' said Blossom.

Kapko's eyes were wide and staring and his lips were twisting.

'What's he saying?'

'When a Drudjer dies they have to seek forgiveness,' Blossom told me.

'Has he time for that?' I asked her.

Ochre snorted.

Blossom told her brother that it wasn't up to him. She sounded angry. 'I'm the one he wronged. It's my decision.'

'Perhaps,' said Ochre, 'there is nothing to forgive. Perhaps you liked it.'

'No. I can't believe you said that.'

'You say sorry now,' he said. 'But what you do speaks louder. Uncle first. Then him.'

She said: 'I didn't love them.'

That pissed me off. She was a heifer.

'Like that makes it right,' her brother said.

'But why I did it. That was right. For you. My brother. You're the only one I love.'

He wriggled as she tried to wrap her arms around him. 'Let me go.'

She told him she was weak. She said she needed his protection. What a load of balls. She was strong, he was the wimp. She was the one who wrapped herself around his body. Let him nestle into her.

And he submitted. Standing still, he let himself be hugged. He didn't soften, he stayed stern and upright, but he let his bony fingers rest upon her back. She squeezed him closer. I imagined that her breasts spread flat against his ribs, her belly swelling as she breathed, his balls and penis crushed into her groin.

I put myself in his place.

How I wanted her.

I wanted her as strongly as I've ever wanted anything. I wanted her with water in my mouth as if I hungered and I wanted her with breathlessness and with a fast and ragged heartbeat as if I'd been running faster than I should have run. I flushed; I sweated and my lips were swelling. Blood, hot blood, hot burning blood that scorched the inside of my arteries and stretched my veins until they were about to rupture, carried chemicals that galvanized my flesh and super-sensitised my skin and told my testicles to pump my sperm into my prostate ready to explode out of my rigid cock.

I couldn't breathe. I couldn't move. I didn't think.

I plunged my hand into my pocket and I touched the barrel of my gun. The little voice that told me to be careful was engulfed by floods of longing and I gripped it and I jerked it upwards so they saw it.

'What the fuck,' said Ochre.

'In the hall,' I said. My voice was thick, as if I'd gargled treacle.

Blossom looked at me.

'It isn't loaded,' Ochre said.

'With bullets, just, I have, reloaded, now.' The words had all been lined up in my mouth but as I spoke they seemed to stumble on my tongue. 'Into the hall.'

'What's going on?' asked Ochre.

Blossom didn't need to ask. She knew.

'It isn't loaded,' Ochre said again.

I turned to Kapko and I pulled the trigger and the bullet spurted from the barrel and the noise was like the room exploded and the man who had misused me jerked and slowly, as the echoes died away, fell sideways leaving bits of bloody body sticking to the wall.

Though any fool could tell it was all over, Ochre hurled himself at Kapko and he started doing all his doctor things like checking if the corpse was breathing. Blossom was beside him on her knees and he was telling her to press down on a bit that blood was pouring from. And she was doing what he told her to. They were together. They had found ...

'Get up,' I said. 'Get naked.'

They ignored me.

So I yelled. And then I said: 'Stand up. Stand up. If you don't do exactly as I say ... Stand up. I'm telling you.'

And Blossom heard me and she turned and started standing and she clutched her brother's arm. He looked at her and then at me and then he too began to stand.

'Get over there.' I pointed to the corner of the garage Sodz had colonised.

They moved. They were obedient. They stood, their backs against the wall, and looked at me. The pair of them were splashed with blood. I watched as Blossom tried to wipe her hands by rubbing them down and then up her thighs.

'I didn't want to shoot him but you didn't leave me any other thing to do.'

'Put down the gun,' said Ochre.

'I was only doing what you wanted. You'd have killed him if you'd had the guts.'

That last word, inadvertent, sickened me. The shot had ripped his belly and his shining bowels had been displayed.

'Take off your clothes,' I told them.

'What?' said Ochre.

'On your knees.'

He shook his head.

She touched him gently on his wrist. 'I think we'd better, brother.'

'Either that, or watch each other die. I'll do it!'

Ochre nodded. Knelt. 'Let Blossom go.'

'Stand up. That isn't what I wanted. Stand. Take off your clothes. Get naked.'

'But you said.'

'Stand up! The pair of you. Don't make me hurt you. Both of you. Strip off. I want to ...'

Blossom started stripping. First her blouse: two of its buttons missing from last night. Great bloody handprints stained the whiteness of the cloth. Before she took her bra off she placed both her hands onto her breasts so they were blooded too. And then she reached around her back. Unhooked. Her breasts surged forward as they were released.

'B-Blossom,' Ochre said, a strangled voice. I glanced at him. He couldn't take his eyes off her. I felt triumphant.

'No,' he said.

'I have to,' she replied.

She kicked her shoes off, reached down to her hip, unhooked her skirt. It fell. She clambered out of it. She stood in just her panties.

'No,' he said. 'This isn't right. I'll close my eyes. My eyes are closed. I won't, I won't watch this.'

'Your turn,' I said. I poked him with the barrel of the gun. His eyes sprang open in alarm. 'Take off your clothes,' I said.

She begged. 'Please. No.'

'Come here,' I told her. 'Turn around.'

Her thong was stretched across the twin mounds of her beautiful backside. I reached out with my spare hand and caressed her arse. I hooked my thumb into the waistband of the thong, just where it bridged the valley, and I tugged. 'These too.' She pulled them down her thighs. They slipped below her knees and she stepped out of them.

I was as hard as I have ever been.

Her brother's eyes were fixed upon her slit.

'Take off your clothes,' I told him.

He just looked at me.

'I want to watch you fuck her,' I explained.

'I can't,' he said. He started crying.

She stepped forward. Reached for him. 'It's OK, brother,' Blossom said.

'It isn't right.'

'I'll help you. Hold your hands up. Skin a rabbit!' He was mesmerised. He raised his arms. She peeled his sweatshirt off.

She stood in front of him, stark naked. As she pulled his teeshirt off, her breasts brushed past his chest. My mouth was open. I was dry. I licked my lips.

He stared at her and she at him. Their eyes were locked together.

He was really rather beautiful, I thought. He had the slender body of a boy: long legs, smooth thighs, flat stomach, skinny chest. Above each hip a groove began that dived into his shorts.

'Kick off your shoes.' He did as he was told. Her fingers dipped below his belly. Blossom hooked her thumbs inside the waistband of his running shorts. She gave a quick and reassuring nod. 'It is all right,' she said and then she pulled his shorts down.

Boy and girl, both naked, sister, brother, bare. I swallowed and my Adam's apple lurched. But he was limp.

'I want ...' I started.

'But I can't,' he said. 'It won't.' His voice was wet with misery. His eyes had freed themselves from her; now they were flicking left and right, from side to side and back again. He's looking for the exit, an escape, I thought. There's no way out. It was as if he couldn't work out which was worse: to get stiff with your sister or be impotent. I thought, I'll have to help him out.

'Go down on him,' I told her.

'What?'

'Get on your knees. Start sucking him. I want to see him stiff. He's going to fuck you.' I went up to Ochre and I whispered in his ear. 'You pay attention. If you fuck her I will let you go. But if you don't or won't or even can't I'm going to put my gun inside her and I'll fuck her with the barrel. That will hurt. And then I'll shoot a bullet up her guts.'

That's when the silent tears turned into sobs. He was a wimp.

She squatted down.

'No. Not like that,' I said. 'Get down upon your hands and knees.' She did. I went behind her. I unzipped my trousers and took out my cock. I was enjoying this. I swapped hands with the gun and started playing with myself. I found it difficult to concentrate. I wondered whether she was wet. I knelt behind her. I was making sure I kept my eyes on him. It was a pleasure. He was starting to enjoy himself. I let go of my cock and reached beneath her. I began to fondle her. I slid a finger up into her crack. She shied.

I saw his wide eyes watching. 'Do you like?' I asked. 'Have you got hard?' He looked bemused. He nodded. 'Then come here,' I said, 'and stick it into her.'

I'll make him do it like a dog, I thought. Like she had made me do it. Not in any other way. He wasn't getting anything I hadn't had.

He pulled her off him. It was shining with her spit. He walked around her clumsily as if his legs were stiff. His cock bobbed up and down as if it nodded: yes. I moved to let him kneel behind her. She reached back between her legs and took his cock and guided it into her hole. He gave a squeaking gasp as it slid in. He started pulling out but then I slapped his butt.

'I want to watch you fuck her.' As he pushed back in again I placed my palm against his buttocks, making sure he penetrated her. She caught her breath. A little squeak. I let my fingers fumble underneath his balls and touched her perineum and her labia to make sure that he was inside her all the way. And he was big. And she was stretched. 'Okay. Now, slowly, slide it out. That's it. Now slam inside her. Yes. That's it. You have to make her grunt. That's what she wants. Come on. Again. And harder. And again. Again. Again. And faster. And again. Be bad. Be beastly. Like an animal. Again.' I gave the tempo and I started playing with myself. I was as big as I have ever been. I watched the split between his buttocks squeeze and separate and squeeze and separate as he thrust into her. I stroked and stroked.

She started grunting: as he pumped her, air was being jolted from her lungs. She shrieked. He yelped. She mewled, he barked. She lowed, he brayed. He grunted and collapsed on top of her and she howled: 'No.'

The faintly fishy fragrance of her snatch was matched by sperm's sour smell.

They lay all tangled on the floor. The brother and the sister, boy and girl, the fucker and the fucked. And uncle. Dead.

I felt deflated. Emptied. Dead.

It wasn't funny anymore.

I tucked myself back in, zipped up. I put the gun back in my pocket, picked my keys up from the table. I walked out. I turned and locked them in.

CHAPTER THIRTY:
THE TRIAL

I wasn't late but Faith was there already, standing, hands on hips, her right foot tapping out the limits of her patience, like she wanted me to know that she was nervous. Like I wasn't tense enough myself.

'A shave,' she said, 'might have been sensible. At least a shower or a change of clothes.'

'I've not had time.'

She raised her eyebrows. 'What have you been doing? I've been prepping Sodz.'

'Perhaps,' I told her, 'I'd be neater if your boyfriend hadn't locked me in the crypt last night.'

'He's not my boyfriend.' But she didn't act surprised. I guessed that Nikov must have told her what had happened. She had been preparing Sodz, so Nikov must have taken him to Faith. They'd not had long. I hoped he'd learned his lines.

She sniffed. 'We'd better take the stairs.'

I didn't care. I knew I was unwashed, uncombed, unpleasant. I'd not brushed my teeth since breakfast yesterday. My mouth was full of nastiness and ugly tastes. The inside of my underpants were sticky; I supposed that they were stained. My armpits hosted matted hair which smelt like seaweed, rotting in a rockpool on the beach. My skin was smudged with half-evaporated sweat. My face felt foul.

As ever, Faith was smartly dressed - a black skirt and a white blouse crisply ironed, translucent tights (with, I suspected, double knickers underneath and on, like one of those church-tethered women who are prim as privilege and seem determined to renounce biology) and brightly polished leather loafers with a slightly higher heel than you'd expect - and made up to perfection. The sort of woman who, however used she'd been, looked spanking new. As if she was a doll who dressed herself.

'Have you got blood on you?' she asked. She pointed. I had placed my hand onto the bannister and where I might have worn my wedding ring there was a heart-shaped brown-stained mark. I had been splattered, I supposed, with Mister Kapko's blood. I hoped that he was not contaminated. Drudjers bear diseases; had he not himself said that the Kennels was an incubator for infections?

There'd been a lot of blood in Mister Kapko. Blood and nasty stuff. Skin hides a lot of ugliness. I'd have to scrub the garage out. I didn't know if I would ever get it clean.

At last we reached what had been Mister Kapko's office. I was glad. I was exhausted. It had been a stressful week. It wasn't easy, keeping people happy. Nearly there. 'Just two more flights to go,' I said. I hadn't meant to speak my thoughts aloud. Why had I?

'One. Just one more flight of stairs.'

'One to the penthouse,' I explained, 'and one ...'

'We are not going to the roof.'

'I thought.'

She made a face. It told me all I didn't want to know. 'The venue's changed. The Boss thought that it would be more appropriate to hold the hearing where the crime occurred.'

'But what about the cameras?'

'What cameras?'

'The cameras, the hidden cameras, the cameras that only Nikov knows about. You said yourself that there was something secret hidden on the roof. You thought that it was treasure.'

'Treasure?' What I hated was the scornful way she said it, like because she'd primped herself she mattered more than me. There's smart, I thought, and there is smartly groomed.

'You said that there was something. You were right. There is a secret system of surveillance. Kapko Industries installed it.'

'On the roof?' Her tone: derisive disbelief.

'That was the reason Gary and his men went rushing to the roof. If they had stopped inside the penthouse they'd have captured Sodz. But they were scared the secret system would be burned. So Sodz escaped. You see? It all makes sense.'

'You're telling me that Gary knew about this secret system.'

'Yes!'

'But you are also saying only Nikov knows.'

'That's right. It's how we'll make the Boss confess on camera.'

'But Gary and the Boss are thick as thieves. If Gary knew he would have told the Boss.'

I hadn't thought of that. It didn't matter though. It wasn't reason to belittle me.

'And we're not going to the roof,' she said.

I understood. 'The Boss found out. That's why he's moved downstairs.'

'Or else there are no secret cameras. Perhaps the Boss just wanted to conduct the trial where the murder happened.'

'Why?'

'Because he loved his wife?'

'He killed her. That's not love.'

She shook her head. It isn't always simple, she was telling me. As if I didn't know.

We reached the final landing. Many times I'd entered Mister Kapko's office through this door but this would be the first time since his death. It seemed impossible that I had killed him. Me? I felt the same as when I'd walked those ten steps from the doorway to his desk the first time, as a callow, jobless graduate. He had seemed God-like. Gods can't die. It hadn't happened, can't have done. It must have been a dream.

And, as in dreams, the door swung open and I stepped inside.

And stopped. The gap from here to there had never seemed so big. The room, no longer used, had never seemed so empty.

There was someone sitting at his desk.

'What's wrong? You look as if you've seen a ghost,' said Faith.

I would have spoken if I could. I couldn't. If I could have moved I would have turned and fled. All I could do was stand and stare.

He'd changed my life. When he employed me, he had gathered all my possibilities into a single strand. Fate has a twisted sense of humour. He had fucked my wife and I had fucked him back.

'Come on,' said Faith. 'We are already late.' She jostled me, to pass me, and I stumbled, and I saw that it was Gary sitting at the desk, where Mister Kapko should have been.

'Are you all right?'

I shook my head. I might as well. The rest of me was shaking by itself. 'Bad memories,' I answered.

'No. You're fucking kidding me. You want my gun? Fuck off.'

A Peacemaker - I recognised him, Malc - was angry with the man behind the desk.

'You can't go in there with a weapon,' Gary said. 'It isn't me, it is the rules; the same for all the jurors. Just while you're up there. You'll get it back.' He pointed with his thumb at Mister Kapko's safe, set in the wall behind him, covered by the painting of a peaceful landscape. Gary, taking Malc's gun, slid the picture sideways, opening the safe. The gun was added to the sprawling heap of brutal metal tubes.

'Go up the stairs, the living room,' said Gary. Then he turned to us. 'You can't come in. The jury's full. There's only Peacemakers allowed.'

'He's on the list,' said Faith. 'A witness.'

I was checked, authenticated, fingerprinted, told to follow Malc up to the penthouse. Faith, however, was allowed no further.

'Don't forget St Jude,' she told me as we parted. 'He's the saint to go to after hope has said goodbye.'

Saint bloody Judas seemed appropriate.

I climbed the stairs as carefully as any school kid creeps into a class of strangers on his first day in a new school. Would I find a place? What were the rules? It didn't help that I would be the only one who wasn't in the Peacemakers. Apart from Sodz. The prisoner.

I paused a moment at the stairhead. I was in a vestibule,

surrounded by five doorways. Straight ahead of me, the door into the penthouse living room was open. Through it I could see a press of bodies: comrades slapping other comrades on the back, friends shaking hands, pals laughing at the jokes of other pals, mates swapping anecdotes. I had a moment's panic. Turning round, I headed in the opposite direction. All the other doors were closed but one of them must lead into a place where I could hide. I opened one at random.

'No. You can't come in.' It was the Boss. I had surprised him. He was crouched and bending over something. 'Go away.'

I gulped. 'I'm looking for the bathroom.'

'Not in here.'

I backed away. I closed the door. He had been leaning over something on a bed. Salome?

'Mr Angelo.'

I spun around. There, standing in the entrance to the living room, the light behind him so it looked as if he had a halo covering his silhouette from head to toe, was Nikov.

'I was looking for the bathroom.'

'Not right now. We're nearly ready. You're the last one to arrive. I knew you wouldn't let me down. I wasn't worried. Come along. I'll show you where you're sitting.'

'But it was supposed to be,' I whispered as we went into the living room, 'up on the roof.'

 'We've made some changes to the plan. You're sitting on the sofa, next to Tomas, over there. The witness bench.' He gave a grin. 'We'll start as soon as Gary joins us. Gentlemen!' He turned away to organise the crowd of Peacemakers.

There were a dozen of them: twelve big bodies. What if they were weaponless? The room was saturated with the scarifying scent of masculinity.

They'd congregated by the entrance so I had to dodge and shuffle past them. 'Sorry. Please excuse me. Do you mind? I'm heading for the couch.'

Resentfully, reluctantly, they stepped aside for me. I heard the muttering: 'He gets a seat; we have to stand. What's that about?' 'Why do we need a witness? Don't we know what's what?' 'That data-guy.'

At last I reached the far side of the crowd. The hubbub was behind me. Feeling like a swimmer stepping from the sea, I looked around.

I'd not been in the living room before. I'd worked for Mister Kapko all those years and never made it up here. This was private. I had only worked for him.

But in the end he'd lived with me. And, in the end, he'd died there.

Sodz was sitting in the centre of the room upon a straight-backed wooden chair to which he had been handcuffed by each ankle and each wrist. His back was to the Peacemakers. He stared ahead towards the panoramic windows. He could see the sky. Today, there was a little bit of blue. The clouds were blossoming. Since sunrise they'd been spreading. Now what had then been white was dirty grey, what had been grey was darkening.

I walked across a sheep-skinned rug so vast they must have made it from the shearings of a flock. There'd been a glass of wine tipped over, Sodz had said, the night the Memsahib had been murdered. But I couldn't see a stain.

Sodz must have been sharp-eyed to see white pearls on this.

The sofa was black leather with the sort of cushions that embrace you when you sit on them. This and the carpet testified to Mister Kapko's taste: extravagance and boastfulness. He'd been that sort of person. At the end, though, he had been a fugitive in hiding, in my garage, owning nothing but a body with a dodgy heart.

I had been merciful.

I sat down next to Tomas. Stared at Sodz. What was he thinking? What was he remembering? Salome? How he'd had her? He had lost her. That's the way it goes. But I'd had Blossom and her brother too. The last man standing gets the girl. I fucking won, and that's not anything to be ashamed of.

And that was when the Boss arrived.

The knot of Peacemakers which had so hampered me when I passed through them didn't in the least impede the Boss. A path appeared; he strolled along it like a self-made monarch swaggering along a boulevard. He nodded to the faces that he recognised, exchanging courtesies with those whose names he knew. He shook some hands, slapped backs, he even punched the air, which took it as a compliment.

And they began applauding.

Then I knew we'd lost.

Our arguments were irrefutable. Sodz was innocent. He hadn't killed the Memsahib. Someone else had, almost certainly the Boss. But that was logic. Reason with a rabble? Swarms don't listen to the facts. That's not the way they work.

Was it too late to run away?

'Stand up,' hissed Tomas but I'd only just sat down and now the couch had captured me. I struggled. In the end he had to help me, stopping clapping for a moment to reach down and haul me from the pit.

The Boss acknowledged the ovation by participating. In a moment, all our claps were synchronised with his. Then, still in time, the Peacemakers began to stamp. The floor was shaking. I was terrified. I was convinced we'd cause an earthquake, bring the building down. But then, almost as soon as it began, the Boss completed it by lifting up his hands above his head. There was an instant hush.

'My friends,' he said. 'I want to thank you all for coming to support me. You can well imagine that today is difficult for me. It's but a few days since my Memsahib died. In there.' He pointed to the bedroom. Heads were turned.

'It's hard enough to lose a loved one. It's even tougher when she's murdered. Blood so spilled cries out for justice. I seek vengeance. It is comforting to me to know that you are with me. I am confident that I can trust you. You're my friends. You're more than that: you are my comrades. Even more: you're Peacemakers. We're Peacemakers. And Peacemakers know what is right and what is wrong and Peacemakers are pledged to make this world a better place. The offal must be plucked out from the carcase so it doesn't taint the venison.' He indicated Sodz.

I wondered Sodz could bear to be the centre of such hatred. There were sixteen people in that room, aside from Sodz himself, so there were sixteen pairs of eyes. Imagine all that anger being stared at you.

'I am not asking you, my friends, to take revenge on my behalf. You're Peacemakers. I know you'll make your minds up on the basis of your own beliefs. I'm certain you will do what should be done because it is what must be done. You will decide the punishment that will be suffered by this … Drudjer.'

Here he paused. But nothing happened. So he clapped his hands. He pointed at the door into the room. Somebody coughed. Malc, being closest, took a step towards the door.

Then Gary walked into the room as if he was a priest in a procession. Dignified and reverent, he carried, in both hands, a silver dish, a tray, ornate, engraved, a little larger than a single seat. He held it like a waiter bringing drinks, though there was nothing on it. Not so far as I could see.

But when the dish was handed to the Boss he turned it so its surface was displayed. Somebody gasped. The shiny surface had a dirty red-brown smudge across it. Someone whispered: 'Is that blood?' A ripple - 'Blood.' 'Whose blood?' 'It must be her blood, don't you think?' - spread out across the room and bounced against the walls and shrank back to its starting point.

'The Memsahib's blood,' the Boss announced, 'has dried. It has coagulated. But ...' He walked across to Sodz with tiny steps, but rapidly. He held the tray up high, two handed. Then he brought it down.

I think I heard the crash before I saw what happened.

He had smashed the tray onto the skull of Sodz. So when I looked again the tray was dented, sitting there as if it was a wide brimmed hat. That must have hurt, I thought. Sodz blinked. Then I saw blood. I thought: he's bleeding. Then I saw it wasn't his.

It was the blood upon the tray. I watched it. It began to liquefy. It started flowing. I could see it oozing to the edge. And then it started dripping.

I was mesmerised. It couldn't be. But, drip by drip, I watched it fall onto the carpet. Red, red blood was pooling in among the strands of white, white wool and for the first time I discovered that I doubted Sodz. Let's set aside the evidence. Blood flowed from murder victims' bodies, that was fact.

'Bravo,' said Sodz, 'you are a *prestigiatore*, you're a master of illusions. You have put the con in conjuror. That's all this is: a magic trick.'

'A corpse, when brought into the presence of its murderer, begins to bleed,' the Boss announced.

'So that's the way we're rolling. That's your game. I wondered how you'd play it. But don't you think it's rather risky bringing in your pups, your little sycophantic yap-yap-yapping terriers? You ought to know that dogs are just a twisted chromosome away from wolves and packs can flip to horrors when the master's back is turned.'

'Behold. My Memsahib's blood is spilled upon the ground and cries to me for vengeance.'

'Goodness me. Suppose you're right. It's la demencia, it's lunacy, it's woof woof howling at the moon-acy, it's batshit bonkers, it is empty attic craziness, it is insanity, it's loopiness, it's crackers but if you want to believe it, let's suppose for half a minute you are right. You touched it too.'

The Boss, who, I supposed, expected subjugation from his prisoner, expected meek submission rather than this fusillade of words, was, for a fatal moment, hesitant.

'You touched it too,' said Sodz, 'so if you honestly believe in all this magic of the melting blood then all you've proved is that Salome's murderer is one of us. It's either you or me. It wasn't me. It must be you. You want to flip a penny?'

'Shut the fuck,' somebody shouted from the back. 'You should be fucking silent.'

'No. You're right. I wouldn't want to leave this to the whims of chance,' said Sodz. 'Though fortune's always favoured me there comes a moment when the luckiest of beggars needs to cash his chips. So let's review the evidence. You first. Cat caught your tongue? May I assist? You tell us you received a phone call from Salome, beg your pardon, from your Mem-sahib, seven-thirty-ish in which she told you that a Drudjer was attacking her; at least, that's what you said to Gary when you ordered him to take some troops up to the Tower Block. I crossed the bridge from north to south as is recorded in the log at eight o'clock. And that was after Tomas says that he saw Gary and the troops deployed. I wasn't in the building, not at seven-thirty, not when she was murdered. Therefore, ergo, hence it wasn't me. I have an alibi. I've concrete proof it wasn't me. So if your hocus pocus with the blood is worth its weight and it was really one of us and I'm the one who has an alibi it must be you. I think that proves it. QED.'

Sodz looked like he was melting. Sweat was pouring from him, mixing with the blood. If it was blood.

'But wait. You have an alibi as well. You'll tell me you were in your Town Hall office when Salome was attacked. You were the one to take the phone call. But you didn't, did you? Nikov checked the call logs. No one phoned. That's no one, not Salome, nobody. But you told Gary that they had. You lied to him. You fooled him. You're deceitful, you're duplicitous, you are perfidious. It's one thing, I suppose, to tell untruths to Drudjers. You have lied to your own people. How can you be trusted?'

It was what they'd told him he should say. When Nikov took him from outside my house he'd passed him on to Faith. She'd not had long to school him. Just about the time it took for Ochre to fuck Blossom, and that bucky-boy came quickly. Sodz had learned his lines.

Except it didn't make a difference.

It should have done. If there was any justice in the world it would have done. It didn't though.

The Boss confessed.

'Of course I killed her. She was sleeping with a Drudjer. You.' He turned towards his audience. 'Which one of you would not have done the same?'

There was a rumble of consent.

The Boss confessed. We'd not expected that. We'd concentrated on the murder. He had focused on the treachery.

I knew then: Sodz was going to be lynched. And I would be beside him.

'She betrayed me. She betrayed me twice. The first time, when she gave her body to this Drudjer.'

'Gave? Her body.' That was courage. I respected Sodz. He must have known he didn't have a chance but he kept going.

'Gave. She married me, and marriage grants exclusive rights.' That wasn't clever of the Boss. Don't answer back. It looks as if you're being beaten.

'But she didn't just betray me, she betrayed us all. The Peacemakers. Our movement. There were secrets that I must have spoken in my sleep. She told this Drudjer. Secrets of the Peacemakers. He sold them to his Drudjer contacts.'

'That's not true. She loved to gossip, did Salome. Told me all about herself. I knew the pony she had ridden as a little girl, I knew she hated blackberries, she told me all about the first time she got drunk. But nothing else. Most women tell me how their husbands grunt and groan, the odour of their sweat, their preference for doggy or for dressing up, how swiftly afterwards they shrivel, slump and start to snore. She didn't tell me anything like that. And as for secrets. Nothing. She was loyal.'

Sodz began to wriggle. 'Would you mind? My leg is numb. I think it's gone to sleep. I don't suppose you could massage it?

Just a rub? Not possible? Perhaps you could unchain it, then. I can't escape. How could I, with a dozen of your massive mates between the door and me?'

The Boss had started pacing up and down. He'd started snorting. I could see his fists were clenched.

'It seems a little OTT to chain not just my wrists but ankles too. I'm at your mercy. Nothing I can do. Right now you have the power over me of life or death; that's more or less omnipotence. A little comfort doesn't seem too much to ask. Unlock my legs. I'd like to stretch them out.'

The Boss, his bull-neck bulging, steaming visibly, was getting really rather red.

'I might as well admit it: I've not always done the right thing. What felt good, that's more or less how I decided what to do. It's not conventional morality. So, yes, I guess I'm bad. I think bad thoughts: I'm jealous and I'm greedy and I'm often horrid when I talk to people and from time to time I lie. I've taken things - who hasn't? - that were claimed by someone else. I've even not done things I should have done and that's a sort of sin as well.'

The Boss stayed silent, smothering his anger.

I was sweating. It was like a steam room. It was like the pressured calm before the thunder. Something was about to break.

'Of course I've sinned,' said Sodz, 'and, if you let me live, I'll go on sinning, like we all do, all the time.'

It seemed the Boss was swelling. Would he burst?

'My wrists are hurting. Would you mind releasing me? I understand your point of view. I know you're full of rage and wrath and angry to the point of craziness. And I take full responsibility. It's all my fault, I blame myself, I'm not accusing anybody else. I beg you all to judge me not too harshly. If you can, forgive me. If you can't, forgive yourselves.'

The Boss stopped, staring through the window, hands behind his back, his fingers locked, his knuckles white.

'But here's the thing. Salome wasn't guilty. Not of anything. But she was killed. And I was not her killer.'

'No!' The Boss swung round, he strode across to Sodz, he swung his hand and slapped Sodz round the face, a smack so savage that it pushed Sodz over and he toppled to the floor, him and the chair, still tied together.

'Stop talking!' bawled the Boss. He stood, hunched over, hands like claws, prepared to snatch or punch or throttle, restless twitching legs kept ready, if required, to stamp or trample. Breathing heavily.

There was a silence.

'Boss,' said Nikov and the Boss looked up and Nikov beckoned and the Boss, although he shuffled like a zombie, went to Nikov. They conferred but they were talking in a whisper so I don't know what was said.

It seemed that Nikov was suggesting something. As I watched, the Boss, as if exhausted, nodded.

Nikov glanced around, saw me, and handed me a set of keys. 'Unlock him.'

That sort of thing is easier to order than perform. It took a little longer than I liked. I didn't know which key was which. The locks were small; the keys were delicate; it mattered which way up they entered. Making matters worse, I was aware I was the focus of attention; I could sense some hostile stares. I fumbled. Quite a lot.

Sodz didn't say a single word. He wouldn't even look at me.

When it was done I helped him up. He took some time to

stand. He told me he had pins and needles so he rubbed each wrist in turn and then he rubbed his thighs two-handed. Even then he wobbled. 'Not too steady on the pins,' He said. 'It's like I am a sailor come to landfall at the end of a long voyage.'

'I have spoken to the Boss,' said Nikov, talking loud as if he was on stage announcing the results, which, in a way, he was 'and he has made the judgement that the Drudjer should be hunted.'

Round the room there was a stirring of excitement. Hunted? What was that supposed to mean?

'We'll set him free,' said Nikov. 'He will be allowed to leave this room and go downstairs. I'll count to ten and after that we'll follow. Anyone who catches him can punish him in any way they see appropriate.'

There was a whisper of excitement from the Peacemakers, the dozen jurymen, men good, men true, their muscles flexing and their juices flowing at the thought of hunting Sodz, of hurting him.

'Hang on.' Sodz had a look of desperation in his face. 'You must be joking. Give me half a chance. You've only just unleashed me. I'm not ready.'

You had better be,' said Nikov. 'One.'

Sodz flung himself towards the door, colliding with a Peace-maker who grabbed him.

'Let him go,' commanded Nikov. 'Two.'

Sodz burst away and tumbled through the doorway. I could hear him running down the stairs.

'Three. Four.'

Where will he go? I wondered. To the Kennels?

'Five.'

But weren't they booby-trapped? Sodz wouldn't know about the footbridge, that the guards had vanished.

'Six.'

He might go to the garage.

'Seven.'

And the Peacemakers would follow him. They'd find the Drudjers. They would find the corpse.

'Eight.'

Malc said: 'Fuck! Our guns are in the fucking safe.'

'Nine.'

Then the Boss said: 'Gary, go downstairs right now and get the safe unlocked.'

'Ten.'

The room, so crowded, emptied, in a burst. All of a sudden there was only me, the Boss and Nikov.

'Tally ho,' the Boss said. 'To the roof. We'll watch the chase from there.'

CHAPTER THIRTY ONE: THE FALL GUY

'Where is he? Can you see the dirty little Drudjer?' said the Boss. He stood there at the parapet, his shoulders back, chest pouting, with a greedy look upon his face. He sucked air inwards through his mouth, exhaling through his nose in throttled snorts. He held his hands behind his back, left's fingers wrapped round right's wrist, clutching, squeezing till the blood was dammed. His right thigh twitched; he bounced his left foot up and down.

'There.' Nikov pointed. 'Look. He's heading for the bridge.'

'Then call the guard,' the Boss demanded. 'Get the guard to head him off. Why don't you call him, Nikov? Do I have to do it all myself?' He turned to me. 'You. Over there.' He pointed to the corner of the roof. 'You tell me if you see the pack. I want to know the moment they appear.'

'He means the chasers,' Nikov said. 'He means the other Peacemakers.'

'Don't tell me what I mean!' The Boss was furious. 'Don't change the subject. Where's the bloody guard?'

'We took him off the bridge,' said Nikov. 'He was needed as a witness.'

'Was he? Didn't hear him do much witnessing.'

'We didn't think we needed anybody on the bridge. Right now

the only people crossing are our soldiers.'

'Fleeing from the bloody army. And the bloody Drudjer's nearly reached the bloody river and the bloody hunters aren't in bloody sight.'

The tension of the moment agitated me. 'They've just appeared. They're coming through the door. Four, five, six, seven ... fourteen. Yes. I think that's all of them.'

'They took their time.'

'They must have stopped to get their guns,' said Nikov.

'Drudjer is already on the first bit of the bridge.'

'They'll catch him.' Nikov was much calmer than the Boss.

'They will? I wouldn't be so sure of that.' The Boss produced a pistol. Pulled the trigger. Bang, bang, bang. The sudden smell of cordite. I discovered I had ducked. But he was shooting at the fleeing figure of the Shark. The body of the Boss, all brawn, absorbed the jolt.

Another bang, another shot. 'A running target with a handgun? It's a fair old distance. It will have to be a lucky shot,' said Nikov.

'They're spreading out,' I told them. 'They don't know which way he's ... Now they've seen him. Now they're after him. I think it's Malc. He's in the lead.'

The Boss had moved into the classic forward firing crouch. He sighted, pulled the trigger once again. His face was furious with focus. Bang! And then, bang, bang, bang, bang!

'He's on the apex of the arch,' said Nikov.

'Damn!' The Boss was out of ammo but he pulled another clip out of his pocket and replaced it in the handle of the pistol. It took no longer than a moment but already Sodz was running down the farside of the Bridge towards the High Street. Just a few more paces and he'd have some buildings he could hide behind.

Another bang. The noise was loud enough from my side of the roof; their ears must be exploding.

'Now they're after him, they're catching up,' I called.

Bang, bang! 'I've got him! Look. He's down. He's fallen. Yes.' The Boss, his pistol-holding fist held high, was dancing in a stamping sort of way. 'A lucky shot? I've always been a lucky shot. Get luckier the more I try.'

I hurried forward so that I could see. I saw.

Sodz flat. Sodz belly down. Sodz on the tarmac. Arms spread wide. Shaped like a Y. Face in the dirt.

That's how it finishes.

'I promised her,' the Boss was saying, swollen-eyed. 'I told her I would make her Drudjer lover pay for this.' He danced, if you could call it dancing, with his cheeks puffed out, his chest and belly bulging, and his arms aloft. He punched his feet into the roof as if he wanted to impress it. Like he owned it. Like he meant to rule the world.

I looked at Nikov and he looked away.

He'd been appraising me.

What was he thinking? That I might betray him, I supposed. Who knew of Nikov's plan to overthrow the Boss? Sodz did and he was dead. So that left Faith, perhaps, and me.

He'd silence me, the first chance that he found.

The only thing that I could do was tell the Boss and do it straightaway.

My mouth was open and my lungs were full. I was about to

speak when Nikov said: 'He's up. He's getting up. He must have tripped.'

The Boss, not in the least light-footed at the best of times, stopped dancing with a sudden vehemence that shook the roof. He bawled: 'I bloody got him. Look.' He pointed. 'Can't you see? He's hurt. There's blood.'

Sodz wasn't running anymore. His right leg dragged. His hands were reaching down to grasp his thigh. To stop the blood? To help him walk? He staggered. Leant a moment on the wall. He'd never make it. He was far too slow.

The Peacemakers were closing in.

The Boss was lining up another shot.

Another crack. We saw what seemed to be a small explosion: dust and chippings flying through the air. The bullet must have hit some brickwork.

'That was close,' said Nikov.

I saw Sodz look round. I couldn't see the feelings on his face - he wasn't near enough - but I could see him hesitate. The Boss had fired in front of him, as though to cut him off. I wondered whether that had been intended.

Bang, bang, bang. Another little fusillade of shots. Sodz made his mind up. With a mighty lurch he heaved himself, his damaged leg behind him, round the corner of a building.

I was, just for a moment, disappointed. Now I couldn't see. If Sodz was lynched we would have had a grandstand view. Now they would have to track him through the passages and alleyways.

'Somebody must have tampered with my sights,' the Boss exclaimed.

'You've slowed him down. The lads will get him now,' said

Nikov.

'Malc's already on the bridge,' I told them. 'Tomas too. But ...'

That was strange. That hadn't happened. Couldn't have. Not possible. I'd seen it but I couldn't quite believe my eyes.

'But what?'

'They've stopped. They're in the middle of the bridge. They're looking at the northern bank. They know he's there. Malc's kicking at the railings on the bridge. He looks frustrated. Furious.'

I understood.

'He's told them there's an armistice,' I said.

The Boss, his sweaty palm still clamped around his handgun's grip, turned through a quarter of a circle so that he was facing Nikov. I was, for the moment, in the background. That's a better place to be. Particularly at the moment when the Boss had just been thwarted and his lust for blood had not been satisfied.

I didn't want to draw attention to myself but on the other hand this was my chance. Perhaps my only opportunity.

The way I saw it, Nikov wouldn't want the Boss to know about the plot to topple him. He'd got away with it for now. He'd always tried to play the puppet-master, hidden by the backdrop. That was why he'd left it up to Sodz to make the case against the Boss. And then Boss had seen the way the wind was blowing and had flipped the script. So Nikov did what anybody in those circumstances would have done: played possum and pretended that the world was just the way that it had always been.

And now he needed to protect himself. First chance he had, he'd try to shut me up.

I told the Boss: 'The reason that the Peacemakers have given up the chase is that they have been told they aren't allowed across the river.'

But he didn't blink. The black hole of the pistol's barrel didn't waver. His eye, as dark as any target, never faltered. He had known. The Boss had always known. He knew it all.

The cameras. The hidden cameras. Suppose that they existed. Faith had told me that if Gary knew, the Boss would too. Perhaps he had. Perhaps that was the secret of what otherwise appeared to be omniscience. And maybe it was Nikov who was in the dark.

He must have known that Nikov was betraying him. That Nikov wanted to usurp him. He'd waited. Now his blood was up. He bellowed: 'Baulked. I have been blocked. Blood cries for blood. I will have justice for my Memsahib.'

'You can tell it's all gone wrong,' said Nikov, 'when the only thing that you have left is vengeance.'

'This is justice,' said the Boss.

'You've never known the difference.'

'I know that you've been having talks behind my back, negotiating with the army. Major Whitstable - you see? I know, I always knew. I knew you had a problem with the times: the ceasefire is supposed to start tonight. Of course you hoped to be in charge by then. But, so that you could get your Drudjer friend away, you told my men the truce began this morning, dawn to be precise, so that they couldn't cross the river. That's what caught you out.'

He stopped. He was a big man with a heavy build, strong-boned with slabs of flesh. Indoors he had been dominant. But now that we were on the roof it seemed that he was even bigger than before. He was formidable.

'You really thought you could replace me. Not a chance. Why don't we put it to the vote? We'll call the boys back. We are a democracy. They have the right to choose their leader. You or me. Who do you think they'll pick?'

He stared at Nikov. 'Yes, I killed my wife, but that's the sort of thing that they can easily forgive. I know my men.'

'I've saved us. We were losing. I arranged a peace.'

'You think that's what they want? They'd rather be defeated. They would rather die. There is no honour in a peace like this. There is no pride.'

He stopped and I saw little beads of whiteness round his mouth.

'They laugh at you. They call you Mister Purity. They know, you know. They know you want to stop corruption.'

'We all want to build a better world. That's why we're doing what we're doing. That's the mission of the Peacemakers.'

'You really think that's what they're after? Don't be stupid. What they want is food and drink and sex and sport and how they get it is by theft and looting and extortion and by raping and by killing. They are predators. That's why we have the Drudjers, to provide the prey.'

He held his belly with the hand that didn't hold the gun and he guffawed. 'Stamp out corruption? Did you really think they'd vote for that?'

'You're not so sure,' said Nikov. 'If you were, you wouldn't point a gun at me.'

I thought it might be wise for me to leave. I started going backwards, taking unobtrusive steps.

'You've got the whole thing wrong again. The gun is not because I'm scared of you. It's as I told you: I want justice. You've been judged. You're guilty. Now you will be punished. That's the only way you can redeem yourself.'

'Suppose I jumped,' said Nikov.

It was as if I had been belly-punched. As if I had been emptied. Like I'd stopped.

The Boss was tickled by the notion. 'Do you think an angel swooping down from heaven will catch you in its arms before you mash your skull into the muck?'

'I think I'd have a fighting chance of landing in the river.'

'Would you bet your life?'

'What do you reckon to the odds?'

'I'd give you fifty to a fiver. But you know that it won't save you. It is just as hard to land in water, so they say.'

'I wouldn't want to overshoot. I'd have to work out just how fast to run. It would be useful if there was a try out first.'

He looked at me.

No. No, no, no.

The Boss, who hadn't even glanced at me before, looked now. 'The data guy?'

The life inside me shrivelled. Dread ballooned. A great big blackness filled my brain. I sweated but my arms and legs were frosting over and my bones were being chewed by cold.

They chattered on as if they hadn't noticed that my universe was dying.

Nikov joked: 'You told me I would need an angel. Mr Angelo's the closest I can find.'

'It would be fun to watch him,' said the Boss.

'If I were you,' said Nikov and I understood, though hazily, as if through broken glass, that he meant me, 'I'd run as fast as you can manage. When you jump you have to clear this parapet. You'll have about two seconds in the air.'

I nodded. No, no, no, no, no, I thought.

The Boss was droll. 'That's when you pray. I'd make it brief. And if you've never learned to swim you'd better pray for that as well.'

'I can't,' I stuttered, 'c-c-cant, can't, cant.'

My shirt was sticking to my back. Blood surged and sucked away, my temples throbbed. It felt as if my eyeballs had a pair of thumbs behind them, pushing outwards, squashing them against my eyelids. I began to gasp for air.

This wasn't happening.

The Boss began to giggle. 'Not the data guy,' he said. 'The fall guy.'

Nikov laughed.

They clucked and chuckled like a pair of courting crows. They had no eyes for anybody but each other.

A monstrous hand was rummaging around my gut and squeezing what should not be squeezed.

I was about to shit myself.

This wasn't happening! It mustn't so it couldn't so it wouldn't. In my chest there was a bubble. It expanded fast. It crushed my heart and liquid anger flooded through my body till my skin was smoking.

In my pocket was the gun. Nobody knew I had it. Gary took the sidearms from the Peacemakers but data-guys are not supposed to carry guns; he hadn't even thought to ask me.

I only had two bullets.

But it was my only chance.

I counted: one, two, three. I grabbed the gun. I pulled the trigger. Shot the Boss.

He didn't fall. He didn't fountain blood. He didn't even quiver. But
I could have sworn I didn't miss.

He started turning, facing me. No laughter now. But, honestly, his look of raw surprise was priceless.

So I shot again. He spun around. His gun went flying in a perfect arc across the balustrade and down towards the river, dropping out of sight. The Boss himself collapsed against the wall.

The sky was twisting, the horizon tilting and the ground began to shake. The clouds seemed solid and the surface of the rooftop seemed to melt and bubble like a slab of toasted cheese. My head was ringing like it was the inside of a bell; the world outside was silent.

In front of me, too close to focus, was the face of Nikov, crooked and distorted, screaming.

'What?'

As if from far away I heard him telling me to shoot the Boss again.

He didn't understand.

'I can't,' I said. I offered him a smile instead.

He shouted something. It was muffled. What, I wondered, was the point? We'd reached the end. The rooftop.

Nikov held his hand out for the gun. I gave him it. He took it over to the Boss and tried to finish him. It clicked.

'I only had two bullets,' I explained. The solid things were solid once again, the clouds were fluffy and the sky had settled down. It had the makings of a sunny day.

'Stay here,' commanded Nikov. 'I will go and get my gun. It's in the safe. You keep an eye on him.'

Oh no. Oh no, no, no, no, no. I watched him race across the roof and start to hurdle down the stairs. He thought that I was stupid. He was wrong. He thought that I'd wait here. Not on your life. He'd come back with his gun and kill the Boss. Then he'd kill me.

I was the perfect patsy. I had shot the Boss. Now Nikov could dispose of me: 'shot while attempting to escape'. Then Nikov would be in the clear. What made it even better was that Gary, who had let me keep my gun, would be suspected of collusion.

Nikov had already reached the floor below. I couldn't hang around. I had to flee.

This was my only chance.

I tumbled down the stairs into the Penthouse. I had hardly any time: no longer than it took for him to go down to the floor below, to grab his gun from Mister Kapko's safe, and to return.

I pressed the button for the private lift.

Thank goodness. It was there. The door began to open.

I could hear the sound of Nikov coming up the stairs. His footsteps getting closer.

As I squeezed myself into the lift and jabbed my finger at the button to descend I saw the top of Nikov's head. I pressed again, so that the door would close. I fidgeted. It seemed to take forever but at last it started moving. Nikov reached the landing as it shut. The lift went downwards.

I was praying that he didn't have an override.

I reached the ground. The lift door opened and I fled.

Which way to go? Towards the town? Like Sodz? That wouldn't work. The bridge was blocked by Malc and Tomas and there were another dozen disappointed Peacemakers, blood lust unsatisfied, still loitering upon the southern bank. All Nikov had to do was call out from the rooftop that I'd killed the Boss. I would be meat.

A burst of anger almost stopped me running. It was bloody typical. Sodz got away and I was left behind. I was the one who suffered, All the time.

I found that I was going home.

I didn't really think about it. There was nowhere else to go. Home's where you run to when you're little and you have been hurt. Home's where you should be safe.

Home was the very last place I should go. It was the first place they would look for me.

Where could I hide?

I thought about the hospital, where Ochre fled to after his abortive shot at freeing Xan. But I knew no-one who would help me there. And Nikov had discovered Ochre.

I kept on running but I knew that I'd run out of options. I'd run out of hope.

Faith said, when all seems lost, remember Jude.

It was a possibility.

If I could get across the river.

I remembered that the footbridge was unguarded.

And the far side of the river would be governed by the army by tonight.

If I could hide, just for the next few hours, in St Jude's …

I wouldn't go into the undercroft.

By now I'd started slowing down. I had a stitch. Felt awful. Heart attack? I couldn't stop. I had to cross the river.

Now, at last, the arch came into view, side on. The red brick of the square-shaped pillar, with the ornamental windows framed in green. The marbled ledging where the Officer would squat. I wondered what mad epithet he'd hurl at me today. Then I could see the white stone facing of the arch itself, each wedge-shaped stone imprinted with a letter so that if you read around the curve the name of the now-bankrupt company was still commemorated though the factory had gone, as if the archway was a tombstone, honouring the dead.

As I came closer I could see that there was something hanging from the centre of the arch. At first it just looked like a bundle. It was swinging slightly to and fro.

I thought: I'll have to duck.

That's when I saw.

He'd hanged himself.

EPILOGUE

So here I am. In hiding on the north side of the river, in a chapel, rather smaller than a garage though at least there is a little light that comes in weakly through the tainted windows which display a woman taken in adultery. God savours irony.

I think I'm safe. I rather fancy Nikov might consider it to his advantage that I've run away. I am the perfect scapegoat. If I'm not around I cannot challenge his side of the story.

Please don't think I'm blaming Nikov. In his shoes I'd do the same. It's just more evidence to show that most of them come out of this debacle better off than me. That lying and deceitful Drudjer Xan, for instance, has gone back to Mum and Dad and money, money, money with the inside knowledge of my System which will make them even richer. Nikov will become the new Boss of the Peacemakers; with him in charge they will be difficult to beat. Sodz has escaped to freedom; I expect he'll send us postcards from his beach. And Blossom isn't any worse off now than she was when this started. As for me: I've lost my job, I've lost my home, I've plunged from data-guy the hero to assassin; I have swapped the inside of a garage for the inside of an empty church. Still hungry. As per normal, I'm the only loser.

Even Mister Kapko didn't lose a lot. The man was dying anyway. He was in pain. So I was merciful.

As for the Boss. I didn't kill him. I disabled him. If he was killed, you can't blame me. Though Nikov will. But you can be the judge of that. You know the truth. It was in self-defence.

I can't see how I can be blamed for anything.

Not even Ochre.

Honestly, I don't know how it happened. When I left them they were fine. They'd just had sex, for goodness sake. So, rather more than fine, I would suspect. Full of the good old afterglow.

I locked them in. So they were safe. But when I passed my house, the door was open.

This is what I think. I can't be sure. It is a reconstruction of events. I might be wrong. I think I'm right. It fits the facts.

Remember when I lost my key? It vanished on my way back from the first time Nikov took me to the roof. It must have fallen near the arch. I think the Officer was watching. He's a thieving little jackdaw, perched up in his crow's nest, keeping watch. I bet he picked it up and treasured it.

He kept an eye on us. He knew a lot of what went on.

This morning he saw Nikov taking Sodz away. He may have heard the gunshot. When he saw me leave the house he must have thought it empty. Did he hope to burgle me? Or did he know that Blossom was alone inside? Perhaps he meant to rape her.

So he let a rope down from his eyrie and he clambered down. He dashed across the grass to my front door. Unlocked it. Found ...

I wonder whether they were naked still. Perhaps those dirty little Drudjers so enjoyed themselves that they decided they would have another go. I think he caught them *in flagrante*. Embarrassing. A man like that though, someone like the Officer, who lives like that, is not like us. No self-control. He'd tear his dirty clothes off and he'd fling his dirty body onto

Blossom.

Ochre, I imagine, pausing only to pull on his running shorts, fled from the scene. His first thought was to run away. His route led underneath the arch. He saw the rope. He knew the Officer lived on the arch. Perhaps he thought that he could hide up there. And so he climbed.

It might have been an accident. He might have slipped and got entangled. But the rope was knotted. Not a hangman's knot, not nearly so professional as that. A simple slip knot, one that wouldn't break a neck but tighten, tighten, tighten till it squeezed the breathing from the body.

Picture how his slender doctor's fingers tied the knot. I think he knew what he was doing when he slipped the noose around his neck. Perhaps he had been taught asphyxiation on his doctor's course.

I wonder if he prayed? When Mister Kapko was about to die he mumbled; Blossom said that he was asking for forgiveness; that's what Drudjers do, she told me. There was no one standing next to Ochre as he balanced on the arch's edge, about to topple down into eternity. So there was no one to forgive.

Which means he meant to do it. Why? He'd fucked his sister. Incest. That's taboo. He must have felt enormous guilt.

You can't blame me.

What did I do?

It wasn't my fault Mr Kapko barged his way into my house. That's how it started. All I did was try my hardest to look after them. I ought to be a hero to the Drudjers. Gave them shelter. Risked my life to find them food. They ought to put up statues in my honour. I'm the one who shot the Boss.

The trouble is that nowadays all anybody ever cares about is blaming someone else. If that's your game, blame Xan; she stole my System, fooled us all. Blame Nikov, blame the Boss: they are supposed to be in charge. You want to run things? Take responsibility. Blame Mr Kapko: he's the one who started it.

Blame Ochre. After all, he chose to die like that. He did it to himself. The coward's way. Sodz always said he was a little wimp.

Blame anybody. Blame yourself.

But don't blame me.

It's not my fault.

I was unlucky, that was all.

ACKNOWLEDGEMENT

Many, many thanks to Tariq Perera: among his many other talents he is the world's best beta-reader. And special thanks also to Kath Unwin for proof-reading: any remaining errors are mine.

Thank you also to Sam, Simon, Lucy and Alexa for reading the final draft and making useful comments.

And in particular thanks to Steph, my wonderful wife, for letting me read her the first draft and for supporting me for the many, many months while I was writing and for her continued and constant love.

ABOUT THE AUTHOR

Dave Appleby

I used to be a Science teacher but since retiring I have started writing novels. For a long time I lived in Bedford, UK, in a house with a big window down the side, from which you could see the river, and a door from the hall into the garage. Outside the front  door there was a little square; to walk out onto the main road you had to walk under an old-fashioned archway.

BOOKS BY THIS AUTHOR

Motherdarling

Motherdarling was a monster. Jack, her son, walked out the day he turned eighteen. He's not been back.

Now Motherdarling's dead. Anne has to find the missing Will or Jack inherits half of the estate. She starts to search.

But there are some family secrets that are better left un-covered.

Printed in Great Britain
by Amazon